DOPE GIRLS
AMBITION

MONIQUE LOVE

STREET CHRONICLES

Pu[illegible]y:

G Street Chronicles
P.O. Box 1822
Jonesboro, GA 30237-1822

www.gstreetchronicles.com
fans@gstreetchronicles.com

This work is a work of fiction. The events and characters described herein are imaginary and are not intended to refer to specific places or living persons.

ISBN 13: 9781940574394
ISBN 10: 1940574390
LCCN: 2015947327

Join us on our social networks

Like us on Facebook: G Street Chronicles
Follow us on Twitter: @GStreetChronicl
Follow us on Instagram: gstreetchronicles

DOPE GIRLS AMBITION

Acknowledgements

First and foremost in life, my heavenly Father, again, I say thank you for allowing me to find my dream and seek it wisely. Words can't express my love for you, so I'll say thank you, Daddy (God). Thanks for allowing me to learn through the test and it still did not destroy me. To my Princess Ty'Shai, Mommy loves you and I pray God always keeps us together as you grow and learn…you are my everything.

Thanks and love always to the supporters for believing in me and finding my writings interesting enough to feed your mind.

I would like to thank my mother, Georgette, a very strong woman who showed me the right roads to travel down in life. The things she taught me as a young child I now see myself teaching my Lil Princess today. So I want to thank you Mom. For all the times I said you were mean, I thank you for that because you helped me live longer. I love you Mom.

To my sister Tiara Washington, you are such a beautiful young woman and a great mother to your kids. I just want you to know that no matter what we've been through I'll always love you and you mean more to me then you know.

Jemiya, Lil Javon, Te'asia; Auntie's other side of her heart. I may not have had you but I'll give you the world because you mean so much to me. The three of you are so special to me and I hope we always have our special bond.

To Nette, thanks for all your love and being there for me as well as always having my back. Words can't express how grateful I am for your input on the book. We're going all the way this time.

A very special thanks to the G Street family for making me apart of the team and believing in me. I won't let you down!

Last but not Least…To my supporters and family, thanks for all your prayers. I love you all so much and without all of you I wouldn't be here.

Well, my loyal and faithful readers…sit back and enjoy this journey as you follow Rain through the trials and tribulations, the rise and fall of one girl's determination to live out her ambition. Enjoy!

Rain's Diary

Dear Dairy,

Today has been one hell of a day. I've been ripping and running errands all day for Rico's ass; preparing for this extravagant fucking New Year's Eve party that he throws every year. He does it so that he, and all his baller friends, can show off their mistresses. *Like I don't fucking know what's up.* Shit, the only reason I'm probably invited is because I'm his girl and this is my fucking house too. But, oh trust and believe…when he thinks I'm dumb, I'm not. No matter how many bitches he fucks, or how many times they smile in my face but sucking his dick behind my back, I'm still gonna have the final laugh on them hoe's. *Laugh now; cry later*; isn't that one of the famous Rico quotes? He better live by his own words, because I love him with all my heart, but I won't let him make me out to be a fool. I'm no dumb bitch and I've learned a lot from watching his ass; which, by the way, taught me a lot. Oh shit… gotta go; I'm meeting Tasha for brunch and I still have to pick up Rico Jr. This nigga better be glad I love his ass because I'm all behind schedule.

Later!

Rain's Storm

"*Ring, Ring,"* was the sound of Rain's blackberry jumping in her $400 Gucci bag. *Who the fuck is this now*, she thought as she reached for her phone while driving.

"Hello?"

"*Queen?"* Rico called out.

"Yeah, poppy, wassup?"

"I need you to go by my sister's house and tell her I sent you to snatch up that bag I left there and meet me at the spot with it. Do not look in the fucking bag, queen!" Rico demanded with anger in his voice, "I'm serious."

"Alright, dammit!" replied Rain, "How you know I didn't have shit to do while you calling me barking out orders?"

Even though the sound of Rico's Columbian accent drove her crazy, she still couldn't let him know he had her gone like that. "What's in it for me," asked Rain?

"Shorty, don't play me; don't I always take care of you? Don't I set you straight every time you see me, whether it's business or pleasure? Am I right?"

"Hold up, so what you trying to call me, poppy?"

"My future wifey," replied Rico.

Rain begins to laugh, smiling ear to ear. "Whatever nigga; let me go or you won't get no bag at all."

"Alright, queen!

"Shit, that bitch, Candace, better be at home," thought rain as she dialed the number. *I still got to meet Tasha and pick up RJ from my grandparents' house; time is fucking flying.*

"Hey, Candace, are you home?"

"Yeah, girl, wassup? Your brother said he needs that bag and I'm on my way to pick it up."

"Oh, Okay! I'm here, how far are you?

"Like ten minutes…I'm hopping on the interstate now."

"Okay, see you in a minute."

Rain grabbed the bag from Candace and headed over to meet Rico at one of his spots. *How did I ever get myself involved in a life like this?* Rain thought. I mean, I'm better off than some of these other raggedy ass bitches out here nickel and diming; but you would think I'd choose to run away from this after what I've seen as a child.

La'Rain Shant'e Peters wasn't always living the life that she has now. Straight from the streets of *"Bankhead"* in Atlanta, Georgia, Rain was introduced to drugs and death earlier than any normal young girl her age would probably see. Born February 14[t], 1980 to a drug king pin Donte' Peters and his wife and the love of his life, Jackie; La'Rain was their second baby, but the first and only girl; which made her special in the household. Rain was a "daddy's girl"; everything she wanted, she got…and then some. The leftovers went to her oldest brother, Edward; who was seven years old and wanted nothing more in this world than to be like his dad when he grew up.

By1984, crack had hit the streets hard; and with Donte' being the man he was—feeding the hood and always fresh to death to everyone looking in—it seemed as if the Peters were living the good life. Donte' would have the kids with him while he made transactions with dealers or even when it was time to collect from his workers. Rain and Eddie have seen their father and his goons beat the shit out of niggas for coming up short or getting high off of *Donte's supply* as he would say. A couple times before, Donte' allowed Eddie to be a part of the dangerous shit that he had going on. Eddie was always under his father and thought whatever he did was right. Rain, on the other hand, wasn't feeling that shit at all. Jackie did nothing but shop all god damn day; living the FAB life was all that concerned her. She was always too busy to know what was going on in the house; not that she cared anyway. She had her group of friends, or should I say, "Groupies" that flocked all over her, wanting to have her life; and to her, that was exciting.

A lot of Rain's memories from her past involved seeing her father hurting people, selling drugs and making plenty of money. Donte' had much respect on the streets, and if crossed the wrong way, he definitely had your ass *dealt* with. Rain and her brother were put to bed every night at the same time, which meant adult activities were about to hop off. Donte' and Jackie's friends would come over to party, do drugs, and drink all night long. This was starting to take its toll on Rain. I mean, what child doesn't want everything, but no child wants to lose anything, and that's how Rain felt the first time she saw Donte' kill someone. She was scared he was going to jail. Of course, like any child, she was supposed to be in bed, but the sound of laughter and partying had kept her up. Rain laid there staring at the walls as the sound of Rick James' *Mary Jane* played throughout the house. She noticed the sound of her father's voice arguing from downstairs. As Rain sat on the stairs to listen, she could hear her dad fussing with T-Bone over some money and Donte' wanted to collect.

"This nigga had the nerve to show up at my fucking party like shit's all good," said Donte'. "He must be out of his fucking mind, mane; coming up in here, enjoying shit that *my* money paid for and disrespecting me like that."

Apparently, T-Bone had been making noise on the streets about Donte' and his money; and that's one thing Donte' didn't play with. Rain stood quietly behind the stairs as she listen to her father become enraged by this nigga. Rain watched her dad, Kay-bug, Snook, and James stomp the fuck out that man. They kicked and beat his ass with anything around the house that was within their reach. Broken glass and chairs where all over the place as Rain ran to wake Eddie and let him know what was going on.

"Daddy's gonna kill him, Rain," Eddie cried.

She shook her brother with fear. Eddie jumped out of bed and went to see what was going on now, but as he headed toward the stairs, a loud pop stopped him in his tracks.

Pow."

"What was that Eddie?" asked Rain, scared to death.

"I don't know, Lil sis; but we're gonna go see." Before Eddie could bend the corner, he was stopped by Kay-bug checking in on them as instructed by Donte'.

"Wassup, Lil man, why y'all not in bed?" asked Kay.

"Where's my daddy?" cried Rain.

"Yeah, where is my father? I heard a noise and I want to know if he's okay."

Before Kay could answer, Rain ran past him to go find Donte'. Just as she entered the living room, she discovered what the loud noise they heard was.

"*AHHH!"* screamed Rain. "Daddy, help me please!" she walked in on T-Bones' dead body—beaten to death on the floor.

Snook rushed over to Rain, grabbing her up in his arms and carrying her to Donte'. Eddie just stood there in shock; he had never seen this side of his father and it really shook him up. That night really bothered Rain. It was the first time, but it wasn't the last time that she would see her dad doing something jacked up to another individual.

Donte' was doing good for himself; coming from a poor family with nothing, to slanging weed, crack, and dope…to supplying the streets of Bankhead with work. The streets were happy because everybody was eating. To every outsider, Donte' was the man; but behind closed doors, disaster had already struck.

Jackie and Donte' had decided to wait on having any more kids. They were having too much fun living the good life; but what do you know to Jackie's surprise, her period was late. She was so scared of what Donte' might say, but she decided to take the test anyway. She was three months pregnant, according to the doctor. Donte' was not at all pleased about the news; even though they had money, Donte' made it perfectly clear that he didn't want any more kids.

"STOP! Leave me alone, Rain," Eddie screamed as they argued from their playroom.

"*Sit the fuck down now,"* yelled Jackie, "y'all are getting on my nerves."

Jackie was under a lot of stress. She was pregnant with another boy and Donte's attitude had changed toward her. Not only was he drinking more, but he had picked up a new habit of snorting lines of his own product with his friends.

Just like any other trifling ass man, Donte' blamed it all on Jackie and the baby. What Jackie didn't know was that Donte' was having problems with his connect. He had lost a lot of his respect on the streets; which meant money wasn't flowing like it once was. With Donte' going out of the game that meant the streets wasn't eating and niggas were getting impatient. Donte' was losing control of his empire; the very empire he had worked so hard to build. Jackie was due any day and becoming more difficult to tolerate.

Eddie was getting out of control, hanging with the wrong crowd and trying to imitate his father. Donte' was drifting deeper into depression; using drugs had become his way of life. Day in and day out, he was hardly ever home; which aggravated Jackie even more.

"Georgia 911, what's your emergency?"

I'm home alone and I think my water just broke!" Jackie stated. "Ouch, oh my God, please hurry, my contractions are coming six minutes apart and this shit hurts!"

Okay, ma'am; help is on the way. Please stay on the phone with me until they arrive. You just breathe in and out and try to stay calm!"

Jackie could soon hear the siren's approaching so she went to unlock the door for the EMTs. As the EMTs took Jackie out of the house, Donte' pulled in the driveway; stumbling out of his truck drunk and high.

"What's up, mane? What's the fucking deal with my wife?" Donte' angrily stated.

"Sir, calm down, she's in labor and we're taking her to the hospital. You're welcome to follow us if you like."

"Alright, yo, let me get my other kids straight and I'll be down there."

Donte' called his mother-in-law to tell her Jackie was in labor and to see if she could wait for the kids to get home from school. Diana was so happy; she rushed right over with excitement. Jackie went into labor while in the ambulance; by the time Donte' got to the hospital he had another son—seven pounds, thirteen ounces and long as hell. Donald "Donny" Peters was born on August 17, 1986; beautiful and healthy as can be. Jackie was ecstatic, but Donte' just sat there never showing any emotions toward his son.

Over the next couple of months, things in the Peters' house weren't looking so good. With three kids, Donte's drug addiction and money becoming tight and Jackie sank deeper into being depressed. The fabulous life that she once knew was long gone and things got so bad for Jackie that she started having feelings that maybe family life wasn't for her. She loved her children, but her freedom wasn't something she wanted to give up. While doing laundry one day, Jackie found a bag of dope in Donte's pants pocket. Being stressed, and feeling like she had enough, brought her to the decision to try it. She never thought that she would get hooked, she just needed something to relax her—or so she thought. Jackie never saw it coming; she didn't know what had hit her. What Jackie thought could relax her became the beginning to her end.

"Jackie," screamed Donte' as he slammed the door, "where are you?" Donte' walked into the living room and there she was…passed out on the floor, high. "Mane, what the fuck! You've been in my shit, haven't you, bitch?"

Jackie just laid there staring at him laughing.

"You think this shit is funny?" snapped Donte' as he grabbed her ass off the floor and smacked her so hard she flew across the couch. Just as Jackie began to cry, Rain and Eddie were coming in the house from school. Eddie, who was now fifteen, and Rain, who was eight, had no idea what was happening. Donny was two years old at the time, so he was asleep in his crib.

"Mom…dad, we're home!" shouted Eddie. As the kids walked toward the living room, they noticed that the furniture had been knocked over.

"What's going on?" asked Rain.

"Nothing. Look… take your sister into the room, Eddie," demanded Donte'.

Eddie did just that; he knew something wasn't right and his baby sister shouldn't see it. Eddie, on the other hand, did what any typical fifteen year old would do. He was listening in on his parents to find out what happen.

Bitch, screamed Donte', "look at your dumb ass…so fucking doped out that you don't even know what you just did." Pacing back and forth, Donte' plopped down on the sofa holding his head in frustration, *what the fuck am I gonna do for money now*, he thought.

"What nigga," mumbled Jackie as she stumbled to her feet—clothes hanging off and mouth bleeding. "What the fuck are you talking about?"

"While you in here getting all high and shit…that was some of what I needed to get us back on our feet. We're broke; the streets are dry, and my fucking respect has been taken from me. I don't even know how we're gonna keep this house, let alone pay the bills for this muthafucka. Look at us, mane…a bunch of doped-out has-beens," said Donte' as he began to cry. "I can't Jackie, I can't do this shit anymore, mane; for real."

"I'm sorry baby," cried Jackie as she kneeled down in front of him. "I didn't know things were that bad; you never told me what was up."

"How could I? You were never home to listen to anything all you knew how to do was shop. You're taking what was supposed to be a fun activity and letting it take over you. I mean, don't get me wrong…I fucked up too; but not like you."

Eddie continue listening in on their conversation, he couldn't believe what was happening to his family. He always thought of his dad as superman and to see this going on pissed him off. He began to feel as if he needed to be the one to continue the family business. Never saying a word to his parents, Eddie had a plan…or so he thought. Grabbing his phone, Eddie left; he knew just where to go for help.

"Hey, E," yelled Eddie, "Yo, E."

Eric, Lil E, Smith was the same age as Eddie, but a lot more advanced in the drug game than your average fifteen year old.

"What nigga?" answered E, "You out here being all fucking loud, screaming my name and shit; what you want?"

"Can I holla at you real quick?"

Lil E could tell by the look on Eddie's face that shit was real. "Yeah, come take a walk with me."

"Look, mane, we about to lose everything," explained Eddie. "You know who my dad is on the streets; don't you?"

"Naw, I don't," laughed Lil E, "I know who he was…but where you going with this cause I ain't got all day."

"Alright then," Eddie took a deep breath, "I need to be put on, no bullshit this time. I really need this shit, bruh…for my family."

Lil E stood there with a look of confusion. Part of him wanted to help because Eddie was his boy; but part of him knew what type of name Donte had gotten on the streets and he didn't want any part of it.

"Aight; look…" said E, "I'll look out this time and front you some shit, but if you fuck up my money, bruh…it's your ass cause I answer to someone too, and I ain't trying to get dealt with. Ya feel me!"

"I gotcha, bruh…for real. I won't fuck up."

Lil E went to the backseat of his cousin's car and handed Eddie two keys of dope. "If you bottle this up right, you should make Fifty G's off these two," said E. "Bring me back thirty-six G's and fourteen is yours to keep; so don't fuck this up, bruh."

Little did Eddie know that with his decision to join the game brought consequences; and at that very moment, his life would never be the same again. As the seasons changed, so did Eddie; from a boy to a man. At age twenty-one he jumped, head first, into the dope life without a life jacket; he was living recklessly.

* * * * *

By now, it was 1994 and the drug game wasn't the same. All Eddie wanted to do was get high and slang dope. Eddie had started getting money and it showed. The streets talk, and Jackie knew what was up with her son, but she didn't care. I guess that's what drugs do to you. By now, Donte' had left Jackie and moved to the other side of town—fixing cars. Jackie, on the other hand, was still living in Bankhead in the projects, and doped out; just letting life pass her by. Rain was fourteen now, and becoming her own person; she was set in her ways. Being brought up around all the drama made her very cold inside; to the point where she sheltered her feelings from the world. Being very quiet and never wanting the company of anyone else was becoming very lonely for her, but everyone knew that there was something special about her even though she never showed it.

Now…Mr. Donny was something special; he wasn't your average eight year old running outside or playing video games. He was good at science and experimenting with things.

"Baby Bruh," as only Rain would call him, "you're going to grow up and become somebody one day."

Rain loved her brother very much and it showed. With Eddie gone all the time and Jackie staying high, Donny was becoming more like Rain's son then her brother. Rain knew that it was too late to even consider saving Eddie from their father's past; he was heading for destruction.

Ring, Ring, Ring, was the sound of Donte's cellphone ringing loudly in his ear.

"Who dis?"

"You have a collect call from Edward Peters, an inmate at the Fulton County Jail. Press one to accept the charges."

Donte' sat straight up in his bed with a puzzled look all on his face.

"Hello. Dad, can you hear me?"

"I'm here now. Explain to me what the fuck you doing in there, E ddie. You better not be…" and before Donte' could utter another word, Eddie cut him off.

"Dad, listen. I need you to come and get me out of here, mane. I've gotten in some trouble, and of course you know I couldn't call mom. I'll explain it to you later. Just come and get me please."

It had been the first time Eddie got caught hustling in six years. He seemed to always slide through the system; but not this time.

"Alright, son, I'm on my way now, but when I get your ass out, you got a lot of heavy fucking explaining to do."

* * * * *

Donte' sat, waiting and waiting for them to release Eddie. He sat there in that precinct, looking at all the young boys being brought into lock down like animals.

Mane, I never seen the inside of this place, he thought, *I was always smarter than these pigs; but these dumb ass niggas out here today don't know how to hustle. They think they know so fucking much, but still haven't figured out that real G's move in silence. Lil dumb ass muthafuckas.*

Donte' heard Eddie's name being called for release; as he signed the bail papers, he just kept shaking his head at Eddie in disappointment.

"Let's get outta here, pops. This place gives me the creeps."

"Well, then you shouldn't have brought your ass in here in the first place; now let's go."

Silence is what filled the car as they drove to Jackie's house. Eddie didn't even look at his dad, let alone say, thank you.

"So you wanna tell me what this shit is all about, Eddie? What the fuck are you doing, son? Do you even know? These streets ain't the same as when you were little, and this life isn't for you, son."

"What the fuck are you saying, pops? All this shit is your fault! You're the one who introduced us to the drug game and you're the one who brought that shit into our life, mane. You got my momma all cracked the fuck out and then you dipped on us. Your ass is clean now and doing well, while we are out here struggling. Rain and Donny don't have any clothes and we barely paying the bills; so kill that lecture shit, pops. I'm a man, and I'm doing what I got to do the same way you did."

At that moment, Donte' was lost for words. He just sat there looking straight ahead, not saying a word. That was the first time Eddie had ever spoken to his father that way, but Donte' knew it was the truth.

"Jackie," Donte' called out as he slammed the door to her run-down project apartment. "Come here now, we need to talk about your son," he said as he flopped down on her couch.

"What, Donte'? What the fuck you want now…coming up in here making all that fucking noise."

He could tell that Jackie was high as always; her clothes were hanging half off and she was nodding.

"Damn, can you wake your high ass up long enough for me to talk to you? First of all, where's my kids? And why the fuck does this house look like this?" he questioned.

"I don't know; their asses somewhere around here, but get to the point nigga. I wanna go back to bed," replied Jackie.

"Guess where I just picked your son up from? Jail. His ass done went and got himself locked up trying to follow in my footsteps, which is fucking dumb. He has to go back to court on January 12th, so I hope your ass is sober enough by then to be there with him."

"I'm not going nowhere with his ass," said Jackie as a slight grin came over her face. "Is this what you came in here screaming to tell me? Look Donte', I know what Eddie is out here doing, but what the fuck can I say? He's grown, and he don't listen to nothing from any goddamn body anymore. So be it," Jackie calmly stressed as she stood to walk out of the room, "Is that all…because I really don't want to hear anymore of this, so I guess you know the way out then; huh? Jackie laughed as she turned and walked away.

Donte' just sat there, staring at her with hurt and disgust. He couldn't believe that this was the woman he was once in love with and now look at her. She had completely given up on life and everybody in it. Jackie was at her worst, and Rain sat in the window and watched as the kids ran and played. Rain didn't understand everything that was going on, but she knew her life wasn't normal.

* * * * *

March 16th was the day that changed Rain's life forever. Bird's chirping, sun shining, and the delicious smell from outdoor grills floating in the air, made it one of those days where living round the projects wasn't half bad. Rain sat in her room listening to music and writing poems like she loved to do.

"Hey, Eddie," she spoke as he walked past her door, "where you going?"

"Why, nosey?" Eddie replied with a grin on his face. "What you want now?"

"Nothing, when you come back home can we watch *Disorderly* together like we use to do?"

"Yeah, short stuff. We can do that," he said, bending down to kiss her on the head as he left. Eddie went to meet Lil E at the spot where business was always done. *Damn, where that nigga at,* thought Eddie, *it's getting late and I've already been standing here long enough.*

Eddie tried calling Lil E, but his phone went straight to voicemail. Waiting a little longer, but starting to get impatient, Eddie finally saw Lil E's car pulling in.

"Wassup, nigga? Bout time yo ass got here," said Eddie, "Shit, I was about to bounce muthafucka. So wassup? Where we going?" asked Eddie.

"I need you to go with me to score this shit, my nigga, so we can start eating again; you feel me," explained Lil E.

"Hell, yeah; let's do this shit! I'm down," expressed Eddie. He had much respect for Lil E; mainly because he held him down when no one else would.

What Eddie didn't know was that the score was with some ratchet ass Jamaicans from Harlem whom Lil E knew nothing about.

Knock, Knock, Knock.

Lil E and Eddie stood there nervous as hell; neither one saying anything to the other.

"What the blood clot, man," said the voice coming from behind the big steel door.

"Yo, we here to see Rafeek," said Lil E as the eye slot on the door slide open.

The man just stood there looking at Lil E and Eddie as if they were something to eat.

"Hold on," he said, opening the door so they could enter. The sound of leaky pipes was all that Eddie could hear as they made their way to the back of the warehouse.

"Have a seat, gentlemen" said Rafeek as he sat down in front of them looking like the godfather himself. Lil E placed the duffel bag on the table as he and Eddie took a seat like instructed. "So you boys think you're ready to work with the real Jamaican dun dunna?" he asked with a strong island accent.

"Mane, I was born ready," expressed Lil E.

Eddie just sat there focused and quiet; he didn't really know these niggas and for the first time ever, he wished he'd never come.

"Me not take any shit from no one. I am the original shotta; you understand? Me run the streets of Jamaica just like my plans to take over here."

Puzzled about his demands, Lil E and Eddie never took their eyes off him.

"Me want you Lil niggas to come and work for me on my streets under my terms. Help me build my American empire; but before you agree and your dicks get all hard, there's only one thing you boys should know."

"What's that?" Lil E question, hyped up and ready to be down.

"Me not want no fake ass soldiers in my army; ya dig? Once I give you my supply, you belong to me!" Rafeek demanded, pounding his fist on the table.

Looking at each other slowly, knowing that this muthafucka wasn't about to let them leave out alive, but Lil E wasn't backing down.

"What, mane? You crazy! Get the fuck outta here with all that belonging to shit, shorty. I belong to me and only me; so fuck you! We out. Eddie let's go!" said Lil E, getting up to leave them niggas standing there stupid.

Eddie stood up, never taking his eyes off of one of the Jamaican bodyguards who kept reaching behind his back which made Eddie reach for his shit too!

"Yeah, E mane, let's just forget it," he said, turning to walk away.

Rafeek slammed his fist on the table startling Eddie in his tracks. "Wait one fucking minute, lil niggas. Me don't want to hurt nobody; but now you know too much, and me can't just let you leave and think that this is it. Now we had a deal."

"What nigga?" Eddie interrupted. "I ain't have shit to do with you muthafuckas and I don't even know you. Frankly, I don't give a fuck who you are. I'm out this bitch and ain't shit you can do to make me stay."

As Eddie and Lil E turned to walk away, Rafeek replied, "Sorry, boys, me can't let you do that."

Guns were drawn; pointing in all directions.

"No on turns their back on me and lives to speak about it," Rafeek shouted.

Lil E and Eddie knew, at that point, that it was every man for themselves if they wanted to get out of the warehouse alive.

"Me and my boy don't work for fuck-boy Jamaicans; so fuck you bitch!" Lil E shouted back.

The sound of shots being fired rang out all through the warehouse. Bullets flew everywhere, but they didn't care. Lil E ran one way and Eddie another; they were shooting back at them niggas for dear fucking life.

Eddie could hear Lil E as he screamed out for him, but he kept running; never looking back, nor stopping until it was safe.

"*E,*" Eddie whispered as he walked to find the exit. *Mane, E, where the fuck are you*, he thought, looking over his shoulder to see if a nigga was behind him. Noticing the red exit sign ahead, he ran for the door. *Pop* was all that Eddie heard as he felt his insides burning and his body going numb. Grabbing at his chest and looking at his hands drenched with blood, Eddie went turned around to face his attacker, but collapsed face down on the concrete ground. As memories of his life flashed before his eyes, Eddie died right there in that warehouse, leaving a broken promise with Rain forever.

Discovering Eddie's lifeless body right in front of the door, detectives were all over that place in no time. Everything was roped off so that the crime scene unit could investigate. As the bullet shells were counted, detectives knew more bodies weren't far behind.

"Detective Bradford, over here!" shouted an officer as he discovered a sneaker. Not too far away was Lil E, lying face down in a pool of blood with a bullet to the head.

"Damn shame," replied the detective, shaking his head. "I see them dying younger and younger each day," he replied, knowing this was some one's baby. "Alright, let's wrap this up and get me some identification to inform the families."

The next day Jackie was sitting outside on the porch while Rain and Donny played with their friends. Jackie noticed the detective car pulling up, but she paid it no mind because seeing cops in her neighborhood wasn't out of the ordinary.

"Mrs. Peters?" asked the detective, "Are you Jackie Peters?"

"Yes, I am," answered Jackie, "why? Who wants to know?"

"Can we go inside to talk, please?"

"For what!" she yelled, standing up in front of him. What y'all pigs want now? I ain't done shit wrong."

"Ma'am, is your son Edward Peters?" asked Detective Bradford.

"Yeah. Why?" she replied with an attitude. "What the fuck has he done now?"

"I'm sorry to tell you this, ma'am; but your son was killed last night in a violent shootout with some Jamaican immigrants. Again, I'm sorry," he said, reaching out to extend his hand to Jackie. She just stood there, staring at him in dead silence. As Jackie walked into the house, she felt her vision getting blurry and she felt dizzy. *Bang* was the sound of glass coming from inside the apartment.

"Mrs. Peters?" the detective called out as he ran inside to check on the noise, only to find her face down on the floor where she had collapsed into the glass table, cracking open her head. "Call 911!" the detective yelled out as the blood poured on the floor.

As Rain and Donny walked toward the house, they could see the flashing lights from the ambulance coming from what looked like the front of their apartment.

"Come on, baby bruh!" screamed Rain as she took off running. "Something's wrong at the house."

Rain and Donny ran straight for the house—so fast that they almost passed right by it.

"Mom? Where's my mom!" Rain screamed, bursting into the door.

"Wait, honey; you can't go over there," the EMT demanded.

Donny was standing by the door crying for his mother as she lay, still unconscious, on the floor. He and Rain didn't know what was wrong. Hell, they didn't even know about Eddie yet. One of the neighbors, who knew Jackie, called Donte' to let him know what was happening at the house. Just as he pulled up, they were placing Jackie in the back of the ambulance—hooked to an oxygen machine.

"What the fuck?" screamed Donte' as he ran up to the EMT. "What's wrong? Where's my kids? Where the fuck are my kids!" he said, just before Rain and Donny ran outside to their father.

"Mr. Peters, can I please talk to you?" asked the detective.

"Yeah, mane; where's my oldest son and what the fuck is wrong with my wife?"

"Wait, sir; can I please talk to you first?"

"Yeah, mane; go ahead!"

"Shouldn't we talk away from the kids?" suggested Detective Bradford as the kids looked scared already.

"Hell, no. I'm not leaving my kids, so tell me wassup so I can call my son to meet us at the hospital!" screamed Donte'.

"Mr. Peters, my reason for coming here today was to inform your wife that her son, Edward Peters, was killed last night. I'm sorry, sir."

Looking at him confused, Donte' pushed Detective Bradford. "What the fuck you say, nigga? So you telling me my son is gone?"

"Sir, he was killed in a drug deal gone bad last night," the detective explained.

Donte' began punching a tree with his bare hands as the kids started to cry. "My son…my boy? So you telling me some muthafucka killed my boy?" cried Donte' as he slid to the ground screaming out Eddie's name.

"Mr. Peters…" said the detective, "I informed your wife of this and she ran into the home, falling face first into the glass table," he explained.

"So, now you're telling me that I could lose my wife too?"

"Sir, I don't know that. You will have to go to the hospital to check on her, but I do want to inform you that we will be thoroughly investigating this situation; so we will be in touch. Again, I'm sorry for your loss."

Donte' called Jackie's parents on his way to the hospital and informed them of Eddie's passing. He had also told them about Jackie and suggested that they come to the hospital immediately; which they did. Donte' began getting impatient as he waited in the ER with her parents for information from the doctors concerning Jackie's condition. Pacing the floor, *Mane, what the fuck?* Donte' thought as he walked up to the nurse. "Excuse me," he asked, "can you tell me what's happening with Jackie Peters? She was brought in by an ambulance about an hour ago?"

Politely brushing him off, the nurse answered, "Sir, you have to have a seat; the doctors are with her now."

"Come sit down, honey," requested Diana, seeing the frustration in his eyes.

"Pacing the floor ain't helping nothing," added Blake, "all we can do now is pray and keep the faith that God will bring her through. We don't need to be planning two funerals because I don't think my heart can take anymore."

Rain and Donny had fallen asleep; one on grandpa and the other on Grandma Di.

"Mr. Peters," said Dr. Gamble; the sound of his voice startling the children. "After hours of trying everything that we could, sir…I'm sorry to tell you this, but your wife didn't make it. I'm sorry for your loss."

Donte' just stood with tears rolling down his face because he couldn't believe this shit was happening twice.

"It was the trauma to the brain, sir; as well as years of drug usage that caused her system to shut down."

Jackie's parents were in shock as they stood crying in disbelief behind what their ears where hearing.

"My baby girl's gone?" cried Diana as she and Blake hugged. "Oh, Lord, please don't let this be true."

Donte' attempted to comfort the kids, but that shit didn't work. They wanted their mom back and that's all that mattered. Despite her ways and her actions in the street, Jackie loved her kids very much; she was still a good mother. Tears rolled down their precious little faces and pain filled their hearts.

Rain began to question God; which was something she was taught not to do. "My brother and my mom God? Why? What have I done to deserve this? Haven't I been a good girl?" she sobbed, falling straight to the ground as Blake kneeled down to catch her. "What am I gonna do without a mother, grandpa? What will I do without her?"

Donte' held his son tightly as his heart broke for the second time. He was only eight years old and had to endure this type of sadness, a life without his mother wasn't normal to Donny because Jackie was all he knew.

"Can I go say bye to mommy please?" asked Donny. "I need to tell her that I'm gonna be a good boy for her."

Hearing those words made everyone break down as Donte' grabbed his kids to take them into Jackie's room to say goodbye. Entering the room made Rain feel sick to her stomach as she held her daddy's leg tightly.

"Mommy," Donny called out as they walked over to the bed. Mommy, wake up please!" he cried out as he pushed on her shoulder, realizing she wasn't moving.

"Baby bruh," whispered Rain, placing her arms around him as she cried, "mom's sleeping now, okay? So let her rest in peace."

Jackie's parents kissed her stiff hand; saying goodbye to their child for the last time. They wanted to stay longer, but Diana's high blood pressure wouldn't allow it so they left. It never dawned on Donte' how much he loved Jackie until he knew it was really over.

Whispering softly into her mother's ear, Rain expressed her true fillings to Jackie once and for all. "Mom, I love you. No matter what people say about you, or what I know you did…I forgive you. Life without you will never be the same; but I can promise you that one day I will be something special and so will Donny."

Before leaving the hospital, Donte' had to identify Eddie's body downstairs in the morgue—like seeing his son with a bullet hole to the chest made anything better; but reality set in, and the identification had to be done. The next couple of days were hard for the family. Making dual funeral arrangements wasn't easy for anyone to handle; but having Blake and Diana there made shit a little easier for Donte'. People always say when someone dies it rains; well, on the day of the funeral, God must have given them a double portion; because it poured down. The church was beautifully decorated in pink roses which were Jackie's favorite. She looked just like an angel, resting peacefully in her casket, dressed in a golden-colored dress. Eddie, looking just like his dad, looked good as shit; dressed like he did every day. There were so many girls at the funeral—all crying over Eddie; people had no idea he was a ladies man for real.

The service was really touching as the choir began to sing, *I feel like going home*. Rain and Donny held hands the whole time. Diana, Blake, and Donte' were doing as well as to be expected, seeing that they were saying goodbye to two family members at the same time.

"Pastor Cardwell did a lovely job officiating the service; didn't he?" asked Aunt Bernice as she packed her plate with chicken and potato salad.

"Yeah, he did," interrupted Ms. Sharon who was Diana's best friend since grade school. "They really put Jackie and Eddie both away nicely; they really looked good, but I know those children must be devastated."

As the Anderson house filled with people paying their respects to the family, Diana wondered where Rain and Donny were. Looking all around for them, she finally found them sitting on the porch in the swing.

"Well, hello there. Are you hungry?" she asked. Not getting any response from either of them she added, "Don't you wanna come inside and get something to eat? I have cookies. You want some?" asked Diana.

"You do?" asked Donny, jumping up from beside his sister as she continued to swing.

"Yes, I do, sweetie. What about you, Rain?"

Ignoring her grandma and never making eye contact with her made it obvious to Diana that her little *Rain Drops* wasn't the same person anymore. Tears rolled down Rain's face as her grandma walked back in the house, leaving her alone. Rain was hurting so much from all that happened and she didn't understand why it happen to her; but she made a promise on that day that no matter what she had to do in life, she would have a life much better than what she was having so far.

Rain's Diary

Dear Dairy,

It's been four months since my mom and brother passed away. I miss them so much it's not funny, and I don't feel like I can take much more without them. My brother and I haven't seen Donte' in…I don't know when. I think it's been since a couple of days after the funeral; but that's okay; he's not our dad anyway—fucking dead beat. What type of father just ups and walks out of their kid's lives right after they lose their mom and shit? That's fucked up! It's almost like he thinks he can come in and our lives whenever it's convenient for him. Whatever! It is what it is. I guess we just stuck out here in Brooklyn, living with grandma and grandpa under their roof, with their old fashion ass rules pissing me off. I'm just so angry at the world; but most of all, I'm sometimes angry at God for making me go through this much pain so young. The school here is so stupid. I wish I was back home with my friends and not trapped here going to Bushwick High where I don't know anyone. Sometimes I just wanna scream, because it seems like I have no one to show me love. God, please send me someone to show me love, because I feel so alone. I need someone to talk to so maybe I want be sad all day. I just want a NEW LIFE.

Later!

New Life

Where the fuck is this nigga? Rain thought as she impatiently tapped her fingers on the steering wheel. "He got me out here waiting on him with shit in my trunk that I know nothing about or even what it is. Mane, where is my phone cause I got some choice words for his ass. He was supposed to have been here already, and I told him Tasha's waiting on me," Rain said to herself as she dialed Rico's number; but at the same time, he was calling her.

"Where you at, queen?" he asked. "Because I'm coming round the corner now."

"Whatever, poppy! Your ass should have been here by now," she screamed. "I told you I had plans, mane."

"Look…shut the fuck up! I'm coming now, alright? I told you I'm coming round the muthafuckin' corner; so wait, and don't go in the bag!"

"Aite, nigga; just hurry the hell up."

"Shut your whining ass up, queen. I'm right behind you," he said, pulling up in his 2000 Range Rover—black on black—looking and smelling all good. Slamming her phone down in the seat, Rain got out the car mean mugging the hell out of Rico's ass.

"Fix your face," he said, smiling at her with pearly whites and beautiful lips that drove Rain crazy. "You always bitching, ma," he said, bending down to give her a kiss.

"Move, nigga; I'm pissed," She said angrily but smiling at the same time. "Don't make me wait, poppy; you know I hate that shit."

"Aight, boo; my bad. Okay. Now come here…looking all good and shit," Rico said, reaching out for her to come into his arms so he could tongue her ass down. "Um, Um, Um…girl, see what you did?" he said, adjusting his pants to let Rain know his dick was hard and ready for action.

"Stop, poppy!" Rain laughed as she tried to stop Rico from feeling on her ass. "Don't you gotta go take care of whatever it is you needed the bag for? Plus I got things to do too!"

"Aight, shorty," said Rico as he held her closely; giving her a look of passion, but that big as bulge in his pants was also a sign. He loved Rain so much and couldn't get enough of that ass she was carrying around.

"Let's finish this up tonight; shall we?" requested Rain, bending over to press her voluptuous ass against his manhood.

"Oh, yeah; no doubt, baby. I'm going to beat that pussy up. Daddy got you," he laughed, walking toward Rain's trunk…and I do mean of her car.

Rain and Rico had already moved in together with their son and things were really becoming serious between the two of them. Marriage had been the topic of some pillow talks between them, but like any man, Rico kept his queen guessing.

"Aite, boo; I'm out. How long you gonna be, or should I say, what time should I be home?" he asked with a grin on his face.

Looking down at her phone to check the time, Rain answered, "It's 5:45 now, so let's say eight o'clock; or do you need more time to bullshit like you always do?"

"I got you, boo," he said while poking at Rain's neck. "I told you I got you. I'm gonna fuck you real good tonight and take you shopping for the party tomorrow."

Rain smiled as usual; Rico always knew what to say to get her pussy nice and wet; which made her want him more and more, no matter what type of wrong shit he did.

"Alright, poppy," she giggled while placing her car into drive. "I'll see you later!"

* * * * *

Of course heads turned as Rain pulled up at Gino's Restaurant on 5th Avenue to meet Tasha for dinner. Having girl time with Tasha meant a lot to Rain; it was their way of discussing exciting new things and gossip that went on in the streets of NY. Getting out of that Lexus truck looking good enough to eat, she was dressed to kill in her sky blue Armani suite which fit the curve of her ass perfectly as the heads turned.

"Good evening," greeted the hostess, "welcome to Gino's."

"Hi, my friend should already be here…Latasha Greene," she replied, noticing Tasha's hand flagging her down. "Never mind, there she is," Raine said, walking toward Tasha's table. Rain noticed that Lauren and China were joining them as well.

"Hey, girl," Rain said with a look of shock as she sat to join them. "I didn't know y'all where gonna be here; how are you?"

"I'm good, girl," China replied, "just fussing with this man of mine as usual."

China and Tasha both dated men that worked for Rico, so of course, they would be close to his queen.

"Um, excuse me," said Tasha, clearing her throat, "what the hell took you so long, bitch?" she said, smiling at Rain. "What were you doing? Playing with Rico's ass; weren't you?"

Rain laughed as she sipped her water and shook her head, no.

"Yeah, yeah; whatever, nigga! Yes you were."

"Anyway, ladies," interrupted Lauren. "What's been going on? How is everything?"

Before anyone could respond with their answer, the sound of the waiter's voice taking their drink order disturbed them.

"Let me get a bottle of the finest white wine you have," rushed China, being that she was the drunk of the group.

"And anything for you ladies?" the waiter asked the rest of the group.

"Not at the moment," Lauren responded, "so again, bitches…I miss y'all; since nobody's phone works anymore…" she said, pointing her finger at Rain. They had been best friends since Rain first moved to Bushwick. Lauren lived right across the street from Rain's grandparents, which meant they were always together.

"My best friend barely calls me anymore…Ms. Lauren," grinned Rain, "no text, email, postal mail…no form of communication do I get anymore," Rain laughed. "Why is that?"

"Girl, please don't even go there with me," replied Lauren, "you and I both know that once you moved out the hood and started living good with your boo, I hardly get to see you, let alone talk to you," she continued as the waiter brought China's drink. "Yeah, you're not the same Rain I use to know."

"Please don't give me that shit because yes I am," expressed Rain, at this point ordering herself a glass of wine. "I'm still me, bitch. I'm just busy and I do have a life too, ma'am."

Lauren wasn't used to Rain's distance between them because they were fucking road dogs. If you saw one of them, you saw the other; and being that Rain was the new girl at school, having Lauren made shit a little easier. Rain would come to class acting like she couldn't talk, but Lauren broke her out of that real quick. Lauren was the one responsible for Rain and Rico's hook up; but the thing she never expected was for their relationship to go as far as it did.

They had been together for five years now, and he still felt the same way he did when he first saw Rain.

She's a sexy ass shy thing, Rico would think every time he saw Rain around school; but he wouldn't ever say anything to her and the same was true about Rain concerning Rico. She was feeling him too, but she was too shy to say anything, so she just told Lauren her feelings instead of acting on them. Being the person Lauren was, she got tired of hearing how fine Rico's ass was, so she put it out there in the open to him. The bell had just rung and Rain was waiting for Lauren by the lockers where they'd meet everyday.

Where is she, mane? thought Rain, knowing it never took Lauren that long to get there. But little did she know, Lauren stayed back after class to talk with Rico about her ass. Lauren felt like it was time for Rain to come out of her shell and what better way than for it to be with a boy.

"Hey," Rico called out to Lauren as she grabbed for his arm. "Can I talk to you for a minute, please?"

"Yeah, Lauren Hill, wassup?" he joked. "Where's that sexy ass girl you be with, mane? I want her ass bad, but she so shy," he said. "I wouldn't know how to come off on her ass."

"That's what I wanted to talk with you about, my friend…her name is La'Rain Peters, and she just moved here from Georgia. I was coming to ask you if maybe you would go out with her, but I guess I already got my answer," she smiled.

"So, wassup? Where she at then?" he asked.

"She's waiting on me by our lockers, and I was wondering if you would…"

"Come on," interrupted Rico, "I'll follow you round there."

Rain never saw him coming in her direction because her head was stuck in a book she was reading while waiting on Lauren.

"So, tell me..." whispered Rico into her ear, "is that book good?" he said, causing Rain to almost go into shock. She couldn't believe he was really talking to her. She answered him with a look of confusion.

"Yeah, it's okay," she mumbled. "I was just reading this while I waited on my long-winded best friend."

"Well, since she's late," joked Rico, winking his eye over at Lauren as she watched them talk. "How bout I walk you home today. I mean, that's if you don't have anything else going on or some other nigga waiting..." he laughed, "I'll be glad to do it."

"Okay," she smiled, "that would be so nice of you," she said as they walked off together causing all of the hating ass bitches to stare.

In school, Rico was a ladies man and all the girls wanted him. He was ever young girl's dream and every woman's fantasy; and he knew it too. Five feet, seven inches and one hundred and forty-five pounds of young sexy ass swag; Rico had it going on. Plus that nigga came from a family full of money.

* * * * *

The son of a Columbian drug lord, Ricardo Tulio, known everywhere as Rico, was a little cocky ass nigga; even as a child. Born the oldest of four, and knowing his father's reputation on the streets, made him recognize the power behind his name at a young age. Rico jumped, head first, into the family business; following his father's footsteps.

Rico's dad, Ricky, came over to the States with his parents as a child. Living a poor life wasn't something he was down with, and seeing his father work so hard to provide, but never get really far, pissed him off too. Ricky was introduced to the game very young, after his mom passed, and it didn't take him long to learn the rules, nor stack his paper; but that wasn't enough. He didn't want enough money to just get by; he wanted to retire before he even worked. It wasn't until a vacation visiting his uncle, Teto, in Cuba, that he realized the connections his family had with the drug game.

After running it by his uncle, and getting his approval to make a name for the Tulios out in New York, Ricky was on his way. With his uncle on board and supplying him with some of the purest cocaine the streets had ever seen, Ricky had the crackheads going wild; spending all their money with him and his crew. Ricky shot straight to the top fast; causing other niggas to leave their sets and work for him; which, after a while, lead to everyone buying their weight directly from him.

Ricky became the man; just like he said he would. He made a very good life for his family—all off of drug money. He'd gotten married and had kids all while his empire grew bigger and bigger; which to some people would mean problem after problem, but not in his family. Ricky and Rico were very close as father and son. Ricky passed all of the family secrets and rules of the game down to his son.

Rico was fascinated with taking over for his father one day; but until then, once he was old enough in Ricky's eyes he could start his own crew. Everyone knew Rico. His sister, Candace, and his brothers: Steven and Jose, had money; which made them more popular to their friends. Rico didn't care about that shit because he was walking home with the girl of his dreams—she just didn't know her role yet.

"So," Rico paused, "Ms. Rain, why you so quiet? What I mean is, I see your sexy ass around school all the time, and you never look my way. Why is that?" he asked.

"I don't know," she smiled, looking into his eyes. "I guess I don't have much to say. I mean, I've been through a lot and I still am now. So, I guess I'm just looking for a much happier life than the one I have in front of me; because so far, life has been unfair."

"Uh, huh, I see," said Rico as he sat down on the porch beside Rain. "If that's all you wanted, why didn't you just say so, sexy; because I'm feeling you and I do mean a lot. From the first time I saw you, I wanted to get to know you better; but you were just so fucking quiet. I didn't know how to approach you."

Smiling from ear to ear, Rain confessed her crush to Rico as well; telling him every little detail about the way she felt, but also wondering where his bitches were because she knew that somebody that damn fine had to have one somewhere. Assuring her that he didn't have anyone in his life for her to worry about, Rico explained that he had friends, but nothing serious; he was married to his money for now.

"I think I just found the one," he said, winking in her direction. He was used to getting whatever he wanted and he wasn't about to stop at Rain. From that moment on, they became inseparable; and it didn't take long for word to spread bout the two. Being Rico's girl meant Rain would have to grow up fast and bitches hating came with the territory as well. She did something no other girl could do, and that was to get Rico's attention. Her grandparent's weren't happy with the idea of her dating; which meant they couldn't see each other at her house. They had only been dating for a couple of months, but the way she felt about his ass, you would have thought they'd been together forever. She would lie to her grandparents about staying back after school so that she could go spend time with her boo at his trap spot all evening. She didn't give a fuck about what time she came home; nor if she got in trouble, because seeing Rico made her feel good and that was a feeling so unfamiliar in her life.

* * * * *

Trying to get some sleep and hoping that her headache would go away was all Rain could do. She was almost there, that is until her pager started blowing up nonstop; and of course, it was Rico. Forgetting about the fact that she was supposed to meet him, Rain was knocked out until her grandma came banging on her door to give her the phone.

"Here, girl; wake up! That boy on the phone for you," Diana said, handing the phone to Rain as she jumped up out her sleep.

"Hey, boo; I'm sorry. I came home, laid down, and fucking fell asleep."

"Don't even worry about all that, boo," Rico interrupted, "I need you to come meet me. I need to talk to you. It's important."

"Baby, what's wrong?" she asked, "Are you good," she asked.

"Yeah, ma; I'm good, but I'll be even better when you get here because I really need to fill you in on some real shit that went down."

She could tell by the sound in his voice that something wasn't right and she hated not knowing what it was, but she was damn sure gonna find out.

"Aight, poppy; let me throw on some clothes and I'll be...wait," she remembered, "where the hell are you?"

"Meet me at the spot. I'm on my way there now."

"Aite, poppy; later!"

Rain jumped up, threw on her sweat pants and tee, sneakers and a fleece, grabbed her keys and dipped.

It's cold as a bitch, she thought to herself as she walked to meet Rico. *This nigga better know I love his ass; got me out in this bitch freezing.*

It was December in New York and this was her first winter up north and already she didn't like that shit. Rico could see his baby coming down the block, so he went to meet her halfway.

"Hey, boo," said Rain as she placed her arms tightly around his body. "What's up? You got me scared as hell, mane; so start talking," she said as they smiled at each other.

"Come on," he said, walking her back to the spot. "Let's go inside so we can talk."

"I don't know what's going on with me," he said as they lay on the couch together, "but I want you so bad, mane. You've been my girl since July and I'm ready to," he paused as he reached over and gently pulled Rain toward him, kissing her softly on her neck.

"Whatcha doing, poppy?" she said, laughing as her eyes rolled back in her head from the sensation he sent through her body.

"Why don't you let me show you, rather than tell you, boo?" Rico said as he placed her head back on the sofa—gently caressing her petite breast as he slowly unzipped her fleece to take it off. Rain was so afraid she wanted to stop; but it felt so good.

The feeling of his lips kissing around her medium-sized brown nipples as he passionately sucked them and his fingers slid slowly into her wet pussy to open it up a little made Rain tingle inside. It began to get very hot in there to her; it was like the more he touched her, the more clothes came off until Rico placed his dick gently inside her vagina. He knew she was a virgin, so he took his time with her… enjoying every minute of love making that they made. Being that his fine ass lost his virginity at the age of fourteen, sex wasn't new to Rico; but Rain, on the other hand, was feeling every emotion you could think of.

She was afraid that her grandparents would find out, as well as the thought of becoming pregnant; but most of all she was afraid that after she gave herself to him, Rico would diss her. Deeper and deeper, Rico penetrated as he lifted her beautiful, brown legs in the air; in and out that pussy he delved; even at sixteen, Rico was a beast. He fucked her from the couch, to the floor…shit, at that point, Rain forgot all about being scared; she wasn't a virgin anymore, and the dick felt great; so losing it to Rico made that day, in her mind, last forever.

"Can I ask you a question, boo?" Rico asked as he held her tightly in his arms while they cuddled.

"Yeah, boo; wassup?"

"If I needed you to do something for me, would you look out for me? But before you answer me…I'm asking you this because I need your help, queen."

That was the first time he called her that and agreeing to his terms would be her first step into taking a position.

"Yeah, poppy," she replied. "You don't have to ask; whatever it is, I gotcha, boo," she continued as he laughed at her in amazement.

"One of my boys got tore off with all my pops work on him," Rico explained. "He was on his way to meet me, but the pigs ran up on him and that nigga got tagged."

"Boo," she smiled, interrupting Rico nicely. "What that got to do with me? Just say it, poppy."

"I need you to go with me when I make the money drop to my pop's lawyer, Chuck; then we're going to the projects where I need you to go back by yourself and pick up some work and bring it back to me. See the pigs don't fuck with girls," he explained, "But a nigga shit…they see us thuggin' and we automatic suspect, boo. I can't fuck around and get caught and risk my pops finding out; plus, I need this shit to make the money back that my nigga lost before I can go re-up from my pops again. If he finds out, he'll be pissed; so wassup? Are you in?"

As the room became filled with silence, Rain turned to look him dead in his face; shaking her head, yeah. "I told you once before…I got you baby; so don't worry, okay? You show me what I need to do and I got you!"

Rain had no idea what kind of life that decision would bring to her. And at that point, she probably didn't really care. Rain knew she loved Rico; and she was lucky to be his girl. *By any means necessary*, she would say…that was her motto for keeping her man; and she did just that.

The next day, Rain wasn't herself and it showed bad. Being with Rico had changed her attitude from negative to positive overnight, but today was different for her; plus, she wasn't feeling good so she didn't go to school. Her body was felling different. Hell, she had just lost her virginity and even though the experience was perfect to her; that wasn't the way her body felt because she was sore as shit. Everything from her pussy to her back hurt. *Damn Rico…*even her head was hurting.

"Why weren't you at school today?" asked Lauren as she walked into Rain's room—waking her up from sleeping. "Damn, girl" she said noticing Rain's appearance as she sat up in the bed. "What the fuck y'all do last night? Now I see why you weren't at school today. But anyway…I came by to check on you and bring your homework," she said, shaking her head as she sat down on Rain's bed. "But I wanna know what happen to your ass."

Rain sat up from her bed slowly, showing signs of pain as she told her best friend about her night. "I fucked Rico." she mumbled, burying her face in the pillow so Lauren could hardly hear her.

"What you say? I can't hear yo ass. Move that fucking pillow," she joked pulling it away from Rain's face. "Now repeat that, please," asked Lauren.

"I fucked Rico last night," she said, pausing to look at Lauren's facial expression as she covered her mouth in shock.

"Aww," Lauren giggled, "no, you didn't, bitch!"

"Yes, I did, girl; and it was the best thing I ever had…well, the first thing too," she laughed, pushing Lauren's hand from her mouth. "But now I'm in too much pain and I've been spotting a little."

Still in shock and laughing, Lauren wasn't worried about hearing nothing but details and she wanted to know them as she laid out across the bed, listening to a blow-by-blow description of what took place.

Leaving out nothing, Rain told Lauren each and every little thing Rico did and said from beginning to end. Lauren was all into the story up until she heard her best friend say that he asked her to pick up drugs for him and her dumb ass had agreed.

"What the fuck did you just say?" she asked, and from the look on her face, Lauren wasn't feeling that shit. "I know you not gone do no dumb ass stuff like that, Rain? I know he's your boyfriend and all; but damn, girl, do you love him more then you love yourself?" she asked standing up from Rain's bed to leave.

"Please listen and try to understand where I'm coming from; he loves me and I love him; so why shouldn't I help him out if he needs me too? You know how many girls want to be me right now? And you also remember how long I've felt depressed and felt like no one loves me. So now that I have someone, I'm gonna do whatever it takes to keep him; and I hope as my best friend, you will support me and have my back."

Looking at Rain with such fear in her eyes, Lauren grabbed her shit in anger, "Well, if that's what you choose, then I'll support you; but I don't have to like it," Lauren said as she slammed the door and left. Rain laid there thinking about everything that just happened and she couldn't understand why Lauren was so mad; but she didn't care either. She was falling. Shit, she had fell head over hills in love with Rico and she wasn't about to stop.

"Yo," was the sound of Rico's voice coming through the phone.

"What you doing, poppy?" Rain asked. "I haven't heard from you all day," she began to laugh. "And why is that?"

"Look at you, mane; gone off the dick already; huh? Momma that shit was good; wasn't it?" he asked, making her face turn red as she responded to him.

Smacking her lips, "Nigga, where are you? I've missed you all day."

"Well, that's good because I'm on my way to you with a surprise; something tight as a bitch that I know you're gonna like. Oh, yeah, before I forget…are we still doing what we talked about?"

"Didn't I tell your ass, yes?" she answered, getting up to put on her clothes.

"Well, I'll be there in twenty minutes, queen. So get up now!"

Minutes later, Rain couldn't believe her eyes as she walked outside to see Rico's fine ass looking good as usual. But he was pushing something much better.

* * * * *

A 1995 Mercedes Benz coupe—black and white; with the dalmatian interior and platinum rims.

"Why you standing there looking all sexy? Come here and get in," he smiled as she made her way into the car.

"Baby, oh my God," she said, looking around and checking out the inside. "Where did this come from, boo? It's beautiful; but is it yours?" she asked.

"No," he replied, smiling at her hard. "It's *ours,* babe. I can't have you—my queen—on that fucking train all the time; so I went out and brought us the best, because my girl deserves the best."

Rain was ecstatic with his surprise; jumping into his arms, grabbing his face, and placing her lips on him passionately; never wanting to let go.

"Um, Um, Um…girl," he said, shaking his head while grabbing his rock-hard dick. "Stop, girl; before you make me beat that pussy up again…right here," he laughed, pulling off from in front of her house and heading straight for Marcy Projects, one of the worse places in Brooklyn.

"Why are we here?"

"This is where I wanted to take you so I could show you where and who to pick my work up from. You stay in the car and I'm going to get all the details so that everything goes smoothly when you arrive, because a nigga better not try their hands with you…before I come round this bitch and shut it down."

Rico didn't play when it came to Rain; he really didn't want her involved in his shit to begin with, but it had to be done by somebody he could trust to not rat him out; and what better person then his very own queen?

Rico grabbed his gun and the duffel bag from the trunk. "I'll be right back, babe," he said, kissing her on the forehead as he headed toward the apartments.

Rain sat patiently waiting in the car. *Come on, baby. Where the hell are you,* thought Rain as she began getting worried about how long he had been inside. She thought about calling him, but she knew he was taking care of business so she continued waiting. About ten minutes later, Rico came walking toward the car; as she saw him, she felt a sense of relief come over her as she exhaled.

"Is everything okay, poppy? What happen?" she asked as he got into the car.

"Nothing, we good," he replied, giving her instructions to be there tomorrow at 2:30 and telling her who she needed to see. "Go up to apartment 215 and knock twice; ask for Jeff and let him know that Rico sent you and he'll get you straight. Once you leave, come back to the spot and I'll be there waiting on you."

"But what am I getting? I mean, how much? So I'll know that shit is good before I come all the way back to you."

"He's gonna give you a bag and all you do is open it and make sure that there's seventeen bricks in it; and if not, you call me right in front of his ass and I'll handle it."

"Aight, poppy," she answered, turning to look out of the window, "It's whatever, I gotcha! But where are we?" she asked, noticing the security gates protecting Rico's house, "Who's big ass house is this?" *Damn*, she thought, *this shit off the chain.*

"Yeah, I know," he replied, "This is my house," he said, recognizing her facial expression. "I forgot something, so I'm gonna run in and get it," he explained, "so you coming?"

"If you insist, but I'm not even dressed right to meet your parents," she said, fixing her hair as she stepped out the car. "What if they don't like me?"

"Relax, baby. You're gorgeous. I love you and they're gonna love you too," he assured, "so stop your whining and let's go."

Rain could feel her heart pounding as she followed Rico to the door. All she could think of was if his parents would like her and if they didn't, would that be the end for them.

"Welcome to my home," he smiled, opening the door for Rain as she entered with astonishment upon noticing how nice this muthafucka's crib was. Don't get me wrong, as a child she had a nice ass house too; but this nigga's shit was beyond bad. It was a very modern, nineteenth century mansion; forty thousand square feet, with a large private library, swimming pool and enough land to start a golf course. There was a portable touch pad that controlled almost everything from the TVs to the temperature, and even some of the exercise equipment. Rain couldn't do anything but shake her head as she followed Rico down a long ass hallway that led to Ricky's office. Rico knew his dad well, and as such, he knew that's where he could always find him.

Knocking to make sure it was safe to enter, Ricky gave them the okay to come in, but the greeting wasn't quite like Rico expected as his father reclined back in the chair, lowering his glasses.

Noticing the black girl on the arm of his son, Rico said to his father, "Pops, I want you to meet someone very close to me," he expressed as he placed his arms around Rain's shoulders, pulling her close. "This is La'Rain, my girlfriend."

Rain extended her hand toward Ricky, but he just stared back, "So is this serious?" he said, looking at his son with disappointment in his eyes. "This thing between you two…what is it, Ricardo?

Rico knew his father never called him that unless he meant business.

Rain could tell, right off hand, that Ricky wasn't feeling her. All she wanted, at this point, was for Rico to get her the fuck out of there; but she didn't even have to say shit, because Rico was pissed at his dad's reaction.

"Explain what to you, pops? Frankly, I think you owe her an apology because she is my girl and that's the way it's going to be until we decided otherwise. So if that upsets you, I'm sorry," Rico said, looking Ricky dead in his eye.

Out of all the four children, Rico was Ricky's favorite; so to have Rico speaking in such a tone was not only showing a sign of disrespect; it also let his father know he meant business. Ricky stood from his seat, getting ready to knock the fuck out of Rico's ass for talking to him as if he were a child, over some black bitch who meant nothing to his family. Just as he was about to react, Christina, who had been listening from outside the door wanting on her chance to move in on them two before it got out of hand, came in. There was no way in hell, she was going to let two of her men go at it over nothing.

"Hello, darling," she said kissing Rico on his cheek. "I thought I heard your voice; and who might this lovely young lady be?" she said, reaching to shake Rain's hand.

"This is Rain…I mean, La'Rain, mom; and we were just leaving," Rico said, looking over at his father as they headed toward the door.

"Nice to meet you, honey." expressed Christina as she watched them walk away.

* * * * *

Rico knew Rain was upset because the car ride back to her house was silent and Rain always had something to say; especially when it came to his ass.

"I love you, queen," he said as she opened the door to his car.

Pausing to look back at him, Rain replied, "I love you too, poppy. I really do," she said, trying hard to hold back the tears from her being hurt. She just closed his car door and walked away; never looking back.

She had never been more humiliated in her life. *The nerve of his ass acting like I'm not good enough for his son, and I bet it's because I'm black*, she thought as she lay in bed crying herself to sleep. "As long as I got my boo—and I hope that doesn't change either—fuck everybody else from now on," said Rain, laying her head on the pillow to rest for the job Rico needed to be done.

By any means necessary, were the words that played over and over in Rain's mind as she dressed to go meet Jeff. "I gave him my word and that's one thing I'm always gonna keep when it comes to my boo," Rain said, stuffing extra clothes inside of her starter gym bag that she was going to use to pick up Rico's shit. Nervous is an understatement for what she was feeling, because a part of her wanted so much to call it off; especially after what happen last night. But on the other hand, she knew Rico loved her and she wasn't about to let his father's ignorant ass stand in her way of being loved.

As Rain checked to make sure she had everything straight, she noticed that it was 1:30 p.m.; she called Rico to tell him she was about to dip and to make sure he would be at the spot when she arrived with his drugs.

The train ride to Marcy Projects seemed forever to Rain since her stomach was in knots. She felt like she needed to shit and throw up all at once, but that still wasn't gonna change her mind. She walked through the projects with all eyes on her; even the dealers were checking her out like she was food for them to eat. The bitches made it worse, being that she out looked them, they wanted to know why the fuck she was around there blocking their shine. Rain just kept walking straight to Jeff's door with no one on her mind but her poppy.

Rain stood, looking at apartment 215; scared to knock. But after a few minutes of waiting, she finally convinced herself that this had to be done for her boo. Knocking twice, just like she was instructed, Rain waited nervously as the sound of a man's voice quickly shook her out of her daze.

"Um, it's Rain," she began to stutter. "Rico sent me."

She heard the sound of twenty fucking locks being turned on the door; which meant business to her because she could remember her father having their house locked down like that. As she entered, to her right were five, naked hoes; cutting up dope and never taking their eyes off what they were doing. Three niggas sat counting and stacking up Jeff's paper; all of them were taking care of business; never saying a word.

"So, you're Rico's girl?" asked Jeff, walking up to her like he wanted to fuck her right there.

"Yeah, I am," she replied, "and he sent me to pick up his stuff; so is it ready?"

"It is, but let me ask you this…why a fine young thing like you doing your boyfriend's dirty work? Jeff laughed. "This is a dangerous game, lil girl," he said as he went toward the back room and returned with Rico's drugs.

"I'm big enough to handle anything, and there's nothing I won't do for my man," she snapped back; taking the drugs over to the table to count as Jeff and his goons laughed with amazement watching this lil ass girl handle business that way.

"You straight, lil hustler?" he joked as Rain placed the drugs inside the duffel bag. That was the first time she was called a hustler and at that moment, she really didn't understand it's meaning; but little did she know, this would be the first of many hustling days for her,

"Yeah, we good. Thanks," she said as she hauled ass out of the apartment; never looking back. She prayed that she hadn't missed the train, which by the way, rocked her nerves as well. If there's one thing to be known about New York City, it is that when you're on the train, you had better hold your shit…and she would've hated for Rico to have to kill someone.

Pacing up and down the block, Rico was nervous as shit because he hadn't heard back from Rain's ass yet. *If she gets tore off fucking with me…mane, my pops gonna be pissed and I ain't even trying to deal with his ass right now*," he thought, noticing his queen coming up the block and finally being able to breathe.

Rico ran up to Rain, picking her feet slam up off the ground as she began to laugh. "Baby, can we please take this inside?" he said, pointing to the bag on her side.

"Oh, my bad, boo. Come on," he replied, taking the bag from Rain so he could carry it into the spot. She watched him unload the bag and wanted to ask questions with every passing second. Not understanding where the curiosity came from, all Rain knew was that she wanted to learn more. "How much is a brick worth?" she asked as Rico stared at her with amazement.

Part of him was shocked that she even asked that shit. "A brick wholesale on the street should run you bout eighteen thousand," he began to explain. "If I break it down proper, I can make twenty-five. But when I hit my niggas off with work and they slang that shit right, their cut from each brick broke down is seven G's. You feel me?" he said as the look on Rain's face showed him that she was.

"Damn, that's good money, baby. Fast and easy as long as you don't get caught; right?" she joked as he shook his head in agreement.

"That's right, queen. Always remember that and don't trust no one in these streets because there's haters all around; and you don't have real friends in this business."

If the rules to the game were actually how Rico put them, then at that very moment, she knew that it was them against the world. And if being his Bonnie and he her Clyde was what it took for Rico to see that her love was real, then that's what the fuck it was gonna be.

* * * * *

Rain was so far in her thoughts that she didn't even hear her name being called.

"Oh, so you just gonna sit there and ignore me?" asked Lauren, causing Rain to come out of her memory as the other ladies wondered too where the fuck Rain's mind was.

"Huh? My bad, y'all. I was just thinking about something."

"Well, do share with the rest of us," said China, now opening up her second bottle of bubbly as Rain lowered her glasses exposing her eyes.

"First of all, Lauren, to address your statement, I have a family now, okay? So, excuse me if I'm not available to be around you twenty-four seven and talk shit on the phone all night, because the last time I checked, I have more important shit to do."

"Bitch, please!" laughed Lauren, "Don't sit there talking like you better than me because everybody knows whose money you're spending; and it damn sure ain't yours!" snapped Lauren as Tasha and China just sat there waiting to hear Rain's response. "All I'm saying is that I worry about you and my godson, and I would like to see a lot more of you two sometime," Lauren explained to Rain that she meant no harm. They kissed and made up fast.

"Damn, look at the time," Rain said, getting up from the table to leave. "I gotta go pick up RJ and get his butt home to bed," she said, grabbing her shit and rapping up their conversation. "I'll call y'all tomorrow and get home safe."

Rain waved goodbye as she got in her truck in a rush to get home to that dick Rico promised her earlier. She hurried to pick up RJ and get to the house.

"Mommy, I'm sleepy," whined RJ as she gave him his bath. It was their special time shared between the two of them in which Rain and her son talked about the highlights of his day.

"Okay, baby, let's go get dried off so you can get some sleep and so can I," she replied, carrying her son into his room to tuck him in goodnight. Rain was exhausted and all she wanted to do was shower and cuddle up with her boo, who, by the way, hadn't got home yet.

Rain called his ass to see what was up.

"Yo, you've reached Rico; hit me back," his voicemail announced after several rings.

He knows his ass was supposed to have been here by now. Oh, well. Let me go get my black butt in the shower, Rain thought as she walked into her bathroom, never noticing the sound of her front door alarm going off as Rico entered the house.

"Baby, where you at?" he shouted, walking toward the stairs.

He heard the sound of the shower running; glancing at the sight of Rain's spectacular signature ass dripping wet made his dick hard. She didn't even hear him come in, but she felt his aroused dick rubbing against her perfectly round, apple bottom as his hands slowly caressed her breast. Sucking on one nipple while playing with the other, he began licking around her brownish areola and then proceeded up to her lips. Kissing her slowly back down to her tits, he made a circular motion until he reached her hard, protruding nipples. He then used his tongue all the way cross her belly button; right into that phat pretty clit—taking it slowly into his mouth.

Rico tickled Rain's pearl as she moaned with ecstasy; letting the water run down her body, making it nice and moist for daddy as he felt her pussy vibrating until it exploded all over his face. He then pushed her up against the shower, lifting up her sexy ass legs so that her pussy could finally get its reward. As he placed his ten-inch dick deep inside her tight wet pussy, slowly stroking her walls, he could feel her vagina snuggly squeezing his throbbing dick. As his body went through the motions, in and out, mesmerizing her body with each and every stroke, he finally exploded all up inside her sweet dessert.

Rico carried her into their bedroom, drying her off and placing her on the bed to rest and making her feel even more like the queen she was becoming.

The perfect ending to a perfect night, Rain thought as she laid on his chest, listening to him sleep. She knew, at that moment, that she was blessed; and what better way to make their fairytale perfect then for her to become his wife and continue building his legacy. Rico was all that she needed and carrying his last name would make her life complete!

Rain's Diary

Dear Dairy,

I am so scared and I don't know what the fuck to do. I miss my mom very much right now, and I wish she was here with me more than ever now. I have so many questions I wish I could ask her bout pregnancy. I haven't even told my grandparents yet, because I know their asses are going to flip the fuck out on me; but who cares? What's done is done. Oh, fucking well, Rico's happy and we even discussed the idea of us getting a place together soon. I hope that really happens before Grandma's ass finds out what's going on. I'm torn when it comes to living my life. I really don't want to leave baby bruh up in dis hell hole; but he'll be okay, because they don't say shit to his ass bout nothing.

I hope I don't get real big, even though my appetite has really picked up lately and I know that people can see my weight gain too. Anyway, school is getting on my last nerve; but I'm still going to finish because that's what my mom would have wanted and I never give up. I know it's going to be hard, but a baby comes from God, and I feel blessed that Rico and I can start our own family, so fuck the world! Plus, my baby getting money anyway, so I don't know why I'm worried because we gone be alright. I don't know how I'm going to keep making runs for Rico being pregnant, and it isn't like he's going for that shit anyway, so whatever daddy says goes!

Later!

In These Streets

As her two favorite men slept comfortably in their beds, Rain decided to go cook breakfast; which was something she hadn't done in a while being that she had a full staff on call all day waiting on them hand and foot. Normally, she really didn't see a point at cooking, but for some reason, this morning was different; besides the constant feeling of nausea, she was feeling damn good. A veggie omelet, hash browns, and pancakes were always Rico's favorite breakfast, so that's what she decided to make.

Oh, my God, Rain thought as she stirred the eggs to place them in the omelet maker and a sudden feeling of sickness overcame her. "I know he fuck the shit out me last night, but why does my stomach feel like it's turning?" she questioned, placing the bowl down on the table so she could take a seat. "I haven't felt like this since...oh shit," Rain paused with a look of fear on her face. *The last time I felt this way, I was pregnant with RJ,* she rationalized. With so much going on in Rain's life right now, a baby was the last thing on her agenda. Plus, she remembered how hard it was with RJ and she feared that this might be déjà vu.

* * * * *

Months had passed since Rain's first run for Rico; and by now, she and Rico had become inseparable and their sex life was on fire. Driving a car back and forth to DC, carrying pounds of dope in the bumper was a scary situation for her to adapt to; but just like every other assignment she did for Rico, Rain took that shit very serious. Most of all, she used it as a learning experience for herself. She never understanding why she had to be involved, because Rico took really good care of her; giving her everything she needed. Money was never an issue when it came to his queen. Being in the business wasn't something she originally planned for, but somehow, that lifestyle...or should I say, "Rico" seem to grab a hold of her mind, body and soul. Her infatuation with Rico caused Rain to abandon her dream of one day becoming a script writer; and even though she wasn't done with school yet, being focused on anything except Rico was a dead issue in her mind.

She pressed her hand on the horn of her powder pink, chromed-out SL500 Benz that Rico had bought her once she got her driver's license.

"Bring your ass on, bitch. I'm hungry!" she yelled out the window to Lauren who was rushing her out of her house.

"Hold on, I'm coming," Lauren said, locking the front door behind her.

"What the fuck were you doing? I told you I was on my way."

"And I told you I was coming," laughed Lauren as she put on her lip stick.

"You know beauty takes time. So, where are we going anyway? And wassup with your face? Are you sick?"

Wishing Lauren would shut the fuck up with her survey of questions, Rain just laughed; explaining to her that she had been throwing up all day at school and she didn't know why.

"It could be a stomach virus…I hope," expressed Rain.

"Yeah, right. A Rico virus, bitch; because we all know that y'all be fucking like rabbits and you better not be pregnant," expressed Lauren. She knew Rain wasn't feeling the words rolling off of her tongue.

Concerned about Rain's condition, Lauren talked Rain's ass into going to the clinic to find out for herself, because as far as Lauren could see, the signs were already there. They sat in the reception area and the smell of the free clinic became nauseating with each breath that Rain took. The smell of shit from dirty diapers was horrible and wasn't something she was use to.

"La'Rain Peters," Rain heard her name being called; which, by the way, was a relief and a blessing. Being in that waiting area was becoming pure torture as her and Lauren sat there whispering back and forth. "Hello, La'Rain; my name is Tonya Reed and I will be your nurse today. I see that you are here for a pregnancy test; correct?"

Rain nodded her head in agreement.

"Okay, take this cup and go into the bathroom; but you only have to fill it up just enough to be tested; okay, sweetie?" the nurse asked as the look on Rain's face showed her that she was confused as shit.

She had never been pregnant before and she damn sure never had no diseases. The only thing that scared her was the thought of having a baby. *A baby?* she thought as she sat and waited for her test results. *I don't know shit about raising no baby; and neither one of us are ready to be parents. I just don't know what the fuck to do.* Her mind was deep in thought.

"Ms. Peters, we have your results and they are positive," were the words etched into Rain's memory. The nurse gave her numbers for an OBGYN, as well as the crisis pregnancy center. The latter of which, by the way, wasn't something that she would benefit from because killing her baby was definitely out of the question.

"Thank you, ma'am. Have a nice day," Rain said as she left the room, still in shock.

Lauren spotted Rain coming out of the back area. The look on Rain's face as she stormed out the door gave Lauren her answer way before she could even ask.

"What happen? Are you pregnant?" she asked as Rain sat there staring out of the window; letting the tears fall down her face.

"What am I gonna do with a baby? Rain asked as she reached for her cellphone to call Rico. "I don't know shit about raising a child and what if he doesn't want no parts of this?" Rain began to cry harder as the sound of Rico's voice answered the phone.

"I was just thinking about you, boo," were the first words out of his mouth.

Damn, was the feeling that came over her. He always made her day.

"We need to talk," was all that Rain managed to get out her mouth as she turned the corner to the spot.

She hung up her phone because she saw him coming toward her car to see why she was upset. Seeing her hurt wasn't something he could easily tolerate. Switching spots with Rico, Lauren got out of the car and let her best friend talk to her man alone. Plus… Lauren had her eye on a nice piece of eye candy herself. She walked away to talk to Rico's friend, Tank.

"So, wassup, queen?" asked Rico. "What's bugging you, shorty?" he said, placing his arms around Rain's shoulders.

She began to cry, and placed her face into her hands while telling him the news about the baby. To her surprise, Rico was excited about the idea of starting a family with Rain. He knew he loved her and that one day she would be his wife, so to him a baby only made life perfect.

* * * * *

According to the doctor's calculations, Rain was already eight weeks pregnant when she went to the clinic. Supposedly, she had conceived around her birthday; which meant Rico gave her ass more than that Canary Diamond Bracelet as a gift for life. Rain knew that telling her grandparents wouldn't be easy, so she hid the pregnancy from them all the way until she reached her third trimester; and even then she wasn't going to say shit, but Diana wasn't dumb. She had been paying attention to Rain's wardrobe changes within the last couple of months, but thinking that it was a phase, she brushed it off. Diana kept her suspicions to herself until the moment she walked into Rain's room without knocking, catching her undressed.

Upon seeing Rain's round, pregnant belly standing right in her face, she remarked, "You young kids today will never learn," before shaking her head and placing Rain's mail on her stand.

"I'm sorry," was all Rain could say.

"Save it, La'Rain. Okay? I don't wanna hear a damn thing from your ass right now because you did this. You knew what lying down on your back would get you. I warned you about fooling around with that thug ass boy; didn't I?" Diana angry stated, letting Rain know she was extremely disappointed with her.

"But grandma…I love him."

Rain pleaded with Diana to try and understand her feelings too, but she wasn't hearing that shit. All she could think of was how stupid Rain was being and she wasn't taking it.

"I'm sorry, but you can't stay here anymore, La'Rain. You just can't and I'm not taking on another mouth to feed in this house. I wash my hands of you and this lifestyle that you're choosing. You have really let me down!" Diana screamed, slamming the door so hard it knocked Jackie's picture off Rain's wall. Rain's heart was crushed even more as the frame hit the floor, leaving her with no other option than to get Rico and move the fuck out of her grandparents' house just like they wanted.

Pulling up at the spot was always like showing up at a party, because that's how many niggas Rico had flocking around him dying to be him. Since all of them had a little bit of money, you know the bitches were all around; but it was one of those days for Rico where he wasn't fit to be fucked with. It was payday, and niggas wasn't coming through with his bread like they should.

"Wassup, queen," he greeted her by passionately kissing her as he got into her car. She was supposed to take him and Tip to Flatbush to see what the holdup with those niggas and his money was. Noticing Rain's expression as she drove, he knew something was on her mind and he was gonna get to the bottom of it as soon as he handled his business. Rain sat in the car while Rico and Tip went to collect from Lil Chris. Hearing Rico's voice yelling over top of the music, Rain turned the car stereo down to be nosey.

"What the fuck you mean you don't have my money?"

"Mane, some niggas ran up on me while I was leaving the house and they took all my shit."

"So, you know who they are? Did you see their faces?"

"Yeah, I know them niggas; Lil trick ass fucks. They be at this bitch name Cherry's house," explained Lil Chris, praying Rico wouldn't kill his ass.

"Aite then, until them niggas are *got* your ass don't eat out here; you feel me Chris? In forty-eight hours, if them niggas ain't dead, then that's *your* ass, because I'm getting my money one way or another!" Rico said, smacking that nigga in the back of his head as he and Tip walked off.

These niggas sloppy, thought Rain as she closely watched Rico walked to the car. *My baby don't play about his money; and neither do I. Somebody better find it and pay up. Whether it's cash or ashes; somebody will pay.*

* * * * *

Rain knew being sick was a part of the game when it came to pregnancies; but she never thought she'd be one of them girls that stayed sick the whole damn time. With school and Diana still down her back about moving, Rain didn't know if she was coming or going. Rico had bought everything she needed, and his parents even invited Rain to dinner; which, by the way, went very well. But, of course, you know Ricky was burning with hatred for her ass; especially now that she was going to give birth to a part of him,

Rain still needed to get out of her grandma's house before she stressed the fuck out. Rico could tell by the sudden change in her attitude that his queen needed her own kingdom to run. As she walked up to the door at the spot, Rain could see Rico, Tip, and Chris running in her direction.

"Queen," Rico said, almost out of breath. "Get the fuck inside," he said, pushing her in the door as the others followed him. Rain could see blood all over their clothes and she wanted to know why.

"What happened, baby?" she hesitantly asked. "Where's all that blood coming from?"

"We killed those niggas…that's what happened," Rico explained as he took off the bloody clothes so that Tip could burn them. "Those niggas robbed Chris, which means they robbed me; and don't nobody disrespect Rico Tulio like that. So we paid ole boy, his crew, and that trifling bitch, Cherry a visit. Shit, I bet they know now!" he said, waving the gun in the air as a sign to Rain what he used. "We ran up on them niggas and put a lil piece of steel in their brains for memory; but enough with that shit," said Rico as he sat down on the couch beside Rain. He changed the subject; letting her know that he had found them a place to live. That made her feel relieved; so much so that all she could do was smile. She couldn't wait to be out of her grandparents' house. The only problem was she didn't want to leave Donny.

Rain couldn't believe her eyes when they pulled up at the three-bedroom condo out in Williamsburg Bushwick—a super high-end luxurious condo with a balcony overlooking the city. Of course when Rain got inside she saw that Rico had furnished the whole apartment with all the newest electronics and furniture. Hell, that nigga had even set up the baby's room with everything perfectly decorated for his son, Rico Jr.'s arrival. Seeing that made her so happy; all she could was cry because it brought back memories of her and Eddie living in their nice house as a child. Now she could call this place home for her child and it didn't even take her long to get into the swing of things either. She went to school and came home, being a loving girlfriend and preparing for motherhood; but with the Thanksgiving holiday coming up, and the fact that she was getting ready to pop any day, all Rain wanted to do was eat while she had a reason to stuff herself.

* * * * *

"Come on, queen!" yelled Rico from downstairs, "let's go. I'm hungry and I told your ass I wasn't trying to be there all day because I still gotta go to work," he laughed.

"Hold on, nigga; you try being nine months pregnant and getting dressed," Rain said, posing in the mirror and looking at how much the baby had changed her body. "Here I come now, poppy. So you can shut the fuck up," she laughed as she walked down the stairs.

Rico admired her pregnant glow, but all that shit was put on hold when he noticed something wet running down Rain's leg, "Baby, what the fuck?!" he shouted as she looked down to see that her water had broken.

"I think I'm going into labor. Baby, get me to the hospital now," she said, trying not to panic; but for Rico…it was a lil too late.

Rico was scared as shit, but there was no time for that. He picked Rain up and placed her into his car. Hauling ass to the hospital as the pains hit her harder—making him drive faster—Rico almost went straight through the emergency room entrance. Luckily, he stopped and the nurses got her into labor and delivery quickly. RJ's head was hanging halfway out as Rain pushed harder and harder. While she was in labor, the waiting room became packed with everyone they knew.

"Take a deep breath, Ms. Peters. One more big push," ordered Doctor Cole who was couching Rain all the way.

As she pushed with all her might, Rain thought her pussy was ripping apart as she felt them pulling her son into the world. Hearing the sound of his cry for the first time was the proudest day of Rain's life. Laying his bloody body on top of her, Rain counted his fingers and toes while Rico cut the umbilical cord. At that very moment, Rain knew that their bond would always be unbreakable.

"Queen!" Rico called out as he touched Rain's shoulder, causing her to jump out of her chair from being startled.

"Oh, my God, poppy. You scared me. I didn't even hear you come in,"

"Yeah, I know. That's cause your head was somewhere else; and wassup with breakfast? We drinking eggs now?" he said, pointing to the bowl on the counter.

Rain stood up laughing, "Shut up, boy! I'm about to cook now, so go get your son and bring him down to eat," she poured the eggs into the maker as Rico shook his head at her in amazement and at the fact that he loved her with all of his heart.

* * * * *

See the thing about the game is that the shit doesn't stop. You could be hurting; it doesn't matter, because business will still roll up on you and the junkies still had to eat. Rain knew that golden rule. Even though she wasn't feeling good, Rico still needed his drop made on time for Ricky. He also needed his new shipment picked up and brought to him; and since he and RJ were spending the day together, Rain went to handle her new assignment. She took it as another learning experience about the game; what to do and what not to do. She couldn't understand where her obsession came from. Was it the lavish life she was living, or was it the power that came along with it? Whatever it was that had her attention, really had her gone because she couldn't get enough of seeing Rico stacking paper, and she didn't care how he got it just as long as it didn't stop. There was no way in hell she was gonna end up in the projects like her mother did when Donte' fell off. So to make sure that didn't happen, she kept up with Rico's money and how he spent it.

Rain would make the weekly drops, depositing the money straight into an account set up under the name of Ricky's lawyer, Chuck. She knew how much was there and his figures better stay correct cause that's one thing Rico took seriously… his profit. She'd also make pickups for product on certain occasions or whenever Rico couldn't do it. Shit, she was so far gone in the game that now she was breaking down bricks and dispensing them amongst Rico's workers with instructions on how much to bring back to her king. Being his wife was all that she wanted and she wasn't going to stop trying now, even if it meant using the New Year's Eve party to show everyone that she was born to carry the Tulios' name.

"Queen, will you come on? The guests are starting to arrive!" yelled Rico as he walked down the hall to check on RJ in the nursery.

"I'm coming out now, baby," she said, admiring herself in the mirror while wondering what Rico's surprise was that he'd announce tonight. "Just putting on the final touches; you know I gotta look good for you," she said, walking out of the bathroom and straight into the sight of Rico who was overwhelmed by her beauty once again.

She was absolutely stunning, dressed in a cream and gold colored Vera Wang strapless evening gown. Rico, with his fine ass, looked good from head to toe; also dressed in a cream and gold Armani suit.

Umm, girl...goddamn, was the thought that crossed his mind as Rico took Rain by the arm. "Let's do this, my queen," he said as he escorted Rain down the stairs. They looked just like a royal couple, causing all eyes to be on them; which meant she was the head bitch in charge. All night long, people mingled; everyone was dancing and having a good time and Rain couldn't believe she'd pulled this shit off. Especially because this was the first time she ever planned anything, let alone a party this fucking big. It turned out great; even Ricky made a little small talk here and there. Everything was going specular for Rain, except for on lil thing.

Where the fuck is Rico? Rain thought as she searched through the crowd trying to find him. Then she heard his voice over the mic.

"Can I have everyone's attention, please?"

Rain turned to face Rico, wondering what he was about to announce.

"I would like to thank you all for coming out to celebrate the start of a New Year. I know some of you have heard I have something I want to share with you all, and being that it's 11:50 p.m. already, I guess I'd better come out with it."

Adjusting his shirt collar, Rico was nervous as hell because he could feel his father's eyes piercing through his soul. Ricky's eyes gave him a look as if to say, "don't disappointment me."

Rico continued, "Rain, can you come here, please?"

She made her way toward the front. Grabbing her hand and kissing it, Rico looked her straight in the eyes as if he'd never saw her before.

"La'Rain Peters, you are everything to me and each day that we're together seems like the first day we met."

Her eyes began to fill with water. Rain was in total shock as Rico spoke the most beautiful words she had ever heard.

"You are a great mother to my son and a great partner to me. I would love it if you would do me the honor of becoming my wife," he kissed her hand and got down on one knee.

Rain couldn't believe what she was just asked. Of course, you know her answer was yes. She jumped into his arms, grabbing him tightly and placing her tongue inside his mouth.

Everyone in the room clapped and cheered as Rico and Rain passionately kissed. Everyone that is except that Columbian muthafucka, Ricky. It was obvious that he was pissed; and the look on his face showed it too. Not only had that black bitch dated his son and gave birth to his firstborn grandson, but now she was about to have his last name; something he worked hard to give meaning to out in the States. The idea of a black woman carrying his name, and maybe one day taking over his son's empire, wasn't sitting too right with Ricky. To him it showed disrespect and dishonor from his son.

Without noticing his dad's face as he went to hug his mother before she left, Rico could feel Ricky staring at him so hard that if his eyes were knives, Rico's ass would be stabbed in the back.

"Thanks for coming, dad," Rico said as he reached to give him a hug.

"We need to talk, Ricardo; and yes, I'm fucking pissed," he whispered into Rico's ear as they hugged. "You knew I was deadset against you even dating that girl; and now you wanna go and marry her into the family—carrying our name and power?" he said, not giving Rico a chance to finish.

Rico cut Ricky off, letting him know that now wasn't the time to talk about this, and that there really wasn't anything to talk about. He loved Rain, and nobody could stop him from making her his wife.

Ricky pushed himself away from his son, "So be it! You're gonna do what you want and I can't stop you. But just know this…you will not, and I mean this shit, Rico…you will not have my blessing when it comes to this marriage!" Ricky said as he turned, pulling Christina by the arm as they headed for the limo.

Rico stood there looking at his father with so much hurt in his eyes. Hearing those words from his very own father and knowing that to have his father's blessing on their union was like having the blessing of God, tore at Rico's very soul. His father's blessing carried honor and the last thing he wanted to do was hurt his father, but Rain was the love of his life. She completed him and that's where Rico wanted to be.

"Are you alright?" asked Rain as she came up behind him squeezing him tight. "You don't even have to tell me what he said, because I could tell by the look on his face that he wasn't happy."

Rico turned to face her and they began dancing to their favorite song, KC & JoJo's, *All my Life.* Rico gently placed his finger on her lips, "Don't worry about that, queen. It's the year 2000, and you're gonna be my wife; so tonight, can we please just chill? I just want you to be happy."

She smiled and looked into his eyes, "I am happy, poppy. As long as I've got you, I'm very happy!"

Rain's Diary

Dear Dairy,

Why the fuck are men so hardheaded? I tell Rico time after time that he needs to quit being so sloppy with the wway he does shit sometimes. He just laughs at me like I don't know what I'm talking about, but after all this time of me working for his ass, you would think he'd know to trust my words. After all these years of me watching him in the game it is apparent that I pay attention to everything and I learned from it too. I swear I love him with all my heart, but he needs to stop underestimating me because I've always had his back and that shit want stop now. RJ and AAliyah are getting so big, so fast; and I'm afraid that Rico's gonna miss out on important moments in their life due to him always being gone for stupid shit. I'm tired of all these lonely nights in my bed and that shit's gonna stop now. I'll try talking to him again and hopefully, this time he'll listen to me and do some things the way I'm trying to tell him to do them. If he does, he'll have more time to spend at home with us and less time in the streets chasing niggas for his money. I told him we should start a business or something that can continue the money flow so that he won't have to work so hard to get paid. I'll have my time to shine as well as show him I knew what I was talking about all along. But for now my poppy is still the KING!!!!

Later!

Monique Love

The Transition

Life is good; marriage, kids and more money than you can imagine—what more can a girl ask for? thought Rain as she dressed to go pick up Donny. "I can't believe baby bruh is going away to college already; can you, baby"" Rain asked Rico as he lay on the bed watching his wife's every move. It was the way she smelled, the way she moved, even the way she thought, that drove him crazy; to the point that he couldn't function without knowing her whereabouts. Rico was getting too comfortable in his lifestyle; at twenty-five years old, with money out the ass, and running the streets of Brooklyn with much respect from everybody he encountered, Rico felt as if he'd reached his highest in the dope game and he wanted to go to the next level. Tip and James had a cousin that could put them down with getting this new brand of heroin before it hit the streets. Knowing Rico's obsession with being the best, Tip and James took the offer straight to Rico in hopes of making a deal. Usually, Rico didn't make any moves without talking to his father first; but for some reason, he didn't this time. Instead, he went along with plans to meet up for this shit.

"So, are you still going with me to drop Donny off at college?" Rain asked.

Donny had gotten a full scholarship to Princeton University to study Forensic science and Rain was gonna see to it that he did just that.

"Yeah, queen. No doubt," he replied, standing up from the bed to get dressed. "I can't wait to get his ass in there so he can pull all the bitches with his smart guy swagger," laughed Rico.

"Whatever, poppy. No the fuck he's not! I want him focused on his education; not pussy. So, that's dead; now hurry up so he won't be late for freshman registration. We still gotta pick him up from home."

"Aight, shorty; chill. I'm coming. I don't wanna make him late either," said Rico as she grabbed the keys to go start the car. He followed right behind her. While heading to the truck, Rico's phone rang out from his pocket.

"Yo, who dis?" he answered.

"Wassup, bruh? This James."

"My nigga!" Rico replied. "I've been expecting your call. What's going on?"

"Look… my cousin got the score on that shit we talked about and it's going down tonight if you want in."

"Hell, yeah," said Rico with excitement in his voice. "But what about the amount I asked for? because ain't no reason for me to pull out that kind of money if these niggas ain't straight."

"Yeah, bruh, I feel you; but naw, you good. Everything is everything. So meet me in two hours at the warehouse on Bleeker and don't forget to get Tip from the spot."

"Fo sho! Let me make tracks then," he said, hanging up the phone and looking at Rain because he knew she wasn't going to like what he was about to say. But business is business and she knows how that goes. "I love you, queen," he said, rubbing her ass while hugging her close.

"I love you too, now let's get in the car and go," she said, giving him a look as if to say, *no your ass not nigga.*

"Naw, *we* can't go, but *you* can go," said Rico. Before he could finish, Rain went off on his ass wanting to know why plans were changing.

"Remember that deal I was telling you about with Tip and James' people? Well, it's going down tonight and if I want my share, I gotta be there, babe. So, please don't be mad. I'll make it up to you," he said, winking his eye at her.

It wasn't working because she had finally had enough. "Is that really important, poppy? I mean, look at us…damn! You act like we broke or something. What the fuck!" she screamed. "You're doing fine right where you are and I don't understand what's the rush to bring in a new product anyway. You don't even know these fucking niggas, boo. Come on now, you're being real sloppy right now and I gotta be the one to tell you," she said while getting into the truck.

Rico shut her door, "Queen, I told you I'm getting bored out in these streets and I need a new challenge, boo. Listen to me," he said, turning her head back to face him. "Three years tops, that's all I'm asking of you, boo."

Rain stared into his eyes; part of her wanted to believe him, but she knew once Rico found something new he liked, it wouldn't be that easy for him to just walk.

"Give me that and I promise I'm out and we can start those businesses you were talking about. We can also take a couple of vacations and shit like that. Whatever you want, it's all yours, boo."

"I have everything I want, so don't throw that away, poppy," she begged, pulling his arm as he walked away. "I'm happy, baby. So please just come with me and give it some more thought. Don't switch up the way we've been doing business just because it sounds good; especially when you've never moved this quickly before.

"Look, queen, I already told them yes. Now we can finish this conversation later," he said kissing her soft lips passionately; never wanting to let go. "I'll be straight home as soon as I'm done, my queen," he whispered as he took one last look at her driving away. His comment was said almost as if he felt that something was different about this time. Normally when money's involved, Rico never hesitated to go get it; but for some reason, he did this time.

* * * * *

Rain sat in the truck texting Rico while her brother and grandpa packed her trunk with his stuff for school.

"Your mother would be so proud," Diana cried while hugging her grandson goodbye. "Do your best, baby. I know you will because you're smart, okay!"

"Yes, ma'am. I will and I'll call you as soon as I get settled in," said Donny, climbing into Rain's truck. "Aite, sis, let's be out."

After meeting up with Chuck to get the money for the deal, Rico started feeling a little funny about going through with it. "*The shit queen said makes sense*, he thought as he pulled up at the spot to meet Tip. *I love that girl so much and she has always had my back. I think I need to put more thought into what she's saying*, Rico thought to himself and just as he was about to call Rain back, Tip got into the car.

"Wassup, my nigga?" Tip slapped Rico some dap. "You ready for this?"

"Nigga, you know I was born ready," laughed Rico. "Shit, nigga, I'm your supplier or did you forget?"

"Shut the fuck up!" joked Tip as he lit up the sour D for them to smoke on the way.

"Why the fuck is it so dark?" questioned Rico, noticing that there were no lights outside the warehouse.

"I don't know, nigga. Are you scared?"

"Shut the fuck up, bitch and get the fuck outta my car," joked Rico as they both got out.

"There goes James right there," Tip said as James walked to meet up with them.

"Right on time, my nigga," greeted James as Tip and Rico approached him.

"Let's do this, bruh so I can get back home to my wife," said Rico as they started laughing.

"That pussy has gotcha hooked, nigga and you need to get like me and fuck your money," said James, opening up the door to the warehouse. "Rico meet Majesty," introduced James.

"So you're Rico?" asked Majesty checking Rico out from head to toe.

"Yeah, that's me."

"Well, I've been hearing some wonderful things about you son, you really doing your thing," he said as he shook his head in agreement. "You've got everything…starting cross the bridge…on lock, and I must say, great job!" he continued, giving Rico an applause.

Rico listened while this nigga kept complementing him and he thought, *this nigga must think I'm a fucking child…talking about great job and shit. He must not know who my family is…talking sideways and shit!* "Well, look…now that we're acquainted, can we get down to business because I've got other plans."

"Indeed. Indeed," agreed Majesty as he popped open all four suit cases containing his product. James reached in to sample its quality.

"OOWEE," said James as the pureness of the heroin burned his nose, "this the shit right here! Rico, mane, we gone have them fiends running around selling the clothes off their muthafuckin' backs to get some of this!"

Rico placed the Nike duffel bag on the table, exposing his money so they could wrap the deal up.

"All this looks nice," said Majesty, pointing to the money on the table, "but check this out…seeing as though you're the man and your cash flow is like that, I'm gonna need double of what this is before you can leave with my shit," he said, looking straight at Rico and waiting for his move.

"Nigga, what? You tripping? That's not what we agreed on. I ain't paying shit. Just because you a thirsty ass nigga trying to come up don't mean you're going to beat my head in for real," Rico replied.

Majesty and his goons noticed the change in Rico's attitude and immediately became defensive. Raising their shirts to show their guns, Rico did the same as Tip and James tried reasoning with their cousin.

"Come on now, cuz, we told you this was our man," said Tip.

"Yeah and I fucks with you, Majesty; we family and all, but Rico make sure we live good and I got his back all the way."

Majesty smiled, looking at James as if he was a stranger. "You do what you feel you gotta do. I said what it is and this money right here," he handed the duffel bag to his goon, "is mine; so either you go get the rest of my money or you just loose; take your pick."

Dropping his head and shaking it back and forth, Rico looked up to face Majesty with guns pointed in all directions, Rico knew he still had one last choice to pick.

"Yo, nigga, you forgot one choice," he grinned at Majesty, "or either I kill you!" he said as the reflexes in his finger pulled the trigger. Rico shot one of Majesty's goons straight through the muthafuckin' eye. The nigga didn't even know what hit him as bullets flew from all angles and niggas scattered while still shooting for their target. Majesty shot straight for Rico, hitting him right in the leg and causing Rico to fall to the ground. Just in the nick of time, James' ass came out of nowhere; shielding Rico and killing another one of Majesty's people. Majesty, with his slick ass, tried to come up behind to shoot Rico in the head, forgetting about Tip who stood there, posted directly behind Majesty's back with a Snub Nose aimed straight for his head. Just as Majesty went to release the trigger, Tip's ass shot him right in the neck; causing him to fall forward and sending off the gun in Majesty's hand.

"Oh, shit!" Rico yelled as he rushed to catch his falling body from hitting the concrete.

"Tip, hurry up nigga! Rico stay with me homie, stay with me," said James as he tried to find a wound but there was too much blood, so they put Rico in the car and drove him to the hospital.

Tip sat in the back, putting pressure where they thought he was hit, and talking to try and keep him conscious as the moans of pain filled the car. "Rain and the kids are waiting on you, bruh. So you got to go home; okay? Tip tried to hold back the tears and Rico just laid there staring straight at him with a tear rolling down his face.

"My brother's been shot," screamed James as he ran inside the emergency room covered in Rico's blood. The staff immediately rushed to his side to bring him into surgery, while Tip and James waited. Word traveled fast, and soon the waiting room was packed with all Rico's family and friends. Shit, even Rain's friends where there.

"Hi, you've reached Rain; do what you do," was what she got every time

Lauren tried Rain's cell.

"This Lauren, please call me back; it's an emergency and you need to come to the hospital," was the message she left as they all kept trying to reach Rain and let her know what happened.

I'm so proud of baby bruh, Rain thought as she drove back to New York, "If only mommy and Eddie could have seen this day," she said out loud as she jammed to Alicia Keys' new cd. Rain remembered that her phone was on vibrate and she wanted to see if Storm called about the kids. As she flipped open her Blackberry, Rain noticed she had twelve missed calls and voicemails. In suspense of what they wanted, she went to listen to the voicemails, but before she could, Candace was ringing her phone.

"Hello."

"Hey, where are you, Rain?" said Candace.

"I'm on the highway headed back to the city. Why? Wassup?" Rain asked.

"Don't go home," whispered Candace. "I need you to come to Saint Mary's hospital, Rain and I need you to get here now!" Candace demanded.

The tone of her voice had Rain scared, but she did just as she was told and went straight to the hospital. What should have been a forty-five minute drive, Rain did in twenty.

Rain's mind was going a thousand miles per hour as she walked into the emergency room. She was clueless as shit, having no idea that the life she once knew would never be the same again. As she entered the waiting area, noticing that everyone else was there except for Rico, Rain wanted answers. Before she could ask anything, the doctor walked into the room.

"Mrs. Tulio?" he asked, walking up to Candace as she pointed her finger in Rain's direction. "Mrs. Tulio?"

"Yes," she answered; confused as to why he was talking to her.

"May I speak to you in private, please?"

Before Rain could answer, Ricky jumped out of his seat and headed straight in Rain's direction.

"Hell, naw, you can't. That's my son, dammit! I wanna know how he's doing now!"

Realizing what she heard, Rain went the fuck off, "What the fuck you mean, 'how *he's* doing?' Where's Rico?" she asked the doctor.

"Mrs. Tulio, Ricardo was shot twice; once in the leg and once in the back."

In total shock, Rain's body went numb as she watched the doctor's mouth utter those words. Rain heard nothing but silence. *Is this a joke?* she thought, trying to bring herself out of a trance as the tears began rolling downing her face.

"The bullet entered through his back, hitting an artery and we were able to stabilize the bleeding, as well as retrieve the bullet; but he's still unconscious."

"Can I see him?" she asked, barely able to breathe.

"Yes, you may; but the others will have to wait," the doctor said as Ricky tried to follow behind her.

It took everyone in there to contain Ricky as he cursed and fussed; but Rain didn't care. All she wanted to do was see Rico and make sure he was gonna be okay. Walking into the room and seeing him in that bed, hooked up to all those machines, was a sight Rain would never forget. The tears were flowing uncontrollable as she made her way over to him—wanting so much to kiss his lips; but she couldn't because of all the tubes helping him breathe. Instead, she kissed his forehead, trying hard to compose herself.

"Baby, what happen?" she said as she sat down beside his bed and held his hand. "You promised me you were coming straight home…not here Rico," she began to cry harder, laying her head on his hand. "Why didn't you just go with me? I told you something wasn't right," she cried as she sat there thinking about their happy times together. "How we go from the world's happiest couple to this shit in less than a couple of hours, baby? I was happy. Why couldn't it just stay that way?"

* * * * *

"Damn, I look good. I should be on the cover of a magazine being this beautiful." Mesmerized by the way the thirty-five-hundred-dollar, Louis Vuitton wedding dress fit, Rain stood in the dressing room of the banquet hall preparing for her wedding while the wedding planner made sure everything was running smoothly and guests were being seated properly. Rain and Rico, along with their wedding party, continued to get ready and everything looked beautiful with the color theme of powder purple, gold and white. The Hampton's Banquet Lodge looked like a paradise. Rico couldn't wait to see Rain. *Twenty-four hours is long enough to be apart from her,* he thought while sipping on Hennessy with his brothers.

"I bet she's beautiful and I can't wait to see her."

"Yeah, I know how you feel, bruh. When I married Amy, that was the happiest day of my life," expressed Steven.

"Speak for yourself," Jose interrupted, "I felt trapped when I did it and I'm still feeling trapped; even after the divorce."

They all laughed while raising their glasses to toast.

"To Rico and Rain, may your marriage be as rich as you are, big bruh," joked Steven, looking down at his watch, "oh, it's time to rock and roll. You ready?"

"As I'll ever be," said Rico, bucking the rest of his drink, "let's do this!"

As the pianists played a beautiful soft tune, Rico stood there, watching his grooms men come down the aisle paired up with the bridesmaids and the maid of honor. Rico couldn't help but notice that the two seats reserved for his parents were empty. But he did not have enough time to think about that. Everyone rose to their feet as *Forever in Love* by Kenney G filled the room and the flower girls came down the aisle dressed like angels.

Blake escorted Rain down the aisle. As all eyes were placed on her, she couldn't help but think she was the luckiest girl in the world. With everything that she had been through and the pain in her life, being this happy was a dream.

Rico could feel his eyes water as she walked closer to him. He'd seen her at her best; *but god damn,* he thought, *she's breath taking*. Having Blake give her away made it even better. Hearing the word of union provided by Pastor Taylor and the reading of the vows had the whole room crying. Even Rico shed a tear. He was in love and could no longer hide it.

"By the power invested in me by the State of New York, I now pronounce you husband and wife. You may now kiss your bride."

Rico and Rain both smiled, and Rico kissed Rain for the first time as his wife; causing her to forget all about the pain she was having in her stomach.

The landscaping outside of the Hampton's was already such a beautiful sight, so having it decorated for the reception made it gorgeous; just like the bride. A lot of Rain's family and friends from Georgia came to share her big day. Rico had provided plane tickets and hotel accommodations for all of her guest; even Rain's favorite cousin, Storm, and her Uncle Keith surprised her and came. Rain and Storm were tight as kids. The best part of family activities was the time Rain got to spend with her cousin. Uncle Keith was Donte's brother and Storm was his daughter whom he raised because her mother died when she was baby. People thought Rain and Storm where sisters because they had such a tight bond. They were always dressing alike and had their hair done alike; hell, they even had the same birthday which was very strange to Rain.

It was not every day that you find two people that almost shared the same brain and birthday; and they weren't twins. But the signs and similarities were there; even Storm and Jackie had a bond. Rain believed it was because her mom felt bad that Storm didn't have a mother, so she looked out for her when she could. When Storm moved to New York, she and Rain lost touch; so seeing her all grown up really made Rain's day.

"Oh, my God!" I thought that was you," Rain said, hugging Storm tightly for lost time.

"Look at you, cuz. You're such a beautiful bride," said Storm with her strong Georgia accent, "your momma would be so proud," she said before the hugged each other again.

"Thank you, baby. Now enough about me, how have you been? It's been such a long time"

"I know. Right? I'm making it, just trying to maintain out there in the A."

"I hear that," laughed Rain, "what kind of work you doing now?" she asked as Storm hesitated to answer.

"I've been dancing in a strip club for the last two years, but I really want to go to school for cosmetology because that's my thing. I can do the fuck out some hair; just ain't making enough to pay the bills, so it is what it is," expressed Storm.

"Well, I tell you what..." said Rain, "I can't really talk about this like I want to now," pointing toward Rico coming her way, "but before you leave, I'm going to give you my number, and when I get back from my honeymoon we're gonna get some things done."

"Excuse me," Rico interrupted, "can I please steal my bride back now," he laughed as he held Rain close. "You've had her long enough," he said, extending his hand to greet her.

"Storm," she said, shaking his hand back, "I'm Rain's cousin."

"Favorite cousin," said Rain, blowing a kiss at Storm as Rico whisked her away to the dance floor.

"I love you, Mrs. Tulio;" Rico gazed into her eyes, realizing she was now his wife. "I'm complete now."

"Oh, really?" she laughed sexually, "well, there's one last thing I need to be complete," said Rain, smiling up at him.

"And what's that?" he asked.

"I'm gonna need you to tear this pussy up for the first time as your wife."

"No sooner than we hit the island of Hawaii, queen," said Rico, "you don't have to ask. It's whatever you want for the rest of our lives together," he said as they continued to dance the night away.

Rain and Storm did meet up after the wedding; in fact, Storm stayed in New York to babysit RJ while they went on their honeymoon. Two weeks of nothing but pure bliss and passion from Rico was more than enough for Rain. Indeed, he completed her just like he promised, but niggas was running low back in Brooklyn; so like every good thing, it had to end. Once back at home, Rico went straight to work fixing what went wrong while he was away.

Rain, on the other hand, couldn't understand why she was still so lazy. It was almost like she was still in vacation mode with all the sleeping she was doing. Thank God for Storm still being there because RJ would have been taking care of himself.

"What's wrong with you, cousin?" whispered Storm as she sat on Rain's bed beside her.

"I don't know, girl," she replied, waking up from her sleep. "I haven't been right ever since we got back."

"Are you pregnant?"

"Don't know…could be," she answered, sitting up on the side of her bed, "I never really took the time to get the test and check, but I think I need too."

"Well, go in your bathroom and take the one under your sink," smiled Storm as she noticed Rain's expression that said, *how the fuck you know?*

"Maybe you're right," Rain said, getting up to head into the bathroom, "since I gotta pee, I might as well do it now. I'll be back!"

Finding out she was pregnant with Aaliyah was a shocker; neither Rain nor Rico was expecting another baby right after getting married; but to her surprise, Rain was pregnant before the wedding. Rico, of course, was happy at the thought of having another baby. RJ was daddy's lil man; but having a daughter would really complete their family. With Rain being pregnant again, Storm decided to stay in New York and help her out. She figured there wasn't shit happening back in Georgia anyway, so why not stay in the Big Apple and try to go to school or something. Plus, it wasn't like her cousin wasn't balling anyway, so why not?

It all worked out for Rain; but being that there was still money to be made, she still did her part in making sure business flowed. Having her cousin there was perfect because she could drive her around.

If her brain works anything like it did when we were young, then I know she's picked up on the game by now, thought Rain as she sat by the pool watching RJ swim. "I was just thinking about you," Rain said as she sat her glass of wine down on the table, "where you coming from?"

"Applying for school and some jobs. Oh, by the way, thanks for letting me use the car."

"Oh, you good, girl; that's what I like to hear…you doing positive shit to get money. Speaking of money, I want you to be smart out in these streets," said Rain, "it's things I know that Rico don't have a clue I even understand; and I've learned a lot of stuff from sitting back, paying attention and learning. Everything I've seen, everything I've heard…I learned from, and I'm gonna school you, Storm. Just in case one day it could come in handy for you," they laughed and toasted their glasses to the good life.

After giving birth to Aaliyah and things being back on track for Rico, shit was looking mighty good at home. With Storm in school and Rico always gone, Rain hardly did any work for him at all. She spent a lot of time at home with the kids having "mommy time" and shopping; kind of like when she was young with her mom. "Never repeat the cycle" was a motto Rain lived by when it came to being like Jackie in the game. So, deciding to be different, Rain went to school for business and got her license just in case.

Rico was feeling like the king of New York; accomplishing all his goals without ever working, but things started to get boring and he needed a new challenge with the game. Ignoring his own rules, as well as his wife's advice, Rico decided to do a side deal without his family.

"Never change your game, stick to the plan. Wasn't that what you always said?" Rain asked as she ran her hand across his wavy hair and kissed his forehead. "Poppy, I love you, okay? Baby, you hear me?" she asked Rico as he lay, still unconscious in the hospital bed. "I need you to come home, okay? So you gotta wake up now and show these prick ass fucks that you're still the king," she said, grabbing his hand and trying hard not to cry. She played with his wedding ring. "I'm not ready to divorce you yet, Rico. So fight, baby, because the kids love you and so do I."

Rain placed his hand back down on the bed and she saw him move his finger. "Oh, shit. Nurse!" she screamed, pushing the call bell, "nurse! Poppy, you moved! You heard me?" she asked, wondering why the nurse was taking so fucking long. Rain headed to find the nurse, but as soon as she reached the door, Rico's machines started going off and he stopped breathing. "What the… poppy!" she screamed, running back to his bed, "please, baby, don't leave me!" she begged as the nurses and doctors filled the room to save Rico's life.

"Ma'am, I'm gonna have to ask you to leave the room right now," said one of the nurses practically pushing Rain out the door.

"Get the fuck off me, that's my husband!" Rain fought back as her eyes watched them fight to save Rico's life.

"I think we've lost him," was all that played over in her mind as she opened her eyes looking up in the ceiling to face bright ass lights. Rain thought this was a dream and she was now coming out of it, but she could tell by the knot on her head that she'd fainted from something. All she could do was pray that by the time she got out that bed, her something would be nothing.

"Are you alright, Mrs. Tulio?" asked the nurse.

"Where's my husband?" she asked in the most threatening voice she'd ever used before.

"Mrs. Tulio, you really need your rest. You've had a pretty bad fall so were going to keep you overnight," said the nurse.

Rain wasn't feeling the shit she was talking; all she wanted to know about was Rico. "I'm only gonna ask you one more fucking time," demanded Rain standing up to face the nurse, "I want you to tell me where my husband is now!" she screamed.

"Ma'am, your husband is dead. I'm sorry," she said as she reached out to touch Rain's arm but she pulled away. "I know this is a very difficult time for you right now, but I'm going to have to advise you to try and get some rest."

Never shedding a tear, Rain just stood there staring right in her face as she put on her Marc Jacob sunglasses, grabbed her phone and keys, and walked right past that bitch to leave the hospital. The old Rain was dead; leaving her heart with Rico. The new person behind her glasses was alive and breathing; the only difference was that from that day on...she was heartless.

* * * * *

Coming back to the house for the first time without Rico was a bitch. When Rain pulled up in the driveway, she just sat there, still in disbelief.

"How the fuck am I going to tell my kids that their father ain't coming home again" she said out loud, taking a deep breath and preparing to go into the house, In order to face the pain, Rain took one more deep breath before entering.

"Girl, I've been trying to call you all day" Storm said as RJ and Aaliyah ran over to their mom for a kiss. "I know, it's been off," Rain said, reaching down to pick up her kids. "Mommy needs to talk to you two about something very important," she said, looking back and forth at her kids.

"Mommy, can I call daddy first and ask him when he'll be home to play me in the game?" asked RJ. Hearing the words coming from her son's mouth cut Rain deep.

"Babies," she said, taking a long pause, "daddy was in the hospital because he was hurt real bad."

"What do you mean?" asked Storm, puzzled as shit.

"Daddy had to go away," said Rain as the tears beginning rolling down her face causing Storm to realize what she was saying. Storm placed her arms around her cousin to comfort her.

"You serious? Rico's dead?" she asked shedding tears herself. She had lived with them for five years now and Rico was like the brother she never had.

"Gone where, mommy? asked Aaliyah, too young to understand.

"Your daddy's in heaven," Rain explained, "he's with God and the angels now," she held her kids to sooth their pain, but at that time, everyone in that house needed someone; including Rain.

That day was hard, but Rain knew it was going to be harder to bury Rico. With so much to arrange and Ricky getting on her nerves, Rain didn't know if she was coming or going, but she remained focused. When it came to taking care of business for Rico, she always took that serious; and his death wasn't going to be any different.

The seats of Holy Cross quickly filled with family and friends coming to pay their final respect to the king and Rain did a beautiful job laying her baby to rest. Being that Rico only wore suits on special occasions, she decided to not only do it his way, but she showed New York just how Rico Tulio really got down. A fourteen karate gold casket with the words, "KING OF NEW YORK" engraved at the top was the final resting place for Rico. He laid peacefully dressed in an all-black Gucci linen outfit with his black, trimmed in gold, Cartier frames and inside the casket Rain had placed photos of them together and the kids. All of the family lined up to walk in and take their final look at Rico before saying goodbye. Instead of Rain wanting to be in front of the line, she chose to be last. It wasn't like she was enjoying this shit anyway; plus, she wanted everyone in the room, including Ricky to see her face so they would know that this wasn't going to be over. RJ held his sister's hand as they walked up to see their dad. With tears in his eyes, he placed a soft basketball, which was his favorite toy, in his father's hands and walked away.

"I love you daddy," cried Aaliyah, holding on to her mother's legs as Rain bent to kiss her husband one last time.

"So, this is it; huh?" she whispered, "I thought I told you I wasn't ready to get divorced yet," she rubbed his head, never shedding a tear. She didn't give a fuck about holding up the funeral; this was the last time she was going to talk with her husband face to face.

"I have always loved you, Rico Tulio; and this isn't going to stop the love I have for you. I promise you, poppy, I'm going to find out who separated us, and when I do, I can guarantee you that I'll send them to you," she said, taking her finger and placing it over his lips as she walked to take her seat.

Rico's cousin, Shirley, sang *Amazing Grace*, causing every eye in the church to be wet. Even the hardest thug had tears in their eyes because they knew a true soldier was gone. Ricky, on the other hand, just held his wife close as she broke down in pain. They say the hardest thing for a parent is to bury their child, and Christina felt every bit of that saying. Ricky just stared at Rico as his heart broke more and more. It wasn't a secret that he hated Rain, but this just made shit worse in a sense, because in a way, he blamed her ass too. Rain could feel his eyes burning through her soul, but she hated his ass too; so she didn't give a fuck. Half of her world was lying right before her eyes and she had to say goodbye, so she sat there hard as stone in her Versace black dress fitting each part of her body just right. Her long hair hung slightly over her shoulder, looking like pure silk as her black hat sat perfectly in position. Her Marc Jacob glasses went well with the black and gold, seven-hundred-dollar Christian Louboutin shoes which Rico had bought, but she never got to wear…until now. Rain never showed any emotions the whole time during the service; only turning her head to look at her kids and then right back to Rico.

The pallbearers carried Rico out to a horse and carriage pulled by six white horses. Rain and the kids sat in the front so they could take one last ride with their father. All of the rest of the cars followed as they took Rico's body through the hood one last time. Rico took care of the streets, making sure everybody was good; and the game was hurting behind this shit. So, niggas weren't going to rest until somebody paid.

Placing a rose, one by one, on top of the casket, everyone left the cemetery; saying their final goodbyes. To Ricky it symbolized love, respect, and honor to his son and that's all he ever wanted for his life.

"Excuse me, La'Rain," a voice from behind her said. She turned to face the voice and removed her sunglasses so her eyes could be seen.

"Yes?" she said in the angriest of tones as Tip began to speak.

"Rico was with me and my brother the night he was murdered and I just wanted to personally say, I'm sorry," he noticed the facial expression she was giving him.

"I want to know everything," she said, pointing her finger at Tip's face, "you niggas either know or y'all better find out who was the one in on this shit with your cousin," Rain said, making Tip confused as to how she knew Majesty was his cousin. He also knew now wasn't the time to try and figure it out. "I know your cousin's dead, but I also know that punk ass nigga was teamed up as well. So, just when y'all think I don't know…I do," she said, placing her glasses back on. "So, you can spread the word and y'all niggas better squad up. I'm going to be the hand that's going to continue feeding you and a lot of things are going to change. None for the worse, all for the good. Understood?" she asked Tip as he nodded his head to say yes. "My husband will still remain the king in these streets because his queen ain't done yet," she walked away, leaving Tip standing right there.

Ricky and Christina did the repass at their house; but Rain didn't attend. She knew that they really didn't care for her; plus, she didn't want to be around Ricky's ignorant ass, so she, Storm, and the kids went home. She wanted to start looking for a new house because she felt being there would be too hard for her and the kids to handle. After getting the kids to bed, all Rain wanted to do was sleep. She hadn't slept in her bed for a week and she felt like giving it a try so she did just that. She wrapped her legs around Rico's pillow Rand buried her face into it; inhaling Rico's scent as she closed her eyes and tried to sleep in *their* bed.

*****

Over the past six months, Rain's life was spinning out of control very fast. Getting used to life without Rico became difficult with each breath. Things with Rico's crew were at its worst; and for the first time ever, Rain handled business with the lawyers settling Rico's estate. She opened up accounts under the kids' names; using Rico's insurance money because she wasn't spending anything that was given to her from losing him. Jennifer Jamison was the attorney for the kids and since she was handling all the financial business involving them, she and Rain became real close friends. Rain was preparing to move out of the house that she once shared with her husband which was very hard for her to do; but having Storm there made things a little bit easier for her at times.

"Everything in the downstairs office is boxed up and ready to be moved," instructed Rain, talking to the movers as they prepared to move her things into the new house. "I haven't gotten to the garage, so don't go in there yet," she said as she walked up the driveway back toward the house. She noticed Tip's car pulling in and stopped right in her tracks.

What the fuck does he want now? she thought, wondering why he was there. Tip approached her and she could tell by his actions that something had pissed him off. She knew it had to concern Rico, otherwise why was he coming to see her.

"Wassup, Rain?" How have you been?" asked Tip.

"I'm doing as well as could be expected under these circumstances."

"Yeah, I heard that." said Tip, "we all missing that nigga, Rico, like crazy B, and shit ain't never gonna be the same. You feel me? That's why I'm here."

He explained to Rain Ricky's plans of wanting to set Steven and Jose up with parts of Rico's empire; splitting it down the middle between the two so that the money coming in could still somehow be under Ricky's control. Tip tried to bring Rain up to speed quickly while her back was turned and before she realized the power she really possessed being Rico's wife.

Laughing at how low Ricky would really go to get his way, Rain was burning with anger inside, *this nigga done gone too far now,* she thought, *he's trying to take from me what my husband lost his life trying to build. He gotta be sick if he thinks I'm going to lay down and take that shit like the dog he thinks I am.* Before Rain knew it, she was screaming at Tip, letting him know that she wasn't having that shit.

"I want you to get all the boys together for me, Tip. Let them know it's real and now is the time for me to put everything I've learned into action! I'm taking charge; just like the queen my husband taught me to be. So, those who thought I was gone, let them know we've only just begun, and I'll get back to you with the date. So, just make sure they are ready to go!" she stormed off, headed toward the garage to pack because hearing that made her want to take position faster.

Rain's Diary

Dear Dairy,

It feels good to be the bitch! I know that nigga, Ricky, really hates me now; but who cares? My husband's gone, but that doesn't mean his money has to stop. Plus, my kids are going to eat anyway. Since Rico's been gone I haven't had sex with anyone; but I do let Vick eat my pussy from time to time… and he enjoys the taste of money. It could never be serious between us because he is my protector and the line stops there. I'll never mix business with pleasure; but I will let him suck on this twat though.

I love making my own decisions and the streets are making double the money; which means they appreciate me and I love it! The way things have been going with me and Ricky, he may try to throw some shit in the game; that's why I need to start setting some shit up for myself and the kids, as well as the option of working on my own and not under Ricky Tulio! Well, time to go shopping with Aaliyah. I love my kids so much. Their all I have left of Rico and I will always love and treat them the same way he would if he were here!

Later!

Queen's Way

The light of hope allows those without dollars to dream; and through your life's existence become wealthy because having knowledge is being a Queen. Rain never realized that being black meant being hated until the day that she met Ricky; and after Rico's death, the shit just got worse.

How the fuck this nigga gone try and take what I helped my husband build? thought Rain while calling Tip to make sure the Crew was set for her meeting. "He must be crazy to think I'm that damn dumb, but I got his ass without having to make any noise and I want him to keep thinking I'm this stupid bitch he makes me out to be," said Rain, grinning at herself in the mirror as she stroke the head of Diamond, her tea cup Yorkie. She made sure Storm was straight and ready to attend the meeting, while RJ and Aaliyah visited with Rico's parents, which was perfect because she knew that would keep Ricky busy.

The crew started arriving just like Rain had ordered and not a minute later. Rain sat at the head of her boardroom table, waiting patiently for everyone to have a seat. Tip and James were the last to come strolling in the house, and as they made their way back toward the office to enter, James was struck by Storm's beauty and he knew he had to have her.

"Wassup?" he spoke as Storm walked past.

"Hey," she replied, stopping in her tracks.

"I'm James and you must be…"

"Storm," she answered, giving him a smile.

"Well, Ms. Storm, I can't talk to you like I want to now; but maybe I can get your number so we can hang out," he asked, handing her his phone and she put her number in it as they walked into the room, ready for Rain's meeting.

* * * * *

Once everyone was seated and all eyes were on her, Rain just sat there staring at them all with disappointment in her eyes. "Most of you already know why I called this meeting; but for those of you who don't, allow me to enlighten you," she uttered, reclining back in her chair like a boss with Diamond on her lap, "it takes brains to make money and to be able to survive this business. This is something I know all too well," she said, explaining to the crew what her rules for survival where going to be. "First things first," she paused, pointing her finger at the crew, "I want all you niggas to remain at your spots and everything will stay the same except for the way we mix our product as well as our prices, which Vick will get with y'all on that very soon. My plan is to shut these other dealers down by making our shit call their names," she expressed, "with our quality plus quantity being the shit, there's no way we can lose; and that's what I want y'all to keep in mind because this is the way Rico would have wanted it to be. My safety meant everything to him; that's why it's important we do this shit my way; do you understand?" she asked the crew as they all shook their heads in agreement, as well as the excitement of making even more money than they did at first. "So, I take it we're clear?" Rain said, standing from her seat to leave. A thought came to mind that delayed her plans as she turned around so that they all could see her face. "Oh, and one more the thing…I know somebody in this room knows the person responsible for what happen to my husband," a change in the tone of her voice let niggas know she was hurting, "and I don't care if it takes weeks, months, or even years to do…I want that nigga brought to me so I can handle him personally!" Raine stared into the eyes of everyone at the table to let them know she meant business.

Storm noticed that every nigga at the table damn near broke down behind the loss of their fallen leader. Their actions showed Rain that the crew was down for revenging Rico's death; no matter what had to be done. As Storm surveyed the emotion in the room, she looked over at James. His facial expression wasn't what she expected and it seemed very strange. It was as if he knew something, but wasn't saying shit. Storm didn't have anything to base the feeling she was getting on, there was just something about the look on his face. She couldn't put her finger on what was wrong, so she brushed it off, never telling Rain what she saw.

"Well, Ms. Lady," James said to Storm as he headed for the door, "I would love to get to know you better if you'd grant me that wish."

His comment caused Storm to blush. Since she'd only had hookups since she lived in New York, the idea of steady dick made her pussy moist. "Yes," she answered, "just use the number I gave you. You still got it; right?" she joked, knowing he was feeling her so he would definitely still have her digits.

"Yes, I do," replied James, giving her a hug as he left with the others.

Storm headed for the stairs. Unbeknownst to her, Rain had been standing at the top landing, listening the whole time.

"What the fuck was that all about?" asked Rain. She was mad as hell over the idea of her cousin talking to James' ass. "I don't trust him, Storm. You really need to be careful," advised Rain because she felt like his ass was sneaky from day one. "When it comes to that nigga James," she said, looking Storm dead in the eyes to show that she meant business, "sometimes he's not trustworthy," she explained, hoping Storm would listen.

Storm always trusted Rain's instinct on things; but for some reason, in the back of her mind, she could not hide the thought of wanting to get inside James' head a little bit more. Plus, there was the overwhelming fact that she was feeling him a lot.

"Chill, cuz," laughed Storm, walking up the stairs past Rain, "I'm just fucking with him," she expressed. "And, by the way, he's not my type," she told Rain, knowing like hell she was lying her ass off. "I'm bout my money, honey," replied Storm, walking into her bedroom and shutting the door.

Rain left to go and pick up her kids from Rico's parents' house.

"Mommy," said Aaliyah as she ran up to Rain. Aaliyah had spotted her mother walking into the yard.

"Hey, baby," she said reaching to Aaliyah, giving her a kiss, "where is your brother?" she asked following Aaliyah as she walked toward the porch where Christina and Ricky sat talking.

"He's right there, mommy," Aaliyah said, pointing toward RJ who was sitting beside his grandfather.

After Rico's death, there really wasn't any male figure in RJ's life, so he became closer to Ricky.

"Hello, La'Rain," greeted Christina as she sipped on her champagne, "you look lovely today," she said sarcastically, admiring Rain's attire from head to toe. She felt that her daughter in law could afford to look good at the expense of her son's money; and her comment was meant to be a stab to her ass even more.

"Thank you, Christina," replied Rain as Ricky sat there hating on her with each breath he took.

"La'Rain, may I speak to you in private, please?" asked Ricky as he stood up from his seat. Rain agreed, and followed him into his office to talk. Rain was shocked that he even said anything to her and she was dying to find out why. "How has everything been with you since my son left us all?" he asked, pouring them both a shot of scotch as they took a seat.

"I'm okay," replied Rain, wanting to punch that nigga in his face for the underhanded shit he tried to pull; but she remained calm as she sipped on her shot.

"Well, I was thinking that Steven and Jose should take over the crew," suggested Ricky as he looked Rain straight in her eyes. He took a sip of scotch, "Money will never be an issue because you have my grandkids; but I would rather that someone more experienced handle my son's business, and I just don't think that's you."

With a big ass smile spreading straight across her face Rain sat there listening until it was her time to speak, "Well, first of all, let me just tell you thanks, but no thanks, to your little ass offer, Ricky," she expressed, never showing him any sign of anger. "I don't need a hand out from you or anybody else; and for the record," she softly laughed showing Ricky that to her…he was a joke. "Let me inform you that I'm not that dumb black bitch that you try to make me out to be," she expressed; mad as hell. "I, too, have a father who once lived this life, and I've also learned a lot from watching your son. So before you go giving niggas *my* shit, Ricky," she stood from her seat to leave, "I suggest you converse with me. And just so you know, I've already spoken with the crew and they know all the rules to my game. So next time, plot a little better before you try to be a snake, dad," she laughed at what she just called Ricky; she knew it would piss him off even more. "Your deposits will continue to flow on time," she said, "maybe even sooner than usual," she added as she turned to exit his office.

Ricky stood there, steaming with anger and hatred toward her ass. He knew she had the power to do whatever she wanted with the crew; but what he still had control over was her supply.

"RJ, Aaliyah...let's go!" demanded Rain as she stormed off their porch. She left their house mad as hell. Rain did not say a word to Christina who was looking puzzled, not knowing what had just happen.

* * * * *

Rain wanted to scream. She was furious with that nigga as she drove twice the speed limit to get home. The only comfort she had was that she also knew that he was pissed with her for not accepting his offer concerning Rico's business. She didn't care how pissed he was. The thought of him cutting off her supply came to mind, but she hoped that Ricky couldn't possibly be that cold toward her out of respect for Rico.

What Rain didn't know was that Ricky had a plan of his own; he wasn't going to act too quickly. He wanted Rain to make him some money—the money he felt she owed his family for the years Rico had spent buying shit for her ass. So he just sat back and was, for once, quite as Rain jumped head-first into the family business. The areas that people thought she wouldn't succeed in, were mastermind by her within months. The first thing Rain did was to change the location of Rico's main spot. The area had become a hotbox which Five O now had on lock. Rain became the owner of a Columbian soul food restaurant that she called, Rico's Kitchen and in the back was a big ass storage garage where instead of only storing food, she would linkup with the crew to do and discuss business. Rain sold the exact same shit as Steven and Jose; but she did things a little bit different from the way Ricky wanted it. She felt it was time to play the game her way.

Having the crew mix her supply differently was her next plan of action. Her shit wasn't washed up with Acetone and Kerosene like other niggas were doing. It was almost close to being pure; that's why she chose to call it "Queens Way." Each of her boxes contained two thousand bottles; and selling them for $100 a piece was genius to the crew and the fends because other dealers were selling at the highest price they could get; which to Rain was a good thing for her. She knew that word on the street traveled fast in her hood, and soon niggas would hear about her crew and their prices. It wouldn't be long before their customers would belong to the crew. Queens Way was selling so fast that it was like getting wholesale on the streets. That made Rain a shitload of money really fast and Ricky always got his return on time. Everybody that should have been...was definitely living well. Niggas once again were happy; everyone with the exception of Ricky.

By now, Storm and James had gone out on a couple of dates and things between them started to really heat up. Their relationship pissed Rain's ass the fuck off, *there's no fucking way I'm letting my cousin date that sneaky muthafucka,* Rain thought while driving to meet the real estate agent to pick up the keys to a beauty salon she was buying. She'd always wanted to own a salon, and since Storm had just gotten her license in cosmetology, owning that shit now would be perfect! After meeting Mrs. Thompson, Rain realized that she still had some time before picking up the kids, so she decided to go by the restaurant and check up on things there.

Approaching the street where the restaurant sat, Rain noticed a blue Crown Victoria parked on the corner as she got out of her truck. Rain kept right on with what she was doing as this couple came up and approached her.

"Excuse me," said the man as Rain gave both of them a sour ass look. "Me and my girl were wondering where we could score some drugs," he stated, making Rain suspicious about why they stopped her.

"I'm sorry," Rain stated in her most sophisticated voice, "I don't know what you're talking about or what in the hell made you stop me," she continued, wondering what the fuck was up.

Nothing about her said *drug dealer*, plus she was on her way into the restaurant; so for all they knew, she was going there to eat. With the lady hanging slightly onto his arm as if she was stoned already, the man replied, "Word on the street is that if I want it for cheap, then you're the one to see. You're La'Rain; right?"

How the fuck this muthafucka know my name? More importantly, he called me by my government name which nobody in the streets ever does, Rain thought as the whole situation was starting to make her feel uncomfortable. She was suspicious that they might be snitches for the police. What other reason would they have to fuck with her unless they had a death wish. Rain was flashy and she was now the owner of two establishments which she had the papers to prove; but she knew something wasn't right about this. It was almost as if somebody was trying to set her up.

"I don't know who you're looking for," Rain said, smiling hard at their dumb asses, "but I'm late for a date, so I gotta go," she expressed, still laughing as she walked away leaving them standing there looking dumb.

As Rain walked through the restaurant, she couldn't help but wonder what the fuck that incident was all about. That shit had never happen to Rico and she did things much calmer than he did. Storm, Vick, and Tip were in the back, chilling when Rain came in pissed ass fuck and feeling like she needed to relieve some stress.

"Meeting now!" she demanded, causing Vick to know that something was wrong. "What's wrong, boss," Vick asked. He stood behind her chair so that he could pull it out for her. Then he began massaging her shoulders so that she could relax.

"On my way in just now, I was stopped by these two people looking to score drugs," she explained, handing Vick her glass to get her something to drink. "Out of all the niggas out there on the strip hustling, they approached me and not only that…" she said, taking the glass from Vick and sipping on it slowly, "they called me by my real name and we all know that nobody does that."

A look of shock came over their faces, "So, who do you think it was?" asked Storm, wondering why anyone would be stupid enough to fuck with Rain or her money. "Did you recognize them or their car?"

"No, I didn't. But I did see a blue Crown Vick parked at the corner, but I don't know if that's where they came from. I don't know who they could have been, even though the way they came off made me believe they were some cop snitches," explained Rain.

"Mane, something up with them cats," expressed Tip, "they were either stickup kids or like you said, boss, they working for the pigs. Either way, they're not old business and that's your policy; stick to the old and leave the new alone," he said, letting Rain know he was on point with his shit.

That was something she tried to teach Rico, but he didn't listen; so she made sure she took that rule very serious in her world.

"Well, just put the word out to the rest of the crew," she instructed to Tip, "let them know that under no circumstances are they to serve, or even talk about Queens Way with anybody that we don't already affiliate with. At least until I get to the bottom of this," said Rain. "If anyone needs anything, they can either tell you, or call Vick and he'll get with me. Whatever is going on, I can promise you they won't get the satisfaction of seeing me fall on my face. I can be a snake when I need to be too," Rain said signaling Storm and Tip to leave the room so she could be alone with Vick. After all was said and the orders were given, that's exactly what they did.

"Come here," said Vick, holding his arms open to embrace Rain. She walked into his arms as he lifted her face to kiss her lips. Rain turned her head, causing Vick to catch her on the neck, "Don't worry, baby," he said, knowing that she needed to feel good. He picked her up and placed her on top of her desk. "I'll never let anything happen to you because I'm your protector," Vick assured her as he parted her legs to taste her sweet pussy.

Rain moaned out in passion. Vick could eat the fuck out of some pussy and Rain enjoyed every bit of his tongue game. He twirled his tongue around her clit; licking in and out of her pussy hole like a snake. Rain's leg began to tremble as Vick's head went up and down—sucking the nut out of her and catching it all in his mouth. He swallowed each and every bit of her sweet, but bitter-tasting cum. Rain knew Vick was feeling her in more ways than one, but crossing over that line was sure to be a no no. Beside Storm, Vick was the only person that Rain could trust anymore.

*****

Rain wasn't trying to shine on niggas just to have them hating. She put people on and for the first time since Rico's death, the streets were once again happy; that is until things started changing and people knew too much. Rain and Storm went back and forth processing that situation and shit just wasn't adding up. *Who could it be? Who would want to destroy Rain the most?* To Rain's knowledge, she had no known enemies. The only person she could think of who really disliked her was Ricky. *Was it him? Was he sending strange people to set her up for the cops?* Plus, everyone knew he had those pigs on his fucking pay roll. *Was he finally making them earn their money he paid them to let him be the man?* Rain didn't know who or what to think it was; but she damn sure wasn't going to rest until she did. But there was still some work to be done and Rain wasn't about to let them steal her show.

Organizing the shop was half as stressful as Rain and Storm thought it would be. Since Storm was managing it, Rain let her do the decorating. It was her way of saying, *I'm proud of you* because she had graduated and received her license in hair and now she was doing the type of work that she loved. Storm would still be able to make runs for Rain while maintaining her cliental at the shop. Five stylist, four barbers and two nail techs made up the family at Secret Impressions—all handpicked personally by Storm herself. Some of the girls knew Storm from school, while the other two were her friends from the hood; but they were nice when it came to hair. Storm and Rain held interviews for the rest of the staff, and of course, they had to pick the best that Brooklyn had to offer. The times spent at the shop laughing and gossiping with Storm, the staff, and the customers brought a little light Rain's way again. Even though snow was knee deep on the ground, being around them made Rain feel warm inside with love. Which was something she hadn't felt in the year and a half that Rico had been dead.

Rain became all about her business. She never showed any emotions toward anybody except her kids, Donny and Storm because they were her family now. Walking into Secret Impression's, you never know who you might see. They had cliental from locals on the street all the way up to celebrities; and all their styles were hot! You could get a wrap and an autograph all at once and the customer's couldn't get enough.

James would bring Storm lunch every day. All them slutty ass bitches would be chewing through his swag when he walked in looking and smelling like new money while catering to Storm. Rain, on the other hand, hated that shit. She didn't know what the fuck it was, but from day one, she told Rico that James was sneaky, and there was something about him that changed her mood anytime he came around.

Hot 97 was the station that the shop jammed to daily. As Rain entered, the sound of Angie Martinez's voice filled the shop.

"Hey, babe," greeted Rain, walking over to Storm and hugging her while she finished up Mrs. Braxton's sew-in, "it's looking kind of busy in here."

"I know. Right?" replied Storm as Rain took a seat behind the register right beside Storm's booth, "we've been swamped all day and it hasn't slowed down yet," explained Storm as the alarm from the front door opening caused them both to look up.

"Hey, daddy," said Storm as James walked over and gave her a kiss. "What you bring me today?" she asked, inquiring about her lunch.

"I picked you up the Plato Palisa," replied James, sitting the bag down on the counter. He knew that was Storm's favorite Columbian dish. It consisted of white rice, beans, eggs fried on rice, with a strip of steak. Storm loved it so much that she would eat from Rico's Kitchen twice, maybe three times a week.

"Wassup, Rain," James spoke as she set there mean mugging the shit out of him.

Being nasty wasn't really Rain's thing; besides, there was one very important rule to the game that Rain firmly believed in, and that was to keep your friends close and your enemies closer. Throwing up her hand in the air to speak to him, she never said a word…just looked in his direction.

"Can I talk to you for a minute, please?" James asked Rain.

For a second, she continued sitting there; then she got up and signaled James to follow her into the back room to talk. Their actions caused Storm to become curious about what was up.

"So, talk," Rain instructed, giving him her business look.

"I got a call today from a private number," explained James with fear in his voice, "and they told me to inform my boss that her time was running short and to pass down her crown," he continued as the look on Rain's face showed confusion.

Shit had gotten a little quite since Rain was approached by the strange ass people on the street, but it seemed as if it was back on again

"Did you ask who they were?" questioned Rain, mad as hell on the inside but remaining calm to James.

"Yeah, I did; but they just hung up," he replied. "Look, boss, I don't know what the fuck is going on, but I do know that the couple that approached you the other day just moved in the area. I don't know how they know who you are. So what do you want the crew to do?" asked James as the look on Rain's face showed him she had an idea.

"I want you, Wize and Smitty to do around the clock patrol on them pricks!" ordered Rain, "In two days send me a report back to Vick with everything that y'all find out about their routine. I'll take it from there. This shit started the day I met them two, and I don't know if they are the one's making the calls or not, but I believe in pulling out roots," she said, "and to me that's exactly what they are—roots."

"I gotcha, Rain," said James, giving her his word. "I'm on that shit right now," he said, turning to walk out the room. He gave Storm a kiss and left.

Storm could tell by the look on Rain's face as she walked back up front that shit had just taken a turn for the worse. *Something was about to go down, but what?*

Within the next couple of days, shit with the crew was defiantly on point. Them niggas went hard at collecting information that could possibly be valuable to what Rain had plan. Wize, being the early bird, took first shift, of course. This nigga was up every morning by 6:45 a.m. anyway, so keeping an early eye on those cats to him was like a walk in the park.

Every morning at 8:50 a.m. exactly, the woman left first; dressed in business attire like she had a job in an office and shit. Now the nigga, on the other hand, always dressed like he was part of a crew, with baggy jeans and a fitted on. His attire made it hard for Wize to determine what he did, plus he never left the house until the clock struck twelve on the head. He went across the street to the corner store for milk and lotto; but who the fuck buys milk every day?

By now, Smitty was taking the shift when the woman returned home at approximately 4:15 p.m. She was carrying two brown grocery bags, but from the bulge in them, he knew it wasn't food. She would sit in the window writing in what seemed to be a journal, but Smitty thought that bitch could be taking notes of the entire activities going and reporting back to someone.

Just when James clocked in, the couple clocked out. They were dressed in evening wear as if they had an engagement. James followed them, pulling up to the same restaurant every night. He watched them park with valet and go inside. Not thirty minutes later, the same two guys followed behind them which was strange. James never saw them conversing, but he still felt like there was more to them returning to the same place every night. Time was running out and when Rain set a deadline—especially bout something this serious—she meant business and now it was time to report. Smitty, not really wanting to be the bearer of bad news, did as he was told; passing the news all the way to Rain.

After carefully evaluating all of the details she was told, Rain decided it was time for some action. Carefully planning a little sighting for herself and confirming all that the crew members had gathered, Rain felt it was time to pay a visit to that restaurant. One day, after watching the couple on their daily routine, Rain arrived at the restaurant early. Sitting in a disguise, she spotted the two as they made their entrance and sat down at what seemed to be their usual table.

Look at them bitches, she thought as she watched the couple toast with a glass of champagne. *I'm glad they getting their celebration on because this will be their last one,* she mumbled, noticing the two men approaching right on schedule and taking their seat. "What the fuck are they saying?" Rain asked herself. The conversations in the room seemed to have gotten louder and she was having trouble hearing. She decided to move closer and she still remained unnoticed as one of the guys looked up toward her just long enough for her to see his face.

What the fuck? Rain thought as she remembered seeing his face from somewhere before. "I know that fucking nigga. I just can't remember from where." She began searching her memory, "he was at a party given by the Tulios, but I don't know who he knows in the family or why he even wants to fuck with me."

Rain continued watching him as he slid an envelope under the table to the woman. She placed it in her purse as the four shook hands and the exited the restaurant two by two. Rain wasn't far behind, but as she made her way toward her truck, she noticed James' car pulling off from in front of the restaurant. Now her mind really started to wonder. "Why the fuck was he here?" she said, reaching for her cellphone to call Storm. Before dialing her number, she changed her mind; not wanting to draw heat right now. "I'll get back to that later. Right now I got some fish to fry."

Rain called Vick instead. She let him know it was on and to grab both of the strangers as soon as they open their damn door. She had previously instructed Vick to hide inside their spot, which made that shit extra easy now for him to carry out her plans. Rain sat parked at the corner waiting patiently as the couple made their way inside the house. When Rain heard the sound of a gunshot, she knew it was her signal to pull off and wait for Vick to arrive.

"Right on time, Vick," she said, walking up to him. They stood side by side as the eyes of the couple barely opened to face Rain once again.

"Where are we?" the man tried to mumble, but their mouths were gaged.

The bitch couldn't see, let alone talk. Vick had swollen her face with his fist.

Blood from their injuries and the man's gunshot wound to the knee started to fuck up the floor beneath them. Vick had beated their asses and he proved he was Rain's protector. The feelings he had for Rain made him a lot more dangerous and the only reason he didn't kill them himself was because of his boss' orders.

"You're in my world now," replied Rain with the most devious smile she could have. She walked closer to the two as Vick just stood there watching. "I know you wish you could rewind back to your decision to ever challenge me," she stated, laughing laugh softly under her breath, "and for what, huh? What did I ever do to you or anybody else for that matter?"

The couple cried out in fear and pain.

"Who the fuck sent you?" she asked, smacking the guy in the back of his head, but he still refused to answer her question. That pissed Rain off even more, but she still laughed as she held her hand out signaling Vick to hand her what was in his pocket. He handed her the envelope full of money that he got out of the woman's purse, along with something black that looked like a key chain alarm. "Well, I'm done playing games with you bitches," she expressed, walking beside Vick. He cuffed their arms and turned to leave them bitches wondering what was next.

"Have a nice life" were the last words the couple heard over laughter as Rain shut the door to the abandon field house she had Vick bring them to.

"What's left of it?" said Vick, escorting Rain outside to the middle of the field—far away from the field house. The two stood there smiling as Rain pushed the button on the device that blow them bitches straight to hell. Pieces of the field house, as well as body parts of the couple filled the air. Rain and Vick got in their cars and broke out.

* * * * *

Rain drove to her house with Vick following behind her to make sure she was safe. A flash back of what just took place made her want to throw up in her mouth from being nervous. She walked into the house and headed straight to her room. Rain just sat there on the edge of her bed holding her head as someone knocked on her bedroom door.

"Who is it?" asked Rain, making sure it wasn't one of her staff.

"Storm," she announced, "may I come in?"

"It's open," said Rain, giving her permission to enter.

Storm walked in and saw the look on Rain's face, she knew she'd completed whatever it was she had plan. Storm sat down, placing her arms around Rain's shoulder to let her know that she was there no matter what. Rain began giving Storm a full description of what just happen, while also informing her about the other two guys and recognizing one of their faces from being around Rico's family. She added that she didn't know who he was. Storm just sat there soaking in all the details that she was receiving. She also prayed that shit didn't get any more out of hand that it already had. After she exhaled, Storm helped Rain get comfortable and go to bed.

When Rain woke up that morning, things seemed as if they were back to normal and everything from the night before had just been a dream. She got out of bed to go find Storm and the kids.

"Good morning, babies." greeted Rain as she spotted them sitting at the kitchen table eating breakfast and watching TV. "How did you sleep?" she asked, kissing them both. Rain sat down to join them and Storm. Her staff poured her a cup of coffee while the morning news came on.

"Good Morning, I'm Sharon Cross with New York One News.

Rain told the kids to quiet down so she could hear.

"Our top story today involves an explosion that left two detectives dead."

Rain turned the volume up.

"Today, around 6:45 a.m. police responded to what they thought was a forest fire at Scott's Bluff Field. But upon their arrival, among the debris, they discovered what was left of the human remains of Detective David March and Kristy Shaw; ten-year veterans of the New York police department."

The look on Rain's face showed Storm she knew all about the story on the TV.

"Oh, my God," Rain placed her hands on her head knowing she had really fucked up this time, "what the fuck have I done, Storm?" she asked, realizing that she had just killed two cops.

"Wait a minute," Storm added, "if they were cops, then why were they fucking with you?" she asked knowing that no one in the crew had ever had a problem with the law before. "Who sent them?" she asked, but that question still remained a mystery.

"I don't know," answered Rain, "but I do know I have to fix this before Ricky's dumb ass finds out."

Rain stood from the table to go and get dressed, but the sound of her phone stopped her dead in her tracks as Ricky's number appeared on the caller ID.

"Hello," answered Rain, not knowing if he already knew what was up.

"Where are you?" asked Ricky. The tone in his voice wasn't something Rain was used to getting from him.

"I'm at home. Why" she snapped back.

He demanded to see her right away at his house. He told her not to bring the children with her because it was about business. The sound of the phone hanging up in her face let her know something was wrong. Rain got dressed and headed straight over to Ricky's house none stop.

"Hello," greeted Christina as Rain entered the house after waiting patiently for someone to answer the damn door.

"Hey, Christina," she spoke, "I'm here to see Ricky."

Rain walked toward Ricky's office where she knew he would be waiting for her. She knocked twice; waiting for permission to enter.

"Have a seat," ordered Ricky, pissed off at something.

Rain sat down immediately.

"My son and I," he began to speak, "with the exception of a couple of my very own crew members, where the only ones who knew anything about that field house, Rain," he said as he turned his chair around to face her. "Then my son showed you…even though it was against my better judgment."

Ricky paused, giving Rain a slight smile. She looked at him not knowing where the fuck he was going with all this, but she continued to listen.

"To be honest with you, Rain, this whole time that you have been around my family, starting with my son Rico, was against my better judgment. I had to be the first to let you know that this time you have really fucked up," said Ricky as Rain interrupted his ass stopping him right there.

"Wait!" she yelled, sitting up in her chair and taking off her glasses so he could see her eyes. "First of all, Ricky…FUCK YOU!" she expressed which seemed to be a sign of relief as the words flew out of her mouth. "Yeah, I knew about the field house," she replied, "but that doesn't mean I had shit to do with anything that has happen; so slow your role. And since we're being so honest," her voice got louder, "I've always hated you, just like you hate me; and frankly, I don't give a fuck about what's your better judgment; alright? she expressed, mad as hell and this time it was starting to show. "I'm RJ and Aaliyah's mother and I'm also your Rico's wife," she started laughing before continuing, "and it ain't shit that you can do to change that, Ricky. So you might as well get used to it!" Rain stood from her seat, ready to take off as usual after she got her point across.

Ricky had a different plan this time as he watched Rain open his office door to leave like it was all over. "Oh, one more thing before you leave," expressed Ricky standing from his seat with the world's biggest Kool-Aid smile on his face, "this will be the last time we meet about business," informed Ricky, "once you leave my house today, the next time you return will not be for business because I'm cutting off your supply and that is final! Ricky said as if this was the proudest day of his life.

Rain let go of his door and turned half way around to face him again. She smiled, which was not the response he was looking for.

"You know what, Richard Tulio?" she paused for a moment to breathe and hide her anger, "you have wanted to eliminate me for a very long time, so I guess your wish is granted; huh? she asked that low down bitch. "So hear this, and hear me clearly," she began to tell his ass off one more time, "the crew is still mine and they will continue to eat. I'm gonna make sure of that even if it isn't under your product," she said before continuing, "I know how to make money. So with me gone, nigga…be prepared to see your lost and my gain when I boom off somebody else's product; you stupid bitch! Rain said, slamming Ricky's office door and leaving his fucking house for good.

To whom much is given, much is tested was a quote Rain said over and over again, trying to remain calm. S felt like she was on a ship all by herself; and for once, if she didn't act quickly she thought it just might sink!

Rain's Diary

Dear Dairy,

Life is funny…I can remember being young and fantisizing about a life like the one that I have now. I've manage to defeat all my odds coming up as a child, growing into an adult without a mother or a father, and never working a regualr nine to five job; but I've still manage to learn the true meaning of hustling hard to survive. I clocked in and out every day without answering to anybody, even though there are a lot of somebodies answering to me. That shit ain't easy; especially without Rico. RJ and Aaliyah are getting so big and I've been thingking about changing my life for them. They already have better lives than I had, but I don't want this cycle to continue with them.

Storm and Donny mean so much to me as well, and after all that we're been through, I really want better for them too! This shit with Ricky really has me bugging; but I'm kind of glad it happen because I'm past being tired of his ass anyway. Plus, I'm shocked he didn't do this shit right after Rivo died; but it is what it is.

I'm tripping because he tripped about the fucking field house, but what about the two dead cops? He didn't say shit about that and I'm so wondering why. I wouldn't put it past him if his grimey ass tried to set me up. I've never trusted him anyway, or that snake James either. I just can't prove shit about either of them bitches.

Now James is dating Storm and that shit is really fucking with my nerves. But she is a big girl and has to learn on her own, but I'm still trying to warn her though. Shit crazy right now and it's only getting worse. I'll be alright because I am the queen; and like every other situation I've defeated in my life, I'll continue to do the same with this one as well.

Later!

LAVISH TO DESTRUCTION

Sometimes God uses things in our lives as a wakeup call to bring us back to reality when we're so far disconnected from the truth. For the first time ever, Rain knew exactly what that shit felt like. She never really believed that Ricky would ever cut ties with her. After all the time and money she'd made for his ass, not to mention the fact that she was Rico's wife and the mother of his grandkids. She was a Tulio and she thought that would mean more than anything else, but it didn't.

Since Ricky cut her supply, Rain took some time to reflect on her next move. Advising the crew to continue doing business as usual using the rest of the bricks that they had left, Rain thought of ways to get another connect, but it wasn't as easy as she thought.

"Turn that fucking music down, Tip!" instructed Rain, yelling in his ear through the phone.

"Wassup, boss?" Tip said while he and Chino rode around taking care of business, "you need something?"

"I need to see you today and it's very important," she began to explain, "I'll explain all the details later. But I have some business to take care of; so meet me at my house in about an hour!" she ordered, hanging up the phone.

Rain went to get ready to go out and eat, while Storm and the kids waited patiently for her downstairs. They wanted to try a new pizza place for the kids.

Oh, my God, thought Rain as she, Storm, and the kids stood in line at DINO's Pizza Palace. It was the grand opening down in Flatbush, and that bitch was jammed packed.

"This shit is ridiculous," Storm complained.

"I know. Right?" agreed Rain. "It seems like everybody in New York is here," she said, pointing to the long ass line behind them; but they had no choice but to wait because of the kids. After twenty minutes of waiting, they finally approached the door to be seated. Noticing a familiar face as they followed the waitress, Rain was shocked and she hit Storm's arm to get her attention.

"Look," she whispered to Storm, pointing to the guy sitting at the table with his family, "that's that muthafucka right there that was working with them cops."

Storm shook her head remembering what Rain told her about seeing him around Rico or his family.

"That's his ass?" asked Storm, giving him a nasty look as they all sat down and placed their orders because the kids were starving.

"Yeah, that's him," replied Rain as he and his family got up heading to leave.

Storm noticed that his girl was one of the bitches that was a regular at the shop,

"I know that bitch, too!" said Storm so only Rain could hear her, "she comes to see Dana at the shop every Wednesday. He might just want to fall back when it comes to you before I switch that bitch's perm!"

They both began to laugh.

"We're going to get to the bottom of his ass," assured Rain, grabbing Storm's hand to change the subject. Rain informed Storm that she was going to Jersey and bringing Donny home tomorrow so that they all could spend some quality time together while she tried and figure shit out.

Storm indicated that she thought that would be great. They all sat and enjoyed their meal as a happy family; it was times like this that really made Rain think of Rico.

*****

Approaching the driveway slowly, Rain noticed Tip's car pulling in at the same time as she did. Storm questioned her about him being at the house, and Rain explained that there was a meeting scheduled. They both helped the kids out of the car and RJ ran up to Tip.

"Uncle Tip!" he yelled, hugging him tightly.

"Wassup, lil man? You been doing good in school?" Tip asked RJ, handing him a twenty dollar bill.

"Yes," RJ replied, placing the money in his coat pocket, "I've been doing good; just like my daddy told me to," RJ responded as Tip placed his arms around his shoulder walking him into the house.

"What about you, princess?" he asked, rubbing Aaliyah's soft, pretty hair, "how you been doing?"

Tip helped Aaliyah hang up her coat in the closet as she yawned, letting him know she was tired and ready to go to bed.

Being the great mom that Rain was, she gave each of them a kiss, promising them that she'd be up in a second to tuck them in.

They followed Storm upstairs to get ready for bed and Rain led the way for the guys to follow her.

"Gentlemen," greeted Vick as they entered into Rain's office and Vick helped her out of her mink coat.

"Wassup, Vick?" they both replied, following Rain over to her desk as they took a seat in front of it.

Rain cut right to the chase, because in her eyes, time was money, "I wanted to meet with you to ask about the count on the bricks that we've got left.

"Shit dying out there," explained Tip, "we're down to our last, boss; and niggas starting to get out of hand, fo real. Being that they're getting hungry out this bitch, and the supply getting slim," he paused, knowing Rain wasn't going to like what he was about to say, "some of them niggas been trying to sneak out and do their own thing behind your back," said Tip, "my brother for one; he don't think I noticed, but that nigga's been staying with money, boss. Even I'm getting low in the cash department, and I know he ain't save more than me."

Rain knew something had to be done: quick, fast, and in a hurry before her other crew members decided to be fake like that muthafucka James. But Rain had something for his ass and she was going to reveal it all in due time.

Chino interrupted Tip, thinking that he may have some news that could help her out right now. He began talking in a strong Spanish accent, "My father's best friend is in the trafficking business, boss, and he can get us a good price on the same quality of shit that Ricky's slanging," suggested Chino as Rain looked over at Vick to read his expression as they listen. "I know you don't normally fuck with niggas that we don't know, but he's a Columbian too!" he said, "So you know that shit's gone be good."

"But that's not the point," said Vick, letting them know he wasn't playing when Rain's life was involved.

Vick loved Rain and had really high hopes of one day being with her, and now that she was from under Ricky's wing, he figured that now would be perfect to make shit happen between them; so he was more determined than ever to protect her.

"You boys know how she feels about this whole process of switching over after all these years. I just want you to know that if she does decide to go through with this." he paused and leaned forward so he could be closer to their faces, "nothing…and I do mean nothing, better go wrong."

The look on Vick's face indicated that he was as serious as a heart attack. He never cracked a smile.

Rain sat there relaxing in her chair, enjoying a man taking charge. After a few seconds, she answered, "Alright, Chino, give me a couple days to think about it. I'll call you to set it up and will go from there," she said, "but in the meantime, you and Tip let James know that I'm on to his ass and that if he doesn't straight the fuck up quick, he's gonna really be fed by somebody else."

Rain stood from her desk and went upstairs with her children to rest. The men all followed Vick outside to leave.

Rain put RJ and Aaliyah in her bed to sleep and as she held her children closely toward her body, she tried hard to get some rest; but her mind was racing. The fear of having to make a decision as heavy as the one Chino proposed weighed on her mind. This decision could really affect her life; which also meant it would affect the kids' lives. She was all they had, and she had to do right by them. Rain tossed and turned all night. Between the kids kicking her in the ass in the bed as thoughts of Rico, as well as the switch with connects, playing over and over again in her mind, she couldn't really rest.

*****

Easing out of bed while the kids stayed asleep, Rain got dressed to go and get Donny. As she entered into Storm's room to wake her up so she could listen out for the kids, Rain noticed that Storm was not alone. As Rain walked closer to the bed, she noticed Storm tucked tightly in the arms of James. He hadn't been there before Rain went upstairs the night before to go to bed, so he must have come there in the early morning. An occurrence Storm knew Rain hated. Rain shook her head in disgust and then she just left the room, cracking the door a little as she headed downstairs and poured herself two glasses of Moscato.

Rain was pissed and she felt like she could smell a rat because why would this nigga show up at her house after house after hours knowing that Vick was gone. If Vick wasn't there, that meant lock down unless it was and extreme emergency; all of her crew knew that. She blocked that out of her mind for now and left the house, heading straight for Princeton University to pick up Donny and bring him home for two weeks.

Donny hadn't been home in over a year and a half now, so when Rain saw him walking toward her truck, she couldn't believe how much he had grown up. He looked just like their big brother, Eddie

"Baby bruh!" shouted Rain as Donny placed his bags into her backseat and got in. She hugged Donny close as he sat in her truck, happy as hell to see his big sister. She was all he ever had. Even when they were kids, Rain was like a little mother to him and he loved her for that. He smiled as they did a little catching up on the drive back home.

* * * * *

Rain's mind was once again elsewhere; but she brushed it off for now, determined to spend some quality time with her family.

"Damn sis," expressed Donny as he shook his head in amazement at the size of Rain's new Mansion. "I'm trying to get like you!" he joked, pushing his sister's arm as she parked the car.

"No you're not," replied Rain and she was very serious, "you're headed on the right track in your life and I want you to keep it up."

Rain encouraged Donny to stay on course; placing her arms around his waist as they entered into the house. The kids spotted them and ran straight for their Uncle Donny so fast that they almost knocked him down on the floor. He managed to hold his balance, hugging them both tightly as he laughed, "Look at you two getting so big every time I see you," he said, looking at them both with astonishment as Storm came walking down the stairs.

"Oh, my God, Donny!" Storm said, hugging and giving him a kiss on the cheek, "look at you all grown up and looking just like Eddie and Donte'; don't he, Rain?" she asked as Rain agreed. Storm showed Donny where his room would be so he could get settled in.

"After you get settled, come on down to the theater and we're all going to watch a movie and have some family time," said Rain as she and Storm went to set everything up. It was important to them that they finally be a happy family. For the first time since Rico died, Rain felt like she had a complete circle again and she didn't want this feeling to every go away again!

They all ate pizza, Chinese food and ice cream while they watched movies and talked about Donny's life on campus. Rain and Storm filed him in on the restaurants and the shop, as well as the business of the streets. Life, once again, felt good to Rain!

*****

When Rain's eyes open to face another day, she just laid in her bed thinking long and hard about life and its changes. She came to the conclusion that going through with the deal with Chino's people was her only option left besides getting out and working a real fulltime job. To Rain, that shit wasn't happening and there was no way in hell that she was going to end up back living with the people that she served every day, so she decided to call Chino and give him the okay to set that shit up for the deal.

"Yo," he answered with sleep still in his voice.

"Chino, wake up!" demanded Rain, "rise and grind nigga," she laughed as he yawned loudly into his phone.

"I'm up, boss. Wassup? Are you straight?" he asked.

As she explained to him that her decision was to move further with his connect and to get everything together, Rain also warned him that she didn't want any shit and that everything better go smoothly with these niggas or else that would be their asses. Chino knew that she was serious. Rain also informed Chino that Vick would be coming with her and to meet them at the restaurant at 6:00 p.m. with his father and his friend because she wanted to meet them both together. She reiterated that she needed to meet them in person so that she would know who to kill if she needed to.

Chino agreed to the meeting, believing that she meant business. They hung up the phone and Rain immediately called Vick to fill him in on the plans for the deal. She told him what time he should meet her at Rico's Kitchen and after taking care business, Rain went to take a shower and dress for her day. For some strange reason, she couldn't get Rico out of her mind and it was almost like he was talking to her himself. She dismissed the idea and just smiled as she headed to find everyone else that lived in her house.

"Donny!" she called out, knowing he had to be somewhere with the kids. Just like she suspected, he was outside with the kids playing in the snow.

"Aww, look at Uncle Donny," joked Rain, pointing to the snow man in the yard that they were building. The kids fell out in laughter and she helped them up, giving them each a kiss goodbye. "I tell you what," said Rain, "when I get back home, I'll help y'all place the carrot on the snowman for his nose," she promised as she hugged her brother before letting him know she had to go pick up some money for tonight. Rain got into her truck and left.

Driving around dead man's curve was always scary; especially when it snowed. But for some people in New York it was the only way to get back to the city. As Rain drove to meet Chuck so that she could pick up some money, it started to snow again…real hard. She started thinking about her life as a whole, and the things that she'd been through. She thought about her parents and siblings, her kids, and most of all…her husband and what her life would be like if she hadn't met Rico at all.

The more she thought, the more dazed she became; but a difference in her brakes as she tried to slow down a little snapped her out that shit real quick. Rain managed to adjust the speed and it didn't do it again.

"Let me call Storm," said Rain, dialing the number to the shop as she kept her eyes on the road.

"Secret Impressions, this is Shaniece."

The music blasted loud at the shop.

"Hey, girl."

"Hey, Mrs. Rain," Shaniece happily greeted, "hold on, let me get Storm," Shaniece said as she handed over the phone.

"Hey, lady, wassup?" said Storm, sounding like she was wore the fuck out.

"Nothing. On my way to meet Chuck for some bread for tonight," Rain explained as the snow began falling harder.

Storm realized that Rain must have made her decision on the deal. "Oh, okay. Well, I'm swamped in here; but you're good; right?" Storm asked Rain because the sound of her voice wasn't like it used to be and Rain sounded tired.

"Yeah, I'm fine. Just sleepy, but I'll be alright," expressed Rain with a change in her voice as she started expressing her feelings, "I just want to let you know that I love you very much and thanks for everything," said Rain as the tears rolled down her face.

Memories of her life and all the things she'd been through became her full concentration. The more she talked to Storm reminiscing about their life, the heavier her foot got on the gas, causing her truck to increase speed.

"Even before we found out what we know now," said Rain, "my love for you has always been strong.

"I know that," replied Storm, "and I feel the same way about you too!" Storm expressed softly, laughing as she remembered something they use to say as kids. "You know why?" she asked, hoping Rain would catch on but she didn't until Storm answered herself, "because I got you!" she said as they both laughed.

Rain responded, "And I got you too!"

A gas truck up ahead caused Rain to hit her brakes and slow down; but no matter how hard she stomped them bitches, the brakes weren't working. Rain's truck starting gaining more speed around the curve, "Oh, shit! My brakes!" screamed Rain.

Storm heard the phone drop and what sounded like a crash. That led her to believe that Rain was in trouble. Storm began to scream and cry, "What the fuck? Her brakes?!" she yelled out in fear as she held the phone still calling out Rain's name, but never getting an answer. Storm continued to scream and the sound of her cries got the attention of the whole shop; causing Dana, Kim, and Nicky to rush over to Storm's side. She explained to them what just happen and that she needed to go find Rain because she might have just had an accident.

* * * * *

They all rushed out back to Storm's jeep and they left while Dana called the police. She gave them Rain's cellphone and license plate number. Storm's ass was doing ninety as she headed straight for dead man's curve to start looking for

Rain. She knew that's where Rain last was traveling.

"Slow down, Storm," pleaded Nicky, scared as hell in the backseat as the snow began to fall so hard they could barely see, let alone drive.

Storm didn't care about the weather conditions; all she could focus on was finding Rain and making sure she was okay. The further she drove, the harder it snowed.

What the fuck? Storm thought as she continued around that sharp ass curve for about ten minutes. There was no Rain in sight. "Y'all keep looking for an accident," Storm instructed the other girls in the truck. With each passing moment that she hadn't found Rain, her nerves grew more intense, but that didn't stop Storm as flashing lights up ahead from what looked like emergency vehicles, made her slow down. The closer she got to the lights, the more she realized her eyes weren't playing tricks on her. There was Rain's truck, flipped upside down and turned the wrong way. The sight alone made Storm and the girls freak out. She put the car in park so fast that it puttered before coming to a stop. Then Storm jumped out of the truck running full speed; leaving everyone else behind.

Her heart began to pound as she made her way toward the scene; not wanting to think the worse. She didn't want to start crying again and she didn't; that is until she ran passed that yellow tape. She pushed the officers out of her way as one of them tried to grab her, but Storm was too fast for that shit. Nicky, Dana, and Kim stood there hugging each other and crying as they noticed Storm's body falling straight to the ground as the sound of her painful cry rang through the air. They made their way closer to see what was wrong, and as they approached slowly, there was Storm and in her arms she held the other part of her. She held her heart, her soul, her best friend. The whole scene was unreal as Storm's cry grew louder.

In her arms, Storm held the lifeless body of RAIN!

* * * * *

"Ma'am, please..." the two officers tried hard to pull Storm away from Rain's body. They almost thought they'd have to resuscitate Storm as she cried so hard she could barely breathe, let alone speak. The officers needed to ask Storm some questions, but before she answered, there was one question she had that damn sure better get answered. As Dana and Kim went over to help Storm up from the ground, they found it hard to hold her steady.

"Ma'am?" the officer called out to Storm who was standing there in shock, staring down at Rain's bloody face from the crash.

Thoughts of their last words to each other made Storm start crying again. The officer stood in front of her, blocking the view of Rain's body as the paramedics placed her into a body bag.

"How do you know La'Rain?" asked the officer, trying hard to wrap this up because it was cold as shit.

Storm didn't care how cold it was outside. At that point, she had no feeling in her body at all and all she could think of was Rain's kids and how they were going to take the news of their mother's death.

"She's my..." she paused and changed her words, "she's my cousin," answered Storm, wanting to choke the fuck out of the non-compassionate officer who only seemed to care about getting answers to his questions.

Storm snapped at his ass, "All I want to know is what the fuck happen to her?" she asked, screaming out loudly into the officer's face.

He let her disrespect go, realizing that she must've been in extreme pain at her loss. "Well, apparently she had an accident due to brake failure," he said, "now it hasn't been confirmed yet, but my reason for saying that is because of the excessive amount of brake fluid," he said, pointing in the direction of the tire marks imprinted in the snow leading all the way up to Rain's truck.

The Officer's explanation to Storm made her think of the last conversation she had with Rain. She explained to the officer what took place in that conversation, making sure she covered all the important details, especially the one when Rain screamed out about her brakes. Storm let the officers know that she would be the person to contact if any more information became available. She also inquired about Rain's truck being investigated for fingerprints before she watched the ambulance drive off with her life inside and there was nothing she could do to get it back!

* * * * *

Storm was so devastated that she couldn't even drive herself to the house. Dana drove her home while Nicky followed in her car behind them. Dana tried so hard to hold it together for Storm without breaking down herself, but the shit was hard to do. They pulled up at the house and Dana helped Storm out of the car. Storm handed Dana the keys to the shop to go lock up and so that she could let the others know what had happen. Then she turned and walked into the house. As Storm walked in, she could hear the kids playing in the back room which gave her a second to brace herself for what she had to do.

"Hey, Storm," said RJ as he and Aaliyah sat playing video games on the floor. Donny walked out of the kitchen and as he passed Storm, he caught her cheek slightly with a kiss as he plopped down in the chair.

"Wassup? Why you looking like that?" asked Donny as Storm turned her back to put down her purse to try and keep from crying. "I've got something I need to tell y'all and it's very important," she said, causing the kids to pause the game and give her their undivided attention, "there has been an accident," expressed Storm as she slowly died inside from the words she was about to say. "Rain's dead," blurted out Storm; breaking down to her knees.

The kids ran to Donny, screaming and crying while he held them tightly. He gave them support while still trying to comprehend what the fuck Storm had just said. That was the hardest night the walls inside Rain's house had ever sheltered. But without Rain inside the home, it would never be the same.

After three whole hours of crying, Storm finally got the kids quiet and settled down in bed. Then she and Donny went into Rain's room to go through her important papers so that they could start notifying everyone and taking care of her arrangements. Storm and Donny, being the closest to Rain, decided that a big ass funeral wasn't her style. Even though Rain was popular to everyone, it was also a well-known fact that she didn't really fuck with no one because that's just how she was. They decided to do a quick cremation ceremony with only her close family and friend. Plus, they didn't want to make it too much of a big deal because of the kids; they were already going through enough. They had already lost their father young; and now their pride and joy, their mother, was gone as well. The crazy thing about it all was that Rain wanted to be with Rico so much; and now she was. The only thing was that now neither of them had their kids, but somehow, there was a bit of comfort that Rain knew that Storm and Donny were going to take care of them all.

Storm and Donny continued calling Georgia; letting Donte' and the rest of the family know what was up. Storm also called Rain's attorney to inform her of Rain's death and to see if Rain ever made a will because if she didn't, Storm was going to be in for a rude awakening because once Ricky found out what happen, he would be coming straight for the kids. Storm also had to get information about Rain and Rico's money; which wasn't something she was even trying to hear shit about, but she knew was a necessity for RJ and Aaliyah.

Word traveled fast, and soon everyone in all five boroughs of New York City had heard of the queen's passing; which shocked the streets real bad. It really had them talking when the story of how it happened, and what caused her death took surface. To some people on the streets, that shit sound like foul play. Everybody knew that Rain took real good care of her shit; especially her automobile, because she had to put the kids in it. For something to go wrong with her brakes like she didn't get her car maintenance on a regular, was something niggas definitely weren't buying.

The crew, as well as the business, shut down for three days as everyone mourned the last of La'Rain, a beautiful queen, and the truest definition of a real hustler. They all joined together in a private ceremony for Rain. Storm placed into a beautiful gold and purple urn, pictures of Rain in happier times and they also played on the overhead screen for everyone at the memorial service to view. The guest book was filled page after page with the names of those that came to pay their respect, which Storm thought would be a great way for her to do some investigating of her own for possible leads on Rain's death. She could go back later to check and see if the person or persons responsible for, or even knowing about, Rain's accident would have the balls to show up at the service in memory of her.

Neither Ricky, nor his family, came out to pay their respects; which seemed to piss Storm and Donny off even more because they knew all the shit Rain had done for Rico. Not only that, but their appearance was expected for the surviving grandkids. Ricky owed Rain, if not Rico, that little bit of respect; but it was apparent that he didn't care. They all knew he wasn't fond of Rain, so he was probably somewhere having a party celebrating the fact that she was gone. No one heard shit from that nigga the whole time shit was going on, but he still managed to plan a meeting with the crew on the same day Storm had to meet with Rain's attorney about her estate. That made Storm think he was trying to be underhanded again. But James, being her boo, told Storm all about Ricky's plans which made her start to think as she prepared and left for her meeting while Donny kept the kids.

* * * * *

The vibe inside Ricky's office was not far from scary as the crew, Ricky's attorneys, Jose, Steven and Chuck gathered together to discuss the future of the crew as well as Rico's empire which was now called, Queens way. Ricky sat at the head of the table as the others showed up one by one until they all were present and seated.

"Now that we're all here," Ricky started, explaining to everyone what the meeting was all about, "let's get down to business."

He began to explain to them that he had plans of dividing the crew down the middle and splitting them up amongst Jose and Steven. He also informed them that he would be getting custody of Rico and Rain's kids, which meant he wouldn't be able to have a lot of hands-on with the crew, being that he would be busy raising the kids. That seemed strange to Tip because he never imagined Rain leaving her most prizes possession to that nigga; especially knowing how much she hated his ass; but he didn't say a word.

Just as Ricky continued with his plans about a happier life for himself, to his surprise, the door to his office opened and all heads at the table turned to face a tall, beautiful and slender business woman. No one in the room had seen her before in their lives. Steven asked if he could help her, and she began introducing herself, looking straight at Ricky as she spoke.

"Greetings, gentlemen, I'm Natalie Davenport; Rain's attorney."

The mouth on Ricky wanted to fall the fuck open, but he just sat there leaning with his chin resting on his hand.

"I was informed that you all were having a meeting in regards to my client, the late La'Rain Peters," she explained, "and I thought it wouldn't be fair if any decisions were made before representation for her was present."

Natalie reached into her briefcase, pulling out some papers that seemed to be a contract. In actuality, it was a will; something that nigga, Ricky, really thought Rain wouldn't have.

But Rain did have a will, and Natalie began to read it.

LAST WILL AND TESTAMENT

*T**HIS IS THE LAST WILL AND TESTAMENT** of me, La'Rain Peters, who, being of sound body and mind does use this instrument to state my intentions. **I HEREBY REVOKE** all wills and testamentary dispositions of every nature and kind whatsoever by me here to before made. **I GIVE, DEVISE, AND BEQUEST** all my property of every nature and kind and where so ever situate, including any property over which I may have a general power of which also includes ownership of the crew and Queens Way, to my said Trustee upon my estate to use to his or her discretion in the realization of my estate, with power to my Trustee to sell, call in and convert into money any part of my estate, not consisting of money at such time or times, in such manner and upon such terms, and either for cash or credit or for part cash and part credit, as my Trustee in his or her absolute discretion may decide upon, or to postpone such conversion of my estate or any part or parts thereof for such length of time as he or she may think best, and I hereby declare that my trustee shall have power to retain any of my investments or assets in the form existing at the date of my death at his or her absolute discretion without responsibility for loss to the intent that investments or assets so retained shall be deemed to be authorized investments for all purposes of this my Will. To pay my just debts, funeral, and testamentary expenses, and all estate, legacy, succession and inheritance taxes and duties (if any), that may be payable. My Trustees may, if they consider it advisable, make any such distribution, and as a condition for so doing shall have the right to ask for and receive signed indemnification from the beneficiaries to whom any such distributions are made. **I DECLARE** that in this my will. The term 'trustee' or 'trustees' and all references thereto shall mean and shall be construed accordingly.*

***IN TESTIMONY WHEREOF,** I have to this my Last Will and Testament with all final requests being obeyed by the law.*

Mrs. Davenport continued, and the sound of her voice made Ricky sick to his stomach. He wanted to kill Rain's ass if she wasn't already dead; but if he couldn't get the crew, at least he could have the kids…or so he thought. That is until Mrs. Davenport utter those very words that changed everybody's life in that room all at once; especially Rick's life. He listened as he heard those final words come out of the lawyer's mouth:

***I NOMINATE, CONSTITUTE, AND APPOINT** Ja'Nay Peters, my twin sister, to be the sole Executor and Trustee of this, my Will; and also to be the sole guardian of my two children: Ricardo and Aaliyah Tulio.*

And just as Ricky sat up in his chair, confused as hell, the door cracked opened to his office yet again, and they wondered who the fuck Ja'Nay Peters was. The expression on everyone's face showed Mrs. Davenport that they were lost. They all, including Ricky—even though he was steaming with anger—were confused about who Rain's twin sister was. They turned their attention to the door and what they saw was the answer to the mystery. The door swung open, and Mrs. Davenport read Ricky one more thing directed to him.

"And last, but not least, to Ricky…if you thought I was silenced, nigga…you better think again. I'm still gonna have the last laugh."

Mrs. Davenport opened the door to give them an answer to the question they all were mentally asking. From behind the door, with her long, pretty legs walked STORM!

G STREET CHRONICLES
PRESENTS
STORMS
REVENGE
PART 2 OF DOPE GIRL'S AMBITION
FROM AUTHOR
MONIQUE LOVE
G STREET DIGITAL

INTRODUCTION

Storm laid on the couch as the tears rolled down her face, her mind was racing a thousand miles a minute because shit just wasn't becoming real to her. *Ring, Ring*...was the sound of her cell phone ringing from her pocket. She reached down to grab it, barely wanting to move.

Who the fuck would be calling this late? she thought, and being that Donny was catching hell getting the kids settled down, Storm didn't want to start them up again.

"Hello," whispered Storm, hardly able to speak from all the crying she had done.

"May I speak to Ja'Nay Peters?" asked the woman on the other end of the phone.

"Who is this!" snapped Storm.

"This is Lisa Clarke and I work at Saint Mary's hospital," she began to explain and Storm started to wonder what the hell they could possible want this late. "Ma'am, I really need you to get to the hospital immediately," expressed Ms. Clarke and from the sound of her voice, Storm could tell it was urgent. "There have been some changes that have occurred and I really need to discuss them with you at once," she explained.

Hearing those words, along with the situation at hand caused Storm to become suspicious about the whole thing, but she agreed to come down anyway before hanging up the phone. After peeping in on the kids, as well as letting Donny know what was up, Storm left headed straight to the hospital.

As she walked into the doors of Saint Mary's Hospital, Storm continued trying to piece together the reason her presence was being requested because as far as she was concerned, she'd answered all of the questions they could possibly have asked her and she definitely had seen all that she could handle for one life time.

"So what the fuck does she want with me now?" Storm asked herself as she caught the elevator down to the basement floor so that she could meet Ms. Clarke. Getting off the elevator and inhaling the scents that the basement produced made Storm's stomach do flips as she approached the desk asking for Ms. Clarke personally.

"Are you Ja'Nay?" asked Ms. Clarke, making sure she was indeed the person she should be talking to.

"Yes, that's me," Storm explained, "now do you mind telling me what this is all about?" she questioned showing Ms. Clarke her identification.

"Sure ma'am, follow me please," she instructed Storm as she led the way down a long ass hallway heading straight into a room. Storm had no idea why she was taken back there and before she could even ask anything, Ms. Clarke pulled back a curtain revealing to Storm why she called her down.

"Oh my God!" screamed Storm as the sight before her began to overwhelm her. "Is this some kind of joke?" she cried as she ran over to the bedside tightly embracing her mystery and never wanting to let go. "How, Why? When?" Storm hysterically asked. Confused, she tried hard to get the words out of her mouth, but she couldn't. Ms. Clarke got her some water and then left them alone to talk.

Now Storm was always told about the powers of God, but this was the first time that she'd ever been face to face with His work and the feeling was unexplainable. They talked for a long time, answering each other's questions as well as pasting together the route of the map that was now about to become their life's plan. Storm was told exactly who to call and she did just that, never missing a step and believe you me…if Storm didn't know him personally herself, she would have thought he had wings because that's how fast he came to the rescue. As he walked into the room and his eyes made contact with the bed, they all began to smile because at that moment they all knew that it was on……Again!

The Truth Hurts

Dear Girls,

All my life, I'd always asked God to bless me with daughters, never thinking that my blessing would come as twins. I first want to say to you that I am sorry—number one. I am also sorry that you two had to find out like this, instead of me sitting you down and telling you like a mother should. I guess I'm not as strong of a person as I thought, but my love for you girls is definitely strong.

La'Rain and Ja'Nay—my wind and my fire—I love you two so much, and even if you don't think so after you read this, just know that I do. The decision that was made had nothing to do with the two of you; it was all me and your father—not even your uncle, Keith.

Ja'Nay, my darling daughter, please don't be mad at him because he was only trying to help and he did a very good job of raising you; even I must say. I hope one day you girls can find it in your heart to forgive me as your mother, and I want you to know that no matter what—I've always loved you two. Nothing will ever change that. I just hope one day that ya'll will be together and live your life the way God intended for you two, and that's the way He made ya'll together as twin sisters—La'Rain and Ja'Nay.

I Love You Both,
Your Mother, Jackie

* * * * *

Storm clutched the letter tightly in her hand as she finished reading it again for the two hundredth time. Thoughts of what Donte' and Keith told them took place that special night at the hospital when her and Rain were born filled her mind.

"Push, Jackie baby," coached Donte' as he watched his wife give birth for the second time.

"One more big push, Mrs. Peters," said Doctor Barnett as she reached to pull their baby girl into the world, "I see a head!" she shouted as Jackie gave one more big push using all of her might and it showed through her painful cries. The sound of their daughter's cry was the sweetest sound to them both, but it was especially sweet for Jackie. As they laid the baby's body on top of her chest so she could see and Donte' could cut the cord, Jackie's excitement was overshadowed when the pain that she thought ended had returned once more.

"Oh my God!" cried out Jackie, frightening Donte' as well as the doctors in her room until they soon discovered why she was back in pain.

"Oh wow!" said Doctor Barnett in amazement to what she'd just discovered, "I see another head, Mrs. Peters. I need you to start pushing again," instructed the doctor as the nurses removed the first baby off of her chest.

The smile on Donte's face went away fast; and signs of confusion, as well as anger, filled his heart. He and Jackie had no idea that they were having twins, and as far as he was concerned, they had both agreed that two children were their limit—or did he decide that for them both. Jackie was surprised just like him, even though their reactions were different. As Doctor Barnett pulled their second baby out and announced that it, too, was a girl, Jackie thought that she was dreaming. She'd always wished as a little girl to one day have two daughters and that shit had finally happened, surprisingly—and at the same time.

Donte' stood there looking...not saying a word as the doctor cut the cord of baby number two as she, too, made her entrance with cries. The doctors cleaned Jackie up and the babies were taken to the nursery to be checked. Donte' went outside to have a smoke; by the time he returned, Jackie and the babies were already in their room waiting on daddy. He walked in and the smile on Jackie's face as she held both of her daughters let him know she was already hooked.

"Hey, daddy" she greeted him thinking his reaction would be the same as hers; but boy...was she wrong.

"Jackie," he said, sitting down beside her bed, "I hope you don't think we're keeping them both," he asked, but telling her at the same time.

"What the fuck do you mean, Donte? Ain't no way in hell that I'm giving one of my babies to the system!" yelled Jackie as the tears rolled down her face.

Donte' placed his head in his hands to think. With the life that they were living, three babies would have been too much to handle—as well as slow him down, so he thought. Donte' remembered that his brother and his girlfriend had just lost their baby, so this particular situation gave Donte' a great idea, "I'll be back," he told Jackie as he left out of her room never uttering another word to her.

Donte' had been gone for about two hours; by the time he returned back, Jackie and the twins—La'Rain and Ja'Nay, which, by the way, she decided to name them herself being that she already knew he was pissed—were sound asleep.

"Wake up, Jackie," said Donte' as he gave her a slight shove on her shoulder to wake her up.

As she opened her eyes, she saw Donte' and his brother, Keith, standing before her. "What's going on Donte?" she asked, sitting up in her bed in pain.

"I've solved our problem, baby," he replied with his face lit the fuck up in happiness as he pointed in the direction of his brother. "Keith has agreed to adopt one of the girls and raise her as his own."

Now Jackie didn't want to give up either one of her daughters, but she thought if she didn't, then Donte' would leave her and she wasn't about to let that happen and be stuck raising three kids by herself, so she hurtfully agreed. Keith reached down and picked up the baby out of the crib labeled Ja'Nay and he held her close.

Kissing her softly on her cheek, he looked into her eyes and said, "Don't worry my baby, you'll always be connected to your sister and I'm going to make sure of that," he promised, never taking his eyes off her. "For starters, I'm going to name you 'Storm' as a nickname since we already know hers" he said, pointing over to the other crib, "is going to be 'Rain' for short, and ya'll will always be together in heart," were the words that were on rewind repeatedly in Storm's mind. She sat at the kitchen table reminiscing, while Donny and RJ played basketball outside on the court and Aaliyah sat talking on her cellphone to her friends.

As soon as the thought of how much they'd grown start coming into play, Storm's memories were interrupted by the sound of her phone going off and it was a call from Lizzy!

"Hey, ladybug," Storm answered her phone with a smile on her face, "how is everything out there in Richmond?" she inquired about the business Lizzy had started down in Virginia.

Six years had passed since she and Rain were separated for the second time in their life, and not shortly thereafter, Storm had made the decision to branch her sister's establishments out into different locations. Storm's answer to everyone who questioned her about Lizzy and the fact that she was the one handling the restaurant in Richmond, VA was always the same response every time, "She is the aunt to one of my most promising celebrity customers that introduced us when she found out I was opening up down there," and that was all the explanation she would give their ass because Storm was just like her sister in a sense, they were very secretive people.

"Everything is going well," replied Lizzy, "as usual. Tommy is in the back whipping up a new recipe he invented, so you know I'm going to stay out of his way," she said.

Elizabeth and Thomas Wales have been married for nine years and they live out in the Southside of Richmond, VA. Lizzy is an investment banker, which for those of you who don't know what that is, she raises capital for corporations and municipalities. Her husband, Tommy, was a cuisine chef and his specialty just so happened to revolve around Columbian dishes which made it perfect for Storm to allow them to manage and run the restaurant. Tommy was also an ex-criminal who served time in the pen for six years on a drug case. His crime proved that he had the street smarts. Storm, learning of this, put her genius to work and she used Tommy to look after the Queen's Way Empire that she started down there in the south which, by the way, no one back in Brooklyn knew anything about, not even James.

"Well, I was just calling to check in on you and make sure you were still making your monthly visits in two days" expressed Lizzy, "and I also have some information for you that I feel could possibly be valuable to you," she explained, making Storm all too excited about what the news could be.

"Ok, that's wassup! So I'll see you then," replied Storm, seeming to be rushing off the phone, "I'm about to go to dinner with my brother and the kids, so I'll text you later," said Storm as she wrapped up their conversation. She could tell there was a sudden change in Lizzy's voice when she told her she had to go. It seemed that after Lizzy hearing this and why, her attitude went from and upper to a downer too damn fast, but Storm brushed that off, and then rounded up her family to go eat.

* * * * *

"What's bugging you sis?" asked Donny as they all sat waiting on their orders at *Don't Walk the Plank Fish and Chip.*

"Nothing's wrong, baby bruh," she replied, smiling at him. "Today has just been one hell of a day, that's all," she confessed, but knowing the real reason was about Lizzy. "What about you two," she asked the kids, "how was ya'll day?"

"Mine was great, auntie Storm," replied Aaliyah. "I made the JV cheerleading squad today," she expressed with joy as Storm hugged her tight and Uncle Donny and RJ clapped.

"What about you, nephew?" asked Donny, "any exciting news in your world you'd like to share with us?" they all laughed as Donny grabbed the top of RJ's head, moving it back and forth as he smiled.

"Ain't nothing new going on here," he replied, "same old, same old, just trying to get school over with because it's getting on my nerves and I hate it!" RJ confessed.

Ever since his mother was gone, RJ shut himself up in a shell. He never exposed his emotions, but his positive attitude toward school and life had all turned negative too soon. Rain was everything to RJ, so going on all these years without her was starting to take its toll on his mind.

Aaliyah was just like any other thirteen-year-old girl, loving to shop, but she, too, was missing her mother. She was starting to see young boys in a different light, so a mother's guidance was definitely what she needed at this point; but having auntie Storm and Uncle Donny around made things a little easier, but it couldn't replace Rain.

Storm and Donny knew that providing the kids with the best was one of the most important responsibilities that their sister wanted them to attend to. That not only stood for material things, she wanted the kids to finish school and go to college so that they could become somebody other than what their parents had become. Ensuring that Rain's wishes came true was exactly what Storm and Donny were going to do.

"Well, sir," said Storm, trying hard to remain calm because she was pissed at RJ's remarks toward school, "I'm going to need you to change that way of thinking when it comes to education, ok?" she demanded, and by the look on her face, RJ knew she meant business but he just sat there in his seat sulking. The waitress brought over their meals and drinks, making sure they were alright.

Donny became enraged, "I can't fuckin believe you, nephew!" he shook his head, "You know how much your mother wanted you to complete school and become somebody in life." Donny's voice began to get higher as he continued, "so why would you feel that way?" he asked RJ but RJ never said a word. They could all tell that RJ was feeling some type of way, but being that he was the sheltered type, they could only go on their assumptions.

"Leave it alone, baby bruh," interrupted Storm before their conversation got hotter.

Donny loved Rain with all his heart, and even though she and Storm were twins, he still felt empty inside. Donny honored his sister's wishes, so with him, the kids didn't stand a chance when it came to breaking Rain's rules.

"If he doesn't want to say anything right now, let it be," she said, giving RJ the benefit of the doubt.

"Let's just enjoy our meal as a family," pleaded Aaliyah.

"She's right," said Storm, cutting her off from anything else. "I'm leaving in two days to head to Richmond on business, so let's just have a good time," suggested Storm, but from the sound of sighs coming from around the table, Storm knew that wasn't making any of them too happy. They hated it when she left for business; plus, loosing Rain made them extra protective.

"Big sis, you leaving again?" questioned Donny. "Damn, you just got back from the 'A' and Miami checking—checking business out there; which, by the way, seemed like you were gone forever already. And now you're leaving again?" he asked, sounding sad.

Storm hated disappointing the family, but her trips to Richmond were very important; and besides, checking on Lizzy and the restaurant, she had to get with Tommy about Queen's Way as well.

"I know, baby bruh and I'm sorry," she expressed to her brother and the kids, "but right now, there are some things that I got to do that I can't explain to ya'll right now," Storm continued to express her feelings. "But I promise soon I will be able to explain and every one of us will be happy and I do mean very happy in life. Now let's just eat before everything gets cold," she said as they all looked into each other's eyes and smiled, hoping that Storm was right.

* * * * *

By the time they returned home, Storm had ten messages waiting on her—all from James. She had forgotten her cellphone while rushing, and now this nigga's ass was tripping,

"Where the fuck were you?" screamed James no soon as he answered the phone, not even saying hello first.

"First of all, nigga, slow the fuck down talking to me like that," said Storm. "I left my cellphone at the crib and I was having dinner with my family, so why the fuck you spazzing out?" she asked James heated as a bitch.

"Because I called you like ten times, shawty, and I didn't get an answer, so I got scared, boo," James began to calm down. "My bad, boo," he said, realizing that he was wrong and trying his hardest to make up with her.

"Where you at now?" asked Storm, feeling kind of horny and flattered all at once.

"I'm on my way to you, boo," expressed James. "I just left Tip and the boys finishing up the count for today…"

Before he could continue, Storm cut his ass off quick, letting him know she was home and immediately hung up the phone. Besides the fact of his little explosion a few minutes ago, Storm didn't tolerate that reckless talking over the phone shit, so she cut him off right there.

Storm and James had been dating for about four or five years now, and on certain occasions, that nigga would let the fact that he was dating Rain's sister—the head bitch in charge over Queen's Way—go to his head. But Storm had no problem refreshing his memory when necessary, and the fact that Rain hated his ass didn't help. Storm wasn't letting any man tell her what to do no matter how good the dick was. Ever since Storm took Rain's place, James would trip every time she had to leave on business; and of course he knew her monthly trips to Virginia were approaching, so right about now is when he tries to flip; but those stunts of his didn't matter to Storm. She was left with instructions, and even though her and Rain were fraternal twins, they still somewhat shared the same brain.

Since Storm had allowed things in the streets to calm down, and being that she didn't have to deal with Ricky on business anymore, shit had started seeming smooth. Niggas thought she was asleep on certain issues left unanswered, but that's actually what she wanted them to think. Storm had been doing her homework; and with the help of Lizzy and Tommy, putting together clues to the puzzle didn't seem all that hard. She still had find out who fucked with Rain's brakes and caused her accident, as well as who sent the cops and started the nightmare that her family was stuck in. What Storm didn't know was that with finding out her answers, she would be answering other questions that weren't even asked and lives would be changed forever, some for good and some for bad. But was she ready to face the challenge was the question that she'd contemplated over and over in her mind.

Storm could hear Donny greeting James as he opened the door to come into the house. She decided to lie in bed and pretend to be asleep so she could see just how James would try to wake her up. As the sound of the door cracking let her know that someone was in the room, she knew it was James by the way his lips felt kissing her forehead. She continued to play sleep. She lay there as the sound of James undressing let her know he was about to slide into bedside her and it made her pussy run even more with each thought that crossed her mind about the way he made her fill when he enter into her kingdom. The excitement of her sexual encounters with her man was put on hold once James' cellphone rang and he answered.

"What's up?" he said in a very whispery voice, "nothing, just got home," he began to converse with the caller on the other end. "Oh you do, huh?" James replied and from the sound of his voice Storm knew his ass was smiling. At the point, Storm's butterflies turned to fireflies making her suspicious of who the fuck James was talking to as he continued to flirt on the phone. Storm decided to act like she was moving to alert him of her waking the fuck up and that he better have a good god damn excuse for his convo.

James noticed her movement and immediately deaden his scene, "Let me call you back" James said quickly as Storm turned over to look in his face. He hung up his cellphone and their eyes met. "Hey, boo," he said to Storm, getting into bed and kissing her on her lips.

"Who was that you were talking to?" she questioned. "And why were you whispering?" Storm asked James never mentioning that she had heard the whole conversation. She wanted to hear his excuse and if he was going to lie to her or be truthfully honest.

James tried to play it off, acting like Storm was losing her mind, but she wasn't and she knew it. "Boo it ain't nothing," James began to explain as he kissed her on her soft lips, slowly taking his hands and grasping her soft breast gently while playing with her nipples.

"So who was that?" she continued to ask him still wanting a name.

"It was my homeboy's wife. She makes jewelry and I have her putting a little surprise together for me; alright," explained James sliding his fingers deep inside of Storm's warm, wet pussy.

The feeling of him entering her made her body jerk back in pleasure. James continued sucking on her nipples while stroking in and out of her streaming woman hood. Storm couldn't help but let him know she was enjoying it by letting out a soft moan from pleasure. The more James heated her body, the more her pussy soaked up his hand as he placed his third finger deeper inside her wet, making his dick arouse very hard for her. Storm let him pass with that dumb ass excuse. She didn't say shit about what she had heard; she knew his ass would slip up again and the next time that happened there wasn't going to be any off the hook chances. Storm kept right on inviting James inside of her; she spread her legs wide enough for him to open up that pussy and long dick them walls of hers nice and slow.

Storm's moans grew louder with each and every blow that James hit her with. She gripped his tight ass cheeks firmly and the motion in his stroke made her loosen up even more. James flipped her on top of him as she rode his hard dick just like a cowgirl bouncing up and down. The sight of her big beautiful breast flopping all in his face must have been too exciting for James. The facial expressions he made, plus the feeling of his dick throbbing inside her walls, both let Storm know that he was about to explode. Storm didn't know what it was, but the more she rode him, the more her body became numb. Within minutes, Storm and James were both climaxing together in pure bliss and ecstasy, making sure they each got out every drop that there was to get.

They spent the rest of the night cuddling in each other's arms but for the most part, James' ass slept. Storm just laid there thinking about his phone conversation that she'd heard and wanting to find out its meaning for real. She wanted to look in his phone to check and see who had called, but the secure side of her wouldn't allow her to be so petty; and besides, she was a firm believer of what's in the dark will definitely be seen in the light. She continued to rest there thinking about her sister and life until she drifted off to sleep; but was it in the arms of an enemy?

* * * * *

As the sound of Meek Mills' *I'm a Boss* rang out repeatedly in Storm's ear because her cellphone was constantly going off, she reached under her pillow—half asleep—to grab it so she could cuss whoever the fuck it was out.

It better be good, she thought to herself as she answered, "hello" with a loud, but nasty tone in her voice.

"Good morning, my boss," greeted Chance who was now Storm's protector ever since Vick's ass had vanished.

"I'm on my way to you" he informed her, "so do you need anything?" he asked, making sure she was straight before he arrived. Chance did his job very well and just like Vick had been with Rain, he took Storm's safety to heart; never letting a soul hurt her, not even James.

Chance was Tommy's brother and he had the same street smarts, which to Storm was definitely a plus sign. James heard the sound of Chance's voice through the phone and he quickly sat up out of his sleep. He hated Chance being around Storm, and even though he was her man, the same rules applied as before with the crew members standing their position when it came to the protectors because they too had a job to do.

"Naw, I'm good, Chance," replied Storm as she got out the bed putting on her robe to go shower and dress for the day. "I'll see you when you get there," she replied, wrapping up her conversation.

From the look on James' face, she knew he would have something to say; but instead, he just stared at her, cutting through her skin with each look he gave. She walked past his ass headed to the bathroom and gave him a look as if to say; *say something, nigga,* as she shut the bathroom door and the sound of the shower came on. While Storm was in the shower, James saw a perfect opportunity for him to be sneaky as usual, so he picked up his phone to make a call.

"Hey, beautiful," he said, trying to sound all sexy toward the caller on the other end of the phone, "how did you sleep last night?" James asked, still listening to the sound of the shower as an alert that Storm was still in it. "I miss you a lot," James began to express, "sorry about last night, but she was waking up and we don't want her to find out about us; right?" he asked, making sure they were still on the same page when it came to their relationship. "Can I see you before you go to work?" he asked as the shower suddenly turned off, alerting him that Storm was out of the shower. After getting his answer and setting up his appointment, James hung up his phone and immediately headed for the closet to get something to wear.

James didn't live with Storm, even though as much as he was there you would think he did. He had his own house out in Harlem, so from time to time he would put that shit to use. As Storm came out of the bathroom, there was something about James' demeanor and the way he walked past her and straight into the bathroom that made her feel like he was up to something. But she just brushed it off because business had to be dealt with in the Big Apple before she left for VA.

After adding the finishing touches to perfection, Storm made her way downstairs into the office where she knew Chance would be waiting. Sure enough, he was sitting there looking good as hell, making Storm just shake her head as he greeted her pulling—out the chair out so that she could take a seat behind her desk.

"Wassup, boss?" said Chance as he stood behind her rubbing her shoulders, "Did you sleep well last night?" he asked Storm as she shook her head yes.

"So what's going on with the business?" expressed Storm, cutting right to the chase about the money. "Have you heard from Jerry this morning?" she asked Chance inquiring about the profit reports from all the businesses including Queen's Way.

Jerry Flint replaced Chuck as the accountant for all of Rain's money and establishments after she parted ways with Ricky which meant his people—and that especially included Chuck's ass—handling all of her money.

I don't fucking think so. Storm knew Rain would have never stood for that, so it was only logical that she found a replacement.

"I haven't heard from him yet," replied Chance, but I will be contacting him this morning," he assured. "There's something I want to talk to you about," said Chance as Storm gave him a look as to say, *spill it.* "You know my job is to protect you," he began to speak, "well, word on the street is that *YO* boy, James, is being a snake out in the field," he expressed to Storm. "That nigga been spotted talking with Ricky's son, Jose, for long periods of time and we all know that all ties on your end have been cut with them. So what reason would they have to talk to each other?" questioned Chance as he waited on Storm to respond with what she wanted to be done.

As of now, James was skating on thin ice; first of all, from the suspicious phone call last night, and now to find out that him and Ricky's son had been having surprised visits behind her back, really cut Storm even deeper. Part of her wanted to call his ass and go the fuck off right then and there, but she knew she couldn't because patients patience is the key to all successful plans being carried out so Storm just took mental notes to discuss with Lizzy when she got to Richmond.

"Let it ride out," she instructed, "just keep your eyes on shit while I'm gone and the crew already knows you're in charge so there shouldn't be any problems. But if someone should just be stupid enough to try you, then you do what you need to do because under no circumstances does anyone…and I do mean 'anyone' turn the heat up on our organization; is that clear? asked Storm, making sure Chance knew that the rules applied for James' ass as well as the rest of the crew members.

Storm also instructed Chance to hire Benny Jackson, their private investigator, to follow James around while she was gone; so that once she returned home, she wanted a full report because she was getting tired when it came to his ass being sneaky behind her back. It was high time that she exposed his cats out of the bag. Storm and Chance finished up their early morning business and she then headed to check in on Donny and make sure the kids made it to school on time, which they did. She grabbed her belongings and headed out the door to go to the shop.

* * * * *

Storm walked into Secret Impressions, and besides the smell of hair and spritz greeting her, the staff and customers gave her warm greetings as well. Storm couldn't help but notice that her new stylist, Tiffany, hadn't gotten in yet and it was already past her time to come in. She had only been working at the shop for about three weeks and out of the three, she had spent two weeks coming in work late. Storm didn't know why Tiffany kept coming in late, but she damn sure wasn't going to stop until she got to the bottom of it. She hated having customers waiting on a stylist which was all Tiffany's clientele ever did. Storm gave the waiting customers a bottle of FIJI water and apologized for their wait and then she went to the phone to try Tiffany's cell to find out where the fuck she was. A ringing sound was all that Storm heard in her ear as Tiffany's voicemail picked up every time she tried calling. Storm kept calling and finally, after the fourth try, Storm decided to leave a message; but just as she was about to speak, her other line beeped and it was indeed Tiffany's ass calling her back.

"Where are you, Tiffany," Storm began to question her.

"Sorry, Ms. Storm," she began to explain, "I was running behind this morning."

From the sound of Tiffany's voice, Storm began to think that she was doing a lot more than running behind, it sounded like she'd just finished fucking; but at that moment, all Storm wanted her to do was get her ass there and attend to her customers.

"Well, I hope you're done," expressed Storm, "because there's money sitting here waiting on you and we all know how I feel about bullshittin' when it comes to my businesses," she continued to yell through the phone. "So I hope your ass is walking through this door in fifteen minutes or we're going to have to make some other arrangements as far as your job here is concerned. Understood?" Storm said and Tiffany agreed; promising that she was definitely on her way and they both hung up the phone.

Storm's two customers came strolling in on time, which meant she had to get to work. Exactly fifteen minutes later, and not a minute less, Tiffany's ass came in awfully cheerful for someone who'd just lost two customers. Storm was pissed. After Storm sat Mrs. Jenkins and Sherell under the dryer, she went over to Tiffany's booth to inquire about her tardiness over these last couple of weeks. Storm knew actually how she was going to approach Tiffany, but as she got closer to her, Storm's thoughts became shattered as the smell of a familiar aroma hit her nose.

"What's that smell you have on?" asked Storm.

Tiffany becoming very offensive, "Why?" she snapped her neck questioning Storm, "it's Curve for men," answered Tiffany. "I *it* must have gotten on my clothes when I hugged my man goodbye," she explained.

Storm wasn't stupid at all, and that type of Curve couldn't be brought in stores, you had to order it specifically mixed, and only true ballers could afford that bottle. Storm's mind began to wonder who the fuck was Tiffany's man if he had it like that, and why hadn't Storm ever heard of him before. Instead of asking Tiffany about it, Storm just continued on with letting Tiffany's ass know that if she missed any more appointments, her ass would have to find a new shop to work at. As Storm chewed her out, Tiffany knew Storm wasn't playing. Tiffany pleaded with Storm for her job. Besides the brand new Mercedes she was pushing, she still had a mortgage on that nice ass Condo she'd just purchased two months ago, so maintaining employment at the shop right now was all she had, so that meant straightening up her ways had to be top priority.

After talking with Tiffany, and with her clients still under the dryer, Storm decided to head to the back office and sit down to cool off. The more she sat, the more her heart pounded because something fishy was going on. Storm knew that the scent coming from Tiffany's clothes was indeed the same exact scent that James ass always wore. *Were the two linked together or was Tiffany being honest with Storm?* She didn't know what to do—yet alone think—so she decided to call James and mess with his head a little bit more to see what he let out.

As "Your My Lady" by De'Angelo played into Storm's ear from James' phone line, Storm patiently sat there taking in deep breaths to remain calm. Even with the law, you're innocent until proven guilty, and as of now that's how James stood in her life.

"What's up, boo?" greeted James, sounding too damn cheerful for someone who had and attitude earlier that morning. "What you up to?" he asked, trying to make nice with her.

Storm was way too smart for his ass, "Nothing," she replied with a pause trying to decide what next to say to him. "Where did you go when you left the house this morning?" she asked him steaming mad but continuing to remain calm in the sound of her voice.

"What do you mean, *where did I go?*" he questioned her back. "Why are you surveying me?" asked James, becoming a little more suspicious about Storm's questions.

"Nigga, please," Storm replied, "surveying you?" she began to laugh. "Don't flatter yourself alright. I was basically asking you about your whereabouts this morning, but according to your actions toward me now, I guess you're telling me already; right?" asked Storm, implying to James that being secretive with her right now damn sure wasn't the best choice.

"Boo, you're tripping," James instantly said. "I left the house and went by my brother's, then after him, I scooped up Chino and we went ahead and snatched up that new shipment of work from Ghost, and now I'm on my way to place it into safe keeping.

Ghost—whose government name is Stanley—is the best friend of Hector who is Chino's father and the main reason that Storm still maintains the *best* when it comes to product; even after they parted ways with Ricky. Ghost has been the supplier for Queen's Way North and South, and their partnership was amazing because they both didn't play when it came to their money.

"Well, I was just asking because the new girl, Tiffany, came into work late today and smelling like the same brand of Curve you wear," Storm began to express. "I just thought I'd ask you about it because I'd hate to have to murder you both myself," she assured him that she wasn't playing, "but I got to go, my customers should be ready so I can get the fuck out of here cause I got shit to do."

Before James could utter another word, Storm had already hung up the phone in his face…again. But as sure as the sky is blue, by the time Storm got back up front, Tiffany was outside smoking a Newport and on the phone looking pissed. From the look of her body movements and hand gestures, everyone inside knew she was mad at something; or someone for that matter!

Storm quickly finished up her customers so that she could leave. With all that was going on and that fact that she had a terrible migraine already, Storm was beyond ready to *snap, crackle and pop* a bitch…or a nigga that is. Remaining sophisticated was something Storm had mastered, and it wasn't that she didn't want to handle it, but why not wait on the right time to make a move? That way, the facts are a hundred percent proof.

After beautifying her customers, Storm wrapped up business and left the shop, heading over to Rico's Kitchen to check in on things over there. As Storm approached the front door of the restaurant, she did not believe what the fuck her eyes were seeing. *I know a nigga didn't!* she thought to herself, wondering if someone had gone delusional. Storm felt the inside of her palms start to sweat as she yelled out calling for Crème. Crème, who was the restaurant's manager, was in the back counting the inventory that had just arrived when she heard Storm's yell.

"What's wrong, Storm? Crème asked, shocked at Storm's reaction and the fact that customers were in there when she did it; she knew something must've rubbed Storm the wrong way. Storm didn't know that Tip and Dana were in back until they both came walking up at the same time with Crème as they made their way over to Storm. She was standing by the door and she pointed out to them what was wrong.

"Who opened up this morning?" asked Storm, pointing to the lock on the door that apparently someone had been foolish enough to temper with.

"I did," explained Crème, "but that wasn't like that when I put the key in the door this morning boss," she assured Storm. "It looks like whatever they used, broke off in the lock," Dana rationalized as she immediately began to take the lock apart. For a Lesbian stud coming out of a terrible past and a life full of *you name it she seen or did it*, Dana was brilliant and she was great with her hands; everything she touched, she could bring life to. But because of a bad background, Queen's Way was her job for now.

Storm instructed Dana to go to Ace hardware and get new locks to put on the restaurant and Dana did just that as Tip and Storm went into the office to talk.

"Here are the figures from yesterday," said Tip, handing Storm a big ass duffel containing five hundred thousand in cash which was damn sure collected on time from the crew and their individual workers. Everyone affiliated with Queen's Way knew that payday meant actually what it was, and Storm wasn't taking any shorts, just like Rain didn't.

"How is everything else?" asked Storm, inquiring about the crew's unity as a street family. "Did you hear anything about your brother and Jose meeting up with each other on occasions?" she asked Tip, knowing he would keep it real. But as soon Tip got ready to answer, Crème knocked on the door to get Storm's attention and ask for her assistance handling a rude girl up front.

Storm and Tip just stared at each other as they got up and headed to the front to see what was up. As Storm made her way toward the counter, she could see the young lady eyeing her hard as shit. Storm didn't know what for, but she knew this bitch had better not want to see her over some shit about James or it was really on. Storm greeted the young bitch politely, but polite damn sure wasn't what she got back from her as she began to talk very loudly.

"Look…my name is Stacy and I'm looking for RJ," she began to explain. "I'm good enough for him to fuck but I'm not good enough to know where he lives or even be his only one for the matter."

Now Storm was pretty reasonable when she had to be, but here this bitch was, standing in her face yelling in her mutherfucking establishment and fussing about her nephew who Storm didn't even know was dating, let alone fucking. Storm stayed calm, instructing Stacy to follow her into the office to talk. As they entered into Crème's office, Storm slammed the door and that's when all hell broke loose.

"Who the fuck do you think you are, coming up in here screaming in with your ghetto ass attitude, demanding to see my nephew!" screamed Storm directly into Stacy's face, making her want to piss on herself. As Stacy began to explain to Storm that her reason for coming by was because RJ hadn't taken her calls ever since she told him she missed her period and she didn't know what to do. She also informed Storm that she hadn't taken a test yet because she had no money and she was scared to tell her parents. Storm had to think of something to do. She instructed Stacy to go and get a test, handing her some money to buy it with, then she told her to report back to her with it so that she could see the results for herself.

"In the meantime, I'll handle RJ," said Storm, "so don't worry about him."

Crème watched Stacy's every move up until she left, then she headed in the back to check on Storm, but as soon as she went to say anything, Storm was grabbing her purse and keys only stopping to inform Tip about changing the locks and she dipped, heading straight home to RJ's ass and yes…she was pissed.

* * * * *

As Storm drove up to the house, she couldn't help but think of how dumb RJ was being. A baby so young was really not in his deck of cards, so he knew being that reckless was a no, no in his family. Storm pulled into the driveway and pushed the button to open the garage; well, what do you know, to her surprise, there was RJ sitting in his mom's old truck, listening to the cd that was last played. Storm pulled in next to him and parked, collecting her thoughts before she smacked the shit out of him. She knew something was going on with him and it was high time she pulled it the fuck out.

Tap, Tap, Tap, was the sound of Storm's finger nails hitting the window as a sign for RJ to unlock the door so that she could enter. You could still smell Rain when you got in her truck, and that shit was bringing on emotions for Storm that she didn't need right now so she just held them in.

"Why are you sitting out here?" she asked RJ.

"Because I miss my mom," he replied to her, never lifting his head from underneath his hoodie. "I miss my mom so much right now and I feel like so much is happening in my life that she is missing and I don't know what to do," he expressed.

Storm knew he missed his mom; shit it was only natural, but there was still a little problem that needed to be discussed right away. Storm began to explain to RJ about Stacy's little visit to the restaurant. She wanted to hear what he had to say about it. RJ couldn't believe his ears; he told Storm that this bitch must be crazy. He explained to storm that she was obsessed with him and that they had only had sex twice. He continued saying that one time he used something, but that the other time he didn't, but that he had made sure to pull the fuck out. Storm informed RJ that she'd given Stacy money to get a test, but from what he was saying, there was nothing to worry about and Storm made for damn sure she heard him correctly.

"Yeah, we straight, Auntie. So don't even sweat it," assured RJ as they both got out of the truck to head inside for dinner and so Storm could prepare to leave.

After eating dinner and watching a movie with her family, Storm checked her flight information to make sure everything was set. She touched base with Chance to let him know she was leaving. With all the excitement of the last few days, Storm was past ready to be out of the city. Storm and Donny carried the bags to the car and she gave him a kiss goodbye.

"I'll call you as soon as I land," she promised him as she climbed into her truck and peeled. Storm could not wait to get to Richmond to discuss important things with Lizzy, but most of all she anticipated hearing what it was that could be valuable to the next plan of action!!

"CAP CITY"

Oh, will you please shut the fuck up bitch! thought Storm to herself as the flight attendant gave instructions to prepare the passengers for takeoff. Storm was so anxious to get to VA, and the last thing she wanted to do was hear this bitch babbling but shit, *it is apart of her job.* After listening to the rules of safety and the attendant's voice finally leaving the intercom, Storm placed her headphones on her ears, admittedly turning on her iPhone to relax for her forty-five minute flight. A lot had changed in Storm's life; events that she'd never would have expected to occur, had somehow manage to take place. A lavish life was great to her, but at the same time, Storm wanted a piece of mind as well as to live free. Now don't get me wrong, living without financial worries made things a lot less stressful, but keep in mind that the kind of money they had was dirty; and just as with every dirty job you have in life, at some point you have to wash off, and Storm knew cleansing time was coming.

As she gazed out of the window admiring the beauty of the clouds, Storm couldn't help but think of what it would feel like to walk on one of them, if she could. She imagined it felt like the day she walked in on Ricky's meeting and rained all over his parade.

"Is this some kind of joke?" shouted Ricky, standing straight up from his seat as everyone else in the room tried to catch their mouth's from hitting the floor as they all stared at Storm in pure shock. No one had any idea that Storm and Rain were sisters, let alone twins. Even though there was some resemblance, you never would have thought that they were that much connected. You could tell by the look on James' face that he had shit in his pants and it was because his ass was so sneaky. There was so much stuff about James that nobody even knew about. That's why he tried to always stay his distance in certain things, especially concerning his personal life. Tasha was the only girl that Rain and the crew had ever been around and the others were just well kept secrets, even from Tip. But at this point, him and Storm where getting real close, but how close could they really get if she found out what he was really all about? That was the question running through his mind continually as Ricky almost gave himself a heart attack listening to Mrs. Davenport as she tried to explain further.

"Mr. Tulio, I understand those are your grandkids," expressed Mrs. Davenport as Ricky's assistant Megan handed him some water to try and calm him down. Tip just sat there smirking at his ass as she continued, "But Ja'Nay and La'Rain are sisters, and this will is a legal document prepared by the guardian of Aaliyah and Ricardo. So, yes...everything in this will is Ja'Nay's" she said to Ricky as the sound of those words rolling out of her mouth made Ricky's face turn

as red as his suit.

Storm standing directly in his view wasn't helping anything. Before you knew it, Ricky just snapped, picking up his fucking chair and humming that bitch directly toward Storm and Mrs. Davenport. They both moved out of its aim just in time to avoid being hit. Instead, the chair went smack dead into the door, hitting the glass and causing it all to shatter like his heart. As security filled the room, the hallway became filled with Ricky's workers who were wondering what the fuck was going on. Ricky stood there on fire as Jose and Steven tried to restrain him from going any further with his actions at this point. Storm stood there looking as beautiful as ever as Mrs. Davenport handed

her the copy of the will and she proudly held that bitch in her hands.

Just so that it would add to Ricky's view, since he wouldn't take his eyes off her, Storm turned to walk away, stopping dead in her tracks to turn around to say, "Just to remind you, Ricky…I am not my sister," she began to address, "nor do I carry your last name, so if it isn't about the kids, please stay the fuck out of my way. Queen's Way, and anybody connected to its organization, is from here on out none of your fucking concern; understand me bitch?" asked Storm, pissed as hell and it was time that his ass knew just that. "Ya'll tried to destroy my sister and that shit didn't work, but just know this you conniving muthafucker… as long as I reign over this here Queendom, La'Rain Peters will always have a voice; now plot on that you fat, dirty dick bastard," said Storm as she and Mrs. Davenport turned and walked away leaving Ricky disgusted and furious at Rain, yet again; but at least this time would be the last.

The sound of the intercom announcing the landing fucked up Storm's thought as she started smiling hard as shit. Feeling like a conquer, just as she felt on that very same day, Storm exited the plane heading straight inside to wait for her luggage as well as for the sight of Lizzy, who was coming to pick her up. As Storm stood there waiting, the stares from bitches and their niggas caused her to laugh at them hating ass hood bitches from Richmond. From what she had heard, they never had shit all because they took too much time and energy and placed it into the wrong things like trifling ass men, who promised them a dream, instead of going out and making their own dreams come true; so instead of getting things for themselves, they hated on others who did.

"Hey, girl," said Lizzy, walking up behind Storm as she turned around to hug her out of relief.

"Hey, pooh," she greeted back. "I didn't even see you come up. I was sitting over there on Twitter and then I looked up and saw you," explained Lizzy as she helped Storm to the car with her luggage. "Damn, girl," said Lizzy as she tugged on Storm's heavy ass suit case. "What the fuck you got in here…a body?" she joked as they both laughed heading over to Rico's kitchen.

Storm was quiet for most of the ride, which led Lizzy to believe that something was bothering her. "So how you been lady" asked Lizzy to break the ice. "Is everything going ok out in the Big Apple?"

"Yeah, it is" replied Storm, but that nigga, James, is really trying my patience and I'm gonna end up killing that bitch!"

Storm began to laugh, but Lizzy knew damn well she wasn't playing. "What the fuck has that bastard done now, because you know I'll fuck him up, Storm," expressed Lizzy. "And you know I don't care for him anyway," she said and she meant just that.

"I overheard him on the phone with some bitch the other night and their conversation didn't sound anything like he explained it to be," said Storm and Lizzy could tell that this shit was stressing her and she didn't like it one bit. "I didn't say shit to him about what I heard," continued Storm. "But when I got to the shop the next day, the new bitch, Tiffany, had the nerve to show up late and smelling like the same cologne that his ass wears, and she claimed it came from her man."

Lizzy never said a word as she continued to drive, but by the look on her face, that shit with James wasn't sitting right with her and something had to be done in due time. "Let's continue this later," expressed Lizzy as they pulled up in front of the restaurant and got out. As they headed inside, Storm noticed the amount of cops that were patrolling the area and to her that shit seemed strange.

* * * * *

"Hey there, baby girl. Bout time your ass got here," greeted Tommy as he hugged Storm tightly, picking her up off her feet.

"I've missed ya'll so much," Storm began to express; it was like being with Lizzy and Tommy was a stress reliever to her and she felt free. "Something in here smells good, Tommy," said Storm, admiring the lovely aroma from the kitchen as she made her way into the office with Lizzy and Tommy so they all could get down to business.

Tommy made sure all of the doors were locked as they all took a seat and came to order. "You look very good, Storm," expressed Tommy.

She thanked him, but cut right to the chase, "What's up with all those pigs riding around outside?" questioned Storm, still thinking about what she saw coming in. "Is it like that all the time?"

"I'm glad you noticed that shit," said Lizzy, "because that's the info I told you we needed to discuss."

Storm didn't understand why she would need to worry about the cops; ever since that problem Rain had years ago, shit's been going good. But what Storm didn't know was that the way the commonwealth worked was a whole lot different from commuting in the Big Apple and Tommy was about to explain to her why!

"Let me start off by saying that the boys are doing very well for themselves to have only started Queen's Way South such a short time ago," informed Tommy as Storm and Lizzy listen. "They got everything from Richmond all the way to Fayetteville on lock in just a year," he said, "and besides a little jealousy street beef with another hating ass crew, shit's been very lovely."

"But there's just one little problem," Lizzy cut in, turning her chair directly face to face with Storm. "The Richmond P.D. ain't shit like up North; them bitches be in your shit for no reason what so ever," she seriously continued. "The only way for us to stay out of their way is for us too begin a game of dodge ball." Lizzy said, taking off her $700 designer frames and Storm did the same as she sat straight up in her chair.

"So, what do ya'll suggest?" asked Storm. "It's obvious I don't know anything about Virginia, so I think it's time I start doing my homework on these niggas.

"Well, while you're doing that," said Tommy, "me and Lizzy want to start two more business out here to play decoy for the cops and they won't even know it if we stay smart. Our money can triple in no time if we go at this thing right, and you won't have to lift a finger because I already got locations as well as workers and routines lined up," informed Tommy. "And if ran right, profits would sky rocket in both categories real goddamn fast."

Everything so far sounded real good to Storm; the only problem was she had not been told what the businesses were and until then, she wasn't making any decisions on shit. Giving Tommy a look that said just that, which Lizzy picked up on, Lizzy decided to cut right to it herself.

"We're going to open up a Taxi company as well as a slamming night club," she explained.

"Club Benji is going to be down here on Canal Street," Tommy pointed his finger in its direction, "and I'll take you by there to see the spot," he said.

"Queen's New York style Taxi is very simple, Storm," said Lizzy, "this will be our way of playing the game I suggested to you earlier," she explained. "I want us to start this taxi service for two reasons: one, they don't have taxis like you do back in NY," she continued, "these niggas call a taxi…excuse me," she laughed, "I mean…a cab here and it takes almost two hours just to get picked up. They don't know what it feels like to come outside and wave your damn hand or whistle and have a taxi come pulling the fuck up for you," said Lizzy, tapping Tommy on the knee for his agreement in what she'd said as they all laughed. "Look, Storm, it's like this…we can make a shit load of money this way and that shit would be sweet," said Lizzy. "Just think…the fucking fiends would lose their mind being able to just walk outside, wave for a taxi and get picked the fuck up quick, taken to be served, and then catch another nigga coming back thru."

Storm sat there taking everything in and thinking on it. "We're not just going to pick up a fiend, that's the thing," said Tommy. "Our regulars will know how to get in touch with the boys and the rest will be real taxi customers because we're going to be a legit taxi company," he continued to inform Storm of Lizzy's plan, which was brilliant by the way.

Storm smiled, sliding to the edge of her seat and expressing to Lizzy and Tommy how impressed she was and that it was time to get to work on this because she wanted things in motion before she left VA; even if it meant staying a little longer.

After hitting all the areas of business, Storm and Lizzy had something to eat specially prepared for them by Tommy. After the girls completed eating a beautiful lunch, he held it down at the restaurant while Lizzy personally escorted Storm over to meet the boys and to start putting this taxi company plan in motion!

"These are the Projects?" questioned Storm in confusion as she stared out of the window gazing right into the Projects of Fairfield Court. The Projects in Richmond were damn sure different from the ones in New York. To Storm, the ones in Richmond looked way more like houses. In New York, the Projects were known to be a lot more hoodish and there is definitely real street loyalty; so from the looks of things to Storm, there was "no way" thugs came from around there; but boy, was she wrong. It may be true that the Projects in New York are known to come off way harder in some ways, but what Storm didn't know was that some of the most thuggish, most dangerous, most real money makers came out of Fairfield Court and Richmond as well.

"Are you gonna keep sitting there stuck on stupid?" asked Lizzy as she waited patiently for Storm to get out of the car so they could go in to meet her Richmond Crew.

Storm laughed, but still took her time. "I'm coming, girl; shit!" Storm replied. "Are you sure things are going to work with these boys?" she questioned Lizzy's judgment even though she knew Lizzy and Tommy would never steer her wrong.

Lizzy telling her to, *shut up and come on,* was all Storm heard as Lizzy placed the key into the door of apartment 2326, the chill spot for the boys and the property of one of their baby mommas. Now in Fairfield, if you wanted to find the entertainment or excitement, everyone knew that Selden and Rosetta Street is where the fuck it's at. As they entered into the apartment, the smell of weed cut their breath the fuck off no sooner as they inhaled. They both stood there coughing for one, to get the boy's attention, but mostly because they couldn't breathe and if that nigga, Tommy, was with them, he would have joined in the cypher but the ladies were way too classy for that. Hamp noticed the two of them as they stood there, and he immediately got the other's attention because he knew it was time to come to order.

* * * * *

Jonny Author, a.k.a. Hamp, was the leader of Queen's Way South, so you know he had to be special. Lizzy was like Storm in a sense; she wouldn't let no square lead her train, so you know he had to be a conductor. Hamp and Nate (Nathan Branch) were cousins known in Richmond for their family's name which carried much weight in the Cap City. Their family had been in the game for many, many, years, and had damn sure ran with Richmond's Finest (drug dealers that is) in the hood, but that sure wasn't the main reason. Hamp and Nate's fathers were once all over the news and it wasn't for a goddamn award. They were accused of murdering two niggas—execution style—but not only that, they took the cops on a six-month chase for their asses and the rest is history.

Now the genius with the mind and connects was Blake Cunningham, better known as Whiteboy–crazy ass muthafucker. Whiteboy was an intelligent, rich ass nigga who damn sure didn't have to be in the streets; but for some strange reason, he always felt like he was black, which to his rich mommy and daddy was a fucking no, no. They gave him an ultimatum to either be who he really was, or they were gonna be done with his ass; so he had to choose. Well, as you can see, this nigga dropped out of college from one of the top schools for engineering and took whatever funds he had saved up and dipped out of his parent's life for good. He moved down to what they consider the poor neighborhoods in Richmond and eventually spent all his money on buying drugs and bitches and was left with the choice of dealing.

Paulie (Patrick Davis), Domino (Walter Page), Mickey (Michael Jones), and Lee (Lorenzo Evans) were all best friends and their stories were similar to most black boys that grew up together in the streets of Mosby Court with their crack head mothers and runaway fathers who left it up to the streets to teach them how to be men. They all lived in the circle on Accommodation Street getting in trouble. They stayed in and out of juvenile, which as they grew older, that shit turned to jail because drugs and trouble was all they knew. Last, but not least, there was Smurf (Jamie McDowell), Ant (Anthony Jefferson), and Freddie (Fredrick Stanford)—Freaky Freddie is what they called him because this nigga had a list of kids with crazy dumb ass baby mommas that always came around the block spazzing out with drama and hitting that nigga up for money all at the same damn time.

They were all good niggas who had just lost their way. Being down with the crew was the only family that some of them had ever had, and what made it so bad for some was that this was their only family. They were so used to seeing Tommy, that when Lizzy came around, they knew it meant business because down in VA, Lizzy was Storm's other half.

"Why the fuck every time I come up in here I gotta catch a contact," joked Lizzy as everyone in the room burst out in laughter including Storm before bringing their meeting to order. "Ya'll know when I'm present, it's time for business; right?" she made sure they all answered correctly. "This is the lady I told you about, the hand the serves us all," said Lizzy, giving her intro for Storm. They all greeted her with much respect, just as she'd seen Rain first get when she took the position. "We're here to discuss those changes that Tommy told you would be coming and as of tomorrow, they are here," explained Lizzy. "As of tomorrow, ya'll will be the drivers for Queen's New York style Taxi, which is all created for the moving of our products. Each of your individual crews will still maintain their trap houses or spots; the only difference is you niggas won't be babysitting them anymore. You will be driving the streets," she continued as their attention drew more into what she was saying. "Under no circumstances do any of your crews serve a walk-up, because as of today, that shit is dead so I suggest after I'm done ya'll spend the rest of the evening notifying them bitches because I better not find out any walk-up fiends got served."

They knew Lizzy didn't take any shit, so her word was law around there. "Storm's going back to New York in a couple of days, and before she leaves, we've got to show her this will work," Lizzy said to them all, looking each one dead in the eyes. "You each will have a route and included in that route will be the areas that the majority of your fiends travel. So when their hungry, they'll call you or just come outside and wave for one of your taxis coming through."

The area of Richmond is one big circle, and Lizzy knew that, so the way their routes were set up someone would always be patrolling through if they stuck to the schedule.

"That means," said Storm, "no fucking weed smoking breaks while you're on duty as well as no pussy breaks either. So tell them bitches you got to make some real money now and you'll come back to play later!" she demanded. "Queen's Way, to some of ya'll, might just be a way to get money, but to me…it's a part of my life. My sister, someone very special to me, had to give her all to make this name something special, and ain't nobody or nothing going to fuck that up. Understood?" asked Storm as serious as can be.

Lizzy stood there grinning at Storm's bossiness because Storm, at that moment, reminded Lizzy of herself the way she was running shit. They gave the crew instructions for in the morning and also told them not to make a move until they heard from Hamp or Tommy to move. The ladies kicked it with the crew for another fifteen minutes and then bounced. Storm was tired and wanted to go to Lizzy's house to chill and also call Donny to check up on the kids before she went to sleep.

Speaking of calls, thought Storm as she laid her seat back with her foot on the dash chilling in Lizzy's 2011 Escalade truck, *that muthafucker, James, ain't called me all day. He's probably somewhere creeping, but fuck that shit! There's work that has to be done and I ain't got time to chase no dick. So if he wants to hear my voice, he'd better call me,* Storm continued thinking to herself as Lizzy jammed hard to Escape's "Who can I run to" that oldie, but goodie, that Lizzy just knew she could sing.

As Lizzy pounded her fist on the steering wheel singing the lyrics with much feeling, Storm questioned and laughed, "Must mean something to you; huh?"

"Yeah, girl…umm," she said, shaking her head as she drove, "that was me and…" she stopped herself in her sentence, "Tommy…that was me and Tommy's song," she explained.

Storm gave her a grin because she knew inside all about what Lizzy wanted to say but couldn't. *In due time*, Storm said to herself in her head as they pulled into the driveway of Lizzy and Tommy's bad ass house out in Brandermill. As they both got out, Storm only grabbed her handy bag, leaving the rest of her luggage for Tommy when he got home.

* * * * *

After showing Storm where to get comfortable, Lizzy went to prepare some chic food for the two of them to enjoy while they relaxed. They watched *Just another girl on the I.R.T.,* their favorite childhood movie, but before that Storm headed over to the computer so she could Skype Donny. Lizzy sat on the couch behind Storm watching and waiting as Storm began to chat.

"Hey, baby bruh, you miss me yet?" joked Storm as Donny's face showed that he did.

"Bout time you hit me up, sis. You must have been busy all day not to let me know you were good," he said. Donny was very paranoid, especially when it came to the only sister he had left; her safety meant everything to him.

"Yeah, I have been all day," said Storm. "We're opening up a club down here and I got to help them get things straight before I head back," she continued, knowing he wasn't liking it one bit. Lizzy got up from her seat and went over closer to Storm, being nosey.

"Look who just walked in," announced Donny as RJ entered the house coming over to the computer because he knew that Donny was speaking to his aunt.

Aaliyah came downstairs to join in on the convo as she and her brother began chatting with their auntie. "Hey, auntie," said Aaliyah, smiling hard; but before she could say anything else, RJ cut her off.

"When will you be home?" he questioned her.

"I'll be home soon, baby," she began to explain as Lizzy stood behind her view listening in to Storm's conversation with her family and memories of her own past filled her heart.

"Auntie got a little more business to do with the restaurant and Lizzy, and then I'll be home, ok."

"Tell Mrs. Lizzy I said hello," said Aaliyah, "and when am I going to meet her and her family?" she asked, being that Lizzy's name was well known in their household, but Donny nor the kids had ever meet her before.

"Soon, baby girl," was the reply Storm gave her niece as she wrapped up their convo telling them she loved them all and that she'd call them later tomorrow.

Tommy walked in as Lizzy stood there so deep in thought that she didn't even hear him, but she felt his hand as he touched her shoulder, startling her slightly enough that she jumped.

"Hey, honey," greeted Lizzy out of relief. "When did you get here?"

"I just came in," Tommy replied, walking over to Storm and asking about the family. She filled him in and her and Lizzy sat down to enjoy the rest of their night, but not before handing big Tommy the keys so that he could go and get the luggage. He laughed at the two of them, but damn sure did as he was told.

Give or take an hour into the movie and the two of them enjoying their peace, Storm's cell began to ring out, making her mad because she had just started nodding off. *Well, I'll be damn, at 1:45 a.m. this muthafucker, James, really has the nerve to call now after not attempting to call once all day,* she thought.

Of course you know what Storm's ass did, she hit ignore on that bitch, never saying a word to his ass because truth be told she was getting tired but the bottom line was that she was a boss and ain't no way he was going to pull her strings. She decided to make him wait and think of how she felt when he left her hanging. *Goodnight, muthafucka!*

Storm woke up feeling like something was sitting on her head and not remembering anything from the night before. It could have had something to do with the fact that she and Lizzy had polished off three bottles of Moscato. Then they passed out downstairs, leaving Tommy to have to carry them both upstairs. So of course, her memory was a little faded, but she knew she was safe.

"Damn, nigga…kill yourself!" she said in regards to all the missed calls and messages from James. "Fuck that shit he's talking, there's money to be made," laughed Storm, throwing her phone on the bed and heading toward the bathroom to pop two Ibuprofen, shower and dress to get ready for the day of stacking. "Lizzy Liz," shouted Storm, making her way into the kitchen because she knew that's where Lizzy would be having her morning coffee before she hit the scene. She walked into the kitchen and there Lizzy was smiling, which to Storm meant things were gonna be good today. They sat there talking for a second, and then got their shit and left, heading straight to Club Benji's so that Storm could approve the building.

Meanwhile, over on the other side of town, Nate's ass was feeling himself as usual, tripping on one of his power kicks. Nate rode down Hopkins Road chiefing, and he spots that nigga Steve-o, thuggin as usual, when he decides to pull up on him. Now Steve-o was one of Southside's head goons, and this nigga been making money on these streets for years; but that didn't stop Nate from coming up to him demanding that this nigga pay him fees in order to remain having position of his block. Of course shit wasn't going down like that. Their conversation went from civil to heated in a matter of seconds and shit got bad between them too. Threats were made as well as attempts, but luckily, shit didn't explode. Nate knew how much Lizzy hated confrontation, especially when it jeopardized her life or money, so his starting a beef wasn't a good look.

Nate knew they didn't have to steal people sets; the areas they had, kept them all well paid, so what the fuck was he thinking. Nate and Steve-o kept their guns drawn on each other until they were both out of sight, but it wasn't over, shit had just become real. Nate knew that Hamp wasn't going to be happy about this, but he had to find out. Nate got back into his car and bounced, going straight to his cousin. Storm couldn't believe her eyes as she pulled up in front of her new establishment. The construction workers were hard at work to get things completed.

"This shit is going to be off the chain," she said to Lizzy as she admired the inside layout. The head construction worker walked over to them, taking them both on a tour as well as showing Storm the blueprints to approve. "Oh my God," said Storm as Lizzy smiled because she knew Storm would like it and that she did.

After completing her full tour and signing all the documents to make shit legit, Storm also signed her John Hancock to a check for five hundred thousand dollars so that construction could wrap up because she had to get back to New York. Just as they were leaving, Nyesha, Hamp's wife, showed up with half of the staff in perfect timing so that they could meet the owners. They all took a seat in the sound proof office to start the orientation, when Storm and Lizzy walked in to also attend.

"Good afternoon, everyone, my name is Nyesha Author and I'm going to be conducting your orientation today," she explained, "but before we get started, let's each start off by saying who you are and what's your position at the club as well as one thing about yourself because these are the owners," she walked over to Storm's table, "and they would like to know who's working for them," she expressed before passing the floor to the assistant manager to start.

* * * * *

"What's good? My name is Natalie Miller and one thing about me is that I'd prefer to be called Nizzy. I'm the assistant manager underneath Tommy," she said, sitting back down. Nizzy wasn't much of a talker. She mostly stayed to herself, but don't mistake it for one second, she would bust your shit if crossed wrong; no questions asked.

Next to introduce himself was one of the bouncers, which everyone knew was a very important factor to have in a club. "My name is Main," said a 6'6" tall as a bitch—muscles popping out of his shirt—nigga that damn sure looked like he wasn't to be fucked with, "and I love money," he said.

"I'm Big Gee," this nerdy looking, white boy dressing, nigga expressed. "I'm into computers and building electronics," he said, which explained why no one felt like he fit in. But little did they know, Gee was missing screws in the brain and was waiting on a nigga to try him.

"D-money and Q," introduced the next two in unison and how, ironically, they both shared the same common interest of working to stay out of jail from child support.

"Wassup ya'll? I'm Tam-duke and this is my brother Jay-dub. We're out here representing Duval all day," she continued as her brother just stood there looking ready for anything. "For those of you who don't know that's in Jacksonville, Florida, and we are some paper chasers," she said as they both took their seat.

Last, but not least of the staff that were there were the bartenders, Yetta, Khristy and Tony; who all had the passion for getting niggas drunk off of their very own concoctions which was the reason that they chose the profession.

Storm and Lizzy also said a thing or two to the club crew, letting them know that bullshit wasn't tolerated and if they always remembered that one little motto, they'd always be straight. They also told Nyesha to call when she was done with the business as they made their exit.

"What the fuck you mean you and Steve-o got into it?" replied Hamp, mad as hell at Nate for being so dumb and knowing that now there was going to be trouble. Nate tried to further explain to Hamp what happened, but Hamp didn't want to hear it.

All Hamp wanted to do was to finish up with his basketball team that was getting ready for Hoop It Up so that he could get back to the crew; and here was Nate's ass out there fucking shit up. He knew he'd better fix it before Lizzy found out and fixed everyone herself. Nate held the phone for a second as the sound of Hamp's voice yelling as the phone hung up was all that he could hear. *Has this nigga gone stupid?* thought Nate to himself; but he knew what had to be done so the next time their paths crossed that nigga was going to get dealt with.

"Where is Tommy?" asked Lizzy as she and Storm made their way into the office at the restaurant.

"He's out with Queen's Way showing them their routes for their cabs," said Gloria, one of the waitresses.

Lizzy shut the door to the office as she called Tommy. "Hey, Mrs.," he answered. "What's going on?"

"You tell me," she replied. "How is everything going out there in the field?" she asked as she pushed the speaker button on her phone so that Storm could hear.

"Everything's going good," informed Tommy. "All of the boys have their routes as well as all of the houses are straight, but let's get into details later," suggested Tommy, knowing that the girls didn't talk business over the phone.

At this point, everything concerning business in the Cap City was flowing, and now it was time to see things move; so after the Hoop It Up tournament, Hamp and the boys better be ready, because the mission has just begun.

Every year when Hoop It Up came to Byrd Park you knew it was there. People you hadn't seen in years came out because in Richmond, that was a very big event. Ballers and the bitches came out to play; so of course, you knew there was money involved. Hamp's team won the championship for two years in a row and being that currently they still were the champions, the pressure was on for them to win as they all gathered around Hamp for one last time before the game.

"You boys know what this means for us, so ain't no need for me to lecture you," expressed Taylor, Hamp's assistant coach. "Hamp and I have worked our asses off pushing you boys on this journey and we're not ready for this to end; are we!" he shouted as they all chanted back "Hell no!" "Cap City on three..." he added as they all put their hands together in a count of: 1...2...3, "Cap City!" screamed the team as they all went running out on the court to begin.

Crowd cheering, bleachers packed, and everyone having a good time at second quarter, Richmond was up by ten as Nate, Mickey, Freddy, and Whiteboy finally decided to show up, taking their seats near Hamp's team and chillin'. About thirty minutes after they arrived, Nate noticed Steve-o and two more of his goons hugged up with some bitches on the other side of the court. Nate being Nate, he couldn't let shit go; he whispered to his boys about Steve-o as Hamp watched them chat, wondering what was up. The buzzer went off, signaling time out and also alerting the crowd. They all made their way to the center to mingle; making Nate think that now would be perfect timing for what he had planned. He and the boys, while Hamp's back was turned, posted smack dead in the middle of the court during time out. They had a clear shot of Steve-o and his crew as Nate and the boys opened fire, causing the crowd to scatter. Steve-o noticed who was shooting, so he and his crew began busting back.

Mickey, Freddy and Whiteboy manage to pop all three targets, but only two died instantly as they all turned to run. This gave Steve-o a chance to run to his car. As his shoulder dripped blood up the concrete stairs, he made his way to his car and got in. What do you know, to his surprise, Nate had already beaten him there and was hiding in the back seat. As that nigga Steve-o turned the key to his ignition, his last memory was the coldness he felt from Nate's steel that was pointing so far into the back of his head that Steve-o could feel the pressure in the front. Nate never stopped to think; he pulled the trigger and got the fuck out, leaving Steve-o's brains all on the front windshield as that nigga, Nate, hit the bricks and bounced.

Nate knew his ass was going to be in hot water if this shit got out to Lizzy and he damn sure didn't want to feel the heat from her, so he was going to make sure the streets of Richmond kept quiet – even down to his cousin, Hamp. Nate felt like no noise would be good noise and what Lizzy didn't know wouldn't hurt her; or so he thought. He didn't realize that Storm and Lizzy were vets in the game, and the one thing they could smell was shit…so it wouldn't be long before he told on himself or either someone else would! Even if he managed to keep this thing from them, he'd always have to live with Steve-o's blood on his hands; but the way Nate felt about life, he wouldn't give a fuck until the gun pointed at him; he was heartless!

CLUB BENJI'S

You are cordially invited to attend the Grand Opening of

"Club Benji's"

Mon. & Wed. Go-Go and Reggae Night

Tues. &Thur. - Jazz and R&B Night

Fri., Sat. & Sunday's - Rap & Everything Night (Exotic Dancers on these nights only)

312 Canal Street Richmond, Va.

Doors open at 9pm & party until 4am

No B.S. Tolerated!

Two Floors, V.I.P. Lounge & enough bars to keep the drinks coming all night long.

DJ Street Mike and special performances by Nicki Minaj.

Reserve your V.I.P. table

For more info call (804)375-1234

Feeling nervous was definitely an understatement to the mood that Storm and Lizzy were in on grand opening night as the money green Excursion pulled up in front of Club Benji's and the flashing of cameras, lights and lines wrapped around both sides of the building with Cap City's finest, well-known, and even some unknown people showed their support. *Lights, Camera, Action*, that's what time you would have thought it was as the driver helped Storm out of the Excursion. She stood there looking like new money on that goddamn red carpet as Power 92.1 broadcasted live announcing her, Lizzy, and Tommy's entrance.

It was almost time to cut the ribbon, so they needed to hurry inside to make sure Nizzy had everything running the way it should. As they walked into Club Benji's, the cheers from the crowd let them know that this shit was the bomb because to Richmond, having events this huge wasn't something that happened on a regular. Everything inside was just as Storm imagined it would be; every glass, bottle, table, or chair…shit even every screw was in place and she knew nothing could go wrong tonight because shit was just too perfect. They all went into Nizzy's office and boy was her ass on point. Everybody that should have been there was there, and she was about to begin her final meeting before opening. Storm let niggas know what she'd expected to happen tonight, and Lizzy felt that they couldn't have arrived at a better time because this was their chance to see if Nizzy was a boss and if she had the kind of power they needed to manage one of their establishments. As the three made their way into the office and finally sitting down, Nizzy nodded at them as a sign of respect.

"This is it, the moment we've all been waiting for," Nizzy began as she walked circles around everyone in the room, looking sexy ass a bitch in that all-black, tailor-made, Gucci suit. She was a pimp. "The chance to take over…" she smiled, taking off her NY fitted. "…the chance to enjoy the fruits of our labors; but are ya'll ready to work?" she questioned, never taking her eyes off of them. "If any one of us has plans to assist Storm in taking over Richmond, I just want you to know that it's going to be a lot of hard work. There's a lot of competition out in these streets and we are all we've got, so we have to be ready to do whatever it takes to make our shit shine the best. It's going to take a lot of muthafuckin effort and I really need to know that you niggas understand, because if you don't, you can get the fuck out now; ya dig? We are not going to fail."

Nizzy continued to stand firm, never changing up her demeanor, just like the boss that Lizzy wanted to see as they all grabbed their glasses to toast to bigger and better things.

* * * * *

The whole Queen's Way South, as well as the new Benji family, was all present and ready for the show. Everyone watched in anticipation for Storm and Lizzy—both holding the scissors together—as they cut the Ribbon to their future as business partners. The crowd cheered and the cameras rolled, while DJ Rough did his thing live; giving Club Benji's all of the publicity it deserved.

The crowd made their way inside, ready to get the party started as *Nothing* TM 103 played from the DJ's booth making the niggas all too hype. Bottles popped, getting everybody in that bitch wasted, which was exactly what they all wanted anyway. Within an hour of being open, Club Benji's was already packed to its capacity; leaving a hundred more people outside waiting and pissed. Nobody gave a shit, that muthafuckin club was jumping and they knew they would make a shit load of money that night.

Nizzy kept doing her thing as a manager, making sure everyone and everything was in position. She even had the bouncers on their shit tonight and everything was going so good. She left Storm and Lizzy with no time to think from being pulled all over the club mingling. As Storm sat at the bar finally getting her first moment of piece all night, she began to miss seeing James. Besides the point that she hadn't talk to him after he attempted to call the other night, Storm was missing the touch of a man and not just any man, she wanted hers. The sound of James' greeting was what she'd heard in her ear as she tried to reach him one more time…but it was an epic fail, yet again.

"Excuse me, Ms.," said the voice from behind her, "you're the finest lady I've seen in here all night."

Storm rolled her eyes in the back of her head as she swung her barstool around to face him. "Oh my God," Storm shouted with such astonishment, jumping straight into the arms of James. "What are you doing here, boo?" she questioned him, forgetting all about being mad at that nigga as she rubbed his chocolate brown, clean cut face as if it were a dream.

"I flew in this morning," James began to express, "and I got a room. You know I had to come out and support my boo," he laughed, touching her hair as she smiled. "Every time I turned around, they were advertising about the club on something, so I knew it was going to be big."

For a very short minute, and I do mean short, Storm had drifted away from business and was wrapped up in the way James felt. As he held her closely in his arms, Lizzy spotted them; making her way across the room which was hard because the crowd was still jammed tight.

Lizzy tapped Storm on her shoulder. "Well, well, well, who might this be?" she smiled at James barely as he extended his hand to greet her wassup.

"I'm James," he said. And you must be the infamous Lizzy" he asked as she smiled shaking his hand back.

"Yes, I am. The one and only," she said.

James felt as if he'd met her somewhere before.

"So, what do you think about the club?" shouted Lizzy to James, trying hard to be heard over all the loud music.

"This shit is off the hook. I'm so happy for you girls," he expressed as Storm cut in looking for Tommy, and also wanting them two to become acquainted.

"He's somewhere around here," answered Lizzy. "I'll be right back," she said before walking off to go and find him.

"Yo, bartender," yelled James to Yetta as Storm's back was turned looking for Tommy.

"What can I get you?" asked Yetta as Storm spotted Tommy and walked off toward him leaving James at the bar.

Wrong move!

"You can start off by giving me a shot of hundred proof along with your phone number," James' sneaky ass demanded.

There he goes again being trifling as usual.

"Didn't I just see you all hugged up on Ms. Storm? And now you're over here trying to get all in me!" snapped Yetta, letting him know she wasn't that type of girl. "So let me ask your ass again, what can I get you and you'd better pick quick before your ass gets busted," she said, pointing her finger in Storm's direction as she headed back their way.

But he didn't care…for real.

It's like this nigga had a dick problem. He had trouble keeping it away, because every time you turn around, he was trying to give it away. But playing with Storm was like playing with fire and James damn sure was going to get burned.

He quickly order his drink as Storm walked up behind him, asking him to dance as he took his shot. He grabbed her by the arm and took her on to the dance floor like a gentleman. Boy, didn't he have some game.

Yeah right, so he thought. But he was really dumb because the whole time that he and Storm danced, this nigga had the nerve to eyeball the fuck out of Yetta like she was rice and he was gravy. James made it obvious that he wanted her too, and I mean who wouldn't, she was bad.

Yetta was a 5'4", a 130 pound redbone from Brooklyn with a body like *POW* and a face built just like a model. But that still didn't give him any reason to think that he could just eat every cookie out of the jar; Yetta peeped his game though. As she wiped off the bar, making it ready for the next customers, she saw James grilling her down. She shook her head and laughed at his disrespect toward Storm at that moment. He continued to make love to her with his eyes and winking, but dumb ass should have known better. One thing playas know is that *when in a packed environment, you never know who's watching,* so he should've been more careful because damn sure…Lizzy was standing in VIP looking down and she saw everything from the bar to the dance floor and to her, that shit wasn't cool. Lizzy noticed James heading back over toward the bar and Storm walking in the other direction. It was the perfect time for Lizzy to make her move.

"I need to talk to you…now!" demanded Lizzy, pulling Storm by the arm into a corner behind the bar. "Look," she pointed in the direction of James who was still making googly eyes and trying to harass Yetta.

"Look at what?" asked Storm, confused as to what actually was going on.

Lizzy began to explain, "I stood up in VIP the whole time and watched your nigga hit on Yetta, and there he is doing that shit again," Lizzy expressed as rage filled the eyes of Storm who was zooming in on James' position. She walked off, not saying a word, headed straight over toward him. Remaining unnoticed, she listened in.

"So, you gonna give me them digits or what shorty?" expressed James as the sight of Yetta's eyes became the size of quarters right along with his very own vision as he saw the vision of Storm standing behind him through the bar mirrors. The sight they both saw messed his night all the fuck up.

* * * * *

"What digits do you need from her, James?" snapped Storm as Yetta freaked the hell out. It was clear that Yetta was thinking that she was about to get fired on the first night. But she didn't have to worry because Storm already knew what was up.

"What babe? Mane… here you go," James couldn't even get the shit out of his mouth. "I just got here and already you're about to trip when I was asking her for the digits to my tab," he began to lie again, but she wasn't stupid like he thought and she knew what the fuck was really up.

"Whatever, James. That's not what it looked like from where the fuck I was standing so don't even try to lie."

"Look, mane…ask her if you don't believe me," he said as the look on Yetta's face showed she didn't want any part of this; plus, she needed her goddamn job! "What digits was I asking you for?" he began questioning Yetta, hoping and praying she was one of them down ass chicks and being that she'd already heard his ridiculous lie, he hoped she already knew what to say. "You said my tab was $175; right?"

James peeled two crisp, one hundred bills out of his knot and placed them down on the table, giving Yetta the eye to take it.

"Yeah, that's what I said," she said, taking the money and cuffing that shit up. James' telling her to keep the change pissed Storm off even more, but again, it wasn't at Yetta!

By 3:15 a.m. people had started to leave and the club was becoming empty. Storm, James, Lizzy, and Tommy let Nizzy know that they were leaving because Storm had a flight in the morning. Nizzy gave Storm her word that she wouldn't let her down. Storm hugged them all, saying thanks and goodbye before they all left.

Storm and James went back to his hotel suite and Lizzy—pissed at that of course, she and Tommy went to their home. James could tell that something was bothering Storm because the whole time they drove to the room she was quiet, and he knew that wasn't like her; but he left it alone until he got her inside his room. Holding the door open for her as she walked through the door, he followed behind that phat ass of hers as he shut the door. Storm sat down on the bed taking off her shoes and jewelry never uttering a word to his ass.

"So, Ms. Ja'Nay," James said, sitting down beside her and placing his arm around her neck. "Is there something you want to say, ma'am? You've been silent since we left the club; wassup?" he asked as Storm stood up in front of him. She looked him dead in his fucking face.

"Why the fuck you think I'm stupid?" she asked, "I'm always busting your ass and because I don't have any hardcore facts you manage to slip right by."

James attempted to explain and play dumb, but Storm knew what was up, so she stopped it right there.

"Don't even worry about it, James. I got you. And the day that I find out what I need to find out about your ass, you're gonna wish, like hell, you never met me!" Storm expressed and he knew that the only thing for him to do at that point was to shut the fuck up before he stuck his foot in his mouth any more.

The sight of Storm undressing made that monster of his stand up nice and hard, wanting that pussy.

"What the fuck you staring at James?" she said, being that she'd really had enough this time.

"I'm looking at you; that's what!" he said, "I want some of that pussy," he expressed, walking over to Storm's now naked body and pushing her back on the bed.

"I wanna see that pussy squirt all in my mouth. Right before I insert daddy to please you," he said, taking his tongue and licking all the way from Storm's toes to her mouth…never missing an exit along the way.

Storm wanted so much to show this nigga she meant business no matter how much he made that pussy fart with moisture. She knew he had to be taught who called the shots and that's actually what she did. Storm laid there, taking in each and every new trick that James played with her pussy. As a reward, she drenched his face and his shirt with her juices, and just as he pulled out that nine-inch monster of his…*and oh, how bad she wanted it*, she flipped the script. As soon as he went to put the tip inside of her hot and ready oven, homegirl got up and told his ass, "Never mind…I've changed my mind and I don't want no dick tonight," she said as she pushed him all the way off her. "So, I advise you to beat it or go take a cold shower…because that's the only way you're cumming tonight."

Storm smirked as she rolled over—butt ass naked—and clicked on the TV; leaving that nigga with a hard dick in his hand and egg on his face. That same egg, by the way, was frying from the heat that James was producing out of anger. Storm didn't care about shit at that point; all she wanted to do was go home.

When Storm woke up the next morning, she knew that nigga must've been mad because he slept in all his damn clothes that night. *Oh well, that's what the fuck he deserved. , Now he knows what it feels like to be played,* she thought to herself as she woke him up to answer his phone which was ringing. She also needed to get ready to head back to NY. She shook his ass so hard, he almost fell off the bed but he caught himself in time.

"Yo," answered James, still half sleep, "wassup, bruh?"

"Where you at?" asked Tip, not knowing James' ass was in Richmond, .

"I'm with Storm. Why?" he asked, but Tip didn't say what he needed.

"Nothing… that's a'ight; I'll get Wize to go with me, I'm out," said Tip, hanging the phone straight up.

Tip's reaction made James wonder what that was all about, but he didn't have time to think about it for long, because Storm was rushing him to get his shit. They left the room heading straight over to Lizzy's to say their goodbyes as well as for Storm to collect the rest of her stuff. While meeting with Lizzy, they discussed a few business plans, as well as going over some rules to be followed until Storm returned. They hugged each other tightly and said their goodbyes because they had a flight to catch, plus Lizzy had to get the day of business started. Storm enjoyed her time in Richmond, but boy was she glad to be going back home. She didn't want to leave Lizzy and Tommy with all that shit on their plate, but she knew they would be ok; besides she had enough shit to handle herself back in the Big Apple and time had slipped by long enough.

*****

"Where you at cuz?" asked Nate to Hamp on the phone as he made his way over to the crib.

"I'm at home, nigga; chilling with Nyesha and Josie," he expressed. "You know today is family day."

Even though Hamp did what he did in the streets, he took his family life serious.

"Oh, a'ight, my nigga, I'll holla at you later," Nate expressed as they hung up. Instead of waiting on Hamp, he went to see Smurf. When you live this life, you're going to take a loss; it may be in the form of money, time, or as it relates to family or friends, but just know this rule is for you: *The face of a thief, a snitch, or even a grimy ass nigga, will always come to the surface in this occupation. The more paper you stack, the more hating they stack; that's why you always have to watch the company you keep.*

"So, what's been going on, my nigga?" asked Nate as they both sipped on their glass of Rozay while smoking on a blunt of that loud. "How you like the new operation so far?" he asked, talking about the taxi company.

"I'm lovin' it, mane. That shit is easy money; don't you feel the same way?" asked Smurf, but Nate's face showed him otherwise.

"Yeah, I do, my nigga;, but what I'm saying is that my cousin is sleeping on shit…scared to make moves," Nate began to express.

"Make more moves? What are you talking about now, mane?" Smurf was confused as a bitch thinking that the weed was doing the talking for this nigga because he was talking crazy.

"I know that's my cousin and I know Big Tommy made him a leader, but that nigga being soft to that bitch Lizzy's word, and not trying to take over Steve-o's blocks," he continued. "That nigga ain't here no more to claim shit; so why not?" he expressed.

"And why do it!" snapped back Smurf. "Why the fuck should we make heat for ourselves with the law, as well as beef in the streets; ya feel me?"

"Yeah, I do…but fuck that shit! I want respect as well as money and I don't give a fuck about who I have to kill along the way," said Nate referring to what the fuck went down with Steve-o. He thought that shit was quiet on the streets, which it was; but he knew that silence means trouble in some cases and the streets, indeed, did talk even when they weren't supposed to. Steve-o's people knew who did the shooting and best believe, they were going to react; but when? Smurf stood there taking in all the shit Nate was talking, and from the sound of things, that nigga was hatin' and wanting to have shit all to himself; he was just pure greedy. After Nate left the crib, you know Smurf called and let Hamp know how foul his cousin was living. He wanted to make sure that Hamp could handle the problem and be one step ahead of the enemy.

Steve-o's crew did think they were the shit, even more so after his death when Tooth took over. That was due to him being his right hand man, and of course niggas really didn't know how to ask, and of course that steamed Nate's pit even more. That night at Club Benji's, it was exotic and party night, which meant sexy girls were on the loose. As Thunder, Sizzle, and Desire took their poles, the niggas didn't know how to act. Even though they weren't nude, just in costumes, seeing asses clapping in their faces did the trick. Tooth and his niggas decided to be one of the guests. Without knowing that Hamp and his crew was a part of this establishment, they were all looking to have a nice time. Tooth didn't know exactly who it was, but he knew Hamp's crew, or even Hamp for that matter, was responsible for the death of their leader and that's where the problem came in. Tooth and his boys were maxing, having a good time and damn sure spending money with the bitches; but after three hours of drinks, it soon become boring, causing Tooth to become less interested.

Now Nyesha and Tooth grew up around the same neighborhood and he knew she was married to Hamp, so seeing her in the club was all too easy for him to pick; even without knowing that she worked there. Nyesha and four of her friends were chilling in the VIP as usual, having a ball, and the more Tooth saw her balling out, the more furious he became. He told his boys who she was and what he wanted to do. They all bounced, leaving one behind to spy and alert them when it was time to make their move. Nyesha and Stephanie were parked together, as usual, so after leaving the club, they each made their way to their cars to go home. As Nyesha drove home talking to Hamp, she didn't notice the truck following behind her. As Hamp explained to her that he'd be home in about an hour, Nyesha pulled into the driveway. She thought she'd seen car lights flick off fast from the trees, but then again, she had been drinking.

"I'm home," she announced to Mrs. Sharon who watched Josie for them from time to time. Nyesha let her out, locking up the house to go and shower for bed, but not before checking in on her daughter. As Nyesha sang and showered, getting herself ready for Hamp's arrival, she didn't even hear the bathroom door opening as Tooth and Goldie entered.

"What the…oh my God! Let me go! Get the fuck off of me!" she screamed as she kicked and fought their asses with all her might as they carried her into the bedroom and shut the door.

"Shut the fuck up, bitch!" demanded Tooth as he held his nine directly to her head. Goldie took his finger and played around in her pussy, violating her in so many ways as she cried out softly, trying not to wake up Josie, but it was little too late for that. Josie pushed open her parent's bedroom door—half asleep. All she saw was two men, her mom getting raped by one, and lights from the fist of Tooth who punched her ass in the face, knocking her out. Josie was only fourteen years old and had nothing to do with shit, but at that point, Tooth didn't care; all he wanted to do was make sure they felt pain just like he did from losing his best friend and he wasn't stopping until it was done. Nyesha cried out helplessly as her daughter laid there out cold on the floor, and those two niggas took turns over and over again with her mouth and her pussy; making her wish she were dead.

"You know what?" said Tooth, feeling like he needed more action, "This bitch's pussy ain't even enough to leave this nigga hurt." he joked. "That shit wasn't all that good anyway."

They laughed as Nyesha laid there bleeding everywhere.

"Well, what do you want to do, boss?" asked Goldie as the smile on Tooth's face let him know something else was coming.

Before Goldie could blink, all he heard was a loud *POW* from the gun going off. The bullet hit Nyesha right inside her left nipple, causing it to go through her heart and killing her right there on the bed. Goldie picked up Josie, throwing her limp body across his shoulder and kidnapping her all in the same night. They ran out back and got into their truck, along with an unconscious Josie and dipped as Hamp's truck pull into the front. Hamp never saw anything as he got out and went into the house.

"Babe?" he called out, still hearing the shower running, but no Nyesha. "Nyesha?" he continued to call out, but still no response. As he got to the door of their bedroom, cracking it open and going in, Hamp's whole life—all the way up to that moment--flashed before his eyes. Quickly, he ran over to the bed, picking up Nyesha's lifeless body to hold. "What the fuck, God please!" he screamed and cried out in pain. "Somebody killed my fucking wife!" he said, never thinking about where was Josie at that point, but finally he remembered, "Baby girl?" he called out, opening the door to her room and she wasn't there. Hamp immediately called the police so they could be on their way. As far as he was concerned, whoever did this and took his baby had really gone too far now. He called the crew also to inform them of the shit that went down as he cried.

Tooth and Goldie were gone with Josie. They took her to the old warehouse down Shock-O-Bottom where they were going to have fun with her until Tooth decided otherwise, or until Hamp found them first. I don't know whose squad was the deepest -- the Richmond PD or the crew -- as they all swarmed Hamp's house. He wasn't fit to be fucked with at this point, and the crew tried their best to comfort him, but that didn't work. Hamp finally got up enough strength to give the police a description of his daughter as Nate and the rest of the crew watched. They didn't know who, but they damn sure weren't going to rest until somebody's head was caught for this.

Nate's cell went off from a blocked call. "Who the fuck is this?" he answered, not having time for any games.

A man's voice said, "One point ya'll...two points us, bitch! And if you want to see her alive, back down!"

Click...the sound of the phone hanging up was all he heard after that. Nate never said anything to Hamp about the call, instead he was going to play it off like it was word on the street, but time was running out. Word travels fast in Richmond, so the news of Nyesha's killing got to Tommy and Lizzy's ears quick, which meant they reacted to find out what the fuck had went wrong.

"What the fuck happened, Nate?" asked Tommy as he and Lizzy made their way up to the house where Nate stood outside smoking.

"Where is Hamp?" asked Lizzy as he pointed inside. Lizzy could do nothing but hold him as the tears flowed out of his eyes. He was in pain and at this point, what could anybody do? So after finishing up with the crime unit, Lizzy took Hamp home with them so he could try to get some rest, if possible. That next afternoon, Hamp finally woke up to some shit of missed calls from Detective Western which Hamp automatically responded to.

"Hello, detective; you tried to reach me?" he asked, hoping it was some good news and indeed it was…to a certain extent.

They had found Josie behind Creighton Court apartments; beaten and raped, but she wasn't dead and they needed him to get to MCV hospital right away. Of course you know he did. When word got back to Nate and the crew what was up, you know that shit meant war. Nate put it to Hamp like it got back to him who it was, so by him having Josie back safe said *show time.* That nigga Hamp went psychotic and started killing niggas from their crew left and right, leaving no man behind. Even though Tooth was left lingering for a minute, he knew Hamp meant business and his day would come, and which by the way, it did. Months had gone by since they buried Nyesha and killed Steve-o's whole crew and shit was starting to seem a little better for everybody especially Nate. He managed to talk Lizzy into letting him take ownership of Steve-o's blocks, which meant his fiends too. That nigga's cheese was looking mighty good right now, but what's in the dark always comes to the light and just when Nate thought he was untouchable, somebody dropped a dime on his ass to Hamp quick. Even though that was his cousin, he still told Lizzy and Tommy all about the shit Nate started and that it was because of him that it ended badly. Since Nate *never left Tooth and the crew alone*, plus he never said a word to Hamp about the phone call he got when Josie was missing, at this point all loyalty went out of the window.

Lizzy wanted to do the honors on this one herself, but instead, she gave her blessings and let Hamp loose to do his thing. So he fixed that nigga good. As Nate stood at Hess pumping gas and talking to some bitch, he got a call from Hamp with instructions on a pickup that he needed to complete tonight and he knew Nate's greedy ass would be all for it. As Nate pulled up at the spot, as soon as he popped the trunk to his Porsche and grabbed all fourteen keys for delivery, out of no fucking where the DEA—like a hundred of the niggas—came swarming out on his ass. Their guns were drawn and they yelled at Nate to get down on the ground, leaving him with no other choice but to surrender and carry his dumb ass to jail. So what he was Hamp's his cousin, Nate's ass didn't care. That nigga was on some ol' other shit for real and as far as Hamp was concern, his recklessness had caused enough heartache, so after Lizzy cleared the ok, Nate's ass was removed.

Lizzy and Tommy were glad to see things get back in order because there was money to be made. With the taxi company, club and other establishments booming, they knew that getting money would not be a problem as long as shit stayed still!

The Plot Thickens

The most imperative and crucial element in being a true Queen Pin, hinges on the power and ability of the queen to become invisible when given the chance. It also hinges on the patience to seek the truth until the failure to present authentically comes about, causing the queen to again become visible, and leaving niggas to parish from her deadly plague. She will go through it all before she loose her crown to any muthafucker in the hood. Someone once told Storm that when a plot becomes thick, the situation becomes more complicated. Boy… if she only knew that the plots of people—some still in her circle—had become so thick that if you could throw them, it would definitely stick to the wall. But an old remedy to thickness is water, and Storm was ready to see some folks drown. It had been six months since the opening of Club Benji's and Lizzy's reporting's to Storm were always good things concerning the establishments and everything in Richmond was now going great. Ever since Storm and James got back to the Apple, her attitude toward him had definitely took a turn for the worst and dummy act liked he didn't know why. See jack ass didn't know that Storm had him followed before she left for VA, and when they returned back home, Chance had all of the photos she needed; giving her the evidence to support her theories about James and that bitch Tiffany's affair. All of which was more then she could take, and if you think that's some shit…well, imagine not being able to do shit yet because among those photos where also flicks of James and that nigga, Ricky, meeting up on four different occasions for what seemed to be about money transactions, but why?

Of course you know Storm talked everything over with Lizzy to see if she had any input on her next move. These niggas damn sure weren't going to get away that easy. After putting their heads together, Storm knew actually want she wanted to do. Storm's first plan of action was to befriend that bitch, Tiffany…you know, take her up under her wing; *yeah, sike.* She did immediately get closer into that bitch's inner circle of trust, but only through girl talk Tiffany would let Storm in on, which was more than enough for her. She would always have lunch with her now, three days a week, and that's when Tiffany would spill her guts. Tiffany thought she was smart enough to trick Storm with fake names and bullshit, but Storm wasn't having it even though she still played along. Tiffany had also told James about her and Storm's new found friendship and of course, you know he wasn't feeling it, but he still let it ride, thinking that maybe their closeness would be enough to distract Storm's attention away from finding out their secret. During their lunch dates weekly, Storm would find out some shit about her man that only weak bitches would have lost it on the very first day…but not this bad, bad, bitch!

* * * * *

Tiffany told Storm that her dude has been in the game for years, and that he'd just brought her a new condo out in Jersey, as well as that new car she was driving. Let this bitch tell it, she didn't want for nothing. Tiffany – not knowing that Storm already knew what was up – made that shit even funnier to see her plans carried out for the two of them but first she needed more information. She and Tiffany toasted their glasses, both celebrating two separate things.

"So tell me a little more about this baller," joked Storm, taking a fork full of her water crisp salad as she listen.

"Girl, he's so good to me even though I've bragged before…" *that bitch really thought shit was a game*, "…Damien's so swaged out and hardcore, that he even had the bitch he was fuckin with sister murdered," she continued, making Storm chime in even more out of curiosity and hoping to get to the bottom of Ricky and James. "He really did the work himself, but the bitch's father-in-law was the one who order the hit and getting him to tamper with her fuckin' car… leaving that bitch flipped!"

As the sound of that rattled Storm's whole life at once and because she was so nervous trying to remain calm, that's when she reached for the wine, which right then she needed. It knocked over; spilling everywhere as the waitress came rushing over to clean it up.

Tiffany knew James fucked with Storm, that's why she tried to change his name up; but what that dumb bitch didn't know, and what James reluctantly didn't tell her dumb ass, was that the sister he was talking about was Rain and she'd just completed the puzzle for Storm. *Dumb bitches, SMDH.*

"So, you mean to tell me that your man go hard like that?" she asked, pouring herself another full glass. "Did they get away with that shit?"

Storm was gathering all the information she needed to bring these niggas face down where they stand and that bitch Tiffany just kept right on dishing.

"Girl, hell yeah he did, and he's still getting paid to this day," she continued.

"What do you mean?" Storm asked to make sure she was really hearing right. *Did this nigga really accept money on her sister's head?*

"I mean that nigga been snatching up money from this dude name Ricky since I met him, and you tell me what kind of nigga just give you stacks monthly, so I figure it had to be payment for their deal."

Now can you say Twilight Zone because that's what it felt like to Storm as she tried hard to hold her composure and not kill these bitches tonight, including Tiffany. But instead, she kept it classy until it was time to present them with otherwise. She and Tiffany wrapped up lunch to head back to the shop, only Storm decided not to return back there because she needed to go home and call Lizzy to let her know what she'd dug up.

"Hey, boo," Lizzy greeted, sounding awfully cheerful. "How are you?"

"Girl," cried Storm, shaking Lizzy up a bit, "you won't believe the shit I've just found out," she continued to cry, explaining to Lizzy why. "How the fuck are James and that nigga Ricky the ones responsible for the accident?" she said, trying hard to explain through her tears. "All this fucking time…and he been playing me for a fucking fool and on top of that, he is creeping with that bitch, Tiffany, and she's the one who let the cat out of the bag on his ass," said Storm and just when Lizzy was about to respond, Storm's other line beeped in causing her to have to put their conversation on hold as she clicked over to find out who it was.

"Hello, may I speak to Ja'Nay Peters?" said the woman and Storm asked her who she was.

"This is Mrs. Grady, the principle at IS417, and I have Aaliyah in my office for fighting," she said something else to make Storm say that's enough.

"What do you mean a fight?" snapped Storm. "Is she alright?"

"Yes she is ma'am, but I'm going to have to ask you to come down to the school and pick her up," demanded Mrs. Grady as the loud sighs of Storm's breath let her know she wasn't feeling this shit neither. But, of course, Storm told her she was on the way. She hung up the phone, never clicking back over to Lizzy and rushing straight over to Aaliyah's school.

As Storm walked into the office and asked for the principle, she could tell that the little girl sitting behind her with and ice pack on her bloody eye must've been Aaliyah's victim. From the way she was staring, that little bitch must've knew that Storm was Aaliyah's people as Mrs. Grady come out to get her and she followed her into the office.

"Auntie!" shouted Aaliyah, her hair all over her head as she sat there waiting.

"Don't 'Auntie' me Aaliyah. You know better than to be in school fighting!" yelled Storm taking a seat beside her as Mrs. Grady began to tell her what happened.

"Ms. Peters, I'm sorry to bring you down here, but I felt we should talk face to face," she continued. "Aaliyah and another student were brought into my office during the change of class for fighting, and when I asked why, I was told by your niece, and several other students, that the other girl initiated the altercation."

"So why am I here?" interrupted Storm.

"Well, apparently there was some name calling with things said about your family's activities," the principal said with that *I don't wanna call CPS* look on her face. "Is your family involved in some sort of drug gang?" she asked as the beating of Storm's heart tripled. At that point, Storm took a deep breath.

"Auntie, I…" Aaliyah tried butting in, but Storm stopped her right there, placing her hand up toward Aaliyah in gesture while never taking her eyes off Mrs. Grady.

"Look, ma'am, I don't know what you're talking about," expressed Storm, "but you're not about to sit up here and question me over hearsay from little ass girls hatin on my niece. So before you can say another word to me, ma'am, I'm going to dismiss myself and my niece from your school at this point before I say something you're not going to forget!" she yelled telling Aaliyah, "Let's go" as they headed out of that office quickly. But as Storm headed toward the door to leave, she turned around and said, "Oh and to firmly answer your question, Mrs. Grady, hell naw my family ain't in shit! Unlike you, ma'am, we own our own businesses, so report that bitch!" she said, slamming the door to the office as her and Aaliyah left heading right to the truck to go home.

The first five minutes of the car ride home were filled with absolutely no words at all, that is until Storm, trying her damndest not to scream, went right at Aaliyah's ass for answers as she drove.

"Ok, niece, let's talk."

"Well, Auntie, I was on my way to class with Jennifer, when the girls that call themselves Aces came up to me popping their mouth. I tried to ignore them and I kept on walking when the leader, Ashley, pushed me from behind. She said I think I'm all that because my family got drug money and then she said that's why your mommy dead," Aaliyah began to cry, explaining to her auntie that she just went blank and she turned around and reacted.

Storm continued to drive because at that point she was so furious that she didn't want to give her niece wrong advice, so instead, she just said nothing. This life was starting to affect the kids and something had to be done. Storm and Aaliyah went into the house, and she canceled all of her appointments for that day. All Storm wanted to do was take a nap and hope that once she woke up, shit would have gotten better. The house was so quiet that Storm and Aaliyah both were passed out in their rooms, never realizing how late in the evening it had gotten; thank God Donny came home with his loud mouth on the phone, otherwise Storm might have slept until tomorrow.

"Wake up, big head," said Donny, plopping down on her bed and waking her up for real.

She got herself together and started telling him all about Aaliyah's day at school and of course Donny couldn't believe what he'd just heard.

"What the fuck do those kids have to do with our family?" he asked in rage. "I know one thing," he said, heading down to start some dinner since he felt like cooking for the family, "their asses better leave my baby girl alone before there's trouble."

Mad as hell, he walked off, leaving Storm sitting there until she got up to go and look for RJ, but he wasn't in his room.

"Baby bruh," she called out, walking into the kitchen and sitting down at the table. "Have you seen or talked to RJ all day?" she asked.

Ever since she got the results from that girl's pregnancy test proving that she was a liar, Storm wanted to make sure that he was extra careful with the choices that he made from here on out. She dialed his cellphone twice, but no answer.

"It's 5:45 p.m. and I know he'd better have his ass in this house before it gets late," she angrily expressed to Donny as he volunteered to go out and look for him. Storm declined telling him RJ better not play froggy with her.

* * * * *

Storm helped Donny prepare dinner and everything was looking great. Baked fish, mac and cheese, collards and corn bread…even Aaliyah couldn't sleep through that aroma as she woke up heading downstairs and taking her spot at the table. It was now 8:15 p.m.; they all sat down to start eat without RJ and this nigga still hadn't gotten home. She tried calling his cellphone again and this time she got an answer.

"Where the fuck are you?" snapped Storm and RJ laughed like it was funny, letting Storm know he was high off something.

"I'm out, Auntie," he said. "I'll be home soon, I'm taking care of business for my Abuelo," RJ expressed.

"Your Abuelo!" screamed Storm. "Let me speak to Ricky, he knows better than to have you out late!" demanded Storm, but the laughter from RJ's friends in the background showed Storm he was into something different. *Even though Ricky wasn't anywhere around didn't mean he wasn't the one responsible,* thought Storm and after telling RJ to bring his ass home now, Storm sure put a call through to Ricky.

"Tulio residence," answered Beth, their maid.

"Let me speak to Ricky!" Storm insisted mad, ass fuck as the sound of his voice asking who it was made her cringe.

"What is it now?" questioned Ricky. His rude ass didn't even know who it was, but not that he cared.

"Ricky, this is Storm, why is RJ out so late talking about he doing shit for you?" she questioned and besides that, she knew that Ricky's belief in hustling young was not the same as hers, but he'd better not had bet his luck on RJ.

"What me and my Nieto does is none of your concern, so I suggest you handle your issues with him and leave me the hell alone!" he said as he slammed the phone down in Storm's face making her want to jump in her truck and head over to fuck him up, but she didn't. As Storm hung up the phone, the sound of RJ's bass from his car let her know that he was finally home as he came through the door high as a kite and causing Storm to finally go the fuck off.

"Where the fuck where you?" she screamed at him as he walked into the kitchen, sitting down beside his sister at the table to eat and no… he didn't say a thing.

"You'd better answer me now Goddammit, because I'm not asking you again.

"Look…back off, Auntie," said RJ in response.

For the first time in his life, RJ used that tone with her and Donny didn't find that shit cute. As he walked over toward RJ to jack his ass up, you know Storm jumped in.

"What did you just say, boy?" Storm said, getting into his face instead.

"I said back off with the questioning, a'ight!" he snapped and signing the dotted line to his death date.

"Boy, have you lost your mind talking to me like that!" she screamed and what he said next she wasn't ready for.

"Look, I don't care what you say, Auntie Storm because I'm not telling you where I was," he expressed, "my mother's not here anymore and she is the only one who can tell me what to do, so drop it," said RJ as the punch in his chest from Donny knocked him clean out his chair.

"Carry your ass upstairs, RJ, and sleep off some of that shit!" demanded Donny. "Because the weed is doing the talking for your ass right now and I suggest you leave right now."

Donny meant just what he said as Storm stood there trying hard to hold back the tears because she was fucking overwhelmed. RJ went to his room for the rest of the night, as everyone else at least tried to finally eat; but at that point, all Storm wanted to do was go back to bed. No matter what she went through, she never let it get to her and she always took care of business as well as stayed two steps ahead.

* * * * *

Tiffany thought shit was all good with them; this bitch never once stopped to think if there was a motive, and indeed there was. Storm had gathered all the evidence she'd needed to destroy them both, so with that being said, and her plate being more than full at this point, she needed everything to end. That next morning, Storm was already pissed from the night before, so she decided to take a ride. Not telling anybody, she decided to dress and leave while everyone slept so she could have peace and that's actually what she did.

As she drove on the freeway, jamming to Rihanna, the thought of James not calling or coming by the house crossed her mind. Deciding to do a pop up on that bitch Tiffany's ass, she pulled up and the first fucking car she saw was James'. Now the thought to slash his tires did cross her mind, but it was only a thought because doing that wouldn't have been painful enough. So, instead, she decided to go knock as she walked up to Tiffany's condo with speed. As she lifted her hand on the door, she couldn't help but notice that the curtain was slightly open and she could see James' head lying back on the couch. She reached for her gun to shoot his ass right there, but of course again, that was just a thought as she held her hands up on the glass to look in just to see if this that nigga was sleeping.

She discovered her answer when she saw Tiffany's head going up and down on his dick like a Popsicle, and yes, this bitch was definitely doing her thing on that shit; but she wasn't better than the queen, not at all! Storm stood there in shock as the sight of that bitch's mouth sucking on the tip of James' dick – and his heading was relaxing from enjoying every bit of it – had her stuck for a minute because this time she was seeing it in her face. After having enough and not wanting to spend the night in jail, Storm took off running back to her car, crying and feeling like she was losing her powers. Speeding off and heading home, she cried hard and couldn't breathe.

"No one's home," she sobbed, busting right through the door, heading straight into the bathroom. "I can't take this shit anymore," she snapped as she punched the mirror over the sink and breaking it into pieces. The blood from her now cut up hand bleed badly, but she didn't care; she let that bitch drip. At that point, as she walked out the bathroom to head into her room to clean herself up and plan...*what's RJ's door doing open?* she thought to herself because she didn't hear anyone come in. Storm walked into his room to check, but he wasn't in there, so she just turned to leave. As Storm headed to leave out, she noticed RJ's drawer half open and the back of what looked like a black barrel stuck out so she decided to open it up a little more. She moved the clothes over more to see and what do you know…it was a gun and also a muthafuckin brick.

Tears immediately fell again, "Oh my fucking God. Not my nephew too!"

This shit had finally reached its peak and she felt like she was going to stroke out for the first time in her life. Shit, she wasn't this stressed even when she had to strip and Storm knew what the time had come to do, so she tucked away that shit RJ had and changed her clothes, never calling anybody. She just grabbed her shit and left.

Later on that evening, Donny and the kids came home from their day. Thinking shit from last night was all good, Donny called out, "Storm" as the kids each went into their rooms and RJ discovered what was missing. RJ began to lose it, but he couldn't say shit because he already knew who'd found it.

Donny walked into the hall bathroom, finding the mirror broken and blood everywhere on the sink, his heart starts to race in panic, "What the fuck?" he yelled causing the kids to both come running out to see.

"What happened?" questioned Aaliyah as RJ stood there staring and confused because now he really didn't know what had happened.

Did someone break in and hurt Storm? RJ thought, but he still remained quiet and Donny instructed them both to go chill while he called Storm to find out what was up. Donny called Storm's phone like over fifteen times, and all he got was the voicemail, not even a damn ring. Everyone and everywhere he called, but no one seemed to have seen her all day and that shit was definitely not like her. She hadn't been to work at the shop or even to check in with the restaurant or Chance, so where in New York could she be? The night seemed to go by so slow for Donny and the kids. Not knowing where Storm was caused much agony in the house, especially with RJ. On top of not knowing where his aunt was, the drugs he had were missing too, and this little nigga was so scared along with everyone else, but he managed to get some type of sleep.

* * * * *

That next day, all Donny did was drive around and if he wasn't doing that, he was still making calls; but still no sign of Storm. He tried to ease the kids' mind; he wanted to do something nice for them so they wouldn't worry so much. As they all sat in the family room sharing pizza and watching a movie, they were all stopped when the sound of the front door alarm went off. Donny immediately jumped up, but the sound of more than one set of footsteps coming down the hall grabbed all of their attention quick as the sight of Storm seemed like a brush of fresh air to them all. Donny ran up to her, embracing her with a hug.

"I'm fine, baby bruh," said Storm sounding all too exhausted. "Everything's going to be alright now," she expressed as all eyes in the room turned their focus to the woman with her that was standing there in front of them too. But before anyone could ask a thing, Storm let go.

"RJ, why didn't you tell me you were selling drugs?"

As Storm uttered those words, they burned Donny and Aaliyah's ears because they had no idea, and RJ's face just went blank, not knowing how to respond.

"Look, Auntie, I'm sorry," he began to expressed being smart. "But I didn't have to tell you nothing…ok, and now is not the time to talk in front of company," he said, but the look on the lady's face showed them all different as he continued, "that's between me and my Abuelo, so stay the fuck out of our business!" he cursed Storm, but what happened next sure surprised the hell out of him.

"Watch your fucking mouth, boy," said the lady as the tears started flowing down her face from seeing enough and she couldn't take it anymore. The way those words sounded coming out of her mouth to him it sounded just like his mother Rain. Aaliyah and RJ both started to cry because you know what they say, "a child always knows their mom."

"Who are you?" asked Donny, also confused as to why this lady sounded just like his sister to him; but her face damn sure wasn't the same as she began to answer Donny back.

"It's me, baby bruh."

Donny stared because no one could say his name like *she* could.

"It's me, Rain," said the lady standing there in that room, and hearing her say that for the first time in years made Storm instantly break down. Donny stood there frozen, never saying a word as the kids both cried out in shock and fear, wanting to know if this was true. She didn't look like their mother, so how could this be as she explained. "My name is Elizabeth now," she said.

"You know Lizzy…that's me and I didn't die in my car accident."

Storm went over to comfort Aaliyah as she listened in.

"Someone tried to kill me and I manage to survive, but I couldn't let them know they didn't succeed. "The hospital notified your Auntie Storm and she came down there discovering me and I told her to contact Vick and he then took me to Virginia to escape for my safety and yours," she expressed. "So please don't be upset."

"Is it really you?" asked RJ, standing up from his chair and heading over toward his mom who has now come out to be Lizzy.

"Yes, it is me, baby," she said, embracing him in her arms and letting him feel the touch that only his mother could give. She stared into his eyes and he saw that it was really her. She took his hand and he rubbed her face as RJ cried. "I paid off the lady at the hospital name Lisa Clark to stay quiet and to act like she cremated me. Then Vick and I went to Richmond and had surgery to change our faces. Along with that, we had to change our names and live new lives until I could clean this mess up," she explained. "Now I'm back in your life, but not back to the world. I need you to know I'll never be."

Aaliyah ran up to her, hugging her as a sign not to leave again.

"I'll never leave you again, princess," she expressed as the smell of her little girl filled her heart with love. It had been almost seven years since she'd held her babies and even though they weren't babies anymore, shit…they still belong to her. "Look at me you two," still holding them both, "when I say 'not back to the world' I'm saying…not as Rain anymore," she expressed. "For now on, I'm Lizzy to everyone else, but not to ya'll anymore. From this day on, I'm always and forever going to be in your life and even though I was gone, I was always mommy to you because I've been working through your Auntie Storm all this time. Now's she's tired," said Rain as Storm sat over on the couch looking relieved and Donny still stood frozen as Rain made her way over toward him. "Hold me, baby bruh," she said to him as he cried, doing just that and placing his head on her shoulder just like he did when he was little.

"I'm back, baby. I'm back," she cried, trying hard to hold it together, but she couldn't and after an hour of joyous tears, the whole family was once again together and this time it was going to be for good. Rain was back and ready to put an end to everything that had been wronged. She spent the rest of the night letting Storm rest up for war, while she spent time with Donny and the kids. She informed them that they were leaving for Richmond tomorrow because she needed to get them out of the city before the hurricane came. She also called Tommy, letting him know everything was good and that the family was coming his way. Once they were straight, Tommy was to bring himself along with the Queen's Way South crew out to New York because it was now time for war and the real Queen is back!

The very next day, Rain was ready with a vengeance. She and Storm got up early so that they could help Donny and the kids prepare themselves for their journey to the Cap City, as well as getting ready to suite up for the shit that they were about to bring down in New York for them lingering niggas: Ricky, James and that bitch, Tiffany, who shouldn't have ever thought that they would win.

Rain made sure they had everything they needed as she stood with Storm watching as her heart parted ways with her again. This time would be the finale. Halfway through the gate on their way to board the plane, the kids turned around and hauled ass back to their mom, not wanting to let go again; after all, they had just gotten her back.

"Mommy," Aaliyah cried, "I don't want to leave you again," she expressed.

"It's not for long this time, baby. I promise and when I'm done here this time, there won't be a reason to come back. We're going to live happily together forever, the way God wants," she said as she held her children tighter, really not wanting to let go again now, but she knew it still had to be done. When she turned to face Storm, after watching her family leave her this time, the look they gave each other said, *let the games begin.*

Rain was ready to work out her plan; the plan that cost her seven years in a different life, and the one that she'd had to change so much of herself just to see it lived out, and now, nothing was standing in her way.

Rain and Storm headed over to Chance's house to meet up with him because he had some gathered information to share with them ASAP and it was the start of their plan. Storm knew Chance wanted her from day one and the same went for Rain and Vick, well, excuse me… he's *Tommy* now. Chance opened up his door looking good as a bitch. Storm shook her head as they made their way in and cut right to the chase because they didn't have time to lose. Apparently, Chance knew somebody, who knew somebody else and he was able to get the layout of how Ricky's Empire worked. He also was in need of a new financial advisor that just so happened to be another trade of Rain's, but only as Lizzy, and she was about to make that shit work.

In order to bring Ricky down on his ass, Rain would have to become an insider of his empire and that shit wasn't going to be easy, but she was going to enjoy every bit of taking everything from him that he took from her, all the way down to his fucking life. Chance also went in like a muthafucker for Storm's plot on the other two bitches. This nigga went as far as to hollering at Tiffany himself, but for work purposes only; he didn't really want that gold-digging bitch, he was starting to only have eyes for Storm. Tiffany was all in Chance's ass giving him play, and because he was a step up from James made shit pretty, which meant less working days and more shopping days; so of course she fell for Chance's game... *You Dummy.*

Storm had her own thing planned and boy was it going to be good. She wanted to pay the both of them back to show her appreciation to them both, and this definitely couldn't be done together because in her life, they were indeed on two different levels but that didn't mean it was good. Storm and Rain, after getting all that they needed, told Chance they'd see him later at the meeting and now it was time to locate Tip. Storm called Tip from the car to find out his location, and of course he was at headquarters.

"Wow," said Rain, not believing her eyes that the sight of Rico's kitchen hadn't change. "It's been so long and this place still makes me feel the same when I see it," she expressed to Storm as they got out of the Range Rover. Storm had made some adjustments to the outside of the restaurant, but this was Rain's business and it started from her heart, so of course she'd feel its presence walking in and it was actually like she'd remembered. Crème approached them to bring Storm her messages as Tip waited for them inside of the office.

As Storm and Rain sat down in front of Tip, he was confused as to whom the person was with Storm, but he knew she had to be someone special otherwise business would've never been going down in front of her.

"I called this meeting with you, Tip," said Storm, "because upon my discovery of some very fucked up shit about your brother and I need to make sure you're not a part of it."

Rain listened quietly, and Storm continued to inform Tip on her plan of action and even though he was confused as to what was going on, he knew he hadn't done shit wrong.

"Did you know that Ricky and your brother were the ones responsible for Rain's accident?" Rain still never saying a word, as they look on Tip's face showed he was just as shocked as they were with all of this.

"What the fuck, Storm. Stop playing!" he expressed with a look of hurt all over him from feeling fucked up right now. From day one, he and Rico have had always been close. Shit...those niggas were more like brothers then best friends. Tip was even the one who shot Majesty, killing that nigga for going after Rico and he still remained loyal to Rain even after his death. Tip, being down with hurting her, was definitely a "no, no" and he damn sure explained that to Storm, but still not knowing who the lady was he asked, "So who might this be, a private detective?" he asked and then he got his answer.

"Tip, it's me" said Rain as she smiled hard from hearing what he'd said about her and Rico and how much they meant to him.

"Me, who?" he said, knowing that he'd never seen her face before, but her voice damn sure rang a bell.

"I'm Rain, Tip. They didn't kill me."

Tip tried hard to piece this shit together, but to a hood nigga, Tupac was the only one who ever got away with this shit.

"I'm back, Tip and for war. Your brother and Ricky are going to pay, so we needed to know just where you stood."

Tip just smiled, hearing her giving orders again sure sounded good. I know that there is a thing called *brotherly love,* and in some cases it really does exist, but in the case of Tip and James, that shit was beyond lost because what niggas didn't know was that James fucked Tip's baby mamma, and to this day, James still doesn't have a clue Tip knows. Tip felt like it was time to see him pay for the shit that he does so Tip was all the way in. The BBM from Tommy came in letting Rain know that everything was in place with her family. Also, that Nizzy had them taken care of, and that he and the crew were boarding the flight as they spoke. She informed him to meet her at Storm's house at 9:45 p.m. for their meeting with Queen's Way North. Rain was about to make history, doing something that might not have ever been done before. She was about to bring New York and Virginia together and both on her behalf. The love of the North for Rain and the love of the South for Lizzy…this bad bitch was about to bring the house down. So, after clearing all that up, as well as, snagging that job of Ricky's which mysteriously she came highly recommended for, now it was time to get started. Storm sent a limo to pick up Tommy and the South crew up and Chance had them other muthafuckas all well in place as Tommy walked through the door with the South crew – all in black as they all took their place. Tip and the other crew members started checking them out and wondering why the fuck they were even here because as far as they were concerned, Queen's Way had all the soldiers it needed. What they didn't know was that they too were a part of Queen's Way and Rain. Rain and Storm stood in front of the room with Chance and Tommy standing right behind them and they all came to order.

"Everyone in this room knows exactly who I am," Storm began, "and everyone knows her too," she said as the look on the North crews face showed they were lost. "To some of you, this is Lizzy, and to some her name was Rain,"

Wize and Smitty almost fell out of their chair thinking, *this must be a mutherfuckin ghost,* but one thing they knew was not to interrupt during a meeting, so instead, they listen for a clue as Rain began to speak.

* * * * *

"To verify your information, I am indeed La'Rain," giving them a tone that only she could deliver, "and for the last time, no…I did not die and I'm actually stronger than before and now I'm really ready to play a game," she said as the boss in her voice let both crews know what was up because regardless…her face and her demeanor never changed. "You North boys have always loved and held me down, especially with your loyalty to my beloved Rico."

Tommy's face bolded up from hearing that, even though he knew that was her heart.

She continued, "You South boys have grown to love me too, and I'm not going to stand and question how much, but you all know now who I really am inside and now its time to link up. My face may be different, or even my name to some, but my heart still beats the same blood."

By now both crews are fucked up in the head, and now they didn't have a clue what the fuck was about to go down.

"So now the time has come to fight and destroy those who tried to destroy me, so I need to know who's down?" she asked, ready to give them the explanation as to why. "Ricky Tulio and James are the ones that tried to kill me and for the minds of crew South, I'll fill you in on who they are later to make a long story short, I ducked away and became somebody else and you goddamn right it was fucking hard. I had to leave my kids, and brother; shit, even though I had her…" she said, placing her hand on Storm's shoulder, "I was Lizzy at that time, at brain and heart…so, no…she didn't have me neither."

She continued to confess, hoping the crew would understand and which of course they did. Shit, fuck a queen at this fucking point, to them Rain was a mutherfuckin king with a pussy. They were down with whatever she had planned as she told them blow from blow, not leaving out any details on her plan to work from the inside. She also had work for them to do to stay in business, when it came to these two bitches – all fucking bets were off. She was also tired of this type of lifestyle and felt as if it was time to make a change. Rain and Storm were walking away from it all; they were taking their money and going to live comfortably off of their business, living their life and building their happy family back up and this time they were going to be free.

"So, if you with us and you mean it, then right now and this moment right here, I want ya'll to stand up," she instructed and her army would now become complete.

One by one, they all took salute and not a soul in that room had to think of shit twice before standing, because no matter what name she carried –North or South –the one they always knew her by was always *trust*. A queen will never stare her QUEENDOM wrong and with Rain, that promise she kept it true in any and every fucking thing she would do. Even though she was boxing up her crown to rule, she was going to make sure her crew boys were well the fuck off before she stepped down, but now it was time to, "Do Work!"

ACT ONE

"Excuse me, Mrs. Wales," addressed Megan, "Mr. Tulio will see you now," she said to Rain as she made her way down the hallway and for the first time as Lizzy, Rain was about to face the enemy and his dumb ass didn't even have a clue about who had walked into his life. As Rain knocked on his office door at Tulio Realtor and the sound of his voice telling her to enter made Rain's stomach do flips just like it did years ago. She couldn't stand his sneaky ass, but in order to finally put an ending to his games, Rain knew she had to be patient until the time came to act up.

Now this shit is where things became all too funny because we all remember how much Ricky's ass hated Rain's guts, and even though she had her face done to alter her appearance, a smart person can always tell when you're familiar to them, but I guess his fat ass missed that clue. He was too busy staring all up in her face like she was some food to eat as she made her way over and shook his hand, taking her seat, but never taking her eyes off of him.

Ricky began, "Elizabeth Wales," he looked over her resume, "judging by your paperwork, you're a very intelligent woman who came highly recommended by a close friend of mind. So, tell me a little about yourself and why you will be the best candidate for my company," Ricky questioned her and the look on his face showed her he liked what he saw. For someone who was a racist, he was sure into her smooth Indian brown skin and somehow he didn't hate on her now.

"Well, let me start off by saying how happy I am to work for your company, Mr. Tulio," she began to speak while praying to God that her voice alterations really did their thing because she didn't want that nigga to suspect anything foul on her part. "I've been in New York for eight months now and I still haven't had any luck on employment so I'm blessed to be here today. Back in Virginia, I was in the business of financial investments for eighteen years, and not to brag on myself, but I've made all of my clients filthy rich, sir. And not that you need it," they both began to laugh, "but I plan to increase your profits by three to four times bigger than what it is now if I'm given the chance," she said,, noticing Ricky admiring her thighs, Rain decided to show him more as she crossed her legs so that her split would come open so he really got his glimpse of those beautiful legs, At that time, Ricky's ass was hooked.

"Well, well, well, I like a woman who can talk money," he said, cuffing his hands together in front of him. "Alright, Elizabeth

, I'm gonna give you a chance, but first I want to explain your duties here at Tulio Realtors and you tell me if you feel like it's too heavy of a responsibility for you."

As she shook her head ok, Rain began to listen to this muthafucker as he dug his own grave slowly.

"Here, our cliental consist of million to billionaires who are always willing to pay top dollar on high marketable properties, may it be for businesses or homes. It's our job to close the deal and collect that money no matter what it takes. You will also have some long after hour work days counting and depositing my money and there is no strikes when it comes to fuckin that up; so, let's not, ok? And besides, accuracy is very important in this company. So do you think you could handle working closely with me?" Ricky asked Rain and still never knowing who she really was.

"Not only can I work closely to you, Mr. Tulio, but I'm going to handle your business so well that you, yourself, are going to fall in love with me," she replied back with her sexual and flirtatious smile.

Ricky was definitely buying into the game that this bitch was bringing, so it had to be her face as Rain, that made him hate her so; or was it the fact that she had her claws into Rico's ass getting all of his money and he couldn't stand that shit? But what he didn't know was that inside of the women he saw in a different way, beat the heart that pump blood through the veins of La'Rain and soon he would find out. After wrapping up her interview and switching her phat ass out of his office, he drooled on his desk over the way it bounced with a song in his head, and even he didn't understand where the feelings were coming from, but they damn sure were there.

* * * * *

Rain couldn't wait to go and tell Storm what happened, so she headed over to the shop ready to spill the gossip and to also see if Storm had started on her own plots as well. The atmosphere inside Secret Impressions really jumped that day, it was like everybody in New York wanted to look good for some reason. *Maybe it's a party that I haven't heard about*, thought Rain to herself as she made her way over toward Storm. "Goddamn, boo," joked Rain, slightly pushing Storm's back, "ya'll bitches really doing your thing up in here, it's a packed house," she said looking around at all the dryers that were full and also noticing the six more customers that were waiting on the first available.

"Yeah, girl, sorry I hadn't call you yet, but it's been like this in here all morning," said Storm and just as she went to say something else to her sister, guess who walks in looking and smelling like royalty, it was Chance. He came and headed straight over to Tiffany as a sign that plans were officially in action and the first straw pulled will be her ass. Rain and Storm paid very close attention to what was going on across the room as this bitch just knew she was the shit. All of the other stylists, and even some customers, eye balled the shit out of Chance while wondering to themselves who the fuck he was and also what he'd seen in Tiffany.

"Come here, boo," ordered Chance as he sat in Tiffany's chair spinning around and smacking her ass while she stood in her mirror flat ironing her tracks.

"What baby?" she said, barely even knowing Chance well enough to call him baby, but I guess his money had already earned him that title as she sat down on his lap.

"I've missed you all day," expressed Chance. "For some reason, you're all I can think about shorty; damn you a bad bitch," he buttered her up and of course you know that thirsty bitch brought it, feeling like she was Queen B. Tiffany thought Chance was her meal ticket to an even better life, but this time around her greed for money was going to cost her more than she really wanted to pay.

"I missed you too, daddy, and I can't wait for our trip to Vegas so I can finally give you some of this pussy that I've been saving just for you," she said, but of course she was lying because she'd just fucked James this morning.

As soon as she stood up off his lap, James walked in the damn door. Of course he was there for Storm, but that still didn't stop his ass from breaking his neck trying to see who that nigga was sitting at Tiffany's station. But you know Storm wasn't going to have that. James knew Chance for real, so the only thing that saved them was the fact that Chance threw his hoodie on his head and Storm immediately took James into her office to talk.

Tiffany's skin crawled as she watched Storm and James tonguing each other down from the office bay window, but she had to play it calm. She was too busy into what they were doing, as well as wondering why he gave Storm that knot of money, that she almost dropped the hot wax on Chance.

"What the fuck, boo! Are you sleep?" asked Chance, jumping up from the chair.

"My bad, daddy, I just have a lot on my mind. Can we please finish this later because my customer is ready for me?"

Tiffany was trying to hurry his ass out of there before James came back out and that's actually what she did. As Chance smacked her ass again, which by the way James saw, Chance nodded at Rain out of respect and kept it moving. Rain sat there staring at Tiffany so hard that you could almost smell the anger as it perspired out of her.

"Thanks for the money, boo," said Storm as James tried to lift her legs to suck that pussy.

"Come on baby, you don't have to thank me, just let me taste that nut in my mouth."

To Storm, that shit was dead and the only reason she was being nice was because she didn't want him to become suspicious about her plans.

"By the way, thanks James for the money toward executing your own death plot bitch, and your dumb ass still don't have a clue, but you will," Storm spoke softly underneath her breath.

"What did you say, baby?" questioned James thinking that he had heard her say something as they headed out of her office.

"I ain't saying nothing, boo. I was just singing," she smiled at him as she purposely stopped right in front of Tiffany. Practically sticking her tongue down James' throat again, Storm was making damn sure Tiffany saw this one.

"Umm, girl, damn!" James said, wiping Storm's lipstick off his lips. "Let me go before you leave with me!"

"Yeah, let you go," said Storm, " I have a lot of work to do here but am I going to see you tonight!" she said loud enough for Tiffany to hear; who, by the way, could no longer function as she waited to hear his answer.

"I think that's possible," he replied. "I got some business to take care of later so I'll call you, boo," he smiled, kissing Storm on the lips. He gave Tiffany the eye to say *call me* as he made his exit out of the shop.

Rain was still sitting there taking in everything she saw just like that night at the club when she caught him trying his hands with Yetta and she couldn't wait to see him get burned.

"What's wrong with you, sis," Storm asked quietly as she sat down beside Rain. "Why your face bald up looking all ugly?" she laughed.

"You know why," she answered back, "the whole time you were with James, that bitch sat there watching your every move and I was about to smack her ass in the face with these hot ass curlers."

They both burst out into laughter causing Tiffany to wonder why, so she decided to walk over and make small talk.

"Wow girl, it's been crazy busy in here all day," expressed Tiffany. "Oh my bad... how are you?" she extended her hand toward Rain. "I'm Tiffany, and you are?"

"Lizzy," Rain answered, never reaching back nor cracking a smile, "I'm Ja'Nay's business partner," she blankly expressed.

"Oh cool, nice to meet you. So what do you think about my boo?" Tiffany questioned Storm, "isn't he sexy, girl?" she asked, trying hard to throw Storm off. Little did she know, Storm was the boss of her "so-called" boo and this dumb bitch, again, was totally in the dark.

"I seen him, girl. He is the shit, and oh yeah, you can tell he is a baller," said Storm, rubbing her fingers together as a sign of money and Tiffany stood there blushing.

"This perm is burning me, Tiffany," said Mrs. Tate, causing Tiffany to end their convo and rush right over to her customer. This gave Rain time to fill Storm in on what happened at her interview earlier.

"Girl, you know I had that nigga Ricky, all on my game today," joked Rain. "For someone who didn't like me as Rain, he sure is feeling the fuck out of Lizzy and I'm going to use that to my advantage."

They both smiled because things were falling into place just like they wanted.

"So, when do you start?" asked Storm, inquiring about Rain's first day on her new job and knowing that she couldn't wait to begin.

"Tomorrow," she replied, "and I've already got shit straight in VA to wire all that nigga's cheese right to my accounts as I go along. I also have the maps that Queen's Way will need to all of Ricky's spots so they can tag a different area each day until there's nothing else to get," she explained. They wanted to take everything from that nigga Ricky – the same shit he took from them. Rain wanted it back in return from him and that's exactly what she was going to get. Rain sat there on the computer, waiting on Storm to finish her last two customers when her cellphone began to go off; it was Donny.

* * * * *

"Wassup, baby bruh?"

"Hey, sis," said Donny. "What are you doing? Are you ok?"

"Yeah, I'm good, boo," she said, "How are my babies? Are ya'll getting used to Richmond" she laughed, knowing that Virginia to them was much slower than New York.

"Yeah, their good; just missing the hell out of you," he said, "but I called to let you know what's been going on out here at the club," Donny continued as Rain listen. "Nizzy's been doing her thing out this bitch, holding shit down for you, but last week, she had a situation that we all thought would blow up in her face."

"So, what happened?" she asked, hoping it was nothing too bad that she'd have to fuck Nizzy up over.

"Well, it all happened at the club Friday night," Donny began to explain. "Everything was going good and everybody was having a damn good time while Nizzy kept everything in order. Nizzy was standing over by the bar when Thunder's sister, Kandy, approached her, practically throwing her pussy all up in her face."

Rain knew already from the sound of things that something fucked up went down, but she continued to listen to the facts from her brother before she went the fuck off.

"Nizzy and Kandy talked for a moment as Kandy continued to spit game, trying hard to go home with Nizzy and feel that long tongue twirl in and out that pussy. Well, Nizzy's eyes radared in on that southern phat ass and she forgot all about her girlfriend Tricia real fast. So the next thing I know, sis, their asses were on the dance floor. Whatever Kandy said must've worked, because Nizzy's hands were all on that ass while Kandy backed that thing up good. But just as they got deeper into each other, Tricia taped me on my shoulder looking for Nizzy because she popped up to surprise her and before I could answer, she spotted them getting it in on the floor and she stormed over in their direction."

"What the fuck!" said Rain. "Nizzy know I don't do drama. So what happened, baby bruh? Get to the point!" she angrily snapped.

"All I know is that Tricia pushed Nizzy's ass hard as a bitch, causing her to almost knock Kandy down. Kandy was like, *what the fuck*, but before she knew it, Tricia punched Kandy right in the face and when she went to swing on Nizzy. Main grabbed her arm, holding her back, as Nizzy went the fuck off. But she caught herself; not wanting to make more of a scene. So, instead, she told Main to carry that bitch to her office. I don't know what was said up there, but D-money told me it wasn't pretty from what he heard standing guard outside Nizzy's door. I remember seeing Tricia running out of the club crying and calling Nizzy every hoe in the book; but that shit didn't faze Nizzy one bit because as soon as she came back down, her and Kandy went right back at it in the VIP. If I'm not mistaken, they left together that night," he said. All Rain wanted to know was if everything else went smooth after that, cause if not, she'd hate to have to use her "9" on a nigga and that shit right there was real talk.

After all of that was said, Rain and Donny talked for a few minutes more, then she had to wrap it up because her and Storm were about to leave the shop. They were heading straight over to the crews to give them their orders for mission *Take down Ricky*. Ricky's right-hand man was his best friend, Michael Zaroni, and that nigga was slick as grease. He had made Ricky so much money over the years from the streets that he himself lived like a Tulio. Ricky's Empire stretched all the way to Jersey, and because of who Rain was, they had no problem finding this entire map out. She assigned each of the crew members by sets of two in an area belonging to Ricky's Empire to tag. She wasn't stopping until there was nothing left to get. She wanted to juice that nigga of everything he owned and that included his wife.

The next morning, Rain was hyped as hell to start her new job for Ricky and part of her was nervous as hell. She had to hold her cover and even if this nigga tripped, she still had to stand strong and not let him know who she really, really was and Storm knew that shit would be hard.

* * * * *

As she walked through the doors of Tulio Realtors she was personally greeted by the man himself so that he could show her to her new office that so happened to sit across from his.

"Good morning, Mr. Tulio," she greeted, "hope you slept well last night."

Being that it was early in the morning, she tried to act concerned for the pig, but what she really wanted to do was slaughter his ass and take a bath in his blood; but it was still way too early for that.

"Well, thank you for asking and yes…I did," he replied. "Let me get you settled in because we have our first meeting with my accountant Chuck."

Since Rain hadn't seen Chuck in a long time, she thought that this shit would be interesting as she plotted to fool them both into turning on each other.

"Welcome to your new office," Ricky said, opening the door so that she could enter and as she walked in, all Rain could inhale was the scent of new wood which meant he went all out and had new shit brought in just for her. Ricky had also gotten fresh lilies delivered to her office as a symbol of a new relationship between the two.

"Why… thank you, sir," she flashed him with a smile as he stood over her chair assisting her with becoming familiar with the software he used for handling his clients' accounts. Once she got it down, which didn't take real long, it was time to introduce her to his side business with Chuck. Lizzy knew that this meeting would determine if she could swim or sink in his world.

As they both walked into the board room, her eyes met with Chuck's. After all this time, the nigga was still an old white geek kissing Ricky's ass and he had no clue who was in his presence.

"Elizabeth Wales, meet Charles Gibson, better known as, Chuck around here," Ricky introduced the two as they all sat down to begin.

"How are you, sir," she greeted Chuck.

"I'm fine, Mrs. Wales and might I add it's a pleasure to meet you. I have heard only wonderful things about you," Chuck assured Rain.

"Well, since we're all acquainted, let's get down to business," interrupted Ricky ready to hear about his money.

"Well, sir," said Chuck, "last month's profit looks mighty good I must say. Ricky's Empire brought in 3.5 million starting from the Bronx all the way to Jersey shore," he continued as the look on Ricky's face showed he was impressed at the numbers himself and so was Rain; but of course, she played dumb.

"Mr. Tulio, sir," Rain interrupted, "are we talking about figures for Tulio Realtor or something else?" she asked as Chuck and Ricky both began to laugh at how clueless she was…or so they thought.

"No, honey, it's not," Ricky replied and pardon my inaccuracy, I should have told you about this sooner, but I had to know I could trust you," he said. "Ricky's Empire is something totally different from what we do here and I hope it's not a problem for you."

"So, what is it, sir? Drugs or something?" she began to laugh, acting like she was just joking.

"Yes, you're right; it is drugs," he replied, "and I'm one of the biggest suppliers in New York all the way to New Jersey. It's been that way for years. "You will also be in charge of meeting with Chuck on multiple occasions to keep record of his deposits and make sure they are adding up right. No offence to you. Chuck, but Elizabeth is highly trained to assist you in some of my business."

"None taken, I could use an extra hand," said Chuck looking over at Rain and smiling hard.

"Well great, since everything is out in the open, let's get to work!" said Ricky, handing Rain a spreadsheet with all of his properties, both available and taken, so she could start booking appointments. Rain couldn't believe that this shit was really working out; but most of all, she was amazed at just how much trust she had collected already, which made this shit so much more enjoyable to do.

* * * * *

While Rain held down her new job, Queen's Way honored theirs and they were ready going full force to avenge their Queen and take back what was stolen from her seven years ago. Tip and Hamp were the first two to act. With them being the leaders of both crews, they knew that nothing could be left undone. They had to finish what Ricky started, and this time they weren't going to lose. The first spot they tagged was the South Bronx location; which indeed, made a lot of money for Ricky. Marty Brown and Casey Jones were two of Ricky's most prize able members and those two niggas always went hard. Tip and Hamp sat watch outside of their trap house, waiting to make a move. As they counted the number of fiends that came and went, the calculations of all the money that those niggas were making made their hunger arouse even more then it was and they could no longer hold back.

Tip noticed a nigga running down the block like he was in a hurry to get his fix.

"That looks like that crack head, Marcus," Tip said to Hamp as he lifted his ski mask to see clearer. As his vision became focused, he knew for damn sure who he was, so they decided to grab his ass and make him a decoy to distract the boys while they made their move. Hamp jumped out first, of course, just like a wild VA nigga and Tip was right behind him pulling down his mask as they ran Marcus's way. He didn't even see them coming.

"Run that shit nigga before I bust a cap in your ass!" yelled Hamp with his 357 pressed hard against the back of his head.

"Aww, mane, shit! What the fuck you want from me, mane? I don't have shit!" asked Marcus almost bagging for his life.

"So, what the fuck you doing coming around here with no money?" questioned Tip, trying hard to throw things off.

"I was on my way to book some smack from Casey because he always looks out for me," he confessed, scared as hell of what was about to happened next.

Well, since you can't feed us nigga, you're going to help us get what we want. So walk your half-dead ass up to the door and knock while we make our grand entrance!" ordered Hamp as him and Tip followed that nigga into the yard.

They both stood back on each side of the door as Marcus knocked twice. After making himself known, Marty opened the door and it was on from there. As Marty turned to walk away and Marcus followed behind him, Big Cee went to shut the door and Hamp opened fire, popping his ass twice in the chest. Marcus took off running back out of the house and at that point it was every man for himself.

Marty and Casey rumbled through old boxes, trying hard to find their guns. But any real G knows you should always keep your shit in reach…but I guess these niggas were just too comfortable. Tip shot Marty right through the fucking mouth, not even giving that nigga time for one last breath. Just as Casey went to pull out on Tip, Hamp came up from behind.

"Where the fuck is the work and money nigga?" he asked Casey trying to make the transaction a lot faster, but this nigga wanted to keep on stalling.

"What, nigga? I don't know what you're talking about" he said, even though his homie was scratched out in the corner.

"So, now you want to play horse with me?" questioned Hamp.

Before Casey answered, Tip came back out of the other room with presents.

"I found that shit, nigga, let's rock!" he said as Hamp's finger became locked on the trigger at that point.

"Well bitch, play all you want because we got what we came here for. So give your boss Ricky this message for me once my Queen sends him to hell."

POW was all that Casey heard before his bodily functions came to a halt and that lead went right threw his brains.

"Tell that nigga Queen's Way said, 'fuck you'," expressed Tip as he spit right into that nigga's face and they peeled.

"Woo that shit was fun," said Hamp as they pulled off their masks and Tip drove the truck with speed.

"Yeah, it was my nigga, and they got what they deserved. I bet when it's all said and done, that nigga Ricky gonna wish like hell he'd never fucked with La'Rain Peters," assured Tip. They were on a war path, and from that day forward, it would be popping until all chips were down.

*****

One thing about the street codes is that word travels fast; and not even two hours had gone by before Ricky got the call alerting him about what had taken place.

"Wassup, Mikey? How's it going?" answered Ricky, knowing that every time Ricky called, it was definitely about business.

Boss, we have a situation," said Michael, pissed ass fuck and talking real fast. Ricky immediately picked up on the tone in his voice.

"Whoa…slow down!" ordered Ricky, "now what's going on again?"

"Boss, I don't know how this shit happened, but our South Bronx location has been hit," he explained.

"What the fuck do you mean!" screamed Ricky. "Where the fuck is Marty and Casey?" he asked, wondering how this shit went down.

"Larry called me to tell me what happened and when I pulled up, the police had everything on lock and they still do, my nigga. You can't even get in," expressed Michael. "I'm sitting in my car across the street now."

"So, what about the money and my product? I know a nigga ain't that damn suicidal to steal my stuff from me." Ricky was so mad that he smacked his trophy off the desk and it broke.

"Larry was the first one there and he told me that Casey and Marty are dead and that whoever it was, got away with twelve bricks of ya-yo and $500,000 in cash. The only thing they left was the shit that was broken down and the fiends snatched some of that before the police came."

Ricky was mad as hell; so much so that he hung up in Michael's face and all he wanted to do was kill someone at that point. *But whom?* He didn't know who authorized the hit, but he was damn sure going to find out soon.

"Excuse me, Mr. Tulio," said Rain. Judging from his facial expressions, she knew he wasn't in the mood. "I have those forms you asked me to get signed, sir," she said. "Is everything alright with you?"

"Thank you, Elizabeth," said Ricky. But boy was he not in a good mood at this time. "I'm alright, I just can't believe that some muthafucker on these streets has a death wish for fucking with my money," he stated and the red color of his skin showed his anger.

Rain knew actually what he was talking about. Shit, it was her boys who ran the hit.

"I'm sorry to hear that, sir. Let me know if there's anything I can do to make it all better," she said as she rubbed her hand against his face and turned and walked away with a smile.

All Ricky could think about was the $800,000 loss that he'd just taken and who could be responsible for it. He knew he would find them, but in reality, he didn't have to look real far because *she* was right in his reach and he was too gullible to notice.

* * * * *

Days turned into nights, nights into weeks, and weeks into months and Rain and Storm's plots were on fire. She had been working for Ricky for all about three months now and their work relationship was starting to preheat at 350 degrees. Ricky loved her work so much that it was causing problems for him at home. He and Rain were spending long hours together, as well as having more business dinner dates than usual. Ricky's wife, Christina, damn sure wasn't a fool; she noticed the decrease in her time and sex life at home and she was definitely going to find out who had a hand in it.

"Hello, Mrs. Tulio," greeted Megan. "So nice to see you here today. What brings you by?"

"Thank you, honey. Is Ricky busy? I came by to treat him to lunch."

"He's in his office with Elizabeth," she replied, "those two sure have become real close," snitched Megan.

I swear this girl had diarrhea of the mouth as Christina took off walking toward Ricky's office. She opened the door without even knocking. As Christina entered his office, there he was with Lizzy, sitting on top of his desk in a pose as he sat in his chair admiring his view so much that he didn't even see Christina come in.

"What the fuck is this all about?" questioned Christina as Ricky's face showed he had just seen a ghost. Rain stood up straight to her feet, looking Christina dead in the eyes.

"Hello, I'm Elizabeth," she extended her hand to greet Christina, but all she got was a couple of eye rolls and stares. "Ok…" smirked Rain. "Mr. Tulio, I'll be in my office if you need me," she said as she rolled her eyes back at Christina and walked out.

"What are you doing here, darling?" he asked, walking up to Christina and trying to plant a kiss on her lips.

Christina wasn't having it. She was pissed.

"We haven't been spending a lot of time together and now I can see why," she implied. "I came here to take you to lunch and I catch you in the middle of desert, Ricky. Why was she sitting on top of your desk?"

"Look…I don't owe you any explanation and she works for me. You are just my wife, ok…so you worry about home and leave my business to me!" he snapped.

Christina couldn't believe what she was hearing. This muthafucker had the balls to stand in her face and uphold some bitch over her. She thought his ass had really bumped his head and she didn't know what this was coming from.

"I have a meeting to get ready for so I can't go to lunch," Ricky replied, "and come to think of it, I'll be home late as well."

At that point Christina didn't have any more words to say and she saw the decision he was making. She grabbed her designer bag out of the chair to leave, but before she left she turned around to say one more thing.

"You are all into this lady, Richard, but you gave our son hell—God rest his soul—because he chose to be with a black girl. And now look at your ass… almost loving that chocolate milk!" she angrily expressed. "Fuck you, Richard!" she said, slamming the door as she made her way out of his office and out to car to leave.

* * * * *

Queen's Way was also doing their thing. Ever since Tip and Hamp set things off for them, the rest of the crew members went head first into the plot and the rest was history. Both crews were hungry, and since all of their drug activities had stopped due to the mission, what they collected from Ricky's Empire was theirs to keep. They could do whatever they wanted with the shit because Rain and Storm had enough money that was legit, that dirty money wasn't an option to them anymore. They just wanted to be free. Storm, of course, was handling her business with James, and Chance was really doing his thing with that bitch, Tiffany. In fact, their trip was coming up real soon and the games for her would finally begin.

It was Tuesday night, approximately 12:15a.m., and Rain and Ricky were the last two left at the office putting the final touches on a contract for 1.7 million. After the loss he'd taken earlier, Ricky was trying to get back every dime somehow. As they both walked to the elevators together, Rain could feel his eyes on her body, so she decided to make him sweat; even if it meant making her sick. The elevators went into motion as Rain pushed the stop button in between floors and walked over to Ricky as his eyes became as big as quarters. She pressed her phat apple ass against his dick and began moving up and down.

"I've seen you watching it so I decided to let you feel it for yourself," she said as his manhood became very hard on her ass.

"Elizabeth," whispered Ricky as he rested his head against hers while inhaling the smell of her Chanel perfume. "You are trying to get me into trouble," he laughed, not knowing that trouble was an understatement to what she'd had up her sleeve. Rain had drenched her clothes in perfume so that all Christina would smell on Ricky was her. Just as Ricky went in to kiss her neck, Rain felt that she'd done enough for the night because she knew when he got home all he would think about was her and how good she felt as well as the thought of them going further.

"Ok, boo," she laughed. "Let's get you home before your wife comes looking for you again," she said.

"You're right, my dear," Ricky said, fixing his pants and unstopping the elevators so that they could finally leave.

* * * * *

As Rain drove home, she couldn't help but laugh. "This nigga is so comical," she said to herself as she wished she could be a fly on his wall tonight. Ricky, on the other hand, didn't know where the feelings came from, but he wanted that black bitch so much and now that she'd opened up the door, he damn sure was going to enter.

"Richard, is that you?" called out Christina from the top of the stairs. She'd been waiting on him for two hours because she had something special planned for the two of them.

"Yeah, it's me," he answered back as he made his way up to her. As he walked into the room, there were candles lit everywhere and Christina stood sexy in her $600 lingerie with her breast looking perky and her nipples hard as hell. Ricky knew he was about to have fun, but the only problem was…he couldn't get Elizabeth out of his head. But he damn sure was going to try hard.

Ricky began to tongue Christina down and she very quickly picked up on a woman's scent that wasn't hers.

"Who have you been with?" she asked as Ricky took one of her breast into his mouth.

"Richard, did you hear me? Why do you smell like a woman?"

"Look, darling, don't spoil it. I've been in meetings all day and you know I work around women," he played his hand well and her dumb ass brought it.

As each piece of their clothing began to fall off, Ricky imagined he was about to fuck Lizzy. That was not a good thing to do. He laid out on the bed to let Christina do what she did best with her mouth, and that Columbian bitch couldn't have had any tonsils judging from the way she took in that dick. You could see his hard print inside of her throat and Ricky was enjoying every bit of it. The more Christina sucked, the more he visualized Lizzy backing it up on him. Ricky became so excited at his thoughts, plus the sound of her slurps, that before you know it, Christina's stomach was filled with hot and steamy cum.

Christina licked her fingers. That old bitch was bad! She climbed on top of that dick backwards, bouncing up and down as her breast made a flopping noise that got to Ricky even more and he could no longer hold himself back. He flipped her over and lifted those legs as he went inside to do some damage. The harder he stroked, the wetter Christina got and her pussy juices began to stream out.

"Oh my God, Ricky! I love you," she moaned.

You're not going to believe what he said next. "I love you too, Elizabeth," was the words he spit out and boy…I know he wished like hell he could swallow his words.

Smack! was the sound of Christina blessing his face as she pushed that nigga up off of her and she got the hell up.

"Chrissy, wait…let me explain!" he said, jumping up after her. The only time he called her Chrissy was when he was in hot water; but this time, his pot had turn completely off the stove and this nigga knew he'd fucked up.

"Fuck you, Richard! You fucked that bitch; didn't you?" screamed Christina in rage. "I fuckin hate your ass right now," she said as she grabbed her clothes and got dressed.

Ricky walked over toward her, pulling her arm and turning her around to face him. "Listen Mi Mujer, I have not been unfaithful to you, but I made a mistake and I'm sorry," he begged, but Christina wasn't buying that shit. She felt as though he was lying, but if he didn't fuck her, he must have wanted to. Otherwise why would her name come out of his mouth.

"Richard, I need some time away from you," she cried out hysterically, "and don't even try to find me," she said. "But while I'm gone, I suggest you get your priorities in check or our next step will be divorce court because I'm done and I want come second to nothing or no one."

She grabbed her keys and her pack bag and left Ricky's ass standing there wondering what was happening to his world. Just like the Great Walls of China, bits and pieces of his life were crumbling down and if he didn't repair it, soon there wouldn't be anything left!

Revenge is best served Cold

"Welcome to JFK," said Me'Chole, the airport attendant. "How may I help you today?"

"Two first-class tickets to Las Vegas," said Chance as Tiffany stood beside him smiling hard.

"Name, sir," the attendant asked nicely.

"Charles Sanchez," answered Chance, waiting patiently for Me'Chole to key in his information.

"Here you are, sir. I have you pulled up right here," she said as she printed out their tickets.

"You ready for this?" whispered Chance in Tiffany's ear.

"Baby, I was born ready and I can't wait to ride on that dick you've been saving for me," she said as they both began to laugh.

"Here you are sir, two first-class tickets on Continental Airlines Flight 403 that will be boarding at Gate 7 around 1:52p.m." Me'Chole explained and Chance thanked her as him and Tiffany headed for the plane.

"Damn, boo, somebody's really trying to get in touch with you," joked Tiffany sarcasticaly at the sound of Chance's text messages going off. "Well," she paused giving him a sideways look, "are you going to answer it?" she said as they prepared for take off.

"I'm with you, boo; so fuck whoever that is," he replied, but he already knew who it was. Chance had a set ringtone for everything and everybody, so he knew what time it was without having to look. "Can we just enjoy our trip, baby?" asked Chance as he softly gripped Tiffany's B-cup breast and kissed her on those thin beautiful lips, letting her know that he was horny from the two shots of Patron he had. "I don't want to give anyone my attention but you," he said.

Hearing those words made Tiffany feel like a queen as she immediately began to tongue his ass down.

"Excuse me…" said the flight attendant as she cleared her throat to get their attention.

"Oh, my bad, wassup?"

"Can I get you something to drink?" she asked.

Tiffany didn't like the way she eyeballed Chance, it was if she knew who he was. "No you can not!" she screamed. "All we want is each other!" snapped Tiffany as Chance began to laugh.

The flight attendant didn't give a fuck, she was straight hood and would have beat Tiffany's ass, but she just ignored that bitch and looked straight at Chance and said, "Anyway, let me know if you need anything," she grinned at him as she began to walk away.

That's when Tiffany got balls. "What bitch?" she jumped from her seat as if she was ready to fuck her up, but Chance pulled her ass back down instead.

"Calm your ass down, girl," he expressed as he slowly slide his finger up under her skirt and right into that phat juicy pussy. He inserted two of his fingers as Tiffany's eye's began to roll back into her head and she moaned, "Stop playing, boy, before I make you meet me in the bathroom."

"Shit, you aint saying nothing," he expressed as he took his third finger inside of her deeper. That caused her pussy to open up deeper and wider. He licked on her neck which caused her to slowly remove his hand as she got up heading toward the bathroom and signling for him to join her. She twisted her ass with each step.

Chance sat there for about five minutes so no one would know what was up. He took his phone out of his pocket because now was a good time to check his texts; which, by the way, came straight from the boss. He began to read, *Plan in action; as soon as you land, check in and leave out. But occupy that bitch until you hear back from me.*

He replied to her, *ten four.* As he got up heading back toward the restroom, he thought of how much fun this was going to be. He said the words underneath his breath, "Pussy and head before destruction," and he laughed as he opened the door only to see Tiffany's naked body standing there with one leg up on the toilet and one finger playing inside her pussy. Chance knew then it was game on as he pulled out that thick long monster and locked the door for safety. Tiffany's hoe ass droped right to her knees and being taking her tongue, licking up and down and around and around the entire body of his shaft. Then she took both of his nuts and placed them into her mouth to suck as she tea bagged the fuck out of them muthafuckers.

He began to gurnt, "Goddamn, bitch! Suck them shits!" he said, and she did just that. She liked the dirty talk because hearing that made her suck even harder. Tiffany took her hand and grabbed that now fully erect dick; gently sliding it into her mouth and leaving none of it out for air. Chance couldn't believe how good this bitch gave head. *Damn shame it all has to go to waste*, he thought as Tiffany rotated the muscles in her mouth, never using any teeth as she relaxed her lips around his tip and moved her head back and forth.

As soon as she felt Chance's dick begin to throb, she stood up and bent over the vent for leverage and that was Chance's Q to enter her and he did just that. He fucked that pussy nice and hard while pulling Tiffany's hair with one hand and gripping her breast with the other. She moaned so much you would have thought she was a virgin.

"Throw that ass back, bitch! Give that phat ass pussy to daddy!" he ordered. "Don't run, stay your ass right here!" he said and Tiffany's ass did just that. She couldn't believe how good this shit was. "This dick good; aint it bitch?" he said as she stattered to say yes, but was bearly able to breathe ."Take it, take it, take it!" he said as he jammed that ass harder and she gripped the sink almost pulling it from the wall. Just as she began to reach her peek, a knock at the door slowed up the process, but that shit wasn't going to stop Chance. He was going to get his rocks off no matter who the fuck was at the door.

The passager began to grow inpatient. "Are you almost done in there?" she asked trying to get the fuck in. "Hello…anybody in there?"

"Hold on, bitch, shit!" yelled Tiffany as the sensation of daddy's dick pulsating let her know the cream was coming on.

"Oh, shit, bitch! Bring your mouth here and drink this nut!" he said as he pulled his dick out and Tiffany leaned toward it as he placed it right into the back of Tiffany's throat.

The taste of hot creamy cum shot down into her stomach and she sucked it all out and never let anything drop unless it went into her mouth. Chance was shocked, he couldn't believe how much of a pro this project bitch really was, but they didn't have time to do shit but smile as they both rushed to get dressed. They finally left the bathroom and headed back to their seats, laughing the entire way there as everybody's eyes targeted in on them both, but you know they didn't really give a fuck.

* * * * *

Vegence is sweet were the words that Storm was always told, but she never knew just how good it would taste until she placed it on the tip of her taste buds… and boy was she hooked. People say that when it comes to your plot, you should dig two graves; one for the enemy and one for yourself, but when it came to Storm, she was one step ahead of the game. Believe you me, she would'nt be sleeping in neither one of them muthafuckers because they had already been assigned and now the time had come for her to assure that the enemies laid in them permanetly.

"Welcome to the Royal Hilton," said the front desk attendant. "Las Vegas' most luxury hotel experience. Can I have your name please?"

"Charles Sanchez," replied Chance as Tiffany clung tightly to his arm while resting her head on his shoulder. She patiently waited as her king gathered their keys to the weekend palace and she couldn't wait till it begin.

"Alright, Mr. Sanchez, here are the keys to your room," the attendant said. "You will be on the thirteenth floor and the elevators are located around the corner to your left," she handed him his black card and two key cards to room 1347. The bell boy followed the two of them up to their room as he carried their luggage. He waited for a tip because it was obvious to him that Chance was a baller. Like everyone else in his life, the bell boy wanted his share of the profit, but of course, Tiffany's stupid ass slammed the door in his face, not wanting to share any of Chance with anyone else and that especially went for his money.

"Oh, no…don't sit down." Chance pulled Tiffany up from the bed by her arms. "Let's go out and see the city; plus, I'm hungry as shit!" he expressed.

"Me too, boo. I could eat a horse," said Tiffany as she fixed her hair and makeup, making sure she was fit to go out on Chance's arm. He took her by the hand and they both dipped off.

As they headed for Tropicana Avenue to hit up the Casinos, Tiffany remenbered that she'd always wanted to ride the rollercoster on top of the Stratosphere Tower and that now would be perfect timing.

"Let's stop here first, baby," said Chance pointing his fingers toward Top of the World, one of Vegas' most highly recommendable restaurant. "I have to eat before we can do anything, baby," he expressed as they walked up to the doors heading straight in to dine.

"Oh my God! Daddy, it's beautiful in here," expressed Tiffany as the hostess escorted them to their table. Since there was a packed house, he took their drink orders for the waitress.

"I'll be back, boo. Gotta go drain the monster," he said as he got up from the table and give Tiffany a kiss. He headed straight to the bathroom and pulled out his cellphone to make a call.

"Hello," answerd Storm, sounding good as fuck to Chance. "I've been waiting on your call, so tell me…are we good?"

"Yes, we are," he stated with confidence. "Right now we about to eat at Top of the World and then it's off to gamble until you say otherwise, boss," Chance assured her.

"Well, you two stay busy and I'm about to get started," she said. "I'll call you back when it's time for the next step."

Chance agreed and they both hung up so that he could go back to the table before Tiffany's impatient ass came looking for him.

"You've reached Lizzy, hit me back" was what Storm got twice when she called to see where her sister was. Since there wasn't an answer, Storm went ahead beginning step one.

"Welcome to the Royal Hilton."

"Hi, my is Diamond," said Storm, dressed in disguise from her head to her her feet. "My brother is a guest here and I need to get into his room," she expressed to the clerk.

"Ma'am, I'm sorry, but I can't give you a key unless he, himself, left orders for us to do so," the clerk explained.

Storm, being a boss, wasn't used to rejection, so you can imagine the anger she felt at that point, but she manage to keep her cool. She did what she does best; sliding five, one hundred dollar bills on top of the counter and looking the clerk dead in the face she said, "Let me ask you again, can I have the keys to Charles Sanchez's room?"

The clerk stood there on pause for a minute; scared and happy at the same time, but she sure could use the money. "Look…you didn't get this from me," expressed the clerk as she handed Storm a key. "Room 1347 and whatever you do…please don't get caught because that's my job," she said as she quickly grabbed the money and tucked it safely into her pocket.

Storm grinned and walked off. As she walked into the room, all that was on her mind was the mission at hand; but to her surprise, there was the missing link to her plan already sitting there waiting on her to arrive.

"How the fuck you get in, nigga," laughed Storm as Rain sat there sipping on a Cranberry and Vodka from the mini bar inside Chance's room.

"Damn, I wish I'd known you were here," she said, "that bitch at the front desk cost me $500.00 just to get a key," she shook her head at Rain.

"I took Vick's jet out here this morning and I got the room right next to Chance. When they left, I was able to get housekeeping to let me in by saying that I was his wife," Rain explained. She damn sure wasn't dumb when it came to her plans.

"I got to hand it to you, sis," said Storm, "you really are a boss and being around Rico all those years really taught you a lot."

"Bitch, please!" laughed Rain as she headed into the closet, taking out bags. "I taught myself, he just exposed me to the life," she expressed, "but let's get this show on the road please."

Storm began setting up their scenery for the proformance that would soon take place. They decorated the room with a trail of rose petals from the door leading to the bed in the shape of a heart along with candles all on the tables. This bitch Tiffany was really going to think she was the shit, and that Chance was truly digging her; but *bitch think again*.

Storm laided a beautiful white neglegee at the foot of the bed and a set of golden handcuffs, and a blindfold to match, while Rain checked Tiffany's bags to see if she had anything inside that could answer any more questions for her and Storm.

"Silly bitch," said Rain as she pulled out Tiffany's diary. "would she bring this to Vegas?" she laughed as she handed it to Storm and they began to read through it; not knowing what was waiting for them inside.

July 3rd

Dear Diary,

I love James so much and the more we're together, the more I wonder why he's with that bitch, Storm, because she has nothing on me! I'm ok though until he leaves her alone. I got my new boo, Chance, and I'm also starting to get strong feelings for him as well. He is more trustworthy than James. I mean...shit, anytime a nigga can brag on getting his cousin to kill his bestfriend and don't care at all, that muthafucker is trully heartless to a certain degree; but he sure does have some good dick and I can't let it go right now. Oh, well, it is what it is, and besides, that's not my problem. As long as he keeps me laced and continues paying my bills, we will never have any issues; so as of now, he's cool with me.

Well, it's time for me to pack so I can head to the airport because I cant wait to get to Vegas and away from Secret Impressions cause them bitches in there really be working my nerves and I'm past done with it all.

Bye for now!!!

Storm looked over at Rain as the tears began to fall from what she'd just read. "Sis, that bitch ass nigga set my Rico up to die after all that he did for him," she sobbed as Storm threw the dairy back into the bag and hugged her sister tightly as they both angerly cried. Storm couldn't believe this shit and this was the man that she wanted to marry, but you might as well say he was a murderer; and now that they knew what he'd really done wrong, his ass would pay for real. "I'm good, sis," smiled Rain as she wiped her eyes. "I've always known he wasn't Rico's real friend, and believe me his ass will get what's coming to him."

They both made sure everything was back in order and headed next door to Rain's room to get ready.

* * * * *

I'm so fucking stuffed, boo," said Tiffany and she rubbed her hand across her stomach as a sign. "I don't think that rollercoster would be a good idea right now."

Chance pulled out his phone to check his text that had just went off and it read, *Game on.* He knew it was time for action.

"Well, let's go back to the room and finish what we started on the plane," he suggested as he left $200.00 on the table for their $90.00 bill. Boy…the waitress was happy.

"I can't wait to get some more of daddy's dick, that shit was bum as fuck," Tiffany expressed as she reached down to grab it in her hand and he began to laugh.

"Is that right?" he grinned. "That dick good; ain't it?" he asked and she shook her head as an answer. "Well, I got a surprise for you back at the room," said Chance, getting her even more excited then she was already.

"Let's go then," she said as they headed for the door to walk back to the hotel.

As they entered their room, even Chance was surprise because he really had no clue what was about to happen. From the looks of things, Storm damn sure wasn't playin and it was about to go down.

"Damn, daddy, when did you have time to do all of this?" asked Tiffany, kissing him softly on his lips.

"Don't worry about all that. Just take that phat ass into the bathroom and change into this," he said, handing her the neglegee, "so I can watch you dance for me!" he demanded and Tiffany did just as she was told.

"We're here. What's next," he texted.

Storm replied, "After that bitch puts in some work, handcuff and blindfold her ass, then get us because we are in the next room."

Chance replied, "I'm on it, boss."

He sat on the bed as Tiffany made her entrance into the room, starting the music on Pandora's radio. "I'm in love with a stripper" played loudly from the speakers as she began to bounce that ass all in his face. Even though this was a plot, he sure was enjoying it as Tiffany squeezed her D cup breast together; rubbing both nipples across his lips. He licked them both, making her pussy juices flow harder then before.

Lay on the bed and let me cuff you," suggested Chance as a game.

Tiffany climbed on all fours like the dog that she really was; laying back on the bed and letting Chance place the golden handcuff around each of her wrists and locking the other end to the bedpost. He then placed the blindfold across her eyes, tieing it tight and turning her on as the foreplay continued to make her even hotter then before.

"What are you doing, daddy?" she questioned him, but not wanting him to stop.

The music continued to play, "I'm going to change your life tonight." Chance whispered along with the music, "Just you wait and see," he said as Chance tapped on the wall lightly and the door to his room soon opened.

Storm and Rain entered; both looking good as a bitch dressed in their all-black Armani suites fitting every part of their curves to a T. Chance couldn't keep his eyes off of Storm as Tiffany laid there clueless.

"Baby, what's going on?" she asked, wondering what was taking him so long.

"Shut up, boo. I'm almost done and you're about to get everything that you deserve," he expressed as Storm and Rain stood at the foot of the bed.

Chance did the hornors of unvealing Tiffany's eyes and just as she looked up to gaze at him smiling, he slightly moved to the left and what she saw next made her shit on herself. At this point, she was confused and helpless; but whatever was going on, it couldn't be good.

"Oh my God, Ms. Storm, what are you doing here?" she asked with her eyes big as hell, "and how did you know where I was?" Tiffany said as she jerked her arms trying to get free. But that bitch was stuck.

"Shut the fuck up, bitch!" yelled Storm, "and before I tell you anything…" she said, taking out her baby pink 380 and pointing it directly at Tiffany, "you better not scream or I'll kill you where you lay, you trifling bitch!"

Hearing that scared the fuck out of Tiffany and the tears began to flow as she stared right at Chance.

"What is this?" she asked.

Chance stood behind Storm and Rain smiling hard ass a bitch.

"Don't ask him shit, bitch! And for the last time, shut the fuck up!" said Rain, "My sister has something to say!"

"Silly rabbit, tricks are for kids and you thought you were pulling one over on a boss," laughed Storm, "but it's cool, hoe. Look who has the last laugh because you and James thought ya'll were slick, bitch. But I been knew you two were fucking," she expressed.

From the look on Tiffany's face, she had no words at that point. She was busted and there wasn't shit she could do to get her ass out of it now.

Storm got heated as she continued, "I took yo hoe ass in and gave you a job even though you showed up late everyday and you lost more clients than you could keep and this is how you repay me with your fake ass friendship? The whole time I knew bitch!"

Storm reached her hand toward Rain as a sign to hand her the silencer. "You played yourself, bitch; from the beginning to the end. Even Chance is one of my goons. Hell, he is in charge of protecting me. Yet again, you were clueless and look what that shit is about to cost you."

Pop, Pop, Pop was the sound as Storm quietly sent steel right into each one of her eyes and the last one through the mouth. She ended that bitch's journey right there in Vegas and she felt good after doing it.

They all smiled at Tiffany's slumped over body and Rain uttered the words, "See no evil, speak no evil, bitch!" as they turned to walk out the room.

Storm and Rain gave Chance a nod as a sign of job well done.

"Clean that bitch up and dispose of her remains. Where…I don't care, just as long as she can't be found," said Rain. No one had any idea that Tiffany was out of town so Storm knew she really wouldn't be missed.

Chance took Tiffany's body and threw it into a housekeeper's dirty laundry cart that he'd found on the thirteenth floor. After stripping all of the linen from the bed, as well as gathering all of Tiffany's belongings and throwing them on top of her, he pushed the cart on the elevators and out the side door. Heading straight into the back of a parked, but running garbage truck, he pushed the button, causing it to crush all of the trash that was inside and that now included the body of Tiffany.

Rain and Storm had already packed and headed straight back to New York on Vick's private jet. Just as the flight got started, Chance sent Storm a picture text of the garbage truck as the blood and guts mixed in with the debris. The one thing that stood out as a sign that it was done was the rose tattoo on Tiffany's leg that now wasn't attached to the crushed body anymore. Storm showed Rain the picture as they toasted with their glasses to a perfect TKO in round one. But round two was right around the corner and it was time to prepare. Chance took a shower and cleaned himself up; getting his shit and checking out, heading right back to the Big Apple as well.

* * * * *

It didn't take long before the twins were back at home and all Rain could think of was her kids. "Yo, who dis?" Nizzy answered the phone still half asleep.

"Wake your ass up, girl with your lazy ass."

As soon as she heard Rain's voice, Nizzy's ass sat straight up in the bed. "My bad, boss, what you need?" Nizzy asked quickly.

"How are my kids and baby bruh doing?" asked Rain because she hadn't spoke with Donny in days and that sure wasn't like him.

"Everything is fine; the kids are chilling, having a ball, adjusting to this VA living and Donny's ass been booed up with his new lady, Bria all day," expressed Nizzy. "Ever since they started dating, he ain't really been coming to the club that much because he's either with the kids and her, or shit just with her majority of the time. But we cool out here."

Nizzy had been holding shit down for the girls and of course they laced her pockets right for that shit because she did a damn good job.

"Alright then," said Rain sounding like she was disappointed. "When you see or speak to my brother, have his ass check in with me ASAP."

They both hung up so Nizzy could go back to sleep and Rain had to get ready for work. The sound of Storm's phone blowing up back to back let Rain know she really didn't want to talk so it must've been James.

"Wassup, shorty? Why didn't you tell me you were back?"

His dumb ass thought she was in Richmond the whole time as Storm looked at her phone like this nigga must be tripping, but she still had to play along.

"I thought you were busy, boo. So I just came home and went to sleep," she was definitely lying.

"So am I gonna see you soon?" inquired James, but Storm shut his ass down quick because she wasn't seeing him anymore and the next time she did it was going to be the last time.

"I got a lot of business to take care of with Lizzy today, so maybe we can tomorrow," she said as Rain let her know she was leaving for work. Storm waved back goodbye.

"Ok, that's cool, shorty," he answered her back. "Well, later then."

"Yeah, later," she replied, hanging up in his face as she too had a couple of heads to do at the shop. With Tiffany gone, there would definitely be some lingering customers of hers that were in need of a hairdo, and Storm was going to grab them for herself.

As Rain sat there being Lizzy at her desk filing papers and keeping mental notes as well, she began to think of what life was like being loved and the love she was talking about wasn't what she was already getting. She was fairly loved by the streets, but the kind of love she was missing was sweet, and the only person that came to mind at that point was Vick. He had been a part of Rain's life for many years now, and from day one, he loved her; but that wasn't the case for Rain.

When Vick came into her life, as you already know, Rico was dead and the thought of being in a relationship with anybody at that point didn't cross her mind. But now that shit was changing for her as Vick began to ring her phone and that was enough to bring her out of the trance.

"Hello."

"Hey, Mrs. and how are you?" he asked as his voice made her smile.

"I'm good," replied Rain. "How are you?"

"Happy now that I've heard your voice," he said as they both began to laugh, "I'm chilling with the crews over a Smurf's house, counting and dividing all of the profit from Ricky's bitch ass crews. Which, by the way, still had no clue of who ordered the hit on their asses and now they are all dried up on the streets," he expressed.

Just as Rain was about to respond, Ricky came storming into her office and she could tell by the look on his face that he was pissed about something.

"Elizabeth, we have a problem." Vick could hear Ricky through the phone.

"Let me call you later," she said, ending her call to give Ricky her undivided attention.

"What's wrong, boss? What can I get you?" she was great at acting so concerned about him.

"Elizabeth, last Tuesday I gave you 2.6 million to deposit, as well as another

4 million from Chuck, so why is the account saying something totally different?" he said as the anger in his voice began to rise.

Rain was much smarter than to get caught out so easily, so you know she had a plan. Opening the drawer on her desk and pulling out papers that look like reciepts, she said, "Mr. Tulio, I don't know what's going on, but I'll damn sure find out!" she expressed. "As far as the business I did for you, here are the deposit slips from those transactions," she said as she handed them to him. "So I did what I was suppose to do, but if there is something fishy going on, I can find out, sir."

The dedication she showed Ricky turned him on even more as he smiled and said, "Yeah, you do that, Liz," as he headed for the door. "As soon as you find out anything, you let me know because it's bad enough that someone has hit all of my street locations and wiped my boys clean of drugs and money. I'll be damned if they take my legal businesses too," he said as he left.

Rain stood there staring out of her office window smiling at the city. She knew it belonged to her and after everything was done, she would hand over her crown with honor and for once, live a normal life.

Business was booming as usual at the shop, and every time Storm looked over at Tiffany's empty station, flashbacks of Vegas played over in her mind. She couldn't believe that shit was actually done and what made shit so sweet to her was that it was by her hands at that. You see, Rain had always been the more dominate one that would do whatever needed to be done to prove her power if it was ever tested. Storm, on the other hand, always had it in her to do the same, but she never really had to use it. Ever since she and Rain had reconnected with each other, and having Rain around, Storm knew she was safe.

"Excuse me, Storm," said Dana. "There are two customers sitting up front and they both have appointments with Tiffany's late ass, but no one can seem to locate her," she explained.

"Look, Dana…fuck that bitch, because when she does come back, I'm gonna fire her anyway, so we might as well start snatching up all her cliental," expressed Storm and Dana didn't give a fuck because she knew just how Storm was when it came to her business and money.

Dana took one client and Kim took the other because them two bitches could do the fuck out of some hair; plus, Storm had other shit to do. Storm hurried to complete all of her customers on time so that she could go and get ready for dinner with her sister, Vick and Chance. It had been a long time since they all hung out together, so tonight was really going to be fun.

*****

"Good evening, welcome to Venice Resturant," greeted the hostess. "Table for two?" he asked, looking straight at Storm and Rain like they were fresh food to eat; but the girls weren't paying his ass any attention.

"Actually, we're meeting our friends here to eat…Thomas Wales," she expressed as the hostess checked the list to see if they already had reservations.

"Ahh, yes. They are already here. Please follow me this way," he said as he escorted them to their table.

The men could see them approching from a mile away as they stood from their seats to greet them. "You ladies look amazing," said Chance as he pulled out Storm's chair so that she could sit while Vick did the same for Rain.

"Yes, ya'll do," agreed Vick as he took his lips and softly placed them on Rain's cheek to give her a kiss and she thought it felt real good.

"You guys looking good yourselves," stated Storm as Rain shook her head in agreement. She took a sip of her champagne, causing her already feelings for Vick to become stronger by the moment and she was afraid she couldn't hold back any longer. It was obvious from the constant smile on her face that she wanted more to come out of their friendship, but she didn't know how to say it.

Storm and Chance made googly eyes as well, but damn sure not as strong as their siblings. Even when the food arrived to the table, it seemed as if Rain and Vick were in a hurry because they bearly even touched their plates. After two hours of mingling at the resturant, they couldn't hold back from each other any longer and now was the time to go as they headed outside to leave.

"Come on, sis, let's go!" shouted Storm as they all waited patiently for valet to bring their cars around. Vick and Rain stood together whispering softly.

"You take my car, Storm, and head on home. I'm going to ride with Vick," she expressed as Storm and Chance stood there grinning at the thought of them two finally getting together, which it was about damn time.

Arriving at Vick's hotel door—and this time it wasn't for business—the thought of that made Rain's heart beat faster then it did during the car ride home. But that still didn't stop their clothes from coming off. They both slowly started undressing the other as they kept a stare into each other's eyes, almost never stoping to blink.

Vick did open his mouth to ask Rain if she was sure about doing this.

Rain sexually stopped him by putting her finger over his lips slowly to hush him the fuck up. Vick was unsure as to why she did that, but he figured it was because she didn't want the moment ruined by a nervous conversation and she wanted to get straight to it.

"Damn, what a sexy ass queen you are," whispered Vick as he spun Rain around admiring the view of her whole queendom right before his eyes. He wanted so much to dig in to her.

Rain, on the other hand, had butterflies in her stomach, but she would still perform. She took her perfectly manicured middle finger and rubbed it gently against her clit and removing it soaking and wet, she put it directly into Vick's mouth so that he could savor every last appetizing taste of her pussy juices; but she didn't stop right there.

Rain was feeling very freaky that night and after rubbing her finger against her clit again, but this time she stuck it into her own mouth to suck the tantalizing sweetness of her own pussy off.

"Don't do that queen; God damn you are turning me on!" said Vick as he gently picked her up and placed her on top of the dresser, her hard, protruding nipples pointing right at his mouth. He began to suck them one at a time, taking his tongue around in a circular motion until he approched that end prize. Vick's lips devoured them just as she had yearned for all of those years. As he continued to palm her breast, he sucked and then made a trail with his tongue all the way down her belly headed straight in between her thighs. He never gave her time to prepare herself for what was about to come; he took that hard ass clit and placed it staright into his mouth, letting it vibrate on the tip of his tongue as he began to softly suck the tip of her pearl. Judging by the sound of moans in the room, you could tell they both were enjoying it.

Rain pushed his head even closer for more pressure, and for the last couple of years that's all Vick had done was eat that cat, so he knew actually how to please that powerful pussy. Sucking and licking on that clit until the juices came squirting out into his mouth, what he didn't catch ran slowly down her legs as he lifted Rain's body up into the air again; but this time, he placed her onto the bed as he laid her down slowly, placing her head to hang slightly over the edge.

Vick walked around to the other side and positioned himself over top of her face. He brought that delicious looking dick down slowly into her mouth and don't think for a second that the boss bitch hesitated, because she didn't. Showing off is what she did do as she took the head of it into her mouth with a heightened desire to receive it's taste. Rain sucked the fuck out of that dick for the very first time and she enjoyed every bit of it. He was a monster to every other bitch he fucked, but this was indeed his queen, and this moment right here was what he'd waited for for so long. He took his time to make it last forever. As Vick dick-fed her passionatly, pushing his man hood deeper into her mouth, she relaxed her throat so that he could get it all in. The more she sucked, the more his knees buckled and soon his body began to tremble and he gave Rain that flavor she'd yearned for so much. As his semen shot streamly down her throat, that shit was scrumptious to her.

Vick slowly removed his now tender dick. "Damn, boo! That shit was better then I imagined," moaned Vick as Rain's oven heated up even more. He grinned seductively as he stood erect in front of that pussy and he couldn't hold back anymore. Vick pushed his dick inside her warm, waiting pussy and it had been years since she'd given away her cookies so that pussy fit snuggly around his throbbing dick. Finally being inside her waterfall almost drove him insane. Rain was a little paralyzed when he first stuck it in, but it didn't take her long to grow attuned to his stroke. She began to grind her hips in the most tantalizing way as she fucked him back. The slapping noise from his balls slamming up against her ass as the moisture from her pussy played a tune every time his dick invaded it, made them both become speechless and all they could do was enjoy the moment. But after a few minutes more of passionate love making, Rain felt that explosion again as Vick began to stutter.

He felt his nutt approaching, "This pussy is the best and I've waited for this day for years," he moaned into her ear softly, gripping her body tight as she clutched him back. Now in a sitting position as she bounced that ass harder causing Vick to cum all up in that pussy, he pushed his dick as far as it could go inside of her, causing them both to climax together.

Rain couldn't believe how much she enjoyed it. She knew for damned sure that their feelings were mutual as they laid there cuddling closely.

She thought, *Is this the start of something new between us or is this just the ending?* As she laid in his arms for the first time as a married couple—Thomas and Elizabeth Wales—and after the war was said and done, could Rain really settle down for real and have a normal life with Vick as his wife?

"Oh, shit! What time is it?" shouted Rain as she jumped up out of her sleep grabbing her phone to check for call.

"What's wrong, baby?" Vick asked Rain as he came out of the bathroom, just finishing up from a shower. He rubbed his wet head with a towel. "It's 9:45, baby," he said, answering her question.

"Shit, I'm late for Ricky's board meeting," she said, jumping up at full speed. "You know I got to stay in character, Vick. I've come too far to blow it all now," she expressed as she went into her overnight stash of clothing that was kept in Vick's room and she headed straight to the shower to get ready.

After an hour of pampering and glamming herself up, Rain kissed Vick as she left his room headed straight to the office non-stop.

Not even fifteen minutes later, Vick heard a knock at the door, "Who is it?" he answered as he looked through the peephole with his gun in one hand because he wasn't expecting any guest.

"It's me, big bruh," Chance replied, as Vick saw his image through the hole and he opened up the door so that his brother could enter.

"Wassup, yo?"

They slapped each other five.

"Nothing much," said Chance. "I heard the misses leaving, so I thought I'd come over," he said, being that their rooms were right next door. "So, how was it?" he said, inquiring about him and Rain's night of passion. Judging from the way they were at dinner, he thought that the two of them damn sure fucked.

Vick stood there smiling, and he said, "Three words for you, nigga…Un Fuckin Believable! Mane, her pussy is good. Um, um, um," he shook his head and Chance was dieing out in laughter because he could have sworn that nigga said three words, but yet, he kept going on and on about her.

"Damn, B, look at you…gone off the pussy already," he said.

"Damn right I am, and she can have me forever!" Vick said, meaning that shit because he was in there now and there wasn't no turning back.

"I bet you Storm is the truth too, nigga!" said Chance, "and when the time is right, I'm gonna tear that pussy up!" he paused and looked dead at his brother, "because, big bro, I think I love her" expressed Chance, "and I can't wait to show her how much."

"And make sure you do that shit, nigga!" said Vick as he grabbed his coat and keys to leave.

"Just as soon as we get that nigga, James, out the way and all that other shit is over," continued Chance, "I'm goin in for the steal."

They both laughed as they headed for the meeting with the crews to talk money.

*****

"About time you showed up, Elizabeth," said Ricky as she made her way into the boardroom and took her seat prepared to work.

"Sorry, sir. I over slept. I haven't been getting much sleep lately," she expressed as he nodded his head to let her know it was ok.

He continued, "Ricky's Empire seems to be under attack and you muthafuckers still haven't found out why or by whom," he looked around the room at everybody. "You street crews are completely wiped out and I don't mean from selling it," he said as his crew members hung their heads down in shame. "Do you niggas have a fucking clue how much of a loss we've taken and I'm the one who has to pay it all back. So from now on, you niggas will eat, sleep, and shit the streets until somebody finds out who's responsible for this shit so we can kill them all."

Rain began to smile at hearing him say those words because she knew he'd never find out, at least not for now. Ricky dismissed everyone with the exception of Rain and Chuck because he wanted to get to the bottom of his missing funds from Tulio Realitor, and somebody better have some answers.

"Ok, you two…let's go. Where the fuck is my money?" he asked as Chuck's face showed he was confused.

"Excuse me?" he cut in. "What do you mean, *where is your money*? I met with Elizabeth on all scheduled occassions so that she could get the money from me, so ask her what's going on," replied Chuck as Rain sat silently; never saying a word. But boy, didn't she have plenty to say.

"Is it my turn to talk?" she asked, pulling a brown folder with papers out of her bag as Ricky and Chuck, whom thought he was in the clear, were both all ears. "It is true that Chuck met with me and it is true that I got the money," she continued. "Here are the deposit slips, as well as video footage," she slid the items over toward Ricky. "There are videos of me at the bank making the deposits, but what I also have are copies of the signed withdraw reciepts with Chuck's signature on them, which clearly proves that he removed your money, sir. So I think again you should ask him about the missing money," she grinned as Ricky's Columbian brown skin turn red and Chuck could see the flames in his eyes. That alone made Chuck just snap as he slammed his fist on the table in rage and jump up from his seat to speak.

This has got to be some kind of mistake, Ricky, because you know I'd never steal from you," he began to utter. "Look…how long I've had your back and now you are going to sit here and doubt me?" he pleaded his case.

"So, where did the slips come from, Chuck?" Ricky asked calmly, so you know that wasn't a good thing because he's never calm when it come to his money. "If what she says isn't true, then how did she get the slips?"

"I told you, Ricky, I have no idea."

"And like I told you, Ricky," Rain cut in, "I have them and I got them from the bank where you took the money from, Chuck," she expressed. Rain knew her mind was pure genius and the fact that she could put together this whole plot to get Ricky. She still remained innocent in his eyes; which made Chuck become even more angrier than before.

"Listen here, Ricky, I don't know what's going on, but you can rest assure I'm going to get to the bottom of this. I feel framed and that's one thing I hate, so whoever's involved," he said, looking right over at Rain, "better watch out!" yelled Chuck as he slammed the door to the office pissed.

Rain sat there with Ricky, she was laughing hard inside because she knew there wasn't any way to trace who was taking the money; everything she did was untraceable.

"Well, sir, if you want my opinion," she said as she and Ricky packed up their stuff to leave. "I think you should be more careful with whom you trust now days," she said as a big smile came over Ricky's face.

"I see you have my best interest at heart, Mrs. Lady, and for that you deserve a reward," expressed Ricky as the look on Rain's face showed she was lost. "I would like to take you to dinner to show you my appreciation for the work you do around here. So tonight, you and I will have a special evening. What do you say about that?"

"I think that would be great, just text me with the details because right now I have an appointment that I have to get to in an hour so now I must leave," explained Rain as she headed toward the elevators and Ricky watched her phat ass as it strolled out of his sight.

"Um, Um, Um," he shook his head as he took a seat in his office. "I've never had eyes for a black women, but Elizabeth's turning me on with her power and that go-getter attitude," Ricky spoke out loudly to himself as he tried to do some work, but all he could think of was Liz as she was becoming more and more difficult to resist. Determination is the twin sister of Brilliance; one is a matter of not giving up and the other is a matter of playing your cards smarter, especially when there's a situation in which something unpleasant continues to exist. Now was time to put on the armor, so Storm and Rain had to suit up.

* * * * *

"Ja'Nay!" yelled out Rain as she made her way into the house and Storm sat at the kitchen table waiting.

"Bout time you got here, bitch," they both began to giggle. "I thought you were going to be tied up playing with Vick all day; and by the way, was it good?" Storm asked as Rain's face turned red as she gave her a look that said, *hell yeah.*

"I been left his room, but I had to go to this fucking meeting with Ricky and my plans are running smooth. Chuck's ass is in hot water and he don't even know how he got there," she expressed. "But enough about that, are you ready for war? Because I'm ready to get on with my life," expressed Rain.

"Yeah, we're good," answered Storm. "And his dumb ass don't even have a clue what's coming his way. I can't wait to burn his bridge down," she said as the thought of James made them both become sick and they were tired of playing his little game. "This nigga had the nerve to call asking questions about the shop like he was concerned," said Storm, "when all he was doing was checking to see if Tiffany was there. And guess what,bitch…she's not!" she told Rain as she shook her head in disgust.

Storm and Rain continued to chat it up a little more, spilling details about the plot because the twins, for the first time since they'd been back together, were tired and they wanted out of this life so that they could be free.

Rain informed Storm that she had dinner plans with Ricky so that he could further dig himself into his grave. After handling business and finding out what time to meet at the house, they both left to finish tieing up their own personal lose ends.

"Come on, bitch move!" shouted Rain with her road rage. "I got shit to do!" she yelled, pounding her fist on the horn as her cell went off. It was Ricky. "Hey, boss, I'm stuck in traffic; is everything ok?"

"Yeah, darling, it is," said Ricky. "I just wanted to tell you to meet me at the office in two hours and go straight to the banquet room and I'll see you there," he explained as Rain agreed and hung up with a smile so big the car next to her could see it. She was ready for tonight and everything that came along with it because the more Ricky chased her, the more him and Christina would drift apart and that would be another point for Rain. She loved each and every moment of it, so now it was time to get ready.

Storm had to go out to New Jersery for some business and she was amped up about her night with James and what she had in store for him. She had to make sure everything would be right. As the sky began to turn gray, Rain made her way inside Tulio Realitor and up to the twelfth floor, which by the way, was dark with the exception of the light from burning candles. The scene was set romantically and *for what* thought Rain. This nigga is a clown if he thinks he's getting any pussy from me," she whispered under her breath as she walked into the room.

"Well, hello there beautiful," stated Ricky, walking over and grabbing her hand to kiss it as the aroma of scented oils filled the air and flowers with gift boxes perfectly wraped sat on the table

"Hello to you, sir," Rain began to smile. "This right here is much more then I expected."

Ricky pulled her chair out for her to sit down. "I don't think I deserve all this."

"Well, if you ask me, this isn't enough," he expressed. "Since you started working here, I feel so relieved to have someone that truly cares about my wellbeing. That right there is an honor," Ricky was slick and smooth out the mouth, but Rain was even slicker. "Well, I have a great meal here for us," he said, pointing over to the huge spread of food. "But first I want you to open your gifts," he said, pushing the boxes over toward her. She immediately began to open them. The first box contained a $3,000 Vera Wang strapless evening gown that he thought would be perfect on her. The other had a small envelope inside that contained a check for one million dollars that was supposedly an advancement. His reasoning behind the gift was that she took great care of his money, so he wanted to make sure she was straight. *Clown ass nigga,* he just wanted some ass, but if he really knew who she was, he'd cut off his own dick before he fucked her.

Rain expressed her graditude in the only way that she could as Lizzy. They both started in on dinner and for some one who was pretending, Rain was a very good actress. For her first leading roll, I must say she was great, because Ricky was loving every bit of her. Rain thought that she was going to get away with the night ending just like that, but Ricky had other things in mind.

"Thank you for all of this, Mr.Tulio, but I really should be going now," she said as she stood from her seat to leave.

"Before you go, Elizabeth, there's one more thing I have to give you," he whispered in her ear as he grabbed her closer to him. He kissed her smack dead in the mouth while squeezing that phat ass that he dreamed about.

"What are you doing, sir?" she questioned as she pulled away. "You are married," she expressed and Ricky stood there admiring her womenhood and how she remained a lady at all times.

"Well, I'm not going to force you to do anything, but just so you know…" he paused and licked his lips, "whenever you are ready, I'm here for you and I'll do things to that pussy that you ain't never had before."

He made her stomach turn hearing him utter them nasty words. It was bad enough that he kissed her, and now he was speaking on getting her pussy…*nigga please*, she thought as she grabbed her gifts off the table to bounce. Ricky walked her down to her car to make sure she was off safely, but his dick was still hard. He decided to call Christina to maybe make up with her with sex, but to his surprise, she didn't even answer the phone. For the first time in years, he felt alone, just like at birth; and Rain was going to make sure that that's how he'd died.

The next day seemed to have gone by fast because it was 5:00 p.m. and Storm had bearly gotten everything together, but she finished just in time for the show. She had her meeting with Rain and Chance as well as Vick to check in about Queen's Way. After all the business was said and done, Storm was excited and ready for action. It had been a long time coming and she was more than ready to start her life over fresh. It was time for her to place a call to James and check in.

"You know who this is, do what you do," James' voicemail picked straight up so she tried calling his ass once more. This time the muthafucker picked up.

"What's up, my baby; you ready for daddy?" James flirted as Storm hit him with her little girl giggle.

"Yeah, baby, I am. Where are you now?" she asked and James played right into her games.

"I'm on my way over to your house to eat you."

That nigga really thought he was slick.

"Um, ok, sounds good to me. I'll see you when you get here, my love; and just in case I'm in the shower, the key is under the mat. You know I have to make sure that pussy is fresh for you," said Storm, and based on James' moans over the phone, his dick was standing in salute already and he couldn't wait to play with that cat.

Not even thirty minutes later, Storm could hear the front door alarm, which let her know he was inside of the house.

"Good evening King," greeted Storm as she stood at the top of the stairs looking delightful in that new dress that Ricky brough for Rain. Underneath, she was complety naked, which James found out when he ran his hands up her dress and straight into that shaved pussy. Her juices wet up his hand and he sucked the flavor off his two fingers which made his dick stand up even more.

"You look good, baby. Damn, a nigga was missing you and I couldn't get you off my mind," he was a good gamer, but Storm was hipped to that shit already. The only reason he was all over her like that was because that freak bitch, Tiffany, wasn't around to let him bust nutts all in her mouth. But Storm just played along.

"Follow me into the bedroom so we can get this party started," instructed Storm as she took her hands pulling James by his belt and leading the way to the bedroom. "Tonight I am in control and you are my slave," she seductivelly stated as she played the role of Madam Extacy. "Take off all your clothes and lay on the bed so that I can cuff you."

"Oh, really?"

James was excited because this wasn't like Storm, and the new her was making him hot, so whatever it was that had gotten into her, he damn sure didn't want her to stop. He did what he was instructed to do and and laid buck ass naked on the bed while Storm cuffed up his hands and feet.

Can you say, entrapment?

He relaxed; laying there grinning, waiting to see what was coming next.

As Storm went into her role as Madam Extacy, taking her fingers and rubbing them across the head of his dick, that nigga James didn't know what to do with himself. She clapped her ass so far in his face that his nose was inside her crack.

Just when he was about to reach his peek, she stopped dead in the middle of what she was doing and said, "I almost forgot, somebody else wants to join us, so just continue to relax until I get back" she said as she walked out of her bedroom shutting the door behind her. She soon returned with someone else with her.

"Goddamn, shorty, a three some!" said James as his eyes got real big from excitement. He zoomed in on the both of the bad ass bitches that were looking sexy as hell. "I knew you wanted me Lizzy, from the first time we met in the club," he expressed his feelings to Rain as she stood there with Storm. Rain was dressed as a police officer with her breast sitting pretty in his face. They both smiled at him. "Well, come on over here and one of you sit that pussy on my face and the other one come suck on this dick!" he instructed, but I guess he forgot who was calling the shots – it damn sure wasn't him.

"You have no idea who I am do you, James?" asked Rain.

"What?" he paused with a silly laugh, "Yeah I do…you're Lizzy. I never forget a face," he said. "So what's the hold up? You bitches bring me that pussy since I can't come and get it."

That's when Rain hit him with it. "Take a closer look, James," Rain said as she walked over closer to give him, giving him a clearer view. She bent down so that he could see the tattoo on her breast, and boy didn't he wish he wasn't cuffed up at that point. He read the words, *RICO* beautifully laid out across a long stem rose, but what really gave it away was the date that was underneath the rose. It was the day Rico and Rain got married.

James began to choke. "Who the fuck are you? Is this some kind of prank, bitch? Why would you pretend to be my homeboy's dead wife?"

"I ain't pretending, bitch!"

Rain took her fist and punched that nigga twice in the mouth, causing his shit to bleed and his gold crown to fall out as his tooth went rolling onto the bed.

"What the fuck! Bitch, you crazy!" he yelled. "Ja'Nay, you're just going to just stand there filing your fucking nails, bitch? I swear to God when I get loose I'm killing the both of you bitches…watch and see!"

Storm and Rain both just laughed at his ass. "Yeah, we know," Storm said. "Just like you killed my sister. Well, at least you thought you did," Storm said, placing her arm on Rain's shoulder.

"And just like you killed my Rico," uttered Rain.

You could hear the pain in her voice as she said those words. At that moment, shit became real for James, because she was the only one that could say Rico's name like that. James' bodly functions went crazy and the piss began to shoot out the tip of his dick because he was scared.

"This whole muthafucking time, bitch, you were a snake in the grass; even down to fucking that bitch Tiffany…which, by the way," Rain handed Strom a bag and she pulled out the ring he had brought that bitch. It was still connected to her severed finger. Storm nicely jammed it up his ass hole, making sure it was covered with some of his own shit and then sticking it into his mouth. "You and that bitch can be together now and she's waiting on you where you are going."

James began to vomit off of the taste of green poop and red blood in his mouth and since his hands where cuffed, there wasn't shit that he could do; it wasn't like he was able to pull it out.

"My sister tried to warn me that you weren't any good; and for all the pain you've caused my family over the last couple of years, we're going to make sure that you feel just as much pain in return."

As Rain said those words, this once thug, turned pussy, and the tears began to roll down his face.

"Well, my job is done here," said Rain as she smiled. "I just wanted you to know that I am alive and well, so this queen has for damn sure gotten the last laugh," she expressed as she turned to walk away. As she did, she gave Storm privacy to finish up. "Handle your business, sis; don't keep Tiffany waiting on him much longer," she said, slamming the door to leave but not before she spit twice in that nigga's face.

"I really loved you, James; and I wanted to be with you forever, and that wasn't enough for you," Storm walked over and reached behind her night stand. "So, I'm going to send you to the bitch you hurt me for, and I hope ya'll live happily ever after in hell!" she said as she swung the axe at full speed, cutting that nigga across the neck. She watched as his head hit the floor with Tiffany's finger still in his mouth.

Storm stood there in tears, but happy as the blood from his headless neck continue to squirt out everywhere. She didn't care about the mess because her work was done and on her end she was free. The people in her life that caused her pain had officially been silenced. She made damn sure there wouldn't be any resurrection when it came to the two of them. That chapter had been closed forever and Storm could now move on!

When it rains it pours

Dear God,

It's me La'Rain, and it's been a long time since we've talked. I think that's because I was afraid of what you would say to me about the lifestyle that I'm living. I know this wasn't a part of Your will for my life; but this world kind of chose me. I've done some bad things for which I'm not proud, but all the pain of losing my loved ones to the drug game made me want to seek revenge. I hope that You can forgive me. I know You still love me; otherwise, why would You save me when people tried to kill me, instead, I feel that You kept me here for a reason. I'm tired God, and I want out this life so that I can finally be a mother to my kids. I feel like after seven years of being away from them, it's time to give them me. Please protect me, God, as I go through the storm, and when it's all done, I will no longer fight., I'll give myself completely to You!

Amen

*****

Rain got off her knees from praying and headed down to the kitchen to make her morning cup of coffee as the thoughts of war took over her. She couldn't believe that the time had really come to put an end to her and Ricky's feud; but she also kept in mind that the shit wouldn't be easy to pull off. So far, so good; as far as her master plan was concerned and Rain hoped the ride would stay smooth. As she sat at the kitchen table thinking, she thought it would be fun to try her old hobby again, because no matter how long of a break she took, it's true she had a passion for writing. She wanted to start her new path off on a positive note, so that she could show her children a better way, so for the first time in thirteen years, Rain picked up a pen to write. Stories and poetry had always been her thing. Writing was one of the many gifts God had blessed her with. She was very creative and even though she hadn't used it in a while, it still remained in place. Rain prepared to write down her feelings in a beautiful poem and it said,

I'm so much better than I used to be. I'm sick of all the drama; it's becoming lame to me. I wasn't always like this, nor was it the will for me, but now my arms are open and I'm reaching out for he, I'm not saying I'm innocent…trust me, I did my share; but I'm all grown up and I realized that I don't want to go to hell. I went to God and asked Him was He still down for me, and He replied, "Yes,

My child; haven't you heard I can be all that you need." My homie, lover, friend and that right there says enough, the only thing I need to remember is to always stand tough.

So now I've decided to change my ways and leave the past alone, and I sit here and wonder when the time does come will all who have claimed to have loved me be gone? So just when I thought God was gone, He came back and said to me, "My child, let them go on ahead, because your blessings come from Me. I am the creator, the world is Mine, so once you've found Me, you no longer have to hide. I will protect you."

"What are you doing up so early, big sis?" asked Storm as she walked into the kitchen rubbing her eyes to see clearer.

"Talking to God," replied Rain. "We need Him more than ever now," she began to express while making her way over beside her sister to have coffee and listen to her vent. "I'm at the end of the road and I don't think I can take much more," expressed Rain and it seemed like magic because as soon as she said that, Storm's cellphone went off and it was Uncle Keith.

"I wonder what he wants," Storm said as she held her phone in her hands, "he never, ever, calls me this early," she said as she decided to answer the phone.

"How are you, Ja'Nay."

"I'm doing ok, dad. So, wassup? It's early, and you've never did this before," she said and even though she found out the truth about her real parents, she still had much love and respect for Keith.

"You need to get to Georgia quickly," he expressed and Storm didn't like the tone in his voice, so she knew something was wrong. She asked him what was going on.

"Donte is in the hospital," Keith took a deep breath, "he's not doing so well and you need to bring Donny and the kids out here ASAP!"

Storm turned to face Rain with her eyes saying, *oh shit*. They continued to stare at each other while she wrapped up her conversation with Keith. "Ok, dad, I'll set everything up and I'll text you with the flight information."

She said goodbye to him and hung up with a million things going through her mind at once; plus, she still had to break the news to Rain.

"What was that all about?" questioned Rain, still half-puzzled by Storm's look. "Who's in the hospital?"

"Daddy is," Storm answered back swiftly, "and he's not doing so good," she expressed as Rain gave her a look that she couldn't even read. "So, are you going with me out there, sis?" asked Storm. Rain gave her ass no words, just stiff posture and a head nod as a sign that she was going.

It had been years since Rain or Donny had seen Donte, so them talking was definitely out of the question; and now the worst had happened—bad news. Rain was feeling a little nervous about what she should say, and again they didn't know she was alive. Storm immediately contacted Donny and told him what was going on and that their tickets would be waiting at the airport. She also told him that they would all meet up in Georgia. Storm had been going back and forth to Atlanta for years due to the fact that they have existing businesses out there to run, and you know they love that money.

Rain and Storm canceled everything that they had planned for the day, and booked all five tickets to Georgia very quickly; there wasn't any time to waste. They made sure Donny and the kids were straight and they all left heading non-stop to ATL.

"Oh, shit, sis, it's still like I remember," said Rain in expression of the beauty of Atlanta's airport. It was just as she'd remembered.

"Sis, you're crazy, where are Donny and the kids?" Storm said, looking around in the waiting area. They were supposed to be right here."

As soon as Storm said that, she and Rain spotted them coming toward them.

"Mom," said RJ as he and Aaliyah ran up to her, embracing her tightly in their arms.

Donny made his way over, but with one little twist joining him. There was a beautiful, brown chocolate girl standing right there beside him; cuffing his arm as the girl's' radars went off.

"Who might you be?" asked Rain, looking at her brother with a grin.

"Calm down, sis," he smiled. "This is Bria Johnson, my girlfriend," he expressed, but saying it kind of low underneath his breath.

"Nice to meet you," said Bria as she extended her hand in gesture. They shook her hand back.

"Likewise," said Storm, and they both gave her a smile.

"Um, Donny, you did good for yourself, she's pretty; but what do you do for a living?" Rain changed up the mood and Donny knew actually where this was going, but the airport wasn't the place.

He knew his sister was about to get her interrogation on, so Donny had to come through blocking that. "Sis, can we finish this when we get to the hotel or when we all go out to dinner," he suggested. "First, let's get to the hospital."

Over time, Donny and Donte had talked and that was to be expected. Donny doesn't know that Donte didn't want him either, so all that other shit he did wrong was forgiven. They started talking on the phone from time to time, so Donny really felt some type of way.

They made sure everyone had their luggage and went straight over to the hospital.

"Ja'Nay," called out Uncle Keith as he spotted them coming through the emergency doors.

"Hey, dad," she replied, wrapping her arms around him tightly as they embraced. They turned around to face Donny and the kids.

"Boy, look at you…get over here," Uncle Keith said, hugging Donny and speaking of how much he had grown.

"Wassup, Unc? How's it been?" Donny asked.

"Cool…everything's been cool until now," Keith expressed as he walked over to love on the kids. He glanced at the strange woman standing there as he turned and greeted her too.

"Hello, there beautiful. And who might you be?" he asked. Rain couldn't do anything but laugh because he didn't know who she was.

"Hello, I'm Lizzy. I work very close to Storm," she explained and the family wondered why she didn't tell the truth at this point.

Donny cut in saying, "I want to see Donte, can you take us to him?" he asked. Keith then replied, "Sure," as he lead the way down to the room.

*****

Seeing him like that for the first time in their life was not an easy thing to swallow and it hurt. Donte was hooked up to oxygen with tubes all down his nose IVs in his arm pumping in fluids. The sight of this brought tears to everyone's eyes.

"Hey, son," said Donte in a barely audible speaking voice.

"I miss you dad, what's wrong?" Donny expressed, "why are you like this?"

Storm stood behind the children with Rain and listened.

"Son, I have AIDS and I've had it for a while now," Donte began to cry and so did the kids because they had really only seen him once or twice.

"What do you mean you have AIDS, Donte?" asked Storm, walking up to the side of his bed. "How did you get it and why didn't you tell us about it?" she said, mad as hell. "Didn't you feel we had the right to know?"

"Yeah, but I didn't want ya'll to worry. We had just lost La'Rain and that was really bothering us all, so I figured I'd just keep it to myself," he explained. "I'm sorry, please forgive me."

"RJ and Aaliyah, come see papa," said Donte, still talking to them like five year olds.

"My, have I missed you two so much," he said, reaching for their hands.

"We missed you, too," they replied.

"Are you going to be ok?" asked Aaliyah as she started to remember seeing her dad in this horrible way.

"You look just like your mother, baby girl; and I really miss her so much. She was my little baby girl," he cried, looking over at Storm to speak. "Ja'Nay, there's something I want to tell you," he expressed while Keith gave him a look to ask, *what you are doing*.

Donte couldn't hold it any longer as he spoke, "Back in the day, I did some things that I'm not proud of and I want to come clean with one."

Storm already knew where he was going with this, and she wasn't about to put him through the pain, so she cut him off. "Daddy, I know."

Keith and Donte both started crying as they stared right at her.

"I know I'm your daughter and that Rain and I are twins. We found a letter from mom telling us we were twins and Auntie Cheryl told us the truth about everything and I forgive you," she expressed as Rain walked over beside her.

"I forgive you too, daddy," she stated as Donte and Keith thought they was hearing a ghost.

"La'Rain, is that you?" He asked, trying hard to sit up.

"Yes, it's me, daddy. It's your La'Rain," she spoke as he stared hard at her face. "I'm sorry I hated you all these years," she expressed.

"But how is this possible?" asked Keith. "We thought you were dead."

"It was all a plot, Uncle Keith, because someone did try to kill me, but they didn't succeed; so I had to go away and change everything about myself in order to hurt their ass this time." she continued, "but daddy, your baby girl was never dead and we forgive you."

The peace that came over Donte at that moment was nothing that he could explain. It felt so good and he knew that they didn't have to hide that secret anymore and that the girls were back together.

"Knock, Knock," Nurse Jenkins interrupted. "Mr. Peters, it's time for your medication," she stated as a sign for everyone to leave the room.

They all decided to go check into the hotel and then out to eat. Rain, Storm and the entire family went out to enjoy a meal at Red Lobster and they even brought Donny's new girlfriend with them so Rain could do some more digging.

"It has been such a long time since we sat together as a family. I just wanted to let you guys know how much I love you," Rain expressed as Aaliyah sat next to her mother smiling.

"We love you too, sis. You know this family wasn't the same without you and we're blessed to still have you," Donny poured out his heart to his sister and Bria seemed to be the only one not enjoying it. She was used to having Donny's attention all to herself, and now that his sisters were around, he became very much focused on them.

Bria went all in, cutting those big beautiful black eyes on the twin's hard as a bitch. The closer they got, the more she felt pushed back. Don't get me wrong, he was starting to fall in love with her, but what she didn't know was the love he shared with his siblings. Bria felt she couldn't compete with that. Donny was taught that family comes first and to never let an outsider come between them. Still, she zoned in as their laughter grew louder from shit she really couldn't relate to, or at least that's what she told Donny and right now he was buying it.

Bria was definitely making her mark in his life, so she just decided to chill. She didn't know that Storm had seen her ass looking, so she began to look right back as if to say, *Bitch. I don't back down so try me.* and that Storm was crazy as hell too. Rain made her move over a table of hot steamy crab legs and lobster, as the kids went to work on the food.

"Mrs. Bria, you've been mighty quiet over there, so tell me…how you and my brother met." asked Rain as she patiently waited for her answer.

"Come on, sis, not again," Donny laughed. "Can you let her enjoy her food please?" he smiled with them dimples on both sides of his cheeks which had always melted Rain's heart in pieces.

"Baby Bruh, I'm just getting to know your girlfriend; is that a problem for you?"

Storm cut in, "Don't you want her and your sisters to be close?" she questioned and everyone at the table began to laugh at her expression. But Bria knew she was on to her shit.

"We met at Club Benji's," said Bria, "and ever since then, we've been inseparable," she teased while grabbing Donny's arm in a cuff and leaning in for a kiss. They began tonguing each other down, and Storm and Rain didn't like it at all.

"Oh, so you're like a regular at the club, I see. So, are you originally from Richmond or did you move there?" Rain wanted to know a little about her past and where she came from. What people don't realize is that where you've been in life can affect where you're going, and Rain wasn't letting any harm come to Donny.

"Yes, I'm from there," answered Bria, continuing on with her three word minimum and trying not to say too much, but that shit still didn't stop Rain. She knew all too well how to pull information out of a muthafucker and besides that, she felt that something was up with this girl and believe me, she was going to find out.

"So, what about your last relationship," she went hard and didn't give a fuck who didn't like it because nothing was going to make her back down.

"Yeah, how did that end?" asked Storm as RJ and Aaliyah found it to be very funny as Mr. Donny's smile began to turn into a frown.

"Damn, sis, come on. Can we play family feud later?" he said in reference to their survey of questions.

Bria began to perspire and her anxiety was high, so her boo saved her just in time. Bria never spoke of her past to Donny, but he was so whipped from getting pussy on the regular from a classy, but street, southern girl and that shit had made him blind.

"Excuse me, sir," she said, giving his ass a grown women look. "I was just looking out for you because I love you and I damn sure don't want to see you hurt. I know you can understand that," expressed Storm.

Donny got up from his seat and moved in the direction of his sisters. Placing his arms around the both of them, he kissed each of them on their cheek.

"I love ya'll too, sis, and I promise I won't forget what you taught me, nor will I allow myself to get played," expressed Donny as Bria sat there smirking and looking like she had something up her sleeve. Now wasn't the time for the sisters to address her ass, so instead, they just enjoyed the rest of their dinner together.

* * * * *

"Mom your phone's ringing," yelled RJ as they all got settled in their hotel room after an exciting dinner.

"Hello."

"Hey, Lizzy, this is Mr. Jefferson," he said with his red neck country boy accent. "I'm the buyer for the property on 29th and Park."

"Yes, sir, I remember you. How are you?" she asked while wondering why the fuck he was calling this damn late.

"I'm doing great now that I've gotten through to you," he began to explained. "The money came through, sweetheart, so now I'm able to close on that property. I was wondering when you will be back because I can't wait to place my John Hancock on the dotted line."

"Well, well, well…let me be the first to congratulate you, but I won't be back in New York until Monday night because I have to make a stop in Virginia first," she explained. "Is that ok with you?" she asked.

"Yes, ma'am, it is," he responded. "I don't want anyone else working on my file but you."

"Well, that's mighty good to hear, sir; so I'll see you in my office on Tuesday at 10:00 a.m."

"Ok, Mrs. Lizzy, see you then."

They ended their call and hearing that news made Rain overly excited. The deal with Mr. Jefferson was the biggest file Tulio Realtors had in the time frame that she was with them. Closing that would make her be really, really good for life.

As Rain lay in bed that night with Aaliyah tucked tightly beside her, the relationship she was cheated out of with her mother was all that took over her mind. She thought about Eddie and what things would be like if her big brother was still around. She knew in her heart that things wouldn't be like this. Thoughts of Donte and him dying really made her sad. She tried to gage what effect it would have on her too. She was tired of this fucking family curse. Nothing, and I do mean nothing, worked for Rain as she tried damn hard to remove the past from her mind for good. *But how can you remove something without closing it first?* But at least she knew just who to tell.

Dear God,

I know I'm still learning how You operate, but I sure do need you right now. I feel like you gave me a second chance only to get it right and serve You. I need guidance, Lord. Show me what it is You want me to do and I'll try my hardest to do it, but I can't live like this anymore. My dream was to become a writer and not a drug lord, so I want Your help to get out and give my children a life that surrounds You I believe in Your power.

In Jesus name I pray,
Amen!

As she laid her head down on her pillow with her nose buried in Aaliyah's hair, Rain finally felt peace as she drifted off to sleep.

"Sis, wake up." whispered Storm as she shook Rain's shoulder causing her eyes to open up to face her.

"What's wrong?" she tried to speak with sleep still in her voice.

"Keith just called, Donte's been rushed back into surgery because he's losing too much blood and it's not looking good, sis. We need to get back to the hospital," she expressed as Rain eased up out of bed and went to get dressed.

Storm headed next door to Donny's room to get him so that they could all leave together. She knocked on his room door, but it took a minute for someone to answer and finally Bria opened up.

"Where is my brother?" asked Storm, gritting on Bria's ass hard.

"He's still asleep, so you can come back in an hour?"

I think this bitch really did bump her head because she forgot who she was talking to.

"Girl, move!" said Storm as she pushed passed Bria to enter the room. Instantly she was hit with an odor. "What the fuck is that smell? Donny, wake up!" shouted Storm as he rolled over to face her.

"WASSUP?"

"WASSUP is the weed smell in this fucking room Donny, because I know you're not getting high!"

Storm was furious about that shit, but before he could answer, Bria cut in confessing. "The loud was mine, not his," she said with a kind of a neck roll.

"And that's fine for you, not my brother because he don't need no bitch, he needs a lady and you damn sure aren't acting like one!" Storm shouted as Donny got up out the bed.

"Chill, sis, it's cool; but what's wrong?" he asked and Storm stood there mad.

"Oh, boy," she laughed, ready to smack the fuck out that bitch. "Get dressed, bruh. Dad's back in surgery and it's not looking too good."

The look on Donny's face was like he'd lost his best friend and he was in shock. He rumbled through his bag for clothes to put on to leave.

"Just you, baby bruh," Storm said as she opened the door to leave. "Your girl can stay here," expressed Storm as Bria walked past going into the bathroom smiling. Storm rolled her eyes as she slammed the door real hard saying, "Meet us at the car!"

Rain was coming out their room just as soon as Storm was knocking. "You got Donny?" she asked in a hurry.

"Yeah, I did and he's coming, but let me tell you about his bitch Bria smoking loud in the hotel room and I bet you she's got Donny's ass trying it too," Storm explained as they made their way inside the car. "But she played it off like it was all her," explained Storm as Rain's eyes turned blood shot red.

"You've got to be kidding me, Storm," she said, but not before she punched the steering wheel. "I just prayed to God for the family last night, and if Donte dies, that will make the third man we've lost to the drug game, sis. I'm not about to sit back and watch Donny be a fourth. I'll beat that bitch's ass if she thinks she's going to get baby bruh off track!" screamed Rain as she noticed Donny coming their way. "He ain't never touched drugs before and that shit isn't going to start now!" she said as he entered the car.

"Wassup, sis?" he greeted Rain as he leaned into the front seat giving her a kiss and mushing the back of Storm's head as he sat back.

* * * * *

"We need to talk, baby bruh," said Rain and at that point she'd had enough. "What the fuck are you trying to prove on the real? You and this girl just don't mix."

"What do you mean, sis?" he asked. "You don't even know Bria like that, sis. And you're not trying to give her a chance either and I don't even know why."

"I'll tell you why…because she's not right for you, Donny and you know it. Come on now, smoking muthafuckin weed?" she went ham while Storm sat there grinning because it was on.

"I didn't…"

"Stop it, Donny and listen…ok? I've been in these streets and you know I have," she continued, "look at all the shit it's cost us."

"Sis, I'm grown. I'm not that little fuckin boy no more and I have to have a life too; so why can't you let me?"

"All I've ever wanted was for you to stay safe, so I'm gonna end this conversation right here," she said as they pulled up at the hospital and parked. "So when you're ready to talk, I'm here; because right now, I'm pissed and I want to calm down so that we don't disturb Donte with this."

They made their way over to Keith who was standing by his car smoking a cigarette and Donny just stayed quiet.

"Hey, UNC," said Rain. "Is everything ok with my dad?" she questioned, but by the look on his face they knew it wasn't good.

"Well, he's out of surgery, but something went wrong and now he's in a coma on life support. I just don't know what to do," his emotions were high as he broke down and cried over his brother's sudden condition. Storm held him tightly as the tears began to flow.

"So what shall we do at this point?" Rain was ready, but some things money just can't buy. "Did he have a will?"

"No, I don't think so," replied Keith. "So I think you children will have to decide."

They looked at each other and now they really were confused. They all went back to Donte's room and as Rain entered, she broke down while making her way over to his bedside.

"Daddy, it's me, La'Rain," she whispered as Donte lay there very still. "Daddy, can you wake up? Move your finger if you hear me," she asked as they all waited patiently for his response but there wasn't any. They didn't know how long his insurance would cover this, but however long it took, Rain wasn't going to pull the plug. Shit…for real, she could pay to keep him on there if she had to, but if God wanted him He'd take him while on the machine.

They all sat in the room laughing with Donte, trying hard to bring him around; but as the hours went by, there still wasn't any change. Donny wanted to watch Wheel of Fortune with his dad which was something they used to do. Rain, Storm, and Keith went out to get something to eat. On the way to Olive Garden, Keith sat in the back seat and watched as the girls interacted together and the sight was so beautiful he began to cry.

"Turn that down for a second," he began to tap on the back of Storm's seat. "I just want to tell you girls how happy it makes me to see you two together at last, and this time, you two are really as one," he continued. "it was very hard to watch you two grow up as close as you were and not be able to tell you the truth, but now you know."

They all smiled at each other while pulling up at the restaurant to get their takeout and they all fell in love with the moment.

"Come on, dad, help me guess this puzzle," said Donny, still holding his father's hand. "This is your favorite category, dad," he laughed, pointing at the TV. "Women Habits" old man, since you think you're a pimp," he joked with his dad as he felt his finger being gripped, but thought nothing of it until he heard, "I love you, son," spoken in a light whisper of a voice that could barely speak.

"Dad, you spoke; say it again," Donny leaned in to hear him clearly. "I love you too, dad, no matter what…I do," said Donny and he knew right then and there that his dad could hear him and knew that he was there.

Once the girls got back, Donny told them what had happened and they thought that as a sign of good news. They all ate and spent the rest of the night reminiscing about the good ole days and hoping that would help Donte recover. They all kissed and hugged Donte and Keith goodbye as they informed Keith that they would be back out there in a couple of weeks. They also asked him to inform them if anything changed with Donte. Storm, Rain and Donny returned back to the hotel to get the kids and their things together so that they can take the next flight out to Richmond because the girls were ready to leave.

"I'm so excited to get home, boo," said Bria as they all took their seats in VIP. "I never thought I'd be so homesick, didn't you miss VA, boo?" Bria asked Donny as he looked at her and laughed.

"I haven't been there long enough to call it home yet, baby," he continued to laugh as he looked over at Rain and Storm who were sitting right across from them, but the look on their faces wasn't a joke.

"I know you haven't, boo; but look what you've got and can call your home," she said pointing at herself, "and I think I'm your future wifey and I'm a VA girl," she joked and lay back upon his shoulder. His sisters' eyes burned holes through her chest with dislike, but they manage to keep their cool.

"So, sis, how long ya'll going to be out in Rich-town?" Donny began to joke.

"Not long, baby bruh; just long enough to get this settled which shouldn't take nothing but a day," she said, "and why? Are you trying to rush me off?"

"Hell no, sis, I'm just asking. You know I can't wait until we're back together," Donny shared because deep down inside, Rain was his everything.

Rain laid her head back to enjoy the rest of the flight. Besides being tired, she didn't want to look in Bria's face anyway. In the middle of a good sex dream involving her and Vick, Rain was interrupted by the sound of the flight attendant's voice alerting them for landing. She was upset because her dream was fucking on fire. Of course you know Nizzy was at the airport waiting to pick everyone up.

"Wassup, boss?" she greeted while pounding fist with RJ.

"Hey, honey, how long you been here?" Rain asked Nizzy.

"Not long," she replied as she helped Donny put the bags in the trunk while everyone else got in. "So how's yo pops, boss?" Nizzy asked about Donte and Rain filled her in on his condition so far, and Nizzy know she must've felt fucked up.

Bria's house was the first on the stop list and she was mad as a bitch that Donny didn't stay with her. He wanted to spend time with his sisters, so he made plans to meet up with her at Club Benji's tomorrow and he gave her some tongue then they dipped. Arriving back at the house, it was already late as hell; so after unpacking and getting the kids settled in, everyone passed the fuck out sleep.

* * * * *

The next day, Rain and Storm went food shopping for the house as well as took the kids to buy some shoes. Rain wanted to make sure that they would be good until she returned to Richmond; and when that happened, it would be for good. Donny was getting dressed to hit up the club and the kids were chilling on the game, so it was time to leave to head back to Richmond. The girls kissed them all goodbye for one more time and they promised that this would be the last.

On the way to the airport, Storm had an idea; she wanted to stop in on Nizzy and Rain agreed so they headed straight for the club.

"Good evening, Mrs. Storm…Mrs. Lizzy," greeted D-Money who was working security for the door that night.

"Good evening, D. Where is Nizzy?" asked Rain. "Is everything running smoothly so far?"

"Yes, ma'am it is and Nizzy is inside somewhere," he explained as the ladies made their way in. Nizzy spotted them as soon as they walked onto the floor. "Wassup, boss, I didn't know you two were dropping by tonight," said Nizzy.

"Yeah, we're not staying long, just checking in on you."

"Well, everything's good here, so go have a drink before you peel," she suggested as they smiled and did just that. As they sat at the bar having a Cranberry and Vodka and chatting with Yetta, Storm noticed someone very familiar all up in Main's face.

"Isn't that Bria over there with Main?" Storm pointed in their direction.

"It damn sure is," Rain began to choke. "I wonder why that bitch is all on him like they know each other or something," she expressed wanting to run over and punch her but Rain doesn't make scenes.

They watched as the two headed out on the dance floor. Bria popped that pussy on Main and they seen it, but to her surprise, she noticed Donny coming in and I don't think she was the only one to peep him because Bria ran off the floor like she'd seen a ghost and Main turned and went the opposite way.

"Oh, shit sis, it's 10:45 p.m. and our flight leaves at 11:30 p.m." Storm reminded Rain, so they grabbed their shit and left. The whole plane ride home, Rain stayed quiet as she gazed out the window and into space. The thoughts of her plans wouldn't quit in her mind and Rain couldn't wait to actually live it.

"Hold my hands dear Lord, never let me go. Your touch was something that I never thought I'd know. So now I need your help to show me the way, because You said it in Your words that I'm entitled to better days. So, here I am Lord, standing front and center, with my arms open wide, I'm here to surrender. Please

Save Me!

Rain had a way of expressing herself through her words and she knew the time had come for changes; but the feelings were very scary. This life was all that she knew and the fear of functioning in a new world made Rain questioned if she could survive without it and money wasn't the fucking issue. We all know her family was set for life, but having that kind of power made her feel richer.

As her and Storm sat talking about living a normal life, Rain decided to place the call to Vick because it was time for war. In every great battle, you must always prepare; especially if you want to win.

"Hey, baby, wassup?" Vick missed his boo.

"It's time," was all that she had to say and he knew actually what she meant.

He laughed, "Alright, so when do you want Queen's Way?" he asked and she told them all to meet at the house by noon.

"I can't wait to start over with you baby," he got quiet. "You make me better, La'Rain and I want to marry you."

She almost dropped the phone from what she was hearing "Vick, are you fucking for real?"

"Real as I've ever been and I fuckin love you, La'Rain."

For the first time in the longest, he'd referred to her by the government name. He called her who she has always been to him and that shit would never change.

"Well, you think about what I said since I made you turn speechless and I'll see you at the house in a little while."

All Rain could say was, "Ok" as they hung up and she was still very stunned.

"What happened, sis?" asked Storm and judging from the look on Rain's face, Vick had said something that had her gone and her sister of course was being nosey.

"He just said he wanted me to be his wife…as myself, not Lizzy, and live a normal life together, sis. Oh my God, this shit is happening too fast," she was confused but it was things that had to be done first in order for Rain to even think of the future. It was now 3:00 in the morning and they decided to go to bed. Rain had a meeting with Mr. Jefferson in the morning and whenever money was involved, you know it was her number one priority; and besides that, they had a meeting with the crew.

Beep, "Mrs. Elizabeth," Megan's voice rang out loudly from the office phone as Rain in her softest voice replied, "Yes."

"There's a Mr. Jefferson here to see you and Mr. Tulio will not be in today, he took sick days off all of a sudden and since you left, he hasn't been back," Megan stated as she give him the ok to go in.

"Hold all my calls until I'm done." said Rain, "and I'll check in with him later."

Mr. Jefferson entered. "Well, hello there," she addressed him. "Do come in," she said, pointing her hand in the direction of a seat.

"My, my, my, Mrs. Lizzy…every time I see you, you take my breath away," said Mr. Jefferson. "You are extremely beautiful."

"Why thank you, sir."

They both began to smile and she was ready to get down to business and put the final seal onto his account.

Rain removed his file from her drawer as her heart raced with excitement. "Here are your deeds, sir," she said, handing him some contracts to sign. He slid her over a nice fat ass check.

"I made it out for 475 million and the extra five million in there is for you," he expressed, not knowing that Rain was taking it all anyway.

"So, what are you going to do with all that property?" she asked, due to the fact that this nigga had just brought the whole damn block.

"My brothers and I are going to open up a chain of stores in one big area so that way the money will continue to flow," he laughed.

"It's called legal hustling. I can dig it," she smiled and being that her and her sister was into the same thing, she knew all about it. She had gotten away with so much money from this bitch Ricky that even if she didn't own businesses, her family would always be straight. "Alright, Mr. Jefferson, you are good to go and congratulations," she said, shaking his hand and also giving him a bottle of the finest wine along with his keys.

"Thank you, Mrs. Wales. I couldn't have done it without you working with me as I got straight, you really are a good business women," he confessed and he grabbed his stuff to go forward in his new life.

Rain didn't waste any time getting out of the office with that check; and Ricky had no idea that the deal was even done. By the time he finds out, it'll be too late for his ass anyway; so at this point, it didn't even matter.

"Perfect timing," she thought as she drove back to the house. "That bitch is already on his ass – sick, or so he says; but what better way than to get him while he's down. Who knows, maybe he won't be able to take it. "Old bitch," she said out loud to herself as she bumped Lil Wayne as she drove.

Rain got back to the house with no time to waste because Queen's Way would be arriving any minute. She and Storm went to get dressed for the occasion being that this was the final meeting, she thought as the driveway to their house became packed with cars. You would have thought it was a gangster's convention. As they took their places inside of the boardroom, Rain and Storm stood side by side at the head of the table. They knew it was time for business. They were dressed in pin-stripe gray and white trench style dresses, with the split going up the front. Their hair flowing long, hanging gracefully on their shoulders as the mafia style hate made it perfect. Vick and Chance went over and took their positions, posted one on each side of the girls as all eyes directed their attention on them.

Rain began to speak. "I want to start off by saying thank you for your hard work; we are a family and I couldn't have gotten this far without having loyal ass niggas on my team," she expressed.

"You're welcome, boss," in four different languages filled her ears as the boys express their gratitude.

"You boys made out real good from Ricky's Empire and that was my gift to you. Each of you has enough money to do whatever the fuck you choose to with it. But you're on your own because this is my final run with you guys. I can't live like this anymore and I hope you understand," she expressed as they all nodded their heads, yes. "I will always be here for you, but as long as it's clean business. So with that being said…" Vick and Chance pulled out the chairs for her and Storm to take their seats as she uttered, "Time to kill once more."

The boys began to smile as they rubbed their hands together with pure pleasure. They loved doing anything for Rain and Storm, so this being their last run was going to be great.

*****

"My New York boys are already familiar with this procedure from when we had that job with the cops a while back," she began. "I need you boys to do a routine check on Ricky for the next three days and you will remain in pairs just like before. I need to know everything that this muthafucker's doing from his morning meds to his bedtime shit on the toilet. If he did it I need to know," Rain continued. "I do know he's out sick right now, at least that's what the fuck he called in and said, so confirm that shit for me too."

Storm cut's her off and she's pissed. "So that means if your bitch got to be a nurse, if you got to sit outside his house…you do whatever needs to be done to find out what my sister needs."

Queen's Way knew she meant business, so after wrapping up everything with the meeting, they all had their shifts to report to fucking work.

"Eight-hour shifts, my niggas, in pairs of two; so let's go muthafuckin get it!"

Monday, Day #1 6:59 a.m.

"Mane, it's cold as fuck out here," said Hamp as he and Tip sat watch outside of Ricky's mansion.

"Quit whining, bitch and hit this loud!" joked Tip. "We got to hang tough through this shit; boss's orders," he expressed as he passed Hamp's ass the blunt.

"Where the fuck is this fat muthafucker? Ain't no lights come in there yet," noticed Hamp and just as he said that, a dark red minivan pulled up to Ricky's gate as the driver pushed in the code causing the gates to open the fuck up.

"Come on, nigga," Tip jumped out as a sign. "Let's go while we can."

I know you remember there are the leaders of each side, so you know they had to do the nasty job. As the gates began to close, they made it through just in time as the lady driving the van got out. She made her way up to the front door. Tip and Hamp noticed that she was dressed as a nurse.

"Is this nigga really sick?" whispered Hamp as they hid on the side of the house dressed in all black with ski masks on.

"I don't know, my nigga; but we will soon find out," said Tip as they ran toward the back of the house and began to look through the window. "There go that nigga right there," said Tip. "Fat muthafucker looks fine to me. So what the fuck he need her for? Young ass should be at home some fuckin where," he expressed as they continued to watch them drink and talk for about twenty fucking minutes. They soon discovered why she was there.

This li'l bitch started playing nurse for this nigga. Mane, the things she did I swear she's not old enough to do as she stood in from of him with nothing but her nurse's cap on. As she began to suck on Ricky's pink dick, "eewww, mane… what the fuck!" both boys were about to be sick.

"This nigga is sick alright," said Hamp. "His old ass is sick in the head, number one, because that bitch looks like she can't be no more than fifteen," he was mad as a bitch and wanted to kill that nigga right then. "Hold your position, my nigga; we will soon find out" he said as they looked back into the window again.

They watched Ricky as he enjoyed getting that wrinkled dick sucked and you know he enjoyed the taste of her pussy right before he pounded her ass from the back. Judging from a time of approximately ten minutes, that nigga couldn't hang anyway.

"Damn, that muthafucker is weak," laughed Hamp. They watched her as she put back on her clothes while Ricky handed her a big bag and she thanked him. This nigga had the nerve to slam the door right behind her. I mean…shit, he could of at least made sure she was safe.

Meanwhile outside, Tip and Hamp waited to catch her ass before she left. as she opened the van door, all she heard was, "Don't scream, bitch or it will be your last," you know that nigga Hamp always going crazy. He lived for shit like that. She sobbed.

"Get in now," he said, tossing her ass head first into the car, and then he got behind the wheel as Tip got in back with her, . Hamp drove three blocks away and then parked.

"Please, don't kill me. What do you want?" the girl cried out from under the pillow case and couldn't see.

"Tell us what we want to know and we won't hurt you. Now, what were you doing at Ricky's house?" questioned Tip as he sat there beside her.

"Look, whatever he's into, I don't have nothing to do with it; he's just my friend, Jayla's grandpa," she expressed while Tip was stunned by what she'd said.

"What the fuck you mean *your friend*," Tip asked. "you talking about Lil Jayla? Candace's daughter?"

She shook her head, yes.

"Mane, how old are you then because she's like fifteen."

Being friends with Rico, he knew all about their family and this is not how they operate.

"I just turned sixteen today, but Mr. Ricky's been fucking me for three weeks now," she continued to express. "We met at Jayla's birthday party and he told me he'd give me a job cleaning up for him just so I could make some extra money. Day one of me coming over to his house, he came on to me, asking for pussy. In exchange, he would take care of me because I live in a group home. So, I sneak out and steal the van just to come see him."

The boys couldn't believe their ears; this nigga had gone too fucking far now.

"Please don't kill me, I promise I want go back there," she kept crying.

"Chill, li'l shorty; we don't want you…it's his ass we want," explained Tip. "By the way, li'l mamma, what's your name?"

"Carmen," she answered with her head hung low as Tip goes into the bag.

"Goddamn, shorty…all this damn money."

"He just gave me that money tonight, and that's the first time he's ever given it to me," she continued, "but for three times a week of having to let this nigga fuck me, shit…that's the least he could do; before him, I only had sex once, so all the shit he makes me perform on him, I don't even know how I do it," Carmen poured out her heart and even though she didn't know them, for the first time, she felt safe.

"Well, look Carmen, take your money and get the fuck outta here; but don't you ever come back again," said Tip as she answered him back with a soft, "Ok."

They opened the doors to exit. "I'm not the only young girl he's doing this to," said Carmen underneath her breath as Tip and Hamp got out asking, "What do you mean?"

"On days when I come, he usually has this black skinny girl that would come the same day or the next night and this girl is a runaway."

Tip thanked her for keeping it real with him as they walked off one way and she drove the other way praying to God they didn't come after her.

"What time is it?" asked Tip as they made their way back to their truck. "12:45 p.m." answered Hamp and he was still upset from what he'd heard. After going through what he did behind his daughter getting raped, that nigga Hamp wanted to kill Ricky's ass right then and there.

Ricky was pulling out of his gates and they decided to follow him.

"Mane, my nigga, Rico, probably turning over in his grave right now from seeing his dad doing this nasty shit," Tip begins to enlighten Hamp. "Rico thought the world of his dad, and he wanted to be just like him. I never thought this nigga would stoop so low."

Ricky made a right turn into a parking lot and sat there as they parked across the street to watch. Their shift was almost over, so they needed to find out fast what was up as Jose's car pulled in and parked right beside his dad. He got out and went into his trunk and carried out two duffel bags into Ricky's back seat then he got in. They watched as those two talked for about thirty minutes, and just then, Doc and Lee pulled up.

"Wassup, my nigga? I see you behind me," Tip informed Doc. "These niggas been sitting there for almost an hour now, and he got two big ass bags in the back."

"10-4, my nigga, we got it from here," expressed Doc, so Tip and Hamp peeled off.

"I can see this is going to be a long shift," Lee sat behind the wheel eating peanuts. "I wonder what them bitches talking about," said Doc as the sound of Jose's voice rang out.

"Alright, pops," they heard him say as he got back into his car and left. Ricky got out and went inside of this building labeled, *Jinx Warehouse* and he took the bags right with him.

"How the fuck we supposed to get in there?" asked Doc as he and Lee continued to sit watch. Lee put a call through to Rain so that they could get her insight on what to do next before they ended up killing somebody. He listened to Monica off of Rain's caller tune then she answered,

"It's Doc, boss," he stated. "Lee and I are on our shift and Ricky just went inside of Jinx's warehouse and he took two bags in with him; but we don't know what you want us to do because we're strapped, so you know what that means," he explained, but Rain ordered them not to do anything.

"Stand your ground and he'll tell on himself, but do not put yourself in danger."

Inside the warehouse, Ricky's ass had a meeting with his big boss, which no one knew anything about because his cousin had been supplying him for all these years. That nigga took one to the chest a year ago, so Ricky had no choice but to change up.

"So, Ricky, what's that I hear you don't have all of my money?" asked Ya-Yo, a Columbia muthafucker that was just like him didn't take any shit.

"I have half right here," he said, handing him the bags. "17 keys of work is also included; that's all I have left after the hit," he stated and Ya-Yo was puzzled.

"The hit?" he paused, "Do you even have a fuckin clue what's going on, Ricky? I've never had this problem out of you before, so wassup now?" he questioned his motives. Ricky was used to being talked to in that manner because of his family, he was always a boss. He informed Ya-Yo that he had no clue who was after him, but that his crew was on it around the clock; so when they found out he would be the first to know, but for now, the product was all that he could deliver."

Ricky was two seconds from getting his ass dealt with, but Ya-Yo let him go instead. He told Juan to show his ass to the door as he shared with Ricky that he'd better have all of his shit next go round or it's his ass.

Doc and Lee spotted his ass soon after he came out, and this time without any bags.

"About time, fat bitch wobbling," joked Lee and they both fell out in laughter, continuing to follow Ricky and from the way he was driving, he wanted to get away fast.

They followed Ricky to Miranda's, an Italian restaurant near his house; and he just went in to pick up his food and headed straight the fuck home. He never left for the rest of the night, so when Tank and Jamie came along, they just sat there getting high. That nigga, Jamie, popped like fifteen diddies just to get a buzz; so from the weed and pills, them two couldn't do anything but sleep.

Tuesday Day #2 7:00 a.m.

Knock, knock, knock was the sound of Pauley tapping on Tank's window. He and Jamie were passed out high.

"What the…oh, mane, Pauley," said Jamie. "I was reaching for my gun," he confessed as they both began to laugh.

"I see you two working hard," said Smitty as he drunk his orange juice and then instructed them to go home and get some sleep. This nigga Ricky took his time leaving the house this morning, and it could be because Christina came by to get the rest of her stuff out that bitch as Ricky tried to beg her to stay. I guess they really were getting a divorce, and this time Christina was fed up. Smitty and Pauley continued to watch as Ricky tried to put the moves on Christina, but she rejected his ass, yet again; leaving him all alone. Finally, after hours of watching this nigga at his house, he left and they were on the move. He headed to Victoria Secret first and after buying some things, they followed him to Candace's house; while he was inside, they made their switch with Wize and Michael and at this point even they wanted him dead.

Another quiet evening that soon became night, but Walter and Chino's shift was the one with the twist. It was about 2:15 a.m. and this tall, skinny girl came walking down the block as Walter and Chino just sat there checking her out.

"Where the fuck is she going this late?" said Walter

She headed toward Ricky's gate, but just as she was about to hit the camera, them niggas ran up and grabbed that ass, not even knowing who she was.

"Umm, Umm…let me go," were the cries that came from underneath Walter's hand as it held her mouth shut and she continued to kick.

"Shut the fuck up, we're helping you out," fussed Chino as they threw her into the truck's back seat and drove off.

As she continued to squirm and cry, the duct tape now held her lips together and the more she cried the more annoyed Chino became.

"I wish she'd shut the fuck up man, damn," he pulled out his phone to call Rain and Walter thought that shit was funny.

She was half asleep as the sound of her voice answered and Chino didn't waste any time.

"This better be good, Chino."

"It is boss, you're not going to believe this," he began. "This nigga Ricky's been doing some foul shit, boss and we got the proof for you right here," he confessed and Rain sat straight up in her bed.

"Meet me at my house in fifteen minutes and bring all the boys with you," she hung up pissed, and now she had to go and wake up Storm. After filling her in on what was taking place, they both got dressed to see what was going on now.

It was now 4:00 a.m. and the knocks on the door alerted her that they were there.

"Wassup, boos?" greeted the boys as they made their way inside and some of them were still half sleep as Rain heard noises from down in the basement. She followed the boys as they headed down there.

Once Rain and Storm hit the bottom of the stairs, the crew had already formed their circle as Vick and Chance stood kind of to the side.

"Ok, what's going on?" she asked, noticing a pair of feet in between all of them as they stepped back so she could see what it was.

"Who the fuck is that?" she questioned hysterically, because this wasn't part of her plan.

"She was on her way to Ricky's and we grabbed her before she went in," explained Walter as Chino took the sack off of her face.

"Latoya!" yelled out Red. "Mane, what the fuck ya'll doing with my li'l cousin?" he pushed in the chair, rushing over to her side as the tears rolled down her face.

"Take this fucking tape off of her now," he demanded as Rain gave them the ok for her to speak.

As Red held Latoya tight, she cried from being scared. They needed her to answer some questions.

"Look at me, Toya," Red lifted up her head. "Why the fuck was you going to see Ricky?" he asked as she began to cry harder.

"I ran away from home four months ago and Mr. Ricky's been giving me money ever since he picked me up from downtown one night," she expressed with pain.

Tip and Hamp actually heard what she said as it caused their mind to flash back to Carmen and the things she told them too. Rain and Storm stood there cuffing their mouths while trying to piece this shit together. They both spoke up with information,

"Yesterday morning, we ran up on this young broad leaving Ricky's house after he finished fucking her and she said her name was Carmen."

Rain cut in, "So you telling me this nigga is a muthafuckin pedophile?" she screamed and now she was crying from anger. "I'm a fucking mother of a little girl, and even though she's a part of his family, I still don't trust that shit."

"And you shouldn't," Tip interrupted. "Carmen said she's friends with Jayla."

Their eyes got extra big now and he could read that shit. "Yeah, you heard me right, boss. Candace's daughter—Lil Jayla," he continued and that right there, for Rain, was enough. She and Storm walked over to Latoya as Storm held her hand to comfort her.

"Red, where is her mom and why hasn't she been found?"

"My aunt is probably worried sick; but I will personally be returning her home," Red expressed, but Rain wasn't finish with her yet.

"This nigga's dipping in the kiddie pool now, fuck that operation off!" she screamed and she was ready for war. "Latoya, I need you to call that muthafucker and tell him you're running late but you will be there," she demanded and Toya did just as she was told.

*****

After organizing everything, Rain allowed Red to leave so that he could take her home and return her safe and sound to her mother. Now the show could begin. Rain went upstairs and got dressed into something tight and sexy because she knew that would grab that nigga's attention. Rain, Vick, Chance, and Storm rode in the same car as the crew members followed behind them. They were going to sit watch outside of Ricky's gates as Rain made her grand entrance inside. She punched in the code to his gate just like she never ever forgot it. Anger burned through her skin even more. This nigga deserved what was coming to him, and at this point, all the chips were down.

Rain kissed Vick, telling him her pistol was on her as she said, *I love you* and got out the car making her way up to his front door. Rain's all-red evening gown melted on each part of her curves just right; but she damn sure wasn't to be fucked with at this point,

Ding, Dong.

5:30 in the morning and Ricky opened up just knowing he was about to fuck Toya. But he was stunned beyond his belief when the women he saw standing there was Lizzy.

"And to what do I owe this surprise?" he grinned as he leaned up against the door frame and Rain stood there flashing her smile.

"I guess you've come around now; huh?" he rubbed his hand across her face as she just stood there grinning. "Well, since you're not going to say anything, can I at least ask you to come in?"

He's such a bitch and his uncle told him long ago that pussy was going to be the death of him. At this point he wished he had listen as he walked behind Rain, staring at her ass like it was food.

"Have a seat, Mr. Tulio," she went right into her scene and he did just that and asked, "Ok, I'm sitting; now what's next since we playing the office assistant."

As he sat there smirking and rubbing his dick, Rain took off her shawl. She started walking around his chair in circles as she gracefully felt on his shoulders.

"All this time," she giggled as she tickled her nails across his ear. "A pedophile…I never thought you would be Ricky, but now you're fucking little girls," she continued, making his ass puzzled like never before. "You were jealous of your son all these years because he had something that truthfully you wanted, but never was good enough to get unless you paid them for sex, you bastard!"

Rain made him hot by now as he jumped up in her face pissed.

"How the fuck do you know?" he went on to say, but he was cut off instantly before he could finish.

"Shut up, you fat bitch! Don't even act like you're innocent because your ass tried to kill me and didn't succeed. Stupid muthafucker!" she said as Ricky charged toward her fast.

He grabbed her by the shoulders roughly, pushing her back against the window and she did nothing but smile.

"You finished bitch?" she said, fixing her hair. "Please do as you feel before your time is up."

"You little bitch, how is my time up when I took care of you long ago," he slammed Rain back harder again. "La'Rain, you hoe," he said as she kneed him in the balls, causing Ricky's hand to release and allowing her to run.

She stood on the other side of the couch laughing as Ricky charged at her ass again, but this time, she two-pieced the fuck out of his face, causing his head to swing sideways and blood to leak from his gums.

He grabbed his mouth as a sign that it hurt. "Come on bitch, is this what you want?"

Rain got in position to put her kick boxing moves into play. "You took everything from me; my husband, my life… bitch everything!" she screamed and cried from being furious. "And just when you thought it was safe, I then returned and took everything from you; your wife, your money…" she laughed as this punk ass bitch grabbed a lamp.

"Bitch, I'm going to bash your head in!" he yelled as he threw the lamp toward her head, but it grazed her instead and then smashed straight into the wall. She went to reach for her purse and that fat bitch snuck her in the jaw, knocking her down on the couch. As they struggled with him on top of her, he choked her harder at this point and she couldn't even breathe. "I told you I'm going to cut your head off, bitch; but not until I make you suck my dick first," he was disgusting, but Rain fought his fat ass back with all her might. She really was no match for him, especially being pinned down like that, she couldn't even get free. Just as Ricky swung his hand up to hit her again,

POW, POW, POW, POW, and POW, five rounds through the back as that nigga's body began to fall forward.

Rain rolled to the left, just in time not to get squished as Vick stood there with gun smoke coming out of his 380 caliber, aiming it right at him, ready for more. He ran over and scooped Rain up, holding her tightly against his chest as he wiped her forehead.

"Baby, are you alright?" he inquired.

She answered him back, "I am now," meaning that since he was there. Vick helped her get the fuck up. She noticed that fat muthafucker slumped over, looking like Swiss cheese as he leaked blood from all of his wounds.

"Roll that bitch over," instructed Rain as she wiped the blood from her face and grabbed a sharp pair of shears from the desk. Vick pushed his big ass all by himself, almost causing his back to go out. Before Vick could blink or even say a word, Rain turned and cut Ricky's dick straight off from the base. *Goddamn, even that nigga's balls were unattached.*

"Now chop this off, bitch," she said as she set it on top of a candle stick and stuck a lit match right inside of his hole. "Burn in hell you worthless muthafucker because now I can live my life."

Rain spit directly into his right eye as it slowly dripped all the way down his face. Vick took her by the hand as they walked out Ricky's house, never looking back; and as of now, it had all come to an end.

* * * * *

The next few days all Rain did was sleep, trying hard to get all her strength back up. Vick worked the streets to see if anyone was talking, but instead, everything was going smooth. He got word of Ricky's funeral date and he felt that Rain would want to know. This was her way of really burying the past once and for all; so you know, she definitely was going to attend. She went all by herself because she was known to them as Lizzy, so she didn't want to draw attention from the others. As the words were spoken over Ricky at the burial ground, his children, grandchildren, hell…even Christina was taking him being gone so well. Rain stood there laughing on the inside, but her face had a smile on the outside too. Everyone walked over to place their flower on top of his casket as they lowered his ass six feet deep, she just stood back, paying close attention because this time, she made sure no one would come back. Each person took an arrangement in remembrance of Ricky's life; but Rain, on the other hand, took her red rose, dropped it on the ground and stomped it. She turned to walk away for good this time because there was nothing left to finish. As she turned to walk away forever, it felt good to finally place the top on the box; now better days were definitely all that would come!

Happily ever after

Each and every temptation that we overcome in life are only representations for you to be stronger; a trail endured and weathered in good spirit was only a test to prove your soul noble. What Rain was taught through all of her ups and downs was that life is not about learning to survive the storm, but rather about learning how to dance through the rain. The sun will shine again if you can only hold on and that is actually what she found out.

In life some people are not blessed with do-overs and that one fuck up can be their last. Being fortunate enough to be a chosen one was what she took and ran with. As she and Storm stood in the hallway of their house, and the movers prepared their item's to be shipped, they couldn't help but remember all the good and bad memories that would forever dwell inside the walls of what once was their home. Storm took care of everything as far as the shop was concerned; she appointed Dana and Kim as acting management, but you can bet your ass she would be back and forth checking on things. They sold the house and took everything that was a part of them to begin their new life in Richmond, and at that point, nobody could wait to start things anew.

As the movers collected the final items to load up, the crews all said their goodbyes. They had all formed a friendship or bond, so even in two separate places they would still be one. It was time to hit the road now and what a sad, by happy, good-bye. Queen's Way South took one private jet and Rain, Vick, Storm and her new man, Chance, all gathered together and boarded the other jet non-stop to Virginia, and might I add, Rain wasn't going to miss New York at all. Everything from her past was now a distant memory and that's the way she wanted it to stay.

You can imagine the excitement that the kids and Donny felt as Rain and Storm headed through the door. They were surrounded by hugs and kisses from all types of directions, and nobody wanted to let go because they knew it was now over and they wouldn't have to say goodbye to their mother again. Vick and Chance took everybody out to dinner as a celebration of a new beginning. *Texas de Brazil* was the dinning place of choice as they all sat together in a section reserved just for them. Vick decided to make a toast by tapping his fork on the glass lightly as he stood.

"I would like to makes a toast to one of the most beautiful, wise, and intelligent black women that ever walked the face of this Earth," as Rain blushed and everyone else smiled. "We've been through a lot together," Vick paused, "wait," he turned to face RJ and Aaliyah and asked, "do I have you guys' blessing to be a part of yawls life forever?" he asked, kind of scared of what their reaction might be. He knew that Rain thought the world of her kids and she took their feelings into consideration before uttering another word.

RJ stood and pulled his sister up next to him as he said, "You have always been a part of our life Vick, so to me, you are already like our dad."

Donny smiled hard as he nodded in agreement.

"My mommy has been through so much pain," expressed Aaliyah, "but with you, Vickster…" they all burst out into laughter at her pet name for Vick. "Ok, ok, I was just joking, but seriously…" she smiled and laid her head on Vick's arm. Looking at him as Rain and Storm couldn't do anything but cry, she said, "With you, I feel we are all safe."

Aaliyah smiled as she and her brother both gave Vick a big fatherly hug and sat down so he could continue.

"Well, alright then," he cleared his throat from getting choked up, "shall we continue?" he smiled as the Violinist begin to form a straight line, playing softly and drawing attention to them from everyone in the restaurant, including Rain's.

When she turned back around to face Vick again, all of a sudden, he was gone and John Legend appeared. He smiled and serenaded Rain with these words: "Oh, I'll stay with you through the ups and downs. Oh, I'll stay with you when no one else is around. And when the dark clouds arrive, I'll stay be your side. I know we'll be alright. I'll stay with you."

Tears ran down her Rain's face because Vick knew that was her favorite John Legend song. She continued to look around for Vick; yearning to see the man that was filling her soul with love. Once Storm turned Rain's chair around to face her prince charming, she too cried at her sister's second chance at happiness and she knew Rain deserved it.

Vick held in his hand a five-carat Pompeii engagement ring he had custom made for her and engraved inside was both of their names. Rain was frozen solid as she held her mouth in shock as Vick begin to say how he felt to her.

"Life without you in it is meaningless and that's why I'm doing this," he expressed as he got down on one knee. "La'Rain Shante Peters," he referred to her, not wanting to mention the name Tulio, "for all my life, even before I met you, it was your image inside and out of my dreams, and now that I have you, I can't let you go. You are and have always been the air that I breathe, so what I'm trying to ask you is, will you make my dreams a reality and do the honor of becoming my wife," he stared deep into her eyes and wiped a tear from her eyes. "Will you marry me?" Vick asked and Rain jumped into his arms screaming yes while every soul in the restaurant, including workers, cried and clapped. You should have seen the women mad at their men for not thinking of that first. Rain didn't care as they stood kissing passionately in the center of the room, they captured that moment forever in their minds.

"And they lived happily ever after," were words that Rain only knew from a book. Allowing those words to be the start of living her own fairytale was more then she could ask for. She vowed that they would try their hardest to make it last because from now on, there wasn't any turning back for her family, "Cause It ain't No stopping them now!"

G STREET CHRONICLES
PRESENTS
A BROTHER'S
Betrayal
PART 3 OF DOPE GIRL'S AMBITION
FROM AUTHOR
MONIQUE LOVE
G STREET DIGITAL

CHAPTER 1

Turning a new leaf

A wise man once said that right in the middle of an ordinary life, love gives us a fairytale. Rain's old life was far from fairy, but a tale it damn sure was. To the world, Rain was just one person; but to Vick, she was his world and as he would say, his soul mate. They were two halves of the same soul and today, they would really make everything legit by joining together in life's journey. They both prayed to God that their love would last forever.

* * * * *

"Twenty minutes until show time!" yelled Stephanie—Vick's cousin and wedding planner—as she rushed through Mount Calvary Baptist Church making sure everything was in place. Vick nervously hesitated to put on his suit as Chance came in to speed up the process.

"Come on, bruh, what the fuck you doing?" Chance laughed at the sight of his big brother being scared. Chance had never really seen his brother afraid of shit, but for some reason today, Vick was terrified.

"I'm coming nigga," he said, standing up and grabbing his Gucci Tuxedo and heading straight to the dressing room to change.

"So have you seen her?" Vick yelled to Chance while he waited on him to get dressed, but wishing he'd hurry the fuck up.

"Seen who, nigga?"

Chance joked, "Mom and dad are already here," he was picking because he knew that his brother was talking about Rain. Chance laughed at his mood change as Vick headed out to join him.

"I'm talking about my wife," he shoved Chance on the back as they headed toward the Sanctuary so that things could begin. "No, Vick, I haven't seen Rain. Damn nigga, she coming." They both laughed at the love all over Vick's face.

"I can't believe I'm doing this again," joked Rain as Storm zipped up her dress, "but this time is forever; hopefully."

"Ain't no hopefully," Storm hurried to correct that shit "it is forever and Vick loves you so throw that second guessing shit out of the window sis, this is your blessing from God; you hear me? And you damn sure deserve it, so don't allow nobody to take that away," expressed Storm as she hugged her sister tightly trying hard not to wrinkle up her dress. "You look so beautiful sis, and don't worry about nothing but smiling." Storm kisses her on the cheek as they both begin to cry. "Live a real life," Storm whispered in Rain's ear as they tried to catch the tears so that it wouldn't mess up their faces.

Knock, knock, knock. The door begins to open. "Elizabeth, it's time," Stephanie announces as Storm gave Rain one more look and she took that walk toward her future.

Now, of course we all know that this is Rain's second marriage and the first one with Rico was real big, but this nigga Vick knew every muthafuckin' body; shit, they even had rich and famous on the guest list and everything was beautifully put together. Since Donte was still in the hospital, Keith had the honor of walking Rain down the aisle. He joined her, waiting for her time to make an entrance.

"You look beautiful, baby girl," he whispered to Rain as he cuffed her arm very tightly. "Thank you, Uncle Keith, I'm so nervous right now, but I want to live my life the right way."

"But baby girl listen," Keith cut in, "you've made it through a lot and you're still standing because God has plans for your life," he kisses her hand as they took a step toward the sanctuary door. Bishop Morton raised his hands as a sign for the two thousand guest to stand out of respect for Rain's grand entrance as the music began to play. Eyes gazed in on the astonishment that came from Rain, her and Vick both smiled hard at each other as she made her way beside him and the guests took their seats.

"Who gives this woman to this man to love, honor, and cherish and making the union pleasing to the mighty eye of God?"

"I do," answered Uncle Keith. "I deliver the blessing over this union for myself and my brother," he says as he shakes Vick hand and kisses his niece on the check. Then he takes his seat as Bishop Morton continued.

"Dearly beloved, we are gathered here today in the sight of God, and in the presence of these witnesses, to join together this man and this woman in holy matrimony. It is an honorable estate, and it is therefore not to be entered into unadvisedly; but reverently, discreetly, and in the eyes of God. Into the holy estate these two persons come now to be joined. If there is anyone here today that can show just cause as to why they may not lawfully be joined, let them speak now or forever hold their peace." Every eye was on the next making sure no one would be stupid.

"Elizabeth and Vick, I require and charge you both as you stand in the presence of God before the secrets of all hearts are disclosed, before this company your pledge of faith each to the other. Do you, Victor, take this woman to be thy wedded wife, to live together holy under the eyes of God? Will you love her, comfort her, honor her, and keep her in sickness and in health, forsaking all others for as long as you both shall live?"

Tears came down Vick's face as he said and I do quote, "I wanted, I did, and I always do" as everyone smiled and cried. Bishop Morton continued.

"Do you, Elizabeth, take this man to be thy wedded husband, to live together holy under the eyes of God? Will you love him, comfort him, honor him, and keep him in sickness and in health, forsaking all others for as long as you both shall live?"

"Wait," Rain cut in, making everyone scared.

"Victor, I know we agreed on no vows, but I have to tell you what's on my heart at this moment," she continued while she sobbed, "I've made it through a lot in my life, never thinking I'd ever find love again and then you came along."

"You loved and protected me in every area of my life; you even gave love and protection to my children," she looks over toward RJ and Aaliyah as they both cheesed hard, "so that alone already stole my heart."

"You are my everything and I'm so glad God gave me a best friend back. So, yes, I also and always do want to marry you," she expressed and even Bishop had a tear in his eye as he asked for the rings. He handed Vick his first and then Rain hers as she placed that iced-out band on his finger, sealing the deal to their journey's beginning.

"By the power vested in me by the State of Virginia, I now pronounce you husband and wife. You may now kiss your bride."

When their lips locked, I swear you could see the sparks fly off as they tongued each other like two porn stars.

"Ladies and gentlemen, it is with great pleasure that I present to you Victor and Elizabeth Sanchez."

The claps and cheers rang out as everyone in there showed their congrats through love as the wedding party begin making their exit, heading over to the reception hall to party.

"How does it feel to be Mrs. Sanchez?" asked Vick as he and Rain continued kissing in the limo while they drove.

"It feels good, baby; really good," answered Rain. "I never thought I'd be this happy again," she expressed, and I just want to say thank you, baby," she laid her head on his shoulder.

"You never have to thank me, boo. I told you before…I got you," said Vick as he held his wife close, never wanting to let go while they made their way to Club Benji's followed by everyone else to begin the celebration of their union.

The black people in Richmond really showed out that night with wall to wall limos and fly-ass rides, causing the whole Canal Street to be blocked off. Nizzy assisted Stephanie in decorating for the reception and the club was looking just like the truth. The party was jumping; the guests arrived on time as Vick and Rain changed clothes upstairs, and then it was time to bring them in.

Ding, ding, ding. Nizzy tapped on her glass as Storm, Donny and the rest of the wedding party, sat down in their assigned spots at the family table.

"Thank you all for coming out tonight to be a part of these festivities, now without any further ado, introducing Victor and Elizabeth Sanchez," Nizzy announced as Vick and Rain walked in.

Everyone cheered them on as they walked over to be seated with the rest of the family just as Storm and Donny hugged them both tight. RJ and AAliyah were excited with joy because today marked the day Vick really became a father to them, and with RJ becoming a man now, he really needed that male guidance.

As the party went on, everyone seemed to be having a good time; even the Queen's Way boys showed up with their families to join in on the union, and ever since Rain got out the game, the boys went on to do their own thing but they all still remained close. Bria stayed so far up Donny's ass the whole time; this bitch even got mad when she saw him talking to his cousin and because she was a girl, Bria automatically suspected foul play, but Storm and Rain weren't having that.

* * * * *

"What the fucks going on over there?" asked Rain as she whispered in Storm's ear referring to the commotion between Donny and Bria.

"I have no idea, sis, but I will definitely find out because no one is going to ruin your day." Storm gets up to walk over toward Donny just as Chance decides to cut her off.

"Hey, baby, I gotta go," he said, waiting on her response.

"What? Wait a minute, where are you going, Chance? Both of our families are here," said Storm, and whatever excuse he was gonna use had better be a good one because Storm wasn't easy to be fooled.

"I gotta go pick up my brother's wedding gift. I just wanted it to be a surprise, boo," he replied and Storm didn't give him any clue if she brought his bullshit lie or not and now wasn't the time to get into that.

"So, I guess I'll see you later then?" she rolled her eyes as she went to walk over to Donny, but Chance grabbed her by the arm.

"So, you mad now; huh?" he flashed his sexy smile and he really thought that shit would help.

"Goodbye, Chance, go be where you really want to be because it damn sure ain't here with me."

Storm left him standing there as she proceeded over in Donny's direction and Chance walked off, now heading over to inform Vick that he now had to bounce.

Vick and Rain, along with his parents, were all sitting together talking as Chance approached the table.

"Momma, daddy…I'll see you guys later, I have to go handle some business," Chance explained as Vick gave him a look to say, *what the fuck*?

"Big bruh, let me holla at you," Chance saw his face as Vick kissed Rain saying, "I'll be right back," and they walked away to talk.

"What fucking business, nigga, that you got, to leave my wedding early!" he questioned, mad as hell right now.

"Mane, bruh, you know what I got to do; they been blowing up my phone all day for me to bring the goddamn medicine, so I'd rather go now, than later," Chance explained.

"Look, bruh, you go ahead, but I think it's time you talk to Storm because I'm doing this marriage thing right and you heard the vows we said today. No secrets, bruh; not even for you, nigga," expressed Vick. "So, don't expect me to hold it much longer," he was for real, but I guess he would have to show him rather than warn.

"Whatever, mane; aight. I got to go," said Chance as he walked out the door slapping Nizzy and Main high-five as he left. Vick knew Storm wasn't going to be happy with this, which meant his wife wasn't going to be either. He returned back to their table.

"VJ, darling," which was what Yvette, their mother, called him, "where did your brother run off too?"

"Mom, you know that boy. I have no clue where he's going," Vick replied as Rain cut her eyes at him deep.

"Don't worry about him, son," said Tony, their dad. "I keep telling your mother, you two are grown and she can't worry herself about you guys all the time."

"You're right, dad," said Vick. "All I wanna do is enjoy the rest of my night with my wife," he extended his hand for her to dance with him. Meanwhile, over on the other side of the room, Storm was talking to Donny about him and Bria.

"Baby bruh, you can't keep letting her take you thru this. If that bitch can't act right, then cut her off," instructed Storm, "because our family don't have time for all that drama."

"Yeah, you're right, sis. But I love her, mane. She's just tripping and I'm going to talk to her," Donny tried his hardest to explain.

"Are you giving this bitch money, Donny?" asked Storm. "And I know you been keeping up on your shit with the studio?" Storm wasn't having that shit, it was always Donny's dream to have something of his owns and now that he has D-Nyce productions, wasn't nothing, or no one, coming between that.

"Sis, stop worrying. I got everything under control. Bria's my girl; so, of course, I look out from time to time, but by no means am I gonna be stupid with the bread," assured Donny just as Bria came strolling her ass over their way.

"Baby, I'm ready to go now," expressed Bria, walking up and putting her arms around Donny and without even opening her mouth to speak.

Rain and Storm let it be known that they didn't like Bria and she knew it, but *so what* she thought she was the bitch in charge because she's the one feeding Donny the pussy.

"Aight, boo, give me five minutes. Let me go over and say bye to Rain."

Donny, of course, had his own house now and Bria had no problem making herself comfortable like it was hers.

"Hey, baby bruh," Rain said, standing to hug him.

"I haven't had time to really see you all day," Donny expressed.

"Well, now you're leaving," Storm snapped back as she sat down in her seat.

"Shut up, Storm," said Donny. "You always trying to start shit," he was referring to her trying to get Rain upset.

"What's going on you two? Now isn't the time," expressed Rain. "Baby bruh, I'll see you tomorrow," she hugged him as Storm was cutting him with her eyes and Bria stood there smirking at her accomplishments, or so she thought. She loved to get them mad at each other, but little did she know, it would take a lot more to break the bond that they had and Bria damn sure didn't have what it took.

All of the guests started to taper off at this point, so Rain and Vick decided to call it a night as well. Being that they had a long flight in the morning, Rain knew she needed to get her rest!

The next day was fucking crazy. Rain and Vick were all over the place trying to get shit in order before their flight. RJ went out with his friend Denise, whom Rain could tell really had her son's mind going and that was cool because she really liked Denise for her son; which that, right there, was a first.

Rain had been gone out of her children's lives for a long time, and ever since her return, she still saw them as babies from time to time; so even though RJ was twenty-one years old now, to Rain, he would always be here little man. Aaliyah, sixteen years old now, turned out very good for herself. Coming from a life full with the things that her and her brother went through, AAliyah was determined to become somebody opposite.

Storm and Donny both were living in their own house with their significant others, and shit on all ends was getting real crazy to the point where the trio wasn't a threesome anymore.

"Hey, sis, you still in this bitch packing?" said Storm as she made her way inside Rain's bedroom where she found her digging in the closet.

"Girl, I just got here like thirty minutes ago. I had to meet AAliyah at Pep Boys to get her oil changed on her truck," Rain explained as she continued digging for her favorite purple dress. "Didn't she let you in?"

"No, I used my key. Was she supposed to be here?" Storm asked, wondering why her niece would leave and not tell anyone.

"She might have gone to the store or something, but she's good; they know I'm about to leave. Found it!" Rain jumps up screaming and scaring the fuck out of Storm.

"Bitch, calm down!" she laughed at Rain dancing around the room.

"Girl, this is Vick's favorite dress on me, so of course, I had to bring it on the honeymoon," she winked, tossing the dress into her suit case and closing it. "Where are you on your way to?" Rain questioned Storm.

"Oh, nowhere…shopping to find something to wear when me and Chance go out to celebrate the opening of his second RIM shop," she said, standing up from the bed and grabbing her five-hundred dollar Juicy Couture handbag which was a gift from her boo. Chance had no problem spending money on buying what she wanted and things between them two seemed to be going great.

"So, when will you be back?" Storm asked as they both carried bags to the trunk so that Rain could go meet Vick at the airport. He had to finish some stuff up at the restaurant and working was what he loved to do.

"Next week, sis, but I'll call you when we get there and please keep your eyes on things for me while I'm away," said Rain as she gave her sister a hug and they each parted ways.

As Rain rode to the airport going over her list to make sure she had everything, her phone begins to go off and she answered.

"Hey, sis, you left yet?" questioned Donny.

"I'm in the limo now baby, what's wrong?"

"Nothing, I just wanted to catch you before you left to say I love you, have fun, and don't come back pregnant Mrs. Sanchez." They both laughed and Rain replied, "Hell naw."

"I'm sorry about leaving last night, sis," he expressed. "When will you be back, because we need to hang like old times?"

Donny was missing his sister so much and he needed her now more than ever.

"I'm down with that, baby bruh. Where you at now?" she asked as Vick called in on the other line.

"I'm at the studio, bout to set these beats."

"Well, I'll call you when I get there, bruh," Rain cut him off. "Vick's beeping in on the other line," she said as they said their, *I love yous* to one another and she clicked over. "Hey, baby. Sorry, I was talking to Donny."

"That's ok, boo. Where are you?" he asked as he gave his keys to valet for parking at the airport.

"I'm on my way to you; I'm about to pull up now, so wait for me in the front."

They hung up the phone.

After getting their luggage checked in and boarding, Rain and Vick were ready to tackle the thirteen-hour flight to the lovely, the beautiful, Island of Bora Bora and they both decided to sleep the whole fucking way there, neither were fans of flying for that damn long, but fuck it…*it is what it is.*

Eight days in Bora Bora was much more than any girl could ask for; shit, that place was really paradise. The Hilton Bora Bora Nui Resort and Spa was their vacation spot of choice as a real married couple—The Sanchez's. Rain was overwhelmed when they entered their Villa and this time Vick's ass really went above and beyond to show it was all about her.

The small, glass floor panels in the overwater Villas enables a view of the beautiful blue water below. A to-die-for bedroom separated by a sliding panel from a small living room with couch, the bathrooms are spacious and decorated with rich natural woods, marble French bath fixtures and garden tub.

Vick put rose petals and candles all throughout the villa, leading up to a tray with an ice bucket containing a bottle of Chateau Mouton Rothschild 1945 with personalized wine glasses that said, "Rain and Vick." Strawberries and Chocolate with body whip crème for Rain to be dessert. A beautiful silk nightie and two gift boxes laid neatly across the king bed as Rain picked her presents up to open them. Vick stood there sipping on his Cognac straight as he watched her open the Jacob & CO bag slowly. He knew her face would light up.

"Ahh, my God…baby, you got it!" shouted Rain and she jumped right into Vick's arms almost causing him to drop his drink as they kissed.

"The heart diamond necklace was Jacob's most recent masterpiece; so you know Vick had to be the first to grab one for his Queen, and she now had thirty-seven carats around her neck. The other box contained a pair of Christian Louboutin Alti pump spikes.

"You can wear those tonight, boo," he said, shaking his head as he watched her standing there admiring how fancy they were. He held her in his arms, never wanting this moment to end as they watched the sun set over the water. Rain wanted to feel this way for eternity!

"Oh my God, Chance, where did you find this place baby? It's gorgeous," expressed Storm as they sat inside Le'Yaca's French restaurant in Williamsburg, Virginia, and believe me…to eat there you had to have money. Dining in that bitch cost a grip.

"I wanted to do something special tonight, boo," he replied "we're doing big things…me and you, and this is just the beginning," he said as their waiter approached the table.

"Good evening, my name is Albertus and I'll be your server tonight," he gave his introduction. "Can I start you off with something to drink?"

Chance, knowing his boo, knew actually what she liked so he did the honor of ordering for them both.

"A…look…while you're at it, son," Chance stopped the waiter again, "go ahead and put us down for the three-course meal, we're celebrating tonight."

"Yes, sir, right away, sir," said Albertus as he hurried ass to the kitchen to put their order in.

"Baby, what's wrong?" Chance asked Storm as they listened in on the live Jazz band playing.

"Nothing, boo."

"But that's not what your face says," Chance was persistent. "Is something hurting you?" he questioned because she had a look of pain in her expression.

"Well, boo, it's just that I've been a little under the weather. I guess I'm getting sick because I'm throwing up a lot since last week," explained Storm.

"Why didn't you say something? You know I would have taken care of you," he rubs her soft, silky hair.

"I know that, daddy. I'm fine, tonight is all about *your* success, so let's just enjoy," she said. "It's probably gonna be gone by tomorrow," she added as he kissed her softly and Albertus approached with part one of their meal. Chance and Storm were doing big things together and right now, she was finally feeling her happiness.

Now, RJ and Denise were a much different story; they called themselves *just friends,* but trust me…they had crossed over that *hump* and now they were very, very close. RJ had *friends* that he got on with from time to time, but none of which he seriously dated.

He was different with Denise; she brought out the best in that nigga and everyone around him saw it. Denise was also twenty -one year's old, the baby out of five girls and three fucking boys. She was in school at VCU majoring in business with dreams of one day owning her own massage spa. Denise's family had money, and she was a regular daddy's girl; but she was focused and had her shit together. She showed RJ the importance of standing on your own, even though she had everything handed to her, she still knew the importance of a dollar.

It was beginning to get late and their movie had just ended, so after dinner, RJ invited Denise back to the crib to chill. Being that neither Vick nor Rain was home, so he just knew he didn't have to be interrogated.

"You've been here six times and never been inside my crib, baby; if we're going to be more than friends, you have got to stop hiding from my mom," joked RJ as he opened up the front door. "Come on in," he invited, "my little sister's in here somewhere on the phone ," they both begin to laugh as RJ escorted her into the family room to chill. The sound of AAliyah walking around upstairs let him know that she would soon be down. RJ sat there with his arm around Denise as he flicked through the channels on the TV and it seemed like the beginning of a smooth night. That is until all hell broke loose. Everything went left once AAliyah entered the room while still talking on the phone.

"Um, who is this Rico? Mom isn't here and you know how she is about having people over our house."

AAliyah stood there, holding her cellphone with one hand, and her hip with the other. RJ continued to surf the channels, paying her ass no mind until she got in his face.

"Hello, didn't you…" and before she could finish her sentence, he pushed her ass out of his face causing her to fall back onto the floor.

"Uh, uh, nigga…have you lost your fucking mind!" AAliyah screamed. "Don't try to show off for some stupid ass girl who's just playing you," she mouth off in the direction of Denise, popping her neck and moving her head like she was seriously mad. Denise sat there wondering what the fuck was going on.

"Mane, Aaliyah, go ahead now…I'm fucking grown which means that I don't have to answer to you; besides, mom didn't leave your little ass in charge, so you need to get the hell out of my face!" RJ reached for Denise's hand to take her upstairs to his room so that they could be left alone while tuning his sister's ass out.

"That's ok, nigga," she cried as she hung up on whoever she was talking to. "I got your ass right now!" She dialed Donny's number. AAliyah called herself snitching on her brother.

"Baby girl, wassup? What you doing calling this late?" asked Donny, picking up his phone on the first ring.

"Unc, this nigga pushed me and he's got a girl upstairs in his room while mom's not home," she begin to express, but Donny was busy. He realized this was between brother and sister he knew he had to get back to work.

"Baby girl, it's ok, just leave your brother alone; he's grown, but I'll have a talk with him tomorrow," Donny said as Bria storms around the house mad.

"Just go in your room and get some sleep, ok baby? And come by the studio to see me later."

There was a pause between the two and finally AAliyah said her reply, "Alright, Uncle Donny. I love you," she said.

"And you know I love you back," smiled Donny as his facial expression changed once he looked over at Bria. He picked up on her mood that she was pissed as usual, and he and his niece ended their call.

"Wassup, baby?" he walks over toward Bria to kiss her, but she put her hand out in his way, which kind of threw Donny off.

"Don't *wassup* me nigga? I've called you like ten times and of course you never answered," she was flaming, but if things weren't going her way, that's how it usually was.

"Hold up, ma, my phone is in the other room and I was on the crib phone with my niece," Donny explained, "So do you mind telling me what's wrong?"

"What's the fucking point now? I made it the fuck home didn't I?" And that's when he became confused. "Wait…what?" he snapped back. "Where the fuck is your car?" he wanted to know.

"Outside, nigga…damn!" she screamed. "The shit wouldn't start so I had to get it towed the fuck home!" she shouted as she stood tapping her feet. Donny began walking upstairs, this was the second incident involving Bria's car and he wanted to know what was up with that. Bria followed right behind him, still screaming, trying hard to make her point.

"So, now your girl is getting rides in tow trucks and you don't even seem to care?"

"Look, my bad…damn, I was in here working," money was Donny's thing; as usual, Bria's smart ass cut across and he gave her a look of a thousand deaths.

"So…the fuck what! You say that like it's a bad thing," he said, getting tired of her yelling like she was his goddamn mother. "The way your hands are always out…shit, a nigga gotta keep some bread!"

He laughed sarcastically as he lay out across the bed while she stood in shock over the comment he'd just made. She knew he was right so his words struck a nerve and at that point, she knew there wasn't any come back.

"Are you going to get me a rental and put my car in the shop to see what's going on with it?" she asked, trying hard to change the subject at this point."

"I'm already on it, shorty. I just rented it for tomorrow," he said while he used the internet on his phone. Donny's attitude was now on zero which Bria picked up on very fast, *so I guess we can all picture what happen next.* Bria went over to the bed and climbed onto his back as he laid there browsing on Google.

"I'm just stressed, boo; I'm sorry," she was good at being manipulative as she massaged his shoulders and kissed on the back of his neck. Donny asked her to get up so that he could turn over; he wanted to see just how *sorry* she was. With all the money he kicked for her, Donny felt the need to get a little more respect.

She could start by putting her mouth on this dick, he thought in his head as he laid there enjoying all of its pleasure.

Bria allowed his manhood to rest deeply in the back of her throat and she was sucking the skin off that dick. Those big ass Jay-Z lips unfolded around the head of Donny's dick. I swear with each stroke, his eyes got bigger from passion and he was about to explode.

"Oh my God, shit boo, damn!" Donny didn't know what to say, that shit was good and he showed her just how well she was doing as he filled her mouth with hot and steamy watermelon. You can call that shit milkshake the way Bria drunk it all up; for a prissy lil bitch, you could tell she got down.

Donny was turned on now, so you know he spent the rest of the night dipping inside of some chocolate pussy. But if she thought for a second she was off the hook at this point, that bitch was totally wrong. Her trap was right around the corner, shit you thought you'd left behind, will sometimes find its way back to you.

*****

The days and nights went on and on. I swear time had a 747 jet because that shit was moving and Rain was having the time of her life. She enjoyed being there so much that she talked to Vick about maybe getting some property out there, "We should open up a lil bed and breakfast out this muthafucka, baby," suggested Rain as she laid in Vick's arms rubbing his chest as the morning breeze made its way through the doors and Vick's Michael Jordan cologne filled the room.

"It is a beautiful place, momma. I really don't want to leave tomorrow, but if you're serious…" Vick pauses and kisses her on the top of her head as he smelled her long, pretty, black hair. "I'll make that happen for you, and then we can spend more time chilling out this bitch." They both began to laugh.

When it came to Rain, Vick lived by the saying, *You can have whatever you like*, so much that him and Rain would have been perfect for TI's video.

After admiring each other's comfort for a few moments more, the lovely couple decided to get up and get dressed so they could head outside for breakfast and then it was on to get massages. Vick and Rain lay enjoying each other inside of a black hammock on the beach. He fed her all types of exotic fruits and grapes while the Villa staff prepared a gourmet breakfast for two. It was obvious the level of affection that Vick and Rain shared; no matter what they were doing, even watching TV, they just couldn't keep their hands off each other and that always led up to sex.

They both crushed the fuck out their food: T-bone steaks, eggs over easy, waffles (the fully-loaded Belgian kind), and fried potatoes with onions and green peppers; damn, they had their very own buffet. Vick had no choice but to eat himself silly, especially being that he was slightly hung-over from the night before, but nothing could take his attention away from Rain and you know he got his shit together quick.

After a wonderful breakfast and massage, Rain's body felt great and she wanted nothing more to do then take a nap. Vick wanted to take her out instead to enjoy their last day on the island and he's always wanted to go Jet skiing but never took the time out to do it. *What better way than to do it now*, he thought and since Rain had been to the Island a million times before with Rico, Vick decided to make her million and one time his first.

The water was crystal blue and beautiful as the 5:00 p.m. sun rays shined through the thick, pretty white clouds as Rain and Vick suited up in their gear; ready to go. They listened in as the instructor explained the rules to riding and showed them just how far to go out.

Vick's adrenaline rushed as the excitement of doing something for the first time in his life came into play. He was honored to share this experience with none other than his first lady, Rain. They had the time of their life Jet Skiing with the Dolphins and that shit was much better to do then to just watch being done. Mane, that nigga, Vick, didn't regret any of it. Rain had so much fun that her hair got fucked up and she didn't even bitch about it. Nothing could have destroyed that very special moment with her man and as far as she was concerned. From this moment on, everything they did was to make memories.

Yarning for some sleep since earlier, Rain really was tired as fuck now, but there wasn't any way they were going to miss out on the night festival taking place in town, so her and Vick went and got ready.

Rain was stunning in her all-white Michael Kors high-low hemline gown with diamond accessories, even down to her shoes; she rocked the Christian Louboutin which is Rain's favorite designer. She wore silver and grey diamond cusp with the clutch bag to match, not that she needed one, but it looked great with her dress and you know Rain had to have the best. She styled her hair in an exotic Chinese pin-up which brought out her sexy ass facial features, making Vick want to undress her before they could even leave the Villa. Rain just laughed, brushing him off until later because for now, it was time to party. The limo escorted the way through the city as they both seemed overjoyed to celebrate with the people of Bora Bora, along with a few choice celebrities. It turned out to be more people than they expected, but even that couldn't bring it all to an end. They all danced and mingled the night away, making business contacts as well. Rain was serious about transitioning over there, so anybody she thought could give advice, my girl was damn sure all ears.

As Rain set at the table waiting for Vick to return with her drink, a tap on the shoulder from a tall, dark-skinned nigga caught her by surprise as she wonder what he wanted. He stood there staring at her with creepy eyes, making Rain feel uncomfortable. Finally, she asked the mutherfucker if he needed something, but that wasn't enough, because he still never uttered a word.

He kept right on looking and finally he said, "You look familiar, have we met somewhere before," the guy asked Rain, but she couldn't understand how that could be.

"Excuse me?" she replied back with a look of confusion on her face and she continued, "I think you've got the wrong person because I'm not even from here," she expressed, hoping that that was enough to make him walk away, but the nigga kept on giving her a survey.

"Are you sure? You look some like my cousin's wife, but I haven't seen her in years. Oh, by the way, my name is Clover…" but before he could finish up walked Vick. He stepped right in between Rain and the strange guy who seemed to have put a frown on his wife's face; and judging from his observation, she was already pissed.

"And who might you be again, sir?" Vick stood strong and firm, ready to fuck a nigga up.

"My name is Clover," he tried to explain again, but was soon cut short from the king.

"And ok, nigga, why you all in my wife's personal space?" he said in reference to him standing too close.

"I thought that she was somebody I know, sir. Ma'am," he leans his head around Vick to face Rain, "I'm terribly sorry for my mix up. You two have a wonderful night." He walks off through the crowd on the beach.

They both turned to face each other as they headed back toward their table and sit down.

"That's fucking wired," said Vick as he took his two shots of Patron to the head. Rain still sat there with that same blank look on her face, it was shit like that that she definitely didn't play with.

"It's good, boo. I got you and ain't no mutherfuckin' body gonna ever hurt you again," he assured her as she began to smile. "See…there goes my queen!" he said, walking over to her with his hand out. "Let's get out of here," suggested Vick, "I've got something to calm your nerves down," he smiled with a sexy and seductive grin and Rain knew just what time it was. She took him by the hand, heading straight back to their Villa to *calm down* (wink)!

Vick must have been doing some real serious shit to Rain on the way back to their Villa because he couldn't even open the door without them tonguing each other down as he held on to Rain's phat ass with one hand and inserting the blue key card into the door of the Villa with the other. Inside the room, mutherfuckin' clothes flew off everywhere as they both undressed each other, but my bitch, Rain, kept on her ten-inch Loubatins. That's all she had on, revealing that caramel-brown body that Vick dreamed about all day. He couldn't wait to explore each and every inch of her.

"Our last night in paradise is going to be one to remember," he whispered in her ear while picking her up off her feet, holding her in mid-air right at his mouth. Vick placed her back up against the wall while putting his big hands underneath her apple ass for leverage. He pulled that pussy close to his mouth and stuffed his face nice and slow into it. He instructed Rain to wrap her pumps around his neck and she did as she was told, locking him in and now his dessert was served. Vick took his tongue and licked around her clit nice and slow, making slurps from her hot, wet and steamy juices that were starting to run from the soft touch of his lips.

He then sucked that pearl like a lollipop and Rain loved every moment of it. She arched her back, pushing her pussy almost down his throat if she could have. Vick inserts his tongue inside that nice, tight pussy that was always the same size from when he last was there, and he knew that pussy was his. His tongue fucked Rain so deep, you could have sworn he touched an ovulary as the touch of his mouth organ tickled on her G-spot made her squirt all over his face as he partook in her flavor all the way down to the last drop.

"Come on, boo," he said, now carrying Rain in his arms, heading straight to the Jacuzzi where he wanted to heat things up; not that he needed to it one bit, Rain's pussy was still dripping wet because she wanted more and Vick damn sure was about to give it to her.

Vick stepped down into the Jacuzzi, placing Rain on top of the seated bench. He then stood in front of her face so that she could have a little fun with Monster and that's exactly what she did as she softly folded those medium-sized lips around the head of her husband's dick. She sucked on it lightly, and tickled the hole with her tongue at the same damn time; mane, these two were showing off tonight.

Rain took in all ten inches of that dick and I mean Vick's shit had length and thickness to it, so Rain got the best of both worlds. All it took was six little strokes.

"God damn, Rain…ok, you win," he whispered and she could feel Vick's dick began to throb and swell. She knew what time it was and stopped. Rain wanted to fuck real bad at this point, and she wanted Monster standing tall in salute just like he was.

She whispered to Vick,

"Fuck me."

He smiled, ready to conquer the challenge at hand.

Vick slid down into the Jacuzzi behind Rain, positioning her pussy hole within angle of his dick. He slowly pushed his way inside her tight opening. Bending her further down, leaning over the edge of the Jacuzzi, with her bottom still in bubbly water. The pressure from her pussy farting as he long dicked her womanhood, seemed to cause some bubbles by its self as she gasped.

"Oh, daddy, no one can fuck me like you Vick. Don't stop please," she begged.

Vick lifted her leg up on his arm and he went in deeper. While the stretching of his dick inside her wet canal made Rain's body tighten around him, she fell into his embrace. She moaned softly as he nibbled on her ear while continuing to stroke that pussy then he stops and Rain could've died when he did that. Vick picked her up, carrying her over to their built-in patio, laying her down on the beautiful Italian white carpet and opening her legs wide enough to get home.

Vick then reinserted Monster back into Rain's now runny pussy, as he slow stroked to adjust to its snug fit and inside, which felt like heaven. His facial expression showed just that, turning Rain on more and she showed it to as her body began to tingle and jerk. Vick fucked the shit out of her. With one hand holding up her leg and the other he moved his finger skillfully over her clit; every electrifying sensation released from her body drove her bananas, causing a craving for Vick to give her more. He did, over and over again. He pulled her closer to him, thrusting deeply as he groaned.

"Oh shit, boo…I'm about to explode. Damn, daddy's gonna put a baby in you tonight with this one," he said as his speed increased with excitement.

"Ahh, shit, Rain," Vick's moans grew louder and with Rain joining him, you'd think they were recording a song. They both reached their peak at the same time, him squirting into her pussy his hot steamy cum as Rain let out all she had to offer on top of that dick, and I think he fucked the life out of her. The rounds continued that night, so much so that they fell asleep together with Vick's dick still inside of her, and that, ladies and gentlemen, is how you make LOVE!...Damn.

CHAPTER 2

Sightless eyes

"Aight Skillz, that was good, but let's try it again, starting from, "All my life, these fucking streets was my daddy," instructed Donny as he worked on laying Skillz's verse for the song while he waited on Main's arrival. Donny heard that Main's rap skills were tight, so he set up a session at D-Nyce studio, with promises to make him rich if he was any good and being a bouncer at Club Benji's would become history for him. When Donny and Keyz put their mind together, they are bound to make history because the two of them together were smart as shit. They continued to work hard when the door buzzer sounded off, it was Main's crazy ass and he was hungry to make that paper.

Malik "Main" Washington was born and raised in Richmond, Virginia, straight from the hood of Highland Park. In the early '90s, he was running shit. He and his goons had a say so over all territories and Main was getting money. It didn't last long because some hating ass niggas tried to set him up to be killed; but instead, Main murdered them bitches and ended up doing ten years in the federal prison. That caused him to lose everything and everybody that said they had his back; shit, even his girlfriend walked away.

Now Main's out, and he has to start over so that bouncer gig at the club came right on time because it wasn't no way his big, tall ass was going to work in McDonalds, so he was determined to catch a lick.

"Wassup, my nigga?"

They slapped Main some dap as Skillz nodded his head from the booth. "You ready for this, kid? I heard you were a beast," said Donny handing Main a drink.

"Look here, my nigga…I was born ready, that's all I did in prison was write rhymes," Main began to enlighten them, "that shit kept me sane."

They all began to laugh and agree as he showed Main where he could have a seat and informed him to get ready because it was almost show time for him.

* * * * *

Immediately, Main pulled out his rhyme book and started reciting his bars to himself, while Donny got back to work. Not even a good fifteen minutes later, the buzzer goes off again and Donny checked the cameras to find out that it was Bria.

"Hey, baby," she greeted him as she made her entrance with a hug and kiss and you know he palmed that ass good.

"Wassup, lil momma?" said Keyz, throwing his hand up in gesture.

"Oh, where are my manners?" said Donny as he turns to walk Bria over to the back. "Hey, baby, this is my newest artist, Main, but we gone call him Mango."

Main lifted his head up from reading over his rap, and at that moment, he knew karma existed as he locked eyes with the girl who left him high and dry—Bria.

"Wassup, shorty?" he smiled as she all of a sudden felt nauseous, waving her hand and telling Donny she need to go to the bathroom as she turns and runs out.

"Excuse my girlfriend, bruh, I've told her ass about trying all that different food with her friends and later she always pays for it," Donny laughs, but Main just smirked; he couldn't believe that shit was working out this good.

"I think I need to go to the restroom myself, dog; where is it at?" he asked as Donny told him where to find it while he finished everything up with Keyz. As Bria was coming out, Main was walking right in her direction and you know that nigga had to stop to say something.

"Long time, no see stranger, I bet you never thought our paths would cross again. So, you can imagine my surprise when I found out that my producer's girlfriend is also my goddamn girl!" he laughed, trying hard to touch on her, but she jerks away.

"Your girlfriend?! Main, please…your ass was gone for ten fucking years," Bria whispers making sure Donny couldn't hear her. "I made no visits, I didn't write you or anything after the first two years; so, that right there, nigga, should have told you I was done."

Bria and Main had been dating for six years before he got locked up, and it was clear that they were very much in love, *or so he thought*, but the way it seems now looking back, Bria was in love with his money and lavish lifestyle, so when that all ended she just dipped.

At one point in time, Main was her world, and she would have done anything to make him happy. A part of Bria still had feelings for him; shit, I mean they split up with an open wound. The other part of her was happy with Donny now, but when it came to Main, there was always guilt.

"So, that's how you gone try and do me, when you're the one who left me hanging?" Main said as she proceeded to walk away, "you owe me, Bria. So I don't think that this is it, and if you don't want your new rich man to find out about us, your best bet is to play along!" he shouted as she opened the door to the studio heading back in with Donny. "See you soon," Main smiled as he goes right in and takes his piss.

"Baby, I've got to go," Bria nervously expressed as she grabbed her Jimmy Choo bag to leave.

"Ok, baby, are you alright?" Donny questioned because she looked as if she'd seen a ghost and in reality she just had, but he just wasn't dead. Bria knew some shit might go down if she didn't play along with Main's motives.

"I'm good, boo, my stomach is just upset so I'm gonna go home and try to rest."

She kisses him on those soft, manly lips, just as Main walks back in.

"You leaving the party so soon?" he joked with his eyes locked in on hers. Bria shakes her head, *yes.* "Well, it was nice meeting you, Mrs. Lady. I'm sure we'll meet again," Main smiles and walks into the back. Bria was so upset that she couldn't take anymore, so she turns, hug, Donny and left.

Main couldn't believe how his luck was working out. *Maybe coming back up won't be so hard after all,* he said to himself. *That bitch gone run me a couple of stacks, so each time she collect, I will too.*

Meanwhile, Bria made it to the house ok. She pours a glass of wine and sits down to think.

"What the fuck am I going to do? This muthafucka can ruin everything for me," she began to tear up in fear. "Maybe I should just tell Donny the truth," she picks up her phone to text him.

Baby, we really need to talk.

Bria sent, not knowing Donny wasn't around his phone. He had left it on the table in the back with Main and when the message came through Main saw it.

"This bitch must be crazy," he said as he read Donny's text. After erasing it, he saved Bria's number in his phone and then he sent her a text back from his phone.

Your man is busy right now, but your other man got the message, and before you say anything to Donny about us, I think you would want to meet me first. 9:00 at the Kroker Spot. Be there and if you're not, then worry about him finding out everything. R51 q

Main threatened in his text, and as Bria read it, she knew he was speaking the truth of what he would do. At this point she had to go.

I'll be there.

She texted back, throwing her phone next to her on the bed. As she sat and broke down in cries, she wondered how this nightmare could've found her after so many years. But whatever it took to keep Donny as her man, Bria was prepared to do it.

It had now been four weeks since Storm told Chance that she wasn't feeling well and shit still hadn't seemed to change. Lately, Chance's time became slim to none; he blamed it all on his two shops. Storm noticed that for the past couple of weeks, he had been getting home later and later each day; but she thought nothing of it because she was smart, she did things in her own time and jumping to conclusions wasn't her style.

If found out otherwise, a nigga would definitely get dealt with, but with Chance, she wanted it to be forever. "Ja'Nay Peters," she finally heard her name being called by the nurse after sitting in the waiting room for so long. Storm followed her down the hall and into room three, where she explained the reason for her visit.

"I kind of think I got a stomach virus or food poison because it's been four weeks and I can't keep anything down," said Storm and you know what question came next.

"When was your last menstrual and is there any chance you could be pregnant?" Nurse Kerry asked, almost causing Storm to fall off the table.

"Hell naw. Excuse me…I mean, no, ma'am," Storm elaborated, "I just went off my period three days ago and I haven't missed one yet."

Nurse Kerry told her, "Get undressed from the waist down," as she handed Storm a specimen cup to fill with urine so that they could run some test and find out what's wrong.

"Knock, knock, Ms. Peters," Doctor Bradley enters the room ready to give Storm her diagnosis. "How are you feeling, Ms. Peters?"

"I'm good," she replied. "I'll be even better once you make this pain go away," the look on her face showed that she was really serious.

"Unfortunately, Ms. Peters, abdominal pain is very common in the first stages of pregnancy," Doctor Bradley revealed those words as Storm felt like what he was saying was some kind of joke.

"Are you fucking serious, Doctor Bradley? All this fucking time I've been knocked up?" she said, shaking her head as she cried real hard.

"My estimates show that you're closer to six weeks, but because you haven't missed your cycle, I want things to be accurate. I'm going to schedule you to come back for an ultrasound," he explained and after checking to see if she had any more questions, Doctor Bradley told her she could get dressed.

Storm sat outside in the car for a moment as she tried to collect her thoughts. With everything going on in her life right now, Storm thought a baby would slow her up.

"Hey, baby, where you at?" asked Storm at the sound of Chance saying hello on the other end of her cell phone.

"I'm in Chesterfield at the new shop, is everything ok?"

"No, not really. It depends on how you take it, but I don't want to talk over the phone," she expressed as her voice became weak again causing Chance to feel that something was up.

"Ok, I'll meet you at home in an hour," he said and they expressed their love and said goodbye. Storm stopped at CVS to put in her prescriptions, all she wanted at this point was to be home.

See mane, already a bitch is lazy and this is only the beginning, she thought as the song "Sister" from the movie *The Color Purple* played loudly on her phone. Storm really needed hers right now.

"Hello," she says, ready to break down again when her sister's phone is finally answered.

"Hey, sissy, what you doing?" asked Rain and at that moment Storm couldn't hold on to her tears any longer and her emotions came out in her words.

"I'm pregnant, sis," she blurted out, causing her sister to drop her phone. "Oh shit, wait…" Rain picks it up smiling. "Ja'Nay, are you really serious right now?" she asked and she was happy for her sister's great news. "Nay?" No response. "Ja'Nay Peters?"

"What sis?" she finally yelled out. "I don't know what to say."

"Well, it sounds like you're not happy about this and if you don't mind can I ask why not," Rain questioned. "This is a blessing from God and it's not like we can't afford another mouth to feed, sis, so what is it that has you stressing out?"

"Well, for starters, I haven't had the chance to tell Chance yet, and I don't know what he's going to say," Storm continued to cry and her sister tried to shed some light on the situation.

She knew her sister was just over reacting. "He's going to love it, sis. Don't worry, I promise everything's going to be alright. Vick and I want y'all to come over tonight and I'm going to cook you something to eat."

Storm agreed and they hung up. Storm got her meds and dipped so that she could get home to meet up with Chance.

*****

"Babe!" shouted Chance as he slammed the door behind him, walking into the den where Storm was asleep. He stood at the doorway watching her look so peaceful as she lay balled up on the couch. "Wake up, boo," he kisses her softly, causing her eyes to open up and seeing his face made Storm immediately break down.

"What's wrong, my lady?" he said as he hugged her tightly, trying hard to get her to calm down.

"Boo, I'm pregnant," she murmured with her mouth down on his shirt but Chance still heard what she had said.

"You are, boo?" he sat her up to face him as he wipes away her tears and she shook her head, *yes*.

"So stop all that crying it's not the end of the world," expressed Chance as his face lit up like it was Christmas.

"Baby, I didn't know if you were ready to be a father," she stressed that fact and Chance's reactions went from happy to very uneasy. He went to say something, but instead, he took a real long pause.

"What, baby? What is it?" asks Storm, but Chance just brushed that statement off.

"It's nothing, baby. I get it, but to answer your question, yes, I'm ready to be the father of your baby," he expressed, but he still had a worried look sitting on his face and Storm didn't have a clue what was coming.

Rain had already called Donny and the rest of the family to inform them of the news and you know that they all were very happy. She decided to invite everyone over for dinner to celebrate, but of course everyone had something to do. Donny couldn't make it, he was working late, but he did indeed send his congratulations and said he'd be by tomorrow. RJ and Denise went to Virginia Beach for the weekend; he was now going to meet her family at their family reunion. AAliyah was at cheerleading practice, and from there, she was staying the night at Ry'qual—her best friend's—house, so tonight it would be just the four.

"Got it smelling good up in here, sis in law," announced Chance, as he and Storm walked into the house heading straight for the kitchen,

"Hey, baby, I hope y'all ready to eat," Rain laughed at Chance as he stood there rubbing his belly as a sign.

"Aww, come here," she said, walking over toward her sister, kissing her cheek and rubbing her belly at the same time. "We're having a baby," she did the happy dance and Storm let out the first laugh she did all day. Chance stood there smiling as Vick handed him a beer.

"Let me holla at you, lil bruh," asked Vick as they headed outside on the patio to talk.

"Wassup, Bruh?" Chance put his arm around his brother, "What's on your mind?" he asked.

"You tell me, Chingy. Do you even know what the fuck you're doing?" Vick pushes away as Chance wonders what he's referring to because the only time he calls him *Chingy* is when he's mad.

"What you talking about, bruh?" he still played dumb so Vick went ahead and said it for his ass.

"How the fuck you gone have a baby with Ja'Nay and you haven't even told her about your son?" the question was out and that's why Chance froze up to Storm earlier that night.

"I know that shit already, big bruh. Shit, I almost slipped up earlier," he releases some stress, finally sharing how he felt toward it. "If I tell Storm now, she's going to leave me B. I know I should have been honest with her in the beginning," he was scared. He didn't expect their relations to move from business to pleasure as fast as it did and now he'd really fucked up.

"You need to fix this quick, Chingy. I mean that shit, before it blows up in your face and Lizette finds out, because you know that she will tell Storm." Vick wasn't playing, he knew that if that shit did come out badly that it would get his wife involved and he already knew what to expect if that should happen. When involving her family, she would return back to her old life and murder quick. Chance continued to listen as Vick tried to talk some sense into him, than finally, it was time to eat. They heard Rain's voice call out, so they all gathered to bless the food.

The rest of the night went smoothly, Storm even began to lighten up and smile. *Maybe being pregnant wasn't going to be so bad after all*, she thought as she watched the family all having a good time. Chance was acting like a proud father on the outside, but inside, he was scared shitless. He didn't know how he was going to tell Storm about his son, but however he decides to do it, he'd better do it soon!

I can't believe I'm sitting in this bitch waiting on this nigga, thought Bria as she texted Main's phone to let him know she was there and this nigga replies, *me too*. Bria looks around to see if she spots him, and damn sure…he was coming, walking over toward her from the bar.

"On time, I like that in my girl," said Main as he slid into the booth positing himself right in front of Bria and smiling.

"How did you know when I got here before I texted you?" she asked, "and I'm not your fucking girl!" she said, making sure to correct his ass.

"Girl, I been here since 8:00 p.m." Main kept smiling, knowing he was pissing her off and the ball was definitely in his court.

"Ok, Main…I'm here, let's get down to business. What the fuck do you want?" she angrily asked and knowing Main, it was going to be fucked up.

"Why the rush, sweetheart? I have not seen you in like ten years. I mean… damn, can two old friends catch up?" he said as the waiter walks over to get their order.

"Let me get a shot of Patron and a Heineken," said Main, "and oh, she'll have a Strawberry Daiquiri."

This nigga is a trip. I know he ain't just order for me, thought Bria as she sat silently shaking her head.

"Ok, sir, can I interest you two in something to eat as well?" the waiter asked, and Bria knew Main's big ass sure did. I swear the more he ate, it all went to his muscles.

"Yea, let me get a Fish Boat."

It was the best fucking fish meal in Richmond and Bria knew she wanted some of that shit, but she wasn't eating because the sight of Main really made her stomach cringe.

"Look, Main…I don't know why you ordered all that stuff, nigga; we ain't on no goddamn date!"

That was enough. Main felt like his good gesture was being unnoticed and Main fuckin' snapped.

"Bitch, please…you played me," he said, leaning in toward her, speaking in a whisper. "I gave you everything that I fuckin' had; the majority of my money went on your gold digging ass, so don't sit in here trying to get all uppity with me," he was mad and hurt at the way this chick was acting and the more she showed attitude it pissed him off. Bria's ass had nothing to say because she knew she was wrong and now the time had come to pay Karma.

"You're going to sit here and eat with me until I'm ready to give you my terms," demanded Main as the waiter came over with their order. Bria picked and picked over her share of the Fish Boat, but Main, on the other hand, straight crushed.

"Damn, that was good," Main bucks his beer while rubbing his stomach because he was full. Bria, as usual, sat their quiet; sipping on her daiquiri. The thought to leave kept crossing her mind, but just as she went to speak he interrupted her thoughts.

"Well, Ms. Bria, I must say it was nice having dinner with you."

This nigga was crazy; Bria hadn't said a word in almost an hour, so what made him think she would now talk.

"I see you still not going to say nothing so I'm going to treat you like you're acting," expressed Main and Bria saw his mood change up. I want twenty-five hundred a week from you, bitch, until I say that's enough."

"Main, nigga…you must be crazy if you're thinking I'm giving you that kind of money," she laughed at his stupidity. "I'll tell my man myself first," Bria said, but Main still felt like he still had her right where he wanted her.

"That's cool, Bria if you want to take that route, but make sure you tell him you're a killer."

Here comes the boom and Bria felt it smack her face when she heard Main bring that up. She began to choke.

"What's the matter, cat got your tongue?" he smirked as the tears came rolling down Bria's face.

"You know what happened—the truth, Main," she pounds her fist on the table, "so why would you bring that up?"

"Because I felt you needed a reminder, Bria. Don't fuck with me!" he threatens, giving her ass a stern look.

"But it's your fought that I'm involved in that shit and now you wanna act all innocent!" she argued back, but he didn't care; he still had the facts that if they got out, could ruin Bria's ass period.

"Look here, honey…that may be true, but don't forget, I'm the only one with proof," he slid out the booth to leave, but stopped to say, "starting the first of the month, girl, I want my money or you can kiss your man and freedom goodbye." He walks off leaving Bria sitting there in tears and to pay for all their food, he's a dirty bitch.

What the fuck is going on and who is Bria really? she thought about herself now that Main brought up a dark past that she had buried, and if it got out, life as she knew it would become deceased!

*****

A man can find love with a woman many times in his life, but the magic of feeling the love for that special one for the first time will be a blessed experience he'll remember for an eternity and RJ had been bit by the bug.

"Did you have fun tonight, boo" RJ asked as he walked Denise up to her hotel room door.

"Yes, I did Rico, it's always fun when I'm with you," she expressed, still trying to hold back on her feelings because neither of them wanted to mess up their friendship. RJ took his hands and placed them on each side of her cheek and pulled her face in closer. He tongued Denise ass down, making that pussy want him even more.

"Let me say goodnight now," she said, "or I will be giving up some pussy tonight."

Denise was a virgin and she'd always said only that special one would get her cookies. RJ smiled while walking backwards toward his door, he didn't want Denise out of his sight. He felt good doing something outside of his normal family routine; plus, meeting her family was a good move for him because this time he felt she was the one.

The next morning, or should I say afternoon, RJ was awakened from the sound of Denise's Uncle Bobby banging on the door letting him know it was time to interact.

"Come on, young fellow," he spoke through the door. "It's time for the men to play some ball and you, young man, I picked for my team."

Because of his height, everyone picked him first.

"Ok, Uncle Bobby, give me ten minutes," he begins to get out of bed so that he could get himself together. When RJ got outside, all of Denise's uncles, cousins, and brothers stood in the parking lot outside as they argued over who was riding with who.

"Good morning, handsome," a familiar voice said from behind.

"Hey, I know that sound anywhere," he smiles and turns around to see Denise as she walks up and gives him a big wet kiss, causing RJ to want to join her inside of her room. All of a sudden, he heard his name being called as the sound of Denise's brother, Tre, yelling telling him to come on.

"You're riding with me, bruh," he said as RJ gave his baby another kiss and was out.

Now remember, I told you Denise's family had money, but what they don't know is that RJ's family does too and he never told her about his family's past. All Denise knows is that his dad was murdered but he never, ever, revealed the details of how it happened. He'd always say, "I don't want to talk about it" and she'd just leave it alone. He also only told her about their restaurant and salon in Richmond and Georgia. She didn't care, so no research was done, all she knew was that she was in love and she was becoming sightless!

"Mom, you really look beautiful today," said Legally, Denise's elder sister and the suck-up one out of the group; she made it her business to be noticed by their mom at least once a day.

"Thank you, dear," Gloria expressed as she sipped her glass of Champagne as they all enjoyed pedicures.

"So, Denise my dear…you're the shining star this weekend with your new male friend and all," she said to her daughter as Denise sat up forward in her seat.

"Thank you, momma I'm really falling for him and I think I may have found the one," she said, blushing hard as a bitch and of course Legally and Tiara started to stare her down. For some reason, them two sisters hated on Denise the most, and it might have something to do with the bond she shared with her father.

David, Denise's dad, owned a lot of stocks and bonds he invested in, he did so much that this man gets checks in the mail every day. David had a nasty ass attitude toward the rest of his girls, but Denise could get anything that she wanted out of him. He never raised his voice at her and he always flashed her around. David is always out of town on business, so he hasn't had the honor of meeting, or even hearing about RJ yet. All of Denise's other sisters could date, but not Denise's ass; she had rules. She had to stay a virgin until her father gave his blessing at her wedding and to me that shit sounds twisted.

Denise also wasn't very close to her mom and as a wife looking in she acted like David and Denise were more.

"Leave her alone and stop looking at her like that you guys," Charity and Rena, her other sister, began to protest. Despite what mother and their other sisters thought, they felt like family meant love. "I'm so happy for you sis," Charity said.

"Yes, we both are, so let's just enjoy this pedicure and go, I'm getting hungry now," Rena expressed.

"Plus, your father should be here soon," Gloria cut in that made Denise's heart beat fast.

"Wassup, mom?" said an out-of-breath RJ as he answered his phone.

"Hey, son…when will you be back home?" Rain questioned her child.

"Tomorrow, mom; I'm chilling though, I just got back from playing ball with her fam," he explained taking off his sneakers and white tee.

"That's good, baby. Well, I'm not going to hold you up alright, I just miss you. I need to see your face."

She loved her kids.

"I miss you too. I'll see you at the crib tomorrow," he gives her his love as he hung up the phone to get ready. They were all meeting for dinner at 8:00 p.m. and he was about to meet her dad.

RJ sat patiently in his car changing CDs, while he waited for Denise to come down. A tap on his window startled him and it was her other brother DJ. David Jr. was the eldest of the boys. He, Tre, and Sharod were very, very close and they looked up to their dad as a superhero sometimes, but they too wondered why it was always about Denise.

"Scared you huh, lil nigga?" joked DJ. "Never let no one catch you slipping."

They both began to laugh as DJ tried passing RJ the blunt. Instead of taking it, he refused. "A non-smoker? I can dig that, lil nigga," DJ began to choke from the weed.

"Mane, I used to, but I gave that shit all up," he said noticing Denise and Charity coming down to the car as DJ tried to tell him something.

"My dad isn't that bad," DJ said as he pushes RJ's shoulder, "but I don't know how he's going to feel about you and Denise dating."

"What you mean?" RJ cut in. According to Denise, she'd dated before, but because she wasn't having sex the nigga just dumped her.

"My little sister never dated anyone and she damn sure never brought them home to meet dad," he expressed and RJ felt like this was a trap when he heard them words, but just as he went to speak, the passenger side door opened and Denise got in.

"Hey, boo, you looking good," Denise expressed with a smile.

RJ, still in shock, just grinned, "You look sexy too, boo," he expressed as DJ, Charity, and Charity's husband Josh, got in the car behind them and they all just pulled off.

The family decided to meet at the Terrapin Restaurant in Virginia Beach and boy wasn't it a very nice choice. Everyone else was already inside as they arrived.

"Wait, let me fix you up, boo," she said, straightening the top of his Gucci button up, but his reaction wasn't what she expected as he jerked away.

"I got it," he said with anger in his voice. He fixed his shirt and headed to the table as Denise followed behind him confused. Just as she went to utter a word, the waves of her family stopped her.

"Hello, daddy," said Denise as she walked up giving David a hug and kiss and it seemed like he didn't want to let her go as all the family stared.

"Come on now, honey," Gloria reached for her husband's arm, "you didn't even hug me that long," she played it off as a joke, but she saw the look that David gave her and tried to re-adjust her meaning.

"Denise has a surprise for you," Gloria was being mischievous; she knew that RJ would make David flip. Denise wanted to smack the shit out her for that, somehow she always managed to hate on her.

"Daddy, this is Rico, my friend; but actually it's becoming a little more than that," she explained with her eyes locked in with RJ's in a daze; plus, she was afraid to look at her damn dad.

"Rico, huh?" David's deep voice rang out.

"Yes, sir, it's a pleasure," Rico showed his manners, but David's rude ass didn't show his.

"Are you two fucking yet?" David cut right to the chase and he knew that it wasn't the right time.

"Excuse me, Daddy, but your out of line," addressed Denise. "That's inappropriate to ask either one of us right here," she spoke up firmly for the first time. I guess being with RJ was making her feel free because she knew that someone outside of her family would really care for her and her dad wasn't the only one that could show her what she thought was love.

"Denise Nichole Whitehouse, have you lost your fuckin' mind? I'm your father, you owe me your fuckin' life," David's tone raised.

"Daddy, I'm not trying to be disrespectful," she said with RJ just sitting there heated. After what DJ had just said to him and now this shit right here was whack and he felt like something fishy was going on.

"Alright you two," Gloria was satisfied. "Let's just enjoy our dinner."

But RJ couldn't do that, the family he came from spoke their mind to each other.

"Excuse me, I'm not hungry now," RJ said, getting up to leave from the table.

"Have a seat, young man," David boasts with authority, but now this nigga had the game fucked up. RJ just smiled.

"With all due respect, sir, my father died years ago and like I said, I'm not hungry. So excuse me," RJ turns and walks off as Denise attempts to leave behind him.

"Denise, get back here now," David swiped over his glass drawing attention of the other guest in the restaurant. "You belong to me, get back over here with your father," he continue to use force as Gloria and her sisters were pissed. Here was David again acting like Denise was everything and damn he did have the rest of them sitting there.

Denise gave him back one of the sourest looks I've ever seen and for once she did the unexpected.

"Not this time," she turns and runs out the restaurant leaving shock on every one's face.

"RJ, wait," Denise ran behind him as he walked very fast up ahead, but she continue to chase and call out his name.

"RJ, please wait up, boo," she said, running out of breath, but she finally touched the back of his shirt.

"What, mane…I'm out!" he yelled. "Fuck this shit. I'm good on the drama for real," he looks up in to the ceiling, staring at the lights inside the parking garage as he paced back and forth getting heated.

"Boo, I'm sorry; please listen," she tried pleading.

"Mane, Denise, I can't trust you dog. Wassup with all the shit I've found out since we've been down the beach," RJ wasn't use to this type of shit.

"Keep it real with me and I will with you." *Can't trust no snake*, he could hear his mom's voice saying, and right now, Denise and her secret keeping wasn't playing by the rules of the game.

"Ok, RJ," the hard cries and sniffles from her runny nose is what you heard as RJ makes a face to say, *I'm listening*.

"It's a lot of things that you don't know about me and I haven't been totally honest," she began to explain.

"I think I should start from the beginning."

They stood there talking as Denise began to break down with every word. She couldn't believe she was finally talking about all of this. She never had the opportunity to tell anyone what was really inside her head, but RJ showed Denise different. She wanted to know more of what that *different* really felt like and she wasn't about to lose it over her dad. RJ was furious from what Denise was telling him so far, but before she could get deep into the roots of her problem and explain to him what was really happening, Rain's ringtone on his cellphone interrupted them.

"Hey, mom, can I call you right back?" asked RJ, but he realized his mother was crying.

"Aaliyah's been in a car accident. I need you to come home now!" she cried as RJ took off running to his car and Denise followed.

"Mom, I'm on my way. Is she alright?" he asked as the skid marks he made from how fast he swerved the corners left a trail out the parking garage and he lost his call from no service.

"Mane, fuck!" RJ was doing eighty miles per hour in a fifty-five mile per hour zone. He slammed his fist on the steering wheel as he continued to drive; not saying a word to Denise who finally asked if he was ok.

He answered her, "My little sister has been in a car accident and I've got to get home fast," he explained as Rain called his cellphone back.

"Yo, mom, what happen? What's good?" he was scared, but as Rain began to talk, her voice was a little bit more at ease as she told him the call dropped and what was going on.

"She just got out of surgery; hurry up, RJ."

He told her he was on his way.

Denise sent a text to Rena to tell her what was going on and to ask if she could please get their stuff. RJ didn't care; all he wanted to do was get to his sister, so Denise had to be put to a later date.

"Mom!" called out RJ as he ran down the hall and spotted his family. He requested to see his sister as Rain took him back there and Denise sat in the waiting room with everyone else. The tears were flowing way before he even walked inside the room; all he wanted to do was see Aaliyah's face. RJ needed to know that she was ok; since their argument the other night, they hadn't really talked, and he wanted to tell her that he loved her.

"Peanut!" he called out as he saw her sitting there in the hospital bed, doing crossword puzzles while her leg was up in a cast. The accident had caused the cartilage in her knee to shift, so she had to have surgery to insert a small pin into her knee.

"Hey, big bruh…bout time you got here," she joked as they held each other tight like they had just met.

"I love you, sis and I'm sorry. You mean everything to me," he expressed and Aaliyah told him she was sorry as well. They knew just how strong their love was for each other and it was all they had when their mom was gone. RJ spent the rest of the night chilling with his sister, forgetting all about Denise for right now, but he would definitely get back to her ass.

After getting home from the hospital, Storm wanted to go to bed while Chance held her tight; but little did she know, Chance had a different idea. He told Lizette that he was coming over to see CJ, but with Aaliyah's accident happening, everything got thrown the fuck off and now she was blowing up his phone.

Storm wanted to know who the fuck was blowing up his phone. Chance brushed her off, telling her he forgot to empty the safe at work. Storm didn't care, she was beyond tired. He helped her get into bed as he kissed her saying, *goodnight* and he left, getting in his car and speeding off.

"Mane, what the fuck?" he heard his phone going off again and this time he answered it.

"Hello, Lizette…damn!" Chance screamed. "I told you I had a damn emergency," he uttered as the sound of her heavy breathing pissed him off.

"Shut the fuck up, Chance, you told CJ that you were coming four hours ago, nigga, and yo high-yellow ass ain't came through the door yet!" she yelled back and anyone who knows Lizette, knows her attitude ain't one to be fucked with. She was known for fuckin' bitches up.

"Zette, man, look…you can go on with all that noise, girl. This shit ain't about you, it's about my son, so let him know I'm on my way," Chance hung up, he wasn't about to sit there and hear all that shit from that bitch when all he wanted to do was be in his son's life, but somehow he always managed to have to be in hers too.

"CJ," announced Chance as he walked through the door, still having his own key. CJ came running and jumped into his arms.

"Daddy, you're here," he gives his daddy a kiss as they sat down to play with his racing cars. Lizette just stood there staring with hatred.

After all the begging to get him there, the bitch had a nerve to say, "So, what… your bitch had you tied up, nigga?"

Chance continued playing with his son. He drowned out the sound of her voice and that was pissing her off; so, of course, she tried her other hand.

"CJ, hurry up, it's almost time for bed, son," she said as CJ started to have a fit.

"No nap, mommy. I not sleepy yet. I just want to play with my daddy," he expressed as he jumped back into his father's arms.

"Look, Lizette…leave us alone; you rushed me here, now I'm here, so back the fuck off!" Chance was getting heated. How dare this bitch try to take him away from time with his son? She kept mouthing about how he give his women more time and he needed to apply that same time with little CJ.

Chance got tired of hearing her mouth, so he picked CJ up carrying him into his bed and kissed him and told him he'd see him Saturday. See, Lizette didn't know anything about Storm. All she knew was that Chance dated other girls, but not that he was serious with any; but when he does decide to tell her, the outcome wasn't going to be pretty. Chance was coming down the stairs, heading straight for the door and Lizette kept pulling on his jacket.

"Where you going, muthafucka? You've only been here thirty minutes."

I swear that bitch was bipolar; she was just rushing him because he wasn't giving her any attention. Chance kept going right out the door so that he could leave and she continued to stand in the door screaming. Lizette went running back into the kitchen, grabbing a plate and returning. She threw it in Chance's direction, but he ducked just in time to miss the hit.

"Fuck you, bitch. You ain't never got to come back here. My son don't need your dusty dick ass!"

It was shit like this that Vick was talking about as to why telling Storm was important. Chance seemed to think that he had everything under control and as long as he kept them two apart, he'd be straight.

Storm was already asleep when he got home, so Chance got undressed and slid in bed beside her like everything was ok as he barely drifted off to sleep.

Storm, being pregnant, always had to pee; so when she got up for her 6:00 a.m. bathroom run, she heard Chance's phone vibrating off the dresser and it stopped her in her tracks as she reached down to pick it up. Noticing a text from BM, Storm wondered who that was, so she decided to take a peek at the message.

Fuck you, you're a trifling dead-beat bitch and CJ don't need nothing from you it read and Storm was confused. Before starting drama, she had to think straight first as she looks over at Chance. He was still asleep in the bed and she decided she needed to go get some advice and she headed straight to her sister.

* * * * *

A lie may take care of the present, but it has no place in the future and some bitches will tolerate such emotional dishonesty in communication. They would rather allow men the chance to defend their dishonesty on the grounds that it might hurt others later. Therefore, having rationalized their phonies into nobility, they settle for superficial relationships; but Storm wasn't that type of bitch. She was a firm believer that when it comes to a relationship, *truth fears no question* so Chance had better be ready for his survey to come and he should have learned from what happen to James not to cross her.

If you look at my life, you'll see what I see, Storm sang along to Mary J Blige as the slow melody and soulful singing of a sista who was speaking the truth to her pain at that moment, gave her some kind of comfort.

What the fuck was that? She thought of the text message. *Here I am, twenty weeks pregnant by this nigga, and he's trying to play me?*" She cried as she pulled into her sister's driveway so fuckin' fast that Pierre, the gardener, almost got his ass hit. Storm took off full speed, walking her pudgy round stomach up to the front door; but before she could knock; Vick was leaving for work. He could tell by the way she said *hi* that something was bothering her and he just hoped it wasn't his brother. But Vick wasn't sticking around to fuckin' find out.

Things with Vick and Rain were going magnificently well and they were honestly now living the American dream.

"Rain!" screamed Storm as she stood in the hallway furious. Her screaming caused Rain to run over toward the stairs. Seeing the condition that her sister was in, Rain knew that shit was about to get real.

"What's wrong, baby?" she said, coming down the stairs. She went up to Storm and held her in her arms.

"Oh my God, sis not again; it's Karma from what I did to James," Storm sobbed and Rain became confused. "This nigga cheating on me, sis and I found out while I'm carrying his baby." Storm was done and she felt like this was God's way of punishing her.

"What, Wait…" Rain lifts her sister's head off her shoulder, trying hard not to believe this shit. "Come on in here and sit down, try explaining this to me again," Rain was mad; she had so much faith in their relationship because Chance was around Vick all the time. Storm followed Rain into the kitchen and sat at the table while Rain poured her some water.

"Ok sis, from the muthafuckin' top, how you know that Chance is cheating?" Rain began her questioning as she told her sister what she read in the text and Rain could feel her old ways approaching.

Who the fuck is BM and CJ, was the question at hand. The way Storm explained it to Rain, she felt like they were two different people. She was lost and didn't know what was going on as she cried. But you can bet your ass that Rain was going to help her sister find out.

"OK, ok…look at me, sis. You have to calm down for my niece or nephew in your stomach and you know I'm not going to let nothing happen to that baby," she was mad and all Rain wanted was some answers for her sister and the first person on her list to question was Vick. He was Chance's brother, so of course, he had to know something. Storm asked Rain to come with her to the doctor tomorrow and of course you know she was going. So after getting her to relax and calm down, Rain took her sister to her room to rest. Rain had to go pick Aaliyah up from the hospital because she was getting discharged that day.

The fire was burning deep down inside, but she didn't show it. The last thing Rain needed was something to pull her back into that life of murder; and fuckin' with her family was definitely a way to take her there. She hoped that that wasn't what it was. Besides, with all her sister's problems, this shit might involve her husband's ass lying to her, which might mean things really could change!

CHAPTER 3

What lies beneath?

As we grow up, we learn that even the one person that wasn't supposed to let us down probably will. You'll have your heart broken and you'll even break hearts, that's why you should always be cautious of whom you end up loving because the end results could be painful.

"I always knew looking back on the tears would one day make me laugh, but I never knew looking back on the laughs would definitely make me cry. I wish like hell I'd just left his ass alone and kept it strictly business. How did I not see the lies he told? For the second time in my life, I guess I was just blind."

"Well, Ms. Peters everything looks good to me, so I'll see you in another month," Doctor Charity expressed after completing Storm's pregnancy checkup. Lately, she hadn't been feeling her best between the pregnancy and Chance with his strange bullshit. Storm was under a lot of stress. After going to her regular doctor and getting the proper test done, come to find out she was already four months pregnant.

As Storm waited at the front desk for the receptionist to give her an appointment, her cell began to vibrate from inside her purse as she grabs it and pushes silent. Noticing that it was from Rain, she quickly grabs the card and makes her way out the building to call her sister back.

"Hey, sis. What happen to your ass?" Storm asked. "I thought you were coming to my appointment today?"

"Well, hello to you too, first of all." They both began to laugh. "And second, calm your pregnant, evil ass down," Rain suggested because she knew just how her sister's temper had become; and upsetting her wasn't an option.

"I forgot we had inspection today at Rico's kitchen and after them health department bitches finished taking all fuckin' day, I called you which was now," said Rain. "I also had a little talk with my husband about his brother," Rain explained as Storm drove over to Chance's parent's house to see his mom while Chance was out of town on business.

"I asked his ass was Chance messing with any other girls that he knew of and he told me no," Rain expressed as Storm continued to listen so much that she missed her exit off the interstate heading to Halifax Virginia where Yvette and Tony lived.

"Yeah, that's the same damn thing Chance said to me when I asked his ass the other day. He swears that whoever texted his phone had the wrong number because the only BM he knows is Brian Murphy which is the investor for Riding Rims."

The story Storm got wasn't making since to Rain, so many things just weren't adding up.

"Well, why would Brian text him something like that?" Rain cut in out of curiosity, but Storm's attention had been snatched up by something else.

As she pulled into Yvette and Tony's driveway, she couldn't help but spot Chance's car parked outside as she told her sister she'd call her back. Donesha, which was Chance and Vick's cousin, beeped into Storm's line but she sent her ass straight to voicemail.

* * * * *

The sexiest smile hides the deepest secrets, just like Storm's beautiful eyes cried many tears. Her kind of heart, this time around in her life, was not pulsating to the pain that the future held for her and a little piece of it was waiting behind those doors.

Storm knocked twice before the maid let her in, automatically thinking she was there for Chance as Storm followed her back to the family room.

"Mrs. Sanchez," called out Maria as she pointed in Storm's directions as she announced her presence. You would have thought Chance's heart jumped out of his body from how fast he handed the baby boy he was holding to his mother.

"Hey, baby what are you doing here?" she asked as Chance tightly embraced her with a hug.

"I just got here like an hour ago because we finished inventory early so I just flew back in," he expressed as he rubbed Storm's belly while helping her over to the couch to sit down.

"So, tell me, how was your doctor's appointment, boo; is my Lil man giving you trouble?" Chance joked trying to retract her mind off of what she saw and that shit worked for a few minutes.

"How you know it's your *little man* Chance?" Storm loved the attention from him; she explained that the checkup went great and that the baby was doing just fine. She informed Chance that they've also discovered that she is anemic, which meant she'd have to take iron pills. He smiled and showed excitement ready for their bundle of joy, but Storm managed to hold out on telling him that her next visit was to find out what she was having, she wanted to keep that a surprise.

"Where did your mom go?" she asked, noticing that Yvette left out the room, "and whose baby were you holding trying to get practice?"

Before Chance could answer, his mom came walking in and instantly intervened on the question as she saw the look on her son's face.

"Hey, honey that's my godson," she hugged Storm while eyeing Chance behind her back. "I'm keeping him until my best friend comes back."

Storm's mind began to think." I didn't know Cassandra had another baby?"

"Oh, she doesn't," Yvette snapped back nasty, but gentle, "that's my childhood friend name Towanda's son his name is Zion," Yvette quickly thought out a name. "Oh, I almost forgot, I have a surprise for you," she expressed trying hard to throw Storm off and they knew that talking about her baby would do that and so Yvette used it. She pulled out two bags containing baby items for them and Storm instantly became ecstatic.

"Look, Chance, this is so cute," she shouted as she went through the bags and he smiled hard on the outside, but silently praying and thanking God at the same time as he goes to use the bathroom.

While Storm and Yvette continued to talk, Chance makes his way down the hall, but his destination was not the fuckin' bathroom, instead going into the spare bedroom where his son CJ laid asleep. Chance shuts the door then goes to sit down on the bed beside him.

"I love you Lil man" he whispered into CJ's ear then kisses him gentle on the cheek.

"Daddy, got to go now, but I'll see you next week same time and hopefully this craziness will end soon."

Chance gets up and heads for the door as CJ's little body turns over in his sleep, but not waking up and his daddy leaves the door cracked.

"You ready to go, baby?" Chance asked Storm as he noticed the look of tiredness on her face.

"Thank you for the gifts, Yvette," she says as she hugs her goodbye.

"You are so welcome, honey," responded Yvette as she now hugs her son who whispered in her ear, "Mom call me once Zette picks him up," she smiled and waved as they both left the house.

"This was very sweet of your mom, baby," said Storm as Chance helped her into her car.

"Yeah, it was, boo; but look…go straight home and I'm right behind you so we can spend the rest of the night together."

She smiled. Storm thought that would be the perfect ending to her wonderful day as they tongued each other down and she pulled off with Chance not too far in her rearview mirror. She decided to call Rain back.

"Sissy, are you busy?"

"Hell, naw. I'm watching *Love and Hip Hop;* what you doing? asked Rain and Storm wanted to tell her, but she was sure it wasn't anything to alarm her sister about.

"I'm on my way home from Tony and Yvette's, where is Rico and Aaliyah?"

"Girl, that Stevie-J is so fuckin' comical," Rain's ass was laughing so hard at the shit bitches actually tolerated for TV.

"My bad, sis…Aaliyah's over Karen's practicing routines for their competition game and RJ…I haven't spoken to him all day come to think of it," which was strange, "but I think he's out with Denise."

"He's been getting real serious with her, sis," said Storm.

"Yeah, I know. I kind of like her a lot," Rain replied as the motherly feeling to call her son came over Rain. After making sure Storm had made it home safely, Rain hung up and gave RJ a call. Calling back to back twice, and still no answer, finally on the third try he was calling in to her.

"So, here it is midnight, and I'm just hearing your voice, I know you grown and all, but damn!" she laughs, "What's up with making your mother worry RJ?"

"My bad, mom," his manly, deep voice gave her a laugh. "I was playing ball half the day and now I'm here chilling with Denise," RJ explained and he told his mom he'd be home soon as he ended their call because he and Denise were talking.

* * * * *

"So, baby, what's up for tomorrow? Are we still going to dinner?" she asked as RJ turns his attention back over to her.

"We still have so much to continue talking about and I want to know what it was you started to tell me."

Denise's heart sank to her stomach because she didn't know how to come out and tell him her secret. Since they returned back from the Virginia Beach trip, Aaliyah's accident kind of altered RJ's thoughts; he was busy helping his sister recover, but that doesn't mean that he forgot.

RJ had started spending more time with his family and less time with Denise because he felt a little lied to. He wanted to get to the bottom of her family secrets because something just wasn't right and it was high time Denise explained her dad. RJ decided that they should talk over dinner tomorrow at 8:30 p.m. and Denise quickly stated that she'd meet him there.

"I'm going to be out with my sister tomorrow evening, so when I leave her, I'll come straight to the restaurant."

"I kind of thought that we could ride together."

RJ knew this had something to do with her stupid ass dad, but Denise kept stressing the fact that it didn't. They began kissing each other passionately as their tongues twirled with love and RJ enjoyed the excitement she gave his dick every time they touched.

"Just let me meet you there, boo and I'll come home with you afterward."

They both agreed on that. Denise gave RJ one more peck as she got out the car getting into hers and they both pulled off.

I am in love,
with what we are,
not what we should be
I love your ass naw, for real; I love your ass,
you done got a Lil thick, but I like to hug your ass,
Yo daddy don't like me, I don't give a damn.
What I do remain like a ceiling fan.

Mane, Denise, thought RJ as he continued to rap 2 Chainz; replacing the lyrics to fit his own life, while the warm night air felt good coming through the window while he zoned out.

I could see me with her forever, he thought as he pulled into his driveway to go inside. He made his way into the house and up the stairs as he heard the sound of Neyo playing loudly from his mother and Vick's room. The moans he heard from in between the music let him know that they were busy. He silently laughed while shaking his head as he peeped in on Aaliyah and she was sound asleep. RJ laid out across his bed without turning any lights on, he needed to meditate on his next move in life because he'd be twenty-two years old soon, and it was time to make grown man decisions.

The next day, RJ and Denise both were so busy running around getting ready that they forgot to call each other.

"I miss my baby," Denise said softly as she dialed RJ's cell.

"Yo, ma…wassup? You've been MIA all day, are you still coming to meet me tonight?"

At that same moment, David was coming down the hall and overheard Denise talking on the phone so he began to listen in.

"So, I'm spending the night with you right; RJ? So that we can talk and chill?"

That's when David came busting in the room.

"Who are you talking to, Denise?" he questioned, already knowing the answer as she jumped up from her bed at full speed.

"I…my…" she stuttered to say, but she couldn't even get her fuckin' lie straight. "Why dad?" she quickly snapped back.

"Because you're not leaving this house if I don't know with who."

This nigga, David, really went overboard; Denise is twenty-one years old.

"I'll see you in a few," she said to RJ as they both hung up the phone and Denise went back to getting herself glammed just like her father wasn't even standing there. He got pissed off even more.

"Is that that RJ fellow? You think you're going with him?"

David snatches her hand down from styling her long, black hair, but Denise gives him a look of authority this go round. Gloria comes past just in the nick of time.

"David, darling, there you are. I need your help downstairs," she expressed as his face showed Denise she was lucky. Denise gave his ass a smile like never before as she watched both her parents walk out of her room and she immediately got dressed and peeled. Not even fifteen minutes later, Denise pulled up in front of a restaurant called Kanpai which was their favorite expensive Japanese spot.

RJ waited outside patiently for Denise as he politely escorted her in. Denise always admired how lovely the décor was as the hostess came to seat them both. They decided to take a seat at the Sushi bar where they could talk and enjoy each other.

"Um, hello…why so quiet?" RJ asked Denise as she sat there staring off into space.

"I'm sorry, boo," she said, giving RJ a smile, "but some things are really bothering me."

By now, RJ was getting fed up.

"My bad. I didn't mean to say it like that, it's just that for the last two weeks your attitude has been rocky and I know something is wrong at home."

Denise knew he was right, but just as she went to answer, the waiter came to take their order. RJ put their orders in for both of them. He ordered the Raspberry Champagne along with the Lobster and Chanterelle Risotto. That was an excellent choice.

"Any appetizers?" the waiter asked with RJ waving him off and that's when Denise chimed in.

"Can we please have the Sashmi Tasting?"

Very well," said the waiter as he took up their menus and RJ didn't waste any time going back in.

"So, what's going on baby, because I really want us to become closer, but I feel like I only have half of you."

RJ was in love and it felt like Denise really felt the same way.

"It's a lot I kept from you on purpose, RJ, because I thought if I told you…" the tears streamed down her face, "you'd look at me different and you're the first real love I ever had, but you just won't understand."

"Try me," RJ cut her off and that's when the truth bit him on his ass.

"My father's been raping me ever since I was nine and my mother allowed him to."

His whole face dropped. RJ couldn't believe what the fuck he was hearing as he angrily whispered while banging on the bar.

"So, all this time, that nasty ass nigga been forcing you to have sex and yo mom is cool with that?" It was ridiculous to him because Rain did everything that she could to protect her children. "Denise, you have got to get out of that house. Fuck it, let's just get an apartment together," RJ was pissed and he wanted to whip David's ass right now, but he knew that wouldn't make shit better.

"If I try to move out, he'll kill me."

They were all in on their conversation, so much so, that the waiter came and left their food, but they still hadn't touched it.

"I can't take this shit, Denise; if you're not going to let me be there for you like your man, then I can't sit around and know that you're in that house with him either," he said and she knew he meant every word of it so she decided they should talk more about it at the house because right now all she wanted to do was feel his love.

After a passionate, but upsetting dinner, in which RJ found out a lot about her, they both headed back to RJ's crib. As RJ pulled into the driveway, his uncle Donny was pulling out. He extended him a wave, but he didn't slow down to talk. From what it looked like to RJ, Donny and Bria were in the middle of a heated argument and RJ didn't want any part of that.

"Bria, please…that shit sounds stupid and you know it!" yelled Donny as he did ninety-five miles per hour on the highway, dodging in and out of cars as Bria constantly asked him to slow the fuck down but Donny wanted answers. Apparently, his account was looking quite light compare to how heavy it was before, so this nigga, Donny, was snapping.

"I told you before that I have no fuckin' idea what you're talking about, Donny. I only go into the account when you say so; plus, we all know how your sister can be," Bria rolled her eyes at the thought of Rain. She knew how Rain and

Storm could be behind Donny.

To Donny, things with him and Bria were on fire and it's true he loved her very much; besides music, she was his other passion and she didn't have any problems accepting that. The situation with Main had her all screwed up and Bria couldn't believe she'd got sucked into that nigga's game again, but what was she to do when he's using blackmail from her own skeletons long ago.

"Look, baby…"he played nice as he unlocked the door to their house and they both went inside. "If you used the money, just tell me, Shortie; don't have me call the bank and go haywire all for nothing," he expressed as Bria flopped down on their bed, taking off her Chanel sandals. Donny sat down beside her to finally find out what was up.

Judging from Bria's face, she knew something, but wasn't saying. "Ain't no way one hundred grand just gone up and disappear," Donny holds his head as she continues to sit there and say nothing.

"Ok, baby," she turns to face Donny as he listened in very closely to what she had to say. "I do know where your money went and I am sorry I didn't tell you, but I was going to put it back before you noticed," she explained while gripping his hand, but all Donny wanted was answers.

"Bria, where is my money?" he quietly addressed so that she could stop beating around the bush.

"I used it to buy myself a new car," she said.

The look Donny gave said, *where the fuck is it,* because the car that was outside looked the same.

"I know what you're thinking, boo. It's the same kind of car, but it's just a brand new one." That didn't make sense.

"And what did you do with the other one?" Donny asked.

"I wreaked it last week from being drunk and driving, so you know that makes a terrible mess."

She was trying to be funny, but shit like that wasn't anything to play with and she knew it.

"Why the hell would you do some dumb ass shit like that?" Donny yanked his hand away. "Do you know you could have been killed?" He was really pissed off now; she was gambling with his money and her life. Both of which meant something to him.

"Donny, I'm…"

"Don't say that shit again, Bria. Then you try to hide it and replace the car like it was cool?"

It was all playing out to him now. Come to think of it, he wondered why all last week she was claiming to be broke. But Donny had been so busy at D-Nyce studios that he paid no attention to her or the car. Main and Skillz mix tape was on fire which had Donny busy booking tour dates and release parties. He was just brushing shit off and now he was being hit with all of this and Donny didn't know what to do.

"Baby, I'm sorry" she began kissing all on his face. "I'll never do that stupid shit again, will you please forgive me?" Bria begged, but before he could reply,

Bria took off running into the bathroom holding her mouth as vomit came shooting out and she had no idea what was going on.

"What's wrong," said Donny as he wet the wash rag and started wiping off Bria's mouth.

"Oh my God, boo, I don't know," she was weak as she sat down on the toilet laying her head on the sink.

"Here…drink this," Donny gives her some water and helped her back over to the bed. Maybe you need to rest, baby. So, don't worry about the shit with the money; just next time, let me know what you're doing upfront." he pulls the covers up on her while placing a kiss on her cheek. "I'll be back in a couple of hours. I'm meeting Main at the studio to work," Donny said which hearing that nigga's name made Bria even more fucked up. She softly replied, "Ok," as she closed her eyes to rest away this nightmare.

* * * * *

Time passed by real fuckin' fast and Storm was growing like crazy, so Rain decided to throw her sister's baby shower early just in case because that baby wasn't wasting no time growing and Storm's ass really had gotten big. The doctors had already given her the sex of her baby and she kept it from everyone else including the daddy—this one she was holding inside. By Rain not knowing, she had no idea what colors to pick so she decided to go with traditional baby colors for the shower. Rain chose to have the baby shower at the Historic Mankin Mansion wedding resort and that mutherfuckin' place was fabulous. It was now July in Richmond, so the weather was perfect to make sure Storm had a great day.

Rain's party planner, Stiletto Queen, really did her fuckin' thing with this event. She had been Rain's event planner for the past two years now, and with everything she did, Rain was in AWE. They had arranged the inside with beautiful white rose petals with one hundred and fifty white table and chairs set. Each table had miniature center pieces made out of ice in the image of a pregnant Storm holding her belly. Nizzy's Uncle Dexter had his own catering company which happened to specialize in exotic cuisines, so Rain hired them to do the food.

Stiletto Queen has a bad ass graphic designer on her team, and this bitch could really do the damn thing. She could design with creativity that no one was using, so Rain decided to meet up with her for the invitations and see what they could come up with.

"Good evening and welcome to Stiletto Queen's office," greeted Nancy, the receptionist.

"I'm here for my appointment with Tamika Washington," said Rain as Nancy called back to inform Tamika.

"She'll be right up."

Rain stood waiting, but not for long as she was then greeted by the one and only herself. Tamika was the kind of female they didn't make anymore; this girl was all brains and beauty.

"Hello there, Mrs. Sanchez. I've heard so much about you and it's nice to finally put a face with the name."

They shook each other's hand as Rain followed her down the hall to her office.

"So, Mrs. Sanchez how can I help you?" Tamika takes her seat behind the desk as Rain pulls out some photos.

"I have these images and I wanted to see if you could do something with them for the front of the invitations," she slides them over to Tamika who immediately started smiling which to Rain meant good.

"Did you see the cover of *Vogue* last month?"

Rain shook her head, *no*.

"Well, I myself took those pictures and designed that issue and these kind of remind me of those images," Tamika pulled out the magazine and handed it to Rain.

"Nice work, Ms. Washington; you really are the best."

They both laughed while Tamika took in all of the compliments. She turned the computer around so that she and Rain could go through some layouts so that Tamika could get started. They spent thirty-five minutes going through them all and after Rain finally picked out all of her pictures, Tamika already knew what to do.

She informed Rain that they would be ready in a day and that she'd call her when they were ready to be picked up.

"Thank you so much for your help Ms. Washington."

"No problem, I love what I do," Tamika assured her as she gets on the elevator and leaves.

As she got back into her car, Rain thought she was seeing shit as she spotted Chance putting some bags in his trunk from what looked like JC Penny's.

What the fuck he doing all the way out here, she thought to herself and that's when Rain saw and eyeful. She continued to sit and watch as this short, light-skinned girl approached him and the little boy with her quickly jumped into Chance's arms.

"That had better be a cousin or something," Rain's radar went off and she was starting to feel uneasy. She thought about calling Storm to tell her, but she didn't want to get her upset over nothing; so instead, Rain drove over to them.

When Chance saw her car pulling up, her ass eyes got big ass shit and he admittedly put the child down on the ground. He walked over to the driver side door to catch Rain before she got out.

"Wassup, sis?" Chance leaned inside her window.

"Hey, what's up? What you doing out here?" Rain questioned and he knew actually what she was referring to.

"Shit, nothing really…just picked up some stuff for my mother and my business partner's sister just stopped me," Chance automatically lied because he knew Rain's next question would be who she was, so to him, it was easier to just say.

Chance and Rain continued to chop it up for ten minutes more as he continued to keep peeking up to see if Lizette was coming over their way, but he did see that she was getting pissed. Chance told Rain that he'd holla back at her later, and then he walked back toward his car. Rain continued to sit there because she wanted to see Chance's next move and he peeped that out real quick.

"What the fuck! Who was that bitch?" Lizette asked Chance as smoke shot straight from her ears.

"Main, that's my brother's wife, you dumb ass," he said.

"That's who's married to Vick?" Lizette asked as to if to say, *how did they hook up*?

"Yes, that's his wife and I don't need them in my business, so take CJ and meet me at my parent's house now," Chance instructed as he walked off and got into his car. Rain saw as Chance pulled off first and then the girl's gold Camry followed.

"Hmm, I wonder what that's all about?" she spoke out loud and then Rain pulled off. That whole situation continued to play over in her mind because she had witness her sister done dirty by a nigga before and it damn sure wasn't happing twice.

"My sister's finally starting to live her life and nobody going to bring that back down or cause her to miscarry her baby," said Rain as she pulled into her driveway and her husband was already at home.

Good, she thought. *It's high time that I get the truth and he'd better tell me what's going on.* Rain fussed as she grabbed boxes off the back seat and Vick saw her trying to lift them all inside.

"Hey, baby…" Vick met her at the door, taking the items out of her hand. They greeted each other with a kiss, "why the long face, my lady? Who made your day sour?"

"Your brother," she snapped back as she sat on the couch.

"My brother?" Vick was lost; he didn't know what the fuck was going on.

"Yeah, your brother. I saw him today when I left from Stiletto Queen and he was much too friendly with this high-yellow bitch and her kid in the parking lot. "When I pulled up on their asses, Chance told me he was doing shit for your mom and that she was his business partner's sister."

Vick couldn't believe this shit was happening, he told Chance that this shit would eventually catch up to him and it could end badly.

"Mane, baby, I don't know what that nigga is up to for real, but I'm damn sure going to find out," he confidentially stated while jumping up and grabbing his keys and phone.

"Where are you going, baby?" yelled Rain, but she didn't get a response; all she heard was the door slamming behind him as Vick left.

"God, please help me. I don't want to go back to that life, but I feel my patience is being tested," Rain said in a prayer as she sat looking out of her bay window. I feel like evil is trying to take over my whole family. Dear Lord, please help me figure this out."

Rain covered herself up with her Snuggie as she laid on the couch to rest and about twenty minutes later, Aaliyah came through the door.

Calling out for her mom, she notices that she was sleeping and for the first time, she didn't look so stressed.

"I'm home, mommy," she whispered as one of Rain's eyes slightly opened and Aaliyah kissed her on the cheek and left her alone.

*****

"Answer this mutherfuckin' phone Chance!" Vick was mad as hell, but he knew just where to fuckin' go. This nigga is tripping; my fuckin' wife could have gotten caught up in this shit," he said, getting out of the car and going straight into his parent's house like a raging bull.

"Yo! Mom!" Vick announced as he made his way into the den to find his mother and brother wrapping up their conversation.

"Hello, darling," Yvette greeted, standing up to hug Vick as they embraced and he gave Chance a nasty ass look.

"Mom, can you excuse us? I need to talk to my brother," said Vick and Chance knew just what this was about.

"Yo B, what the fuck are you doing out here, son?" Vick's New York accent came in strong.

"What you mean?"

"You know what I mean. Rain and Lizette almost came in contact today and that shit could have really went way left field," expressed Vick and he was getting tired of warning his brother about fixing his mistake. Chance's shit was starting to affect his wife, and everyone knew he was for damn sure going to protect her.

"Look Vick, mane, I got this shit under control; and besides, you act like they know about each other," Chance laughed as he took a sip out of his Fiji water, but Vick didn't find anything funny.

"How long do you expect to keep this shit from Storm and y'all are about to have a kid? You know you can't start your family off like that," Vick tried reasoning with him and from the looks of things, Chance wasn't paying him any attention. We as people have to learn you can't make a person do nothing that they don't want to do. All you can do is share the knowledge and it's up to them to apply it to their life.

"Everything that you're telling me, bruh, I already think about," Chance finally says and these are feelings that he's held on to for a long time. "The last thing I want to do is lose Ja'Nay and you know it Vick."

"How was I supposed to know that we would fall in love? I already had Lizette and CJ in my fuckin' life before I ever laid eyes on Ja'Nay and you should know all of this because…"

"I got you the job working for her." Vick said it for him.

"Good, I'm glad you remember."

"I love you, Chingy. I really do, but if it comes to me losing Rain over your shit…I'm telling her everything I know and I mean it."

Chance couldn't believe what he was hearing.

"So you're saying that you'll snitch on your brother for some pussy?" He was beginning to cross the line and everybody knew just how Vick felt about his queen.

"What the fuck you say, mutherfucker? Don't you ever in your life disrespect my wife again!" Vick was so close in Chance's face that I thought they would connect.

"I wasn't…" Chance tried to correct himself, but he had already said it now.

"La'Rain isn't just pussy to me as Ja'Nay might be to you," said Vick.

"I love Ja'Nay too, nigga. What you saying?"

"Then fix it, bitch!" screamed Vick. Yvette must've heard their tones beginning to rise with each other so she told Tony to step in.

"Boys," Tony's deep voice firmly overpowered them both as he walked into the room. "End this now!" he spoke as they listened. "I don't care what or who this is all about, or how it even started for that matter, but I told you two to love one another regardless. Never put anyone before your other. What the fuck happen to that?"

They both began to take a minute and think about their actions and that's when Vick spoke up.

"Pops, I love you and my brother, but what I'm saying to him is right and you know it. I don't want no parts in this shit!"

They had to respect what his wishes were, even if they didn't agree. Vick gave his mother a kiss and he left after saying to Chance one more time, "Fix it," then he slammed the door.

As soon as Vick got back outside to his car, he called Rain.

"Hey, baby…I was just about to call you. Are you alright?"

"I am. I'll be fine," said Vick and he told her he'd be home in fifteen minutes. Vick knew the past between Lizette and Chance was crazy, but he also knew how Rain and Storm could get down and he didn't even want to cross that path with them again.

Storm knew all about the baby shower, so on the day of she was super excited. Part of her gift from her sister was to get her hair and nails done; she even threw in a pedicure which Storm really enjoyed and now it was time to see Rain's hard work.

The day of the shower was a hectic one of course, with all the last minute making sure things were good to go trips that Rain had to make over to the resort; but shit turned out just how she liked it.

"Hey, sis," Rain joked bubbly. "How are you feeling?" she wanted to know because lately Storm had been having some serious Braxton Hicks contractions.

"I'm good this morning, sis. I haven't eaten yet, which is why the baby keeps kicking the shit out of me." They both laughed, but Rain told her to go and fuckin' eat right away.

"Well, I was just calling to check up on you before this evening," Rain expressed, also telling Storm to be ready by 5:00 p.m. Once she hung up with her sister, Rain put a call through to Donny; but before she could connect, it was interrupted by Rain's banker and friend Katrina Monroe. At first, Rain wasn't going to answer it because she had so much other shit to do, but this was her money we're talking about and you know she don't play about that.

"Hey, honey…how are you?" Katrina asked, but there was way more feeling in this greeting than usual, and that's when her mind started to wonder.

"I'm fine, why wouldn't I be?"

"Well, I know you told me to call you first if anything concerning the accounts started to look funny," Rain felt a lump in her throat. "My money…" that's all that she could think of, "what's wrong Katrina?" she was pissed before she even knew why.

"Calm down, there's nothing wrong with your shit," Katrina heard Rain breathe easier.

"It's your brother…his account has a withdrawal of one hundred thousand dollars in a fuckin' month; each week the same day and time, someone was taking out large amounts of cash."

Rain knew just who it was.

"Now La'Rain, before you go off the deep end, I need you to keep in mind that unless we have you on his account, I'm really not supposed to share this information," said Katrina. That was her job at the end of the day, and hell, they all knew Rain was rich. She wasn't trying to get fired over this and Rain understood that as well.

"Katrina, baby, you know I got you on that, boo. As a matter of fact, are you near a fax now?" asked Rain as she answered her back with a *yes* and Rain began faxing over a document. Judging from the way Katrina burst out laughing, Rain knew that what she sent would work.

"When did you get this?"

"About four years ago, once I split the accounts down the middle," Rain answered with the world's biggest smile on her face. Her baby brother was the only brother she had left.

"So we straight?"

"We are straight. I'm slipping this into the file right now, and with both signatures and your name on this as the other account holder, we're good if you want to dig all in his shit."

They both found that funny and Rain ended the call because it was time to get going, shit would be starting soon. She was so mad at Donny that calling him had to wait; besides, she wanted to talk to him in his face.

"Baby, are you ready?" Donny yelled from the bed as he waited for Bria to come out of the bathroom so that they could leave. He needed to go pick up his suite from his tailor and Bria's ass was taking all day. As she walked out into the room Donny immediately noticed that she was crying.

"Bae, what the fuck?" he said as he jumped up and grabbed her, "what's wrong with you, boo?"

She cried harder, lying on his chest and she reached in her back pocket pulling something out and handing it to Donny.

"Say word, Shortie," he couldn't believe what he was seeing and Bria couldn't either.

"Could things really work out for me?"

"Do you know what this means, boo? A family doe," he smiled at the fact that he held her positive pregnancy test in his hands.

"Baby, you're not mad? I can't believe this, I really thought you would say you didn't want it," expressed Bria.

"That's me in there, boo. Of course I want it and I want you too," Donny kisses her intimately as a sign of this being a new beginning.

"Ok, ok…let's get ready. I can't wait to tell my sisters the good news," he stated and Bria knew them bitches weren't going to be happy just because it was by her.

* * * * *

Over at the Mankin Mansion, the guest had started to arrive and everything was looking very lovely. Rain had Storm and Chance in back getting prepped by their glam squad while Vick over seed in the kitchen. Donny, Bria, RJ, Aaliyah, and Denise sat at the family table and everyone else made their way over to their seat by names so that the festivities could begin.

"Thank you all for coming out this evening to honor and celebrate Ja'Nay and Charles new edition to the world," expressed Rain, who might I add, stood stunning in her Diane Von Furstenberg evening gown which was specially made to fit her curves.

"Can I please have your attention to the foyer as we welcome Ja'Nay and Charles!"

They both came walking out as everyone clapped and cheered and after they were seated, the DJ began playing a mixture of the old and new jams; soon everyone was getting it on the floor. People were eating, two stepping and mingling; the party was turning out great, but little did Rain know, something was waiting silently to ruin her damn night.

"Come on baby, one more dance," Vick swung Rain then dipped her.

"Boy, I'm tired ass shit. My feet hurt baby," she playfully laughed, brushing him off. "All I want to do is sit..." but before she could finish, she spotted Donny alone at the bar for the first time all night and now was her chance to move in.

"Excuse me husband, but I need to talk to my brother."

Rain kissed Vick quickly and flew ass over to Donny. "Well, hello there, sir," she stood behind him smiling. "Do you have a minute so that we could talk?"

As Donny turns around and kisses Rain on her cheek, he said, "Of course I do, sis; plus, I have some news for you as well."

His saying that made her think that he would just tell her, so she decided to let him go first.

The pie was thrown smack dead in her face when Donny said, "Bria's pregnant," and that's when her nightmare began. "Say something, sis. You're just standing there."

Donny thought her reaction would be different.

"What is there to say, Donny? I see this is who you want in your life forever and I don't agree," Rain got right to the point which kind of frightened Donny and that's when Storm walked up. Now Donny was surrounded by both of his sisters.

"What's up you two?" Storm wobbled out of breath.

"Oh, nothing much but your brother confessing to me that he got that bitch pregnant!"

Storm's whole jaw dropped.

"What?!" said Storm, but Donny cut her off.

"Oh, so I'm just *her* brother now?" Donny snapped back.

"You damn right, with that dumb ass shit you're doing lately, like blowing a hundred grand on this bitch!"

Donny and Storm's eyes widen out of shock from what Rain had just said, but Storm's ass was in the dark about the whole thing.

"Can someone please continue to enlighten me?" Storm begged, confused as she stood in the middle of them both.

"How the fuck do you know anything about my money?" Donny used a tone with Rain that he never used before; but of course, you know the queen didn't back down.

"Don't worry about what the fuck I know and from whom," she fussed. "Did you or did you not blow that money on Ms. Bitch?"

"I don't have to tell you shit mutherfucker, you can scare the streets, but I'm your baby brother, I know your ass real well and inside you are fuckin' weak."

Storm grabs Rain by the arm real fast because she knew shit had just blow up and it was about to go down.

"Oh, for real? So I'm weak, Donny?!" yelled Rain as she tried to shove Storm to the side and all of the commotion got the attention of the guests as Donny started walking up on her and they were now in each other's face.

"I'm weak?"

"Fuck you, Rain! That's my privacy and you're not respecting it. I'm not a damn baby anymore," Donny stated then before he could even see it coming, Rain punched his ass in the face.

"I'm weak, Donny?" she starts going off and charging at Donny for more and this nigga slaps her ass right back.

"Donald!" screamed Storm, now trying to kill him herself. "Don't you ever put your fuckin' hands on her again, nigga. What is wrong with you?!" she screamed as Vick and Chance now had Rain carrying her off into another room. Vick literally had to pick her ass up off the ground, carrying her ass the fuck away. Rain was snapping out all the shit she did for her brother and he'd hurt her like this over some bitch that didn't mean him no good. I swear his ass must've been gone.

Now he pushed away the one person who would be there no matter what, and now she was out of his life.

"Look, sis…I love you and her, but I can't deal with Rain disrespecting me. I'm a man and I'm about to be a father and she's going to have to accept that," he places his arms around Bria. "She is a part of me now."

Storm stood there looking at him as the tears came down her face. She couldn't believe that this was her brother. She said nothing to him. Storm just took Chance by the arm and turned and walked away. Donny said, "Oh, well," and hunched his shoulders, took Bria and left himself.

"Sis, it's me. Open up," knocked Storm as Rain sat inside the locked dressing room crying. She was so embarrassed she didn't want to see anybody at this point; but most of all, she need to calm herself down because hurting Donny was all that she could think about and that wasn't the way to be.

Click, after ten minutes, Storm heard the latch unlock and she opened up the door to find Rain sitting inside—makeup running everywhere from crying; everybody knew she had to be hurt.

"I'm good, boo. Trust me," she wipes her eyes with a tissue. "I just had to relax before I shot his ass," but she didn't mean that at all that was just her anger talking.

"No, you wasn't La'Rain, you're just hurt," Storm said as she takes her sister into her arms causing Rain to break down harder then she'd ever cried before.

How was she going to live without her brother in her life? But then again, he had to learn life's lessons too. After all the guest left, Vick helped Rain to the car while Storm and Chance followed right behind them and it was time to do nothing but go to bed.

If you split something that's meant to attach apart but leave it close, I bet you it will find its way back together and that's what Rain hoped would be the outcome of this disaster, but in her feelings now, she was done with Donny. *Period!*

Chapter 4

A slap in the face

"I can't believe it's been four months already," joked Rain as her and Storm headed back to Virginia from Atlantic City after a weekend of relaxation and fun.

"I know it's like these eight months went by fast and I can't wait to push this baby out," expressed Storm. "I can't even bend down to tie my fuckin' shoe."

They both laughed, but Storm wanted to talk about something else.

"Have you talked to Donny yet," she asked, but judging from Rain's facial expressions, she could damn well tell her answer.

"What the fuck do I need to talk to him for, Ja'Nay? He's already made his decision; plus, this nigga hit me," said Rain.

"So, accept it if you want to make it right, La'Rain," said Storm.

"Bullshit! No I'm not! I'm not kissing Donny's ass!" she snapped. "After all that I've sacrificed for that boy."

Storm shook her head and threw up her hands.

"Look, sis…my bad, I didn't mean to hit a sensitive spot; but all I'm saying is that he isn't a child anymore and maybe if you listen to what he has to say, then things with y'all can get better," Storm expressed as Rain continued to drive in silence just staring straight ahead. What Storm was saying did make some sense and Rain knew that her mom was turning over in her grave right about now over the fact that her babies weren't speaking.

"Can you think about it please, because I'm going into labor soon and the last thing I need is for you two to not be speaking on my day." Storm begins to cry knowing Rain wasn't even going to have that. She pulled the car over to comfort her sister.

"Calm down, please. You're right," she held her sister tight while tapping her eyes with a tissue. "Everything should be ok by next month; I promise you will not have any problems."

Rain was the glue that held it all together, but at this point in her life, she wasn't feeling sticky anymore and she was tired of teaching everybody how to live right. Storm got herself together and then they pulled off so she could get home and go to bed. Rain dropped her sister off making sure she was in the house and then she left, heading straight to wrap up with her man. With all the excitement going on lately, she needed to feel loved; so what better way than to receive it from her husband.

*****

"Baby, I'm home," announced Rain, making her way into the house as the smell of her man cooking met her at the door. "Um, um, um it smells real good up in here, chief," she said as she and Vick embraced in a hello kiss, but Vick had his hands full of stir-fry veggies that he personally chopped up, along with the pot roast in the oven.

"I missed you, babe. About time you made it back," he expressed as she blushed from his words. "Our bed just didn't feel the same without you in it."

"I know what you mean, baby. I couldn't sleep a wink without you next to me."

They both shook their heads at how gone they were over each other; but it was cute.

"So, did you have fun?" Vick asked his wife, he knew she had been hard at work with making sure Storm and the baby were good, but Donny not being around was taking its toll and Rain just had a good way of hiding shit. The type of person she was wouldn't let her admit it, so Vick knew he had to do something. He took Rain over toward their kitchen table.

"Baby, sit down. I have to tell you something."

Rain instantly got worried, but she did indeed sit down and was all ears.

"I love you so much that when you're hurting…so am I, and I felt like I need to make things right."

Rain was lost; as far as she knew, she and Vick didn't have any problems so what cherry bomb was he about to drop on her now. Rain stayed quiet as she looked in his face, but it wasn't at all what she was thinking.

"I'm making dinner for you, me and Donny," said Vick, jumping back because he didn't know what Rain's reactions would be.

"Why would you do that Vick? You know how I fell about that subject and it's still a touchy situation."

"I know that, boo; but I feel like you two have enough love for each other, that not even Bria, or money, can keep you two a part, La'Rain."

Vick was right; Rain was practically Donny's mother; so you know he had to have been going through his own pain behind their fight. Shit, they both were stubborn as hell.

Just as Rain went to say, *no*, their doorbell began to ring.

"He's here, La'Rain; can you at least please try?" asked Vick as he headed for the door to open it.

Rain stood up and headed up the stairs to their bedroom because she needed a moment of process before talking to her brother and after four and a half months of no communication, she was now more angry then hurt.

"My nigga!" Vick slapped Donny hi-five as he entered into the house.

"Wassup, bruh? Thanks for inviting me over to watch the game," said Donny as he took off his LRG coat, hanging it up inside the hall closet and making his way into the kitchen to sit down.

"Damn, dog…you got it smelling good as a bitch up in here," he expressed as

Vick tossed the freshly-mixed salad that he'd also prepared.

"It's just a little something that I put together," Vick smiled as he sat the bowl out on the dining table and Donny noticed that there were three places sat.

"Let me find out you still set a place for Rain even when she's not here," joked Donny who was now helping Vick with the silverware. "You're that sprung off my sister?" Donny pushes Vick shoulder while still laughing and that's when Vick said, "She's here."

"Say what?" Donny drops every fork, plate, and knife on the fuckin' counter. "Vick, what the fuck is going on for real, bruh?" questioned Donny and that's when Rain came in. She kissed Vick looking straight in her brother's direction as she sits down, while inviting him to also do the same; but in all reality, she didn't want to do shit. The room was so quiet you could hear a pin drop because nobody said a word.

The feeling that came over Rain was saying for her to move forward and be the oldest sister because she really did miss him too. After all, the food was put out on the table; Vick did the honors of saying the grace.

"Let's us bow our heads…Heavenly Father, thank you for the chance to let use three assemble as a family to enjoy this meal. May we always stay together no matter what comes our way in life because you are the Alpha and Omega, in Jesus name we pray Amen."

They all took their seats as Donny stared at his sister; they knew they wanted to embrace but they didn't. The sound of passing food dishes was all that was heard.

"This looks so good, baby," Rain expressed as she took a couple more bites of her food. After trying real hard to let them break the ice, Vick said, "Fuck it" and did it all himself.

"Look y'all…this shit is stupid; you two love each other way too much for that. Your bond is too damn strong and I'm shocked," he continued, "especially at you baby," Vick gives Rain the most sincere look and they both knew he was right.

"Look sis," Donny said, "I was wrong for putting my hands on you and I am very sorry it shouldn't of never fuckin' happen. You have to learn that I'm a man now who's about to become a father, so you need to respect me, Rain."

She continued to sit silently as he asked her for a response.

"I accept your apology and I am sorry too, but as far as my opinion on that bitch of a girlfriend that you got, Donny…I still can't stand her fuckin' ass."

He knew that, but what he wanted was Rain to respect the fact that he could make his own decisions and basically for her to stay in her place.

"Look, Rain…I know how you feel about Bria, but she's my baby's mother now, and you have to accept that, sis."

What Donny asked for wasn't much at all, but Rain could tell when a bitch wasn't any good for her brother and since day one, she has had fucked up feelings when it came to that girl and Donny was just thinking with his dick.

"I don't have to respect shit, Donny; and you still will be my brother!"

"And that is true," said Donny.

"But I can still deal with your ass from a distance too, nigga." Donny added.

"I don't think you're serious, baby bruh. Would you really do that to me?"

Vick had seen enough of this fuckin' madness and that nigga went slam off.

"That's it! you two…that's enough! How do you think that Jackie and Eddie are feeling when they see you acting like this? They would say something if they could; but instead, I am…and the shit is dumb! To see y'all like this…" Vick slams his fist on the table, "is hurting more and more."

He stands up and goes to the bathroom.

Rain and Donny continued to sit at the table both screaming over the, *I wants, you need, and anything else* they could to get their point across. Vick's little plan damn sure wasn't working out after all.

"That's my money, Rain and I don't have to report to you every time I make or use my money. Key word…*my money*, and you need to let me take over that shit.

"Oh, really?" Rain smiles, sliding back from her spot, "I'm glad to know how you feel, Donald Peters. From this here day, you won't have to worry about me butting in your life about shit!"

She stood at the door, ready to walk the fuck upstairs.

"Good!" he yelled.

"Good then she yelled back this mutherfucker gone try and get greasy" she knew this shit wouldn't work as she turned and stomped upstairs "Not saying goodbye or anything else and Bria was the main fuckin' reason.

Donny didn't even wait for Vick to return from the bathroom, he got up from the table and fuckin' peeled.

"Ahh, boy that's what I'm talking about," Vick rubbed his stomach in reference to the shit he'd just took; and to his surprise, the kitchen was empty. Where the fuck is everybody?" Vick heads upstairs and straight into the bedroom where he finds Rain sitting in tears.

"I'm sorry, baby," that's the first thing he said.

"No, It's your fought; all you tried to do was get us back together, but I guess God's going to have to fix us now."

She continued to cry as Donny sat outside in his truck crying as well; he knew Rain loved him more than she loved herself. As he wiped his face while backing out of the driveway, Donny's heart was breaking as well; but he felt like this was how a man puts his foot down. But little did he know that was wrong.

A real man respects the strong woman that holds him down--whether mother, sister, or girlfriend—but right now Donny was breaking all the rules. Now, who's going to genuinely have his back?

* * * * *

"Baby, you home?"

Donny comes into his house and it's quiet, so Bria might be sleeping. "Bria?" he calls out as she quickly comes out of the bathroom like she was up to no god damn good.

"Hey, baby, I was feeling sick," she quickly said while closing the bathroom door behind her as she pushed end on her cell.

"You alright?" he asked her.

She replied, "Yes," while sitting down on her bed just as Donny's cellphone begins to ring. It was a call from Main.

"What up, young god?"

"Wassup, my nigga? I need to wrap to you about something important," said Main, "and I think you want to know because of the people involved."

Donny was lost for fuckin' word so he told Main he'd call him right back.

"What was that all about, boo?" asked Bria as Donny placed his phone back inside of his pocket.

"That nigga, Main, talking about he got some information for me about some people that I know real close."

Bria's heart immediately sank deeper into her stomach. *Did this bitch tell Donny anything?* she thought, but just to be safe she thought ahead.

"Baby, I have a huge favor I need twenty-five thousand to start this new cosmetics line called Vantage and that's the deposit for the chemists to start mixing samples for approval on the line.

"I didn't know that you wanted to do that, boo…that's great!" Donny expressed as he reached in his pocket pulling out a key.

"Go to my safe deposit box in the morning and take a stack out of the yellow bag. Each stack contains fifty thousand just keep the rest as money for you and the baby."

"Don't go into the red or green bags, Bria; just the yellow," said Donny and he dropped down on his knees in front of Bria and lifted her skirt to kiss her now round belly, but he wanted to kiss something else. Bria and Donny hadn't found out what they were having and Storm still hadn't told the sex of her baby yet, the wait is what makes pregnancy fun.

"I love you, boo; but please don't fuck me over," Donny stated as he looked deep into Bria's eyes. She couldn't stomach up the nerve to answer him at that moment; so instead, she reached in for a kiss. Donny and Bria lay in bed that night and she slept but he didn't because of the constant thought of Rain. Donny was feeling like he'd lost her for the second time in his life; only this time, he wasn't doing everything that he could to get her back.

After all of the hard work and preparing, the day had finally arrived and it was time for Aaliyah's final cheerleading competition. This year it was being held in Washington D.C. which the best squads from all over are definitely going to attend and these girls had better be on their A game. Of course Storm couldn't go even though she wanted to so bad, but her feet were swollen like balloons. The doctors had put her on bed rest so Rain decided to invite Donesha with her instead.

"Hurry up, baby girl!" Rain yelled upstairs to Aaliyah as she walked to open the front door.

"Hey, hun," greeted Donesha as they embraced with a hug.

"Hey, we'll be leaving just as soon as your little cousin brings her ass on."

They both laughed at how long it took Aaliyah to get ready. She finally made her way down the stairs instantly speaking to Donesha.

"Mom, I was coming; beauty takes time," she joked and Rain couldn't do anything but shake her head in amazement.

"That truly is my baby," she said as she grabbed her coat and keys; they had to go and drop Aaliyah off at the school to meet the bus.

"Do you have everything you need, Aaliyah?" Rain asked out of concern.

"Yes, I do," Aaliyah short answered her because she was too busy on the phone running her mouth.

*****

"We are, are the mighty, mighty Chargers we…Oh my God, girl…I know you remember those days," joked Donesha as she cheered along with the squads from off the buses.

"Good luck, baby. I'll meet you by the ticket booth after the competition is over," said Rain as she waved and pulled her car off, heading to the Washington D.C. Arena.

"Good morning, welcome to Citibank," greeted the teller as Bria asked to be let into the safe deposit boxes. "Right this way, ma'am," she said as she escorted Bria over to security and after being checked in she was let back into the room. As soon as she entered, she found the correct safe, put the key in and opened its top. Inside, there damn sure were three bags in the same fuckin' color that Donny called out, and Bria knew which one she was told to go in.

Goddamn, these bitches are stuffed to the max, the thoughts of what was in them filled her head. As she opened up the yellow bag, she soon discovered a lot of money. "What the fuck? I know money ain't in the other ones too!" Donny was truly caked up. *Go see Bria*, her inner voice said and she listened and that was stupid. "Uggh, what the fuck," she strained to lift the other two out and judging from their weight, they were heavier. Bria thought about it hard as she went to unzip the blue one first, and just then, her cellphone began to ring.

"Hey, boo," Bria's pregnant ass quickly said. "Yes, I got it. I'm leaving now," she expressed as she stuffed everything back inside the safe. I don't know where the strength came from, but she damn sure threw those bags real quick like they were light. I guess Donny had something to do with that as Bria got her shit and left the bank while still on the phone with Donny.

"Baby, what's in those other two bags?" the suspense was killing her.

Donny replied, "None of your damn business. I know you didn't go into those bags, Bria."

Of course she told him *no*. "I did what you to me to do, that's all; so what… you don't trust me now?"

This bitch was tripping, but I guess after all it was to be expected because of being pregnant her hormones are all over the place. Donny spent the next ten minutes calming her down and then he had to get back to mixing beats and laying tracks. Let Bria tell it, she had a meeting with some potential business partners or was she really meeting Main?

*****

"Hot dogs…get your hot dogs!" shouted the arena concession worker as he tried hard to make a sale out there. I guess the snack bar selling fish and chicken wasn't such a good idea to him.

"Oh shit, Lizzy, look…" pointed Donesha in the direction of some crazy ass moms showing spirit for their daughters, but those white bitches went in overboard.

"Girl, I love Aaliyah, but I'd never be caught dead in that shit!" Rain laughed as Donesha mocked the two women's facial expressions. Rain decided to call Vick before the competition started, but as she felt around for her phone, it wasn't in her pocket.

"Donesha, I'll be back. I have to run to my car and get my phone," Rain informed her as she ran back out to the parking lot at full speed so she wouldn't miss her daughter's team performance.

Upon making it to the car, Rain did discover her phone sitting right in the driver's seat as she picked it up and placed it back into her pocket. Turning around fast so that she could leave, Rain was almost knocked down by some fat ass man.

"Oh, excuse me, I'm sorry," a polite man said as he and Rain made eye contact in between the bump.

That nigga damn sure does look familiar, thought Rain as she watched him walk back to a Lincoln Town car limo with plates from New York. Suddenly, she remembered who he was and it damn sure was the driver of the Tulios for years.

"Good thing he didn't recognize me," Rain said as she made her way back to her seat. Rain never said a word to Donesha; as a matter of a fact, it wasn't her damn business, and sometimes things are better left unsaid and Donesha only knew about Lizzy.

As Aaliyah's squad made their way to the stage, Rain couldn't help but feel joy. Her young lady was growing up fast and that moment was one to reflect on as to why her decision to change was correct.

"Girl, slow down," laughed Rain, taking a sip of her soda. "You keep eating like that and you're going to choke on your hot dog."

But Donesha just kept right on scarfing her food. "Bitch, I'm trying to finish before Aaliyah gets started and I'm hungry, so I'm gonna fuck this up."

Throughout the entire performance, Rain sat there in amazement of just how much talent her daughter had; it kind of reminded her of when she was young. Donesha, along with all the other people, clapped and cheered so loud that it almost gave Rain a headache. In the mist of all the excitement, Rain noticed a familiar voice coming two rows down from her.

Damn, that sound just like Candace, she thought to herself while trying hard to get a look at the lady's face, but the bitch never turned around. Rain had to think quickly, she couldn't blow her cover, but at the same time she needed to know if it was her past.

"Donesha, you're louder than me, scream out Aaliyah's name so she will know we went all in on supporting her," said Rain, which was a brilliant plan to see the woman's face.

If it is Candace, hopefully she'll turn around to see if that was someone she knew screaming and that's when I'll get a look at her ass, thought Rain as her eyes stayed glued on the woman at this time and she was missing a lot of Aaliyah's solo.

"Go, Aaliyah, go…you're the best!" Donesha kept chanting and that's when that bitch took the bait. Rain sat there waiting with her dark tinted Ray Bands on and that's when the lady turned to see who was doing all of that damn yelling.

"It is her," said Rain underneath her breath as Candace gave Donesha a sour look. She didn't know which Aaliyah they were talking about because Donesha wasn't a face that Candace had ever seen, so she turned her snobbish ass back around.

The squad made their way off the stage and that's when it was time to pick a winner. This year's Cheerleading championship award goes to Urbanest. Aaliyah's team won as the crowd went wild; once again, her baby girl did her thing. As Urbanest made their way off the stage, Donesha instantly picked up on Rain's change in attitude.

"What's wrong with you, cuzzo? Seems like you seen a ghost," Donesha laughed it off, but as she saw, Rain wasn't smiling one bit.

"I'm good, just tired of all the screaming," she said as they waited by the ticket booth.

"I'm ready to get out of here," she said as she noticed Aaliyah walking over, but it looked like she wasn't by herself. Rain began to stare even harder as she noticed that was Jayla with Aaliyah and the last thing she needed was to be spotted by one of them.

"Look, get Aaliyah and meet me at the car," Rain said as she hauled ass toward the parking lot in fear. *Why the fuck would Aaliyah bring Jayla near me?* Rain asked herself over and over as she sat waiting.

"Hey, Nesha…where mommy at?" asked Aaliyah, "and oh, this is my cousin Jayla," she introduced as they both spoke back to each other.

"Your mom left once she saw you coming, so come on we have to go."

Jayla's mind started to wonder real fast. "Aaliyah, didn't your mother die?"

Once those words were uttered, Aaliyah started to think and she knew she'd fucked up big time. Her stomach literally dropped to the floor and Donesha was so fuckin' confused as to what this little girl was talking about. Just as Donesha went to say, *her mother's not dead*, Aaliyah quickly ended their conversation and left without answering.

"Oh my god, boo…I'm so glad you called, you wouldn't believe…" and as she went to finish, Vick quickly cut Rain's ass off.

"Storm's in labor," he said as Donesha and Aaliyah got into Rain's car. "You need to get to Henrico Doctors ASAP."

"How, Vick? I'm in D.C.; that's like two hours away."

Of course, he came to the rescue.

"I sent Jack to pick you up in the jet, just meet him in the back of the airport, but you need to go now," he instructed as Rain hung up and sped the fuck off.

Donesha tried to tell Rain what Jayla had said, but instantly she was cut the fuck off.

"Storm's in labor and I'm taking the jet, you will need to drive Aaliyah back to Richmond," she said as everyone in the car became very happy. As Rain drove to the airport, I know Aaliyah felt her mother's eyes piercing through her skin, but now wasn't the time to bring it up.

"Alright, Donesha, get both of my babies home safe," Rains said as she rushed out of the car and Jack met her by the jet.

"Hello, Mrs. Sanchez," Jack politely greeted as he helped Rain aboard the Jet. She was so nervous, but all she could focus on was the sex of Storm's baby which had been a well-kept secret up until now. Donesha and Aaliyah watched as the jet took off, then they left with excitement on getting back to Richmond.

"Oh God, please," Storm whined as she lay in the hospital bed with labor pains eating her ass alive.

"Baby, just try to relax," Chance expressed, which we all know that during labor, that shit ain't possible; but I guess he just wanted to help.

"Where is my sister? I need my other half!"

Just as Storm spoke that, Vick returned with details that he'd reached Rain and she was now on her way by jet. Storm continued to lay there praying that this shit would hurry up and be over; she never knew pain like this before in her life. Even when she was getting fuck to make the baby, it didn't hurt that damn bad and Storm was ready to push.

Thirty minutes later, the nurse came back in and checked to see if Storm's cervix's had dilated anymore. "You're only five and a half centimeters, Ms. Peters. We've still got like four more to go."

Those words hurt like hell because Storm just knew she was ready to give birth, but instead, she tried to get some rest. What seemed like forever, Rain finally arrived at the hospital as she ran down those halls like a crazy women.

"Where is labor and delivery?" she stopped to ask a passing nurse as she directed her which way to go. As she approached the nurse's station, it seemed as if those bitches didn't have anything better to do but talk because no one was doing any work at all.

"Excuse me, where is Ja'Nay Peters' room?" Rain asked nicely, but I guess she had her invisible suit on that day because everybody standing there ignored her ass, which pissed Rain off to the max. As two, out of four, of the nurses continued to talk, Rain reached her hand over and grabbed the clipboard.

"Excuse me, ma'am, you cannot look at that information," the nurse finally saw her.

"Bitch, fuck you! I already asked once for my sister's room number, and y'all bitches ignored me, so now watch this…" she found Storm's name and after getting her room number, Rain threw the clipboard directly at the nurse, leaving her with no other choice but to duck. "Bitch!" she said, as she walked her ass off, just waiting on one of the nurses to jump.

"Hey, baby," Vick greeted quietly, trying hard to let Storm stay asleep.

"How is she?" said Rain as Vick took off her jacket.

"She's been asleep for a little while now."

Rain made her way toward her sister. She reached down and kissed her on the head, causing Storm's eyes to open.

"Sis, you made it."

"You know I would. I wouldn't be anywhere else, how are you feeling?" asked Rain.

"I'm in pain, sis. I wish they'd hurry the fuck up because I feel like I have to shit," Storm expressed as she grunted and Rain took the liberty to look down there herself and see if the baby was crowning.

"Oh my, God, sis! I see a head. Nurse!" Rain began to shout as two of them came running inside the room.

"The head is coming out," the nurse expressed as they looked on; and damn sure, the patch of curly hair from the baby's head was showing and it was time to push.

Vick left out the room to check and see if any of their family had arrived while Rain and Chance stayed in for the birth.

"Ahh shit, oh my God, please help me!" Storm shouted in pain as she pushed with coaching from Rain and Chance.

"You can do it, sis."

"Just breathe, baby."

They both said as the doctor instructed Storm to give him one more hard push. As they held her legs in closer to her chest, Storm pushed with all her might and the doctor delivered her first born son. Chance was so excited he let her leg go to grab for the baby, but the show wasn't over yet. Rain couldn't figure out why Storm still looked like she was about to shit again and the doctor was still digging in her sister's walls.

"Ja'Nay, one more time," the doctor demanded with force this time, but whatever she was doing wasn't working to good.

"We're going to have to turn it around."

Chance and Rain both looked at each other.

I don't believe it, are you for real? Rain thought as she watched the doctor and nurses work on her sister. Soon the doctor pulled his arm back out and in the palm of his hand he cuffed the head of Storm and Chance's second baby, which turned out to also be a boy.

Outside in the waiting room, everyone waited for the arrival of their newest edition as Donny and Vick walked a hole in the floor because they couldn't wait any longer. Vick spotted Chance as he came out of the room with tears coming down his face.

As soon as he approached his brother, Chance blurted out, "Mane, I got twin boys," he smiled and cried while hugging his brother to congratulate.

"So, can we see them now," he asked, "mom, dad, Donny…shit, everybody is already here, my nigg."

"Aight, let them know that as soon as they are done cleaning them up, everyone can come in," explained Chance to his brother and Vick went to tell the news.

"You did great, sis; but I'm still a little upset that you kept the twins from me," Rain laughed as Storm filled out the babies' names.

"Chance and Choice Sanchez, I like the ring of that, boo," said Chance as her room began to flood with friends and family. Everyone came in and showed Storm much love, but the tension between Donny and Rain was definitely thick. They didn't say two words to each other and that bitch, Bria, wouldn't even look her way.

"So, Donny, when will your bundle of joy be here?" asked Yvette out of concern, but Rain wasn't trying to hear that. She immediately got up and excused herself out the room; but the way she did it let everyone know she was mad. Vick knew that his wife was pissed at something, or should I say someone, as he got up to follow right behind her. By the time Vick made it outside of the hospital, Rain's ass was nowhere in sight.

Where the fuck did she go that quick, he thought as he pulled out his cell to call her. *Ring, Ring, Ring*, no answer. She wasn't picking up at all. After the seventh attempt to reach her, Vick was successful and from the sound of her voice she was crying.

"Baby, where are you and why are you crying?" he asked, but Rain remained in silence only sobs and heavy breathing was what he got, and it was obvious that she still held a lot of pain.

"Daddy, how can my brother just sit there and act like his life's all perfect and we're still not speaking to each other?" she cried, "it's killing me right now, baby. It really is."

"I know that, boo. But God's going to take care of it, just wait and see, my darling," he tried to provide comfort with his words, but truthfully, at that moment, nothing was working. Rain knew she didn't want to go back there with all them mutherfuckers, so instead, she sat in the parking garage until everybody left, and once Vick called her, she went back in.

"Where the hell have you been, missy? Two little people have been looking for you," Chance said, pointing to the babies who lay peacefully in Storm's arms. Rain sat in the chair as Chance handed her both babies; she smiled and kissed them both.

"I left to go and handle some business," said Rain as she placed her nose into both her nephew's hair. "Chance and Choice, you two have no idea how special your names are to your mother and I; well, let auntie be the first to tell you. You guys' names mean so much to us in life and that was the motto we lived by to change. I am honored to be y'all's aunt, and there's nothing in this world that I won't do for you. I'll always love you."

They all spent the next two hours talking and loving up on the two new babies, then visiting hours had to come to an end, but their new lives were just beginning.

RJ only spoke with his mom for a brief moment at the hospital, and within that time, he didn't get to mention anything about moving out, but he knew he had to tell her he'd just hoped she gave her blessings. As he laid across his bed talking to Denise, he knew it wouldn't be easy for her to move without being noticed, so he told her to only pack what she needed right away. The rest he'd go out and buy whatever the fuck she wanted once they got settled in.

"Mane, baby, I can't wait to be out of here, Tiara and Legally are working my fuckin' last nerve following me around and shit, trying to see what I'm doing so that they can report to my dad," said Denise. "I've already put some bags in the trunk today because my fathers out of town on business until next week."

To her, that was good, but her nasty ass sisters were still being his spy just out of spite to Denise. While they continued to talk, RJ noticed the alarm to the front door going off which meant his family was home and he needed to go and talk to his mother right now.

"Just meet me at the townhouse tomorrow at 4:00 p.m., but I got to go now," he expressed as they both ended their call.

"But, Aaliyah…how could you be so fuckin' stupid as to bring your cousin, Jayla, over near me?" RJ heard his mom yelling downstairs as he ran to see what was up.

"Mom, I'm sorry alright. I totally forgot, it's been so long, I'm used to having my mother and you should know I wouldn't intentionally bring harm your way mom, that's stupid," Aaliyah expressed her heart with tears and Rain couldn't do anything else but understand.

"Come here, baby."

They both sat down at the table to talk.

"Did you see your auntie, Candace?" Rain asked.

"No, mom, I didn't; and by the time I got to Donesha, I remembered to play it off so I addressed her as if I was with my godmother," said Aaliyah, never mentioning that she'd mentioned something about her mom in front of Jayla, which to me wasn't a very smart move and Rain needed to know if she had to prepare.

While Rain continued to integrate Aaliyah, out in New York, Candace and Jayla were having a little talk of their own that went a little something like this:

"You really saw Aaliyah today, Jayla?" Candace questioned her daughter as they sat at the table having dinner.

"Yeah, mom, it was crazy. I didn't recognize her at first because she looks so different, but I approached her anyway and we immediately connected, but then she said something that even I found a little strange. When I asked her who was she with, she said her mom, but I thought auntie Rain was dead."

"And she is," Candace cut in, "why did you see her or something?"

"Nope, I saw this dark-skinned girl with blond hair," said Jayla, and her saying that helped Candace remember making eye contact with Donesha in the stands. But who was she to Aaliyah?

"Aaliyah said that she was with her godmother, and apparently she was in the car because I didn't see her at all," Jayla continued to explain while Candace took it all in.

"I can't wait to tell my mother about all of this I'm sure it's nothing baby, but I'm glad you saw your cousin because in one more year and you girls will both be grown. I'll see what I can do to maybe get you girls together and we can have one big eighteenth birthday party."

It had been long enough, and Candace was missing her brother Rico hard as a bitch, and that's more the reason why she missed his kids.

RJ and Aaliyah…shit, none of the family knew the truth behind the things that their grandfather Ricky had done; the whole damn family was in the dark and that's why the fact of them not being able to see the children never made any sense. After finishing their meal, Jayla began to do the dishes and Candace used that as perfect timing to give her mother a call.

Now since Ricky's death, Christina had to start all over due to Rain taking everything from underneath Ricky, they didn't leave her shit. Christina lost the three houses and all nine of the cars; even the legit business was taken away. I think the bank even took a couple of her furs and diamonds, but that bitch, Christina, wasn't all that dumb. She had six million dollars tucked away, but she had to play it off for two years. She didn't want the IRS to see her spending big money, so she got herself an apartment and readjusted back to her Columbian middle-class living days; but it was just until all that shit was over.

Of course she wasn't going to date a gritty ass nigga; but on another note, she was done with drug kings too, so she copped herself a franchise owner. I mean this nigga had like a million Chicken Kings. You could find one of them places anywhere you went, so for the most part, Christina was chilling.

"What you doing, mom?" Candace asked as she answered the phone.

"Hey, baby…how are you? Your brother Steven just left from over here," said Christina as she noticed Candace blowing hard in the phone like something was bothering her.

"Mom, Jayla saw Aaliyah today."

"What? Where? I have been looking for them for almost…I don't know how long, now," Christina expressed.

"Mom calm down," Candace cut in because she knew how her mom would go on and on. "We had to go to D.C. today because Jayla had a competition and how about Aaliyah's team was there."

"You saw her?" Christina softly asked and I know Candace heard the pain of missing them in her voice.

"No, mom, I didn't; but I wish I did."

Rico's children weren't kids anymore; they had their own lives now which that side of the family missed out on. Rain and Christina never had any real problems, but Ricky created a mess for everybody else to clean up.

"Jayla saw her after the competition and she said she was with her mom, but it was just some chick that probably knows Storm and is acting like she's Aaliyah's godmother."

"You don't say," Christina's voice changed quickly, "Was it that bitch, Lizzy?" she asked. Christina had it out for Lizzy since day one, and after everything went down with Chuck's white geeky ass, he hired someone to do his homework on Lizzy. "He found out that she knew Storm and that they did some work together, but he never told me just how close they were," Christina said as her mind began to cook up a new idea. Why would someone who works for Storm really need to work for Ricky, but no one has seen or heard from Lizzy to get answers and now this shit has come to the table.

"The woman I saw wasn't who you described to me, mom; this bitch was one of the hood rat bitches."

"Watch your mouth," Christina cut her off at that point

"Sorry, mom, but she was that bad," Candace said, but really Donesha was not. She was a dime, just ghetto as hell, and Candace was just being a hater.

"I'll look into something myself, baby," Christina told Candace. "I'll have Chuck find out where Ms. Lizzy is for me, and then maybe she will lead us to my grandchildren."

Christina and Candace discussed the details for a little longer, then they got off their call because Christina had some shit to start digging up.

"Mom, can I talk to you?" RJ asked, but Rain told him to wait, she was talking to Storm. RJ really wanted to talk right now, but after the screaming match between his mom and sister earlier about his dad's family, he knew it was defiantly a bad time to piss her off; so instead, he grabbed his keys and just dipped.

"Sis, my sons are so beautiful. I can't put them down." She loved being a mom.

"Well, I'm happy for you, boo. Where is Chance?" Rain asked, making sure he was still by Storm's side.

"He went outside to make a call, so I'm going to try and get some rest because once I get home with two babies, I'll never get any sleep," Storm joked and Rain said she was tired as well. She really wanted to tell her sister about all the shit that went on today, but instead, she let her enjoy her moment.

"I love you, Chance and Choice," Storm kissed her two sons on the head with love, something that her and Rain didn't have at that age, and Storm meant she was going to be a better mother to her kids; they were going to be the future kings in their family.

Chapter 5

Long Time Coming

Waking up feeling like you're still in a nightmare is something that I think we all can relate to, and that's just how Rain was feeling. Rain felt as if she was stuck in a hole that was slowly filling with dirt and all she wanted to do was get out. As she sat on the side of her extra king size bed, all she could think of was the shit that went down yesterday; and hopefully, Aaliyah's little mistake wouldn't become a problem. Besides the bull shit at the competition, Rain knew that something was bothering RJ and she needed to find out what it was.

"Junior," called out Rain as she knocked on RJ's bedroom door while opening it. "Good morning, my son," she said. "Would you like to talk now," she questioned as he sat up in the bed from a sleepless night. Shit just seemed like it was happening too fast—too fast for RJ that is.

"Morning, mom. You calmed down now?" he began to laugh at how mad she could get when pissed off. Rain began to smile even harder at his charm because RJ reminded her so much of Rico and that's why she stayed on his ass.

"I'm good, baby; but what about you?" she sits down and places her hand on his knee. "What is it that you wanted to talk about last night?"

RJ rubs his hands across his waves in a sweat because he didn't think he'd be hit with this conversation so early in the damn morning. The time had come and there wasn't any way around it.

So, I might as well tell her, he thought to himself as he slowly took his mom's hand. "There's no easy way to say it, mom, so I'm gonna just spill it. I'm moving out. Me and Denise already have a townhouse together," he said as he sat there quietly waiting on his mother's reaction which RJ knew wasn't going to be good.

Rain took a minute as her heart was beginning to beat fast, but deep down inside she knew that he was grown and it was indeed time for him to want to leave the nest. What she was unsure about was Denise's family and the type of people that they could be, so it was high time that their families met.

"I'm proud of you, son; you've grown to be the man that me and your father wanted," Rain began to express, but the words she uttered shocked RJ's ass big time. "I need you to remember that no matter what...my doors are always open to you and please be smart and safe," was her only command for her son.

RJ smiled, he was overjoyed, all of those fears about telling his mother turned out to be for nothing. Rain was already planning a family dinner party for both families and RJ knew in his heart that there was no way that this shit could happen, especially with Rain and Denise's Dad in the same room.

"Now, mom…hold on. Pump the breaks just a lil," RJ was tripping out. "Can we wait until we move in together and get straight then we can do a housewarming party?" he suggested as Rain smiled and agreed with her baby boy's wishes.

So, let's go," she jumped up, shouting to RJ. "I want to see this new house, please!"

"Ok, I'll meet you at the truck in ten minutes."

* * * * *

Over at Denise's crib, the coast was looking clear and now was her chance to get her stuff. Her father had come back in town early, but he and her mother went out for the evening, which meant she could really make moves. Denise began throwing her shit in whatever bags she could find and what was supposed to be fast was taking all goddamn day because this chick had too many clothes and shoes. Half way through Denise's process, as smooth as it was going, Legally and Tiara showed the fuck up. Of course they were being nosey all in Denise's shit, they made it their business to watch her every fuckin' move.

"Wassup with all of the bags in your car?" Tiara was the first to ask.

"None of your fuckin' business, so leave me alone!" Denise snapped back as she pushed past both of them bitches, but she stopped at the door to turn and say, "You two always trying to find something on me to report to daddy, but guess what…there's nothing to tell."

She slams the door, leaving them two standing there looking stupid. Those two bitches couldn't wait to play detective as they hauled ass into Denise's room and immediately started going through her stuff for clues.

"OMG, Tiara look!" Legally called out, that bitch took all of her shit out the closet, so unless she's donating to charity, what the fuck is up?"

They knew their father would flip when he returned home, and you know them two couldn't wait to deliver the bad news. It was fucked up they hated their baby sister that much, and it's fucked up because she wasn't in the wrong.

"Baby!" Denise yelled out as she entered into their townhome not knowing Rain was sitting there on the new $3,000 couch that she'd just brought for them which shocked the hell out of Denise.

"You like?" he asked, coming up behind her and grabbing her waist.

"Hell, yeah! I mean…excuse me, Ms. Liz. Yea, I love it, baby. When did you do this?"

"My mom and I went out this morning and she wanted to give us a gift," he said, holding his hand out in reference to the new items inside the house and there was still more stuff to come.

"Well, I'm glad you like it," Rain stood and they hugged. "I'm about to go so that y'all can be alone," she said as she kissed RJ and expressed how happy she was again, but it was still a bittersweet moment.

As Rain pulled off waving goodbye to her son, a tear slid down her face. After seven years missed, she felt this was too soon; but it's true, RJ had become a man and she had to let him see life for himself. But that doesn't mean Rain won't be that far behind.

Why the fuck is my house pitch black? Rain thought to herself as she pulled into her driveway and Vick's car was there, so why the fuck was he sitting in the dark? Rain kind of hesitated to open the door, but instead, she still entered. As she punched in the alarm code, she felt a hand rest on her shoulder, causing her to jump.

"Shit, boo…you scared me!" Rain yelled out as her eyes met with Vick.

"That's my whole point," he laughed, helping Rain out of her coat.

"Please follow me," he said as he led the way back toward their bedroom which seemed to be the only thing lit the fuck up in the house. There were candles and a wrapped around bar filled with every type of liquor, fruit and syrup that can be put on *deserts*; well, I guess that the desert would be Rain tonight.

"Aww, baby…is this for me?" she asked, knowing it was.

Who else, boo?" Vick laughed. "You have always been and will forever be my queen, and tonight I'm going to crown you good."

He escorted her to the Jacuzzi so that she could undress and get in. Vick stood and watched as Rain's milk chocolate body slide down into the steamy water.

"Are you coming in?" she asked seductively.

Vick grinned, replying, "No. I'm going to watch you wash that golden pussy and then I'll take over." Vick sat back with his Peach Ciroc in one hand as he massaged his dick with the other while his queen prepared the kingdom for him.

"All done, daddy," she proudly announced, "so what's next?"

She held out her hand for him to take it, but instead, Vick picked her up and carried her dripping wet body into their room and laid her out on the table. With candles still lit, Vick began to place his favorite topping on her body, but only in the area he intended to indulge in first.

First base, Vick gently rubbed some strawberry syrup on Rain's lips and he began to tongue kiss it off. The feeling of his lips caressing hers nice and slow caused Rain's clitoris to begin pulsating which meant that pussy was nice and hot!

"I've missed you all day, daddy," she whispered between kisses.

"Me too, my queen," his manly voice sent vibrations through places that Rain never knew it could reach, but she kept right on enjoying the night.

Second base, Vick grabbed the bottle of hot oil and lightly placed it on Rain. That shit must've been on point because her moans sent all of Vick's blood to his dick, and before he could get finish with her massage, Vick's head was between Rain's legs and he instantly started feasting on that pussy.

Slurp, slurp, slurp. "Damn, queen, you taste so fuckin' good!" Vick tried to say while drinking her love. Rain kept right on thrusting her pelvis into his mouth; the more she fucked his face, the harder he came at that pussy, causing orgasm number…

"Oh shit, daddy!"

Who the fuck can count when multiples were shooting out back to back and he hadn't even stuck the dick in yet. He continued adding the ingredients to his sundae and his favorite was using the diced pineapples.

"Your taste is simply scrumptious, my queen," he said and its funny because Rain and the word *queen* seemed to follow each other everywhere, which leads me to believe that is her true title in life. Finally, Vick produced her sixth of seventh nuts from his head game, and now it was really penetration time.

Vick began to undress, revealing king ransom, that thick ass piece of long dick he carried around. Rain's eyes widen at the sight of his manhood; every time she was in its presence, it was like a wonderful sight, but feeling it was even better. Vick slowly stroked it in and out of her pussy to open it up.

"Umm, daddy, that shit feels so good," she whispered, "and after the week I've had, I really do need this."

"Well, this is what you're going to get," he softly moaned in her ear and on this go round, he slid all the way into her uterus; the tip of his dick slamming a little rough this time was his way of whipping the kitty.

"What you need is some thug love tonight; that will help you get rid of your stress," Vick laughed, but Rain knew he damn sure wasn't playing. Vick fucked the shit out of her for…I know all of two hours. They fucked in every part of that room; at least they tried, because some parts they couldn't fit in. Vick threw the dick and Rain took it; dripping that wet pussy all up and down on his shift. Mane, the nut Vick busted…I swear Rain better hope she's not the next one pregnant.

"Are you really happy, baby?" asked Vick as he held Rain as she lay on top of him breathing hard but starting to slow down.

"Of course I am, why would you ask me that?" she questioned out of curiosity.

"Just something I wanted to ask you, boo, because if you weren't, I'd do whatever I needed to do to make it happen for you."

Rain lifted her head to eye him as she kissed his medium perfect lips.

"I know," was all she said and she rested her head back against his heart beat; and this time, she went to sleep.

"Mr. Peters', Main is here to see you," said Dallas; she was the receptionist at D-Nyce Studios. Donny was in his office; so far gone that he forgot all about his meeting with Main.

"Let him back, Dallas. I'm ready for him," Donny announced as he cleared his desk of his work and Main entered taking his seat, ready for business.

"So, Main, how have you been, my nigga?" he said, slipping him five. "How's life treating you?" he asked.

"I'm good, but I'll be even better when we talk about money. I know a nigga done generated some good figures up in this mutherfucker," he replied, popping shit because he thought he had power. Poor Donny was so clueless to the power he was thinking and he had no idea what laid ahead.

"Now hold on there, soldier; yes, your albums did great…but you and I both know your spending habits exceeded way beyond your artist budget, which leads me to this," as Donny started putting out what looked like receipts as well as Main's new contract.

"Here is the proof to back up everything that I will say to you at this time." Donny took a sip of his Patron silver on the rocks, "Main, your contract on this term doesn't come with advancement money and also your percentage will be down by fifteen percent," his words made shit hit the fan.

Main's big, 6'9" ass stood up, and I swear I thought he would kill Donny; but instead, he tried to remain calm.

"I'm telling you, Dee, mane…you don't want to fuck with my money, that's grounds for a nigga to get fucked up."

Donny was now standing up on his feet.

"Look, nigga…don't be fuckin' threatening me in my own shit. In case you forgot, I own this here, alright my nigga? So you can either play by my rules, or you can get the fuck on because this is my final answer.

Niggas didn't know that Donny had balls and he was tired of people telling him what to do. Main stood there grinning, taking all that shit in.

"You're right, dog; you are in control," he laughed and turned to walk away, "But I will get my fifteen percent one way or another."

"What the fuck is that supposed to mean?" ask Donny angrily, "If you know what's good for you, you'll leave." He pulls his AK-47 out from under the desk so Main would know he stayed strapped.

"I'll go, my nigga. Good looking out, just make sure you send my shit to the right address," Main turns around to leave. Main was pissed and he didn't want to go back to jail because he, too, was strapped; but he decided not to pull out at the time, he had other plans for Donny. Skillz and Keys pulled up to the studio just as Main was pulling off, and from the way he drove that Benz down the street, they knew something was wrong.

"Donny?" called out Skillz as they made their way toward the back of the studio and there Donny was playing around with a switch board, but his expression said something else was on his mind.

"Wassup, boss? We saw that nigga, Main, doing ninety miles per hour down the block; he seemed pissed off," said Skillz, but Keyz already had an idea about what took place. He knew contract negations were today and Keyz had already seen Main's. Donny never answered Skillz, but he did inform him that their album, *Maniac Money* was being pushed back on release which indeed made Skillz wonder why.

"We got three more tracks to lay for that album and its fire," he expressed, knowing how hard he and Main worked on that shit, so of course there were number one hits on it.

"There are some issues with Main's contract right now, and that's that," replied Donny as Keyz sat there eating and not saying a word. Donny was his boy and he put him on to the business, wasn't no way he was going to fuck his bread up for another nigga…shit, his girl just had baby number three. After beating around the bush for about thirty minutes more, Skillz hit the booth; and Donny, along with Keyz, did what they do best—create!

Some people believe in the saying, *an eye for an eye,* and that *revenge is sweet*; what you dish out will come back to you, and Main just didn't give a fuck at this point. He knew what Donny was saying had some truth to it, and a lot of his money he had indeed blown. Nobody knew about Main's fetish for females and money; even with one heart break, it still didn't change him. Bria cost him his money and life the first go round, and now this bitch's nigga think he's going to start the second show.

Oh, hell ,naw, Main said to himself as he popped four diddies and bucked his Ciroc while driving to the fuckin' hood. It had been a minute since he'd been around Highland Park—his stomping ground; when he left Club Benji's and started doing music, a lot of his priorities changed.

Even though his face wasn't always seen, Main always rep for his niggas from around the way, which made them continue to respect him. He knew if there ever was a time or a number on a nigga's head, that he could return back and squad up quick.

Cheese and Mac Man were old head killers that once ran the streets of HP. They now lived together in a house on Fourth Avenue where all the young niggas hung out. Cheese supplied crack and heroin to the streets, so a couple of lil dudes flocked and sold for him. Mac Man stuck to his favorite drug of choice; he smoked and sold only exotic strains of weed, and this nigga would have shit that existed only in California and that made the dudes buy it all the time. It was one lil nigga that was crazy about Main and he looked up to him a lot.

"Lil Haze," knew Main from back in the day when he was first taking over the streets and Main gave him his first pack. When Haze's older brother, Keon, got shot in a drug deal, Main looked out financially for their mom. Haze was a killer who ran the younger niggas around the way and whatever Main said, that's what went.

"God damn, is that all y'all niggas do?" joked Main as he walked right on in Cheese and Mac Man's house. All of the goons were in the middle of a cypher and that's one thing Main didn't fuck with was weed; smoking it that is…but he'd sell that shit to your ancestors. As he made it over to the couch to sit down, he dapped up every nigga in there along the way then he took a seat over in the corner by Haze.

Mac Man's girlfriend, Bianca, brought Main a Corona and that's all she did was serve Mac Man's friends all day, as well as spend hidden money.

"So, what's up with you nigga," Haze joked around, "the way you sounded on the phone made me think you were about to kill somebody."

"I am," Main wasn't kidding as Haze laughed like he was fuckin' playing.

"Y'all know that nigga, D-Nyce; right? This mutherfucker tried to play the kid today," he began to explain. "I had a meeting with dude to discuss my new contracts and my new album, *Maniac Money*…tell me why this bitch ass queer gone hit me with some shit about my artist budget is exceeded and now he has to deduct from my stacks? Long story short, he's trying to fuck me by voiding my contracts for speaking up to his ass, which means he's cutting off my fuckin' bread."

Main was good at mind control, especially when it came to young ass goons. "So, tell me this y'all…am I wrong for taking care of my hood?" said Main and this nigga was a trip for real. He tried to make it seem to them that Donny was hating on him because he looked out for his hood, when technically, Main hadn't really given them shit. He'd hit them with a couple of stacks and some pounds of weed when he had it or when it was given to him by friends, but since Main didn't smoke, he had no problem throwing them the shit it was free.

"So, what we gone do?" Mac Man walks in from the back room; they hated for a nigga to double cross one of their own.

"I got a plan. I just need to know if y'all niggas were in or not, but I guess I got my answer," Main laughed standing up to walk out the door.

"I'll be back. I got to go make a call!"

* * * * *

I got you now, bitch, thought Chuck to himself as he sat in the living room sipping on Brandy and throwing dots at a picture of Lizzy up on his wall; he blamed her for causing him his life.

"We will meet again bitch!" he said, throwing two more darts at her eyes. Damn this mutherfucker really did feel some type of way. In the middle of his aim straight for Lizzy's nose, Chuck's house phone began to go off. Chuck hesitated for a brief moment; he hadn't really been talking to anyone lately, so who would that be?

"Hello," he answered with a stern voice.

"Well, well, well…hello there, Chuck," said the voice of a woman that Chuck needed no time to pick up on who it was.

"Hello, Christina. How are you?" he greeted, but wondered why she would be calling him, "Lovely as always I hope" said Chuck but part of him knew he really didn't care.

"I was wondering if we could have lunch tomorrow?" asked Christina, and of course Chuck's light bulb went off. "We sure can, but is everything alright?"

"Don't worry about all of that; just meet me at 12:30 p.m. on 51st Street at LeBernardin," Christina instructed, and of course that broke ass nigga hurried up and agreed.

"Ok, cool. I have nothing else to do. I'll see you tomorrow evening."

They both had it out for Lizzy; as he hung up, staring back at his wall, he hoped that whatever it was Christina wanted concerned Lizzy.

"I'm coming for you, bitch," Chuck threw one more dot, landing it right in the middle of Lizzy's throat.

"Why am I here?" Bria questioned herself as she sat waiting in the dark ass parking lot for Main and it was starting to get cold.

"I'm so tired of playing this mutherfucker's game when in all honesty, I don't owe him shit!" she continued talking out loud to herself when the tap on the window scared her, even though she already knew who it was.

"Why the fuck you got to play so much?" said Bria as the car door opened and the person got in. She soon discovered it wasn't Main, but before she could react, Bria felt the punch of a male's fist in her face which caused white lights and she was knocked out cold.

Bria was now seven months pregnant, which made Donny become even more paranoid when she was out late driving. He felt like the folks in Virginia couldn't drive for shit.

Right number, wrong time...this is Bria and I'm always busy so leave a message and I'll think of calling you back.

Beep.

"Baby, I've called you six damn times. Where the fuck are you? It's now 11:30 p.m. and your ass ain't home. I hope you're on your way."

Donny couldn't figure out why she hadn't made it home yet; sometimes after work, she'd go and chill over her god sister Penny's house, so he decided to call over there.

"Hello," Penny answered half asleep.

"Penny, this is Donny...have you seen or talked to your sister today?" Donny was nervous about her response; all he wanted was for Bria to walk through the door at that moment. "The last time I talked to her was this morning when she was on her way to work."

"Why?" she asked, becoming wide awake. She didn't play about her sister. Donny took a deep breath followed by a pause, he didn't want to scare anyone over nothing, but this type of behavior wasn't at all like Bria.

"This could be my nerves, Penny, so I don't want to worry you...but you're the closest thing she has to family here," he expressed. "I haven't been able to reach Bria and I'm getting kind of scared," he continued, "the last time I spoke to her she was leaving work, she told me she had a stop to make and then she'd be home. That was three hours ago and she still hasn't gotten home yet," Donny went on an on as Penny's heart jumped through her chest. He knew this by the sound of her phone hanging up in his face.

As the minutes turned into hours, Donny called everyone he knew that Bria communicated with; no one had seen or heard from her at all and that's when Donny felt it was time to call the police.

"Wake up, bitch," Haze's masculine voice said as ice cold water splashed all in Bria's face. The chilling water caused her eyes to open and discover that she was in a basement somewhere.

"Who are you?" she tried to speak from underneath the scarf that covered her mouth.

"What, what's that bitch?" asked Haze as he went to remove the gag. "What are you trying to say, bitch? And if you scream, I'm going to kill you way before your bitch ass boyfriend pays up," he said as she shook her head as a sign she understood. Bria had no idea what the fuck was going on, let alone where her location was.

"Why are you doing this to me?" she pleaded, "Can't you see I'm pregnant and I've done nothing to you? Hell, I don't even know who you are."

"You don't need to know, bitch. Just know this...your man better cooperate with our demands and you'll live to push that baby out," he said as he handed Bria the phone which was already ringing Donny's cell. "Now tell him your ransom is one million dollars if he wants to ever hold his child."

Tears streamed down Bria's face; she was scared, she didn't know what to do as the piss ran down her legs. All she could think about was making it out of this shit alive.

"Donny," Bria called out in tears.

"Bria, where the fuck are you baby and what's wrong?" he asked as her crying freaked him out even more.

"Donny, I've been kidnapped and they want ransom which is a million dollars; please pay baby so I can come home…please," she begged. As she heard the phone drop, Bria began to cry even harder. At that point, she began to worry about Donny.

"Look, bitch…give me that phone!" Haze snatched it from Bria's ears as Donny put it back against his.

"Look here, nigga…you got three days to make the drop around Whitcomb Court, and if you don't, you can kiss your bitch and fatherhood goodbye."

"What's the reason for all of this, mane? Let my girl go. She's pregnant!" Donny pleaded, but all he heard for the second time that day was a click then the dial tone in his face.

Think before you act is a very true statement; but depending on the situation, you might not have time to think of a positive action when all you want to do is kill. The company you keep may not always be trustworthy, but you can always believe in your decision to let them go before disaster strikes. Now that was too late. All Donny could think of was his sister, Rain, and how much he needed her help now. "Never bite the hand that's there for you."

Chapter 6

Black Ice

"What the fuck is taking these niggas so long to call?" expressed Rain as she paced the floor in agony. It had been a week since Bria's kidnapping and Donny was losing his mind. Even though he and Rain hadn't spoken in almost a year, as soon as Vick got word about what was going on, he told Rain. Just like any good sister, regardless of what was going on, she was there for her baby brother. Donny was in the guest room finally taking a nap because this nigga was running off of no sleep. All day long, he would ride around looking for clues on Bria's whereabouts; that's all he could do until these fuck niggas called. Thank God for Keyz taking care of D-Nyce Studios, because Donny was only worried about Bria and his unborn child.

* * * * *

Rain took off running in the direction of the kitchen as the sound of her iPhone went off.

"Here, baby…I think it's them," said Vick as he handed her the phone. The look of fear really filled her eyes.

"Hello," she answered to nothing but silence and heavy breathing. "Look, I don't have time to play no mutherfuckin' games. Now who is this?" she asked as a loud laughter presented itself in her ear.

"Bitch, we got your money but that ain't enough…your boy, Donny's pockets gonna feel this hit!" the nigga had a nerve to say, not knowing that Rain was the last bitch he wanted to play games with. These niggas switched the game up knowing that Donny had a lot of money; they were trying to play him for a fool.

"What the fuck y'all niggas think my brother some type of square that's gone be an ATM for some thirsty niggas?" she was pissed the fuck off.

She was now discovering that this situation was a personal tag toward her brother; which meant she wasn't going to stop until she got to the bottom of this shit.

"Look here, bitch…y'all got seven more days to get me the money or this hoe and her baby will need funeral arrangements!" he slammed down the phone as Vick stood there trying to comfort Rain. She didn't know how she was going to tell Donny what their new demands were when all he wanted was Bria back. The fact that they were going to now hold her longer than planned was really going to make him snap and Rain knew she'd have to fix this quick.

"Please, I have to go to the bathroom," Bria pleaded as Cheese sat there and kept right on eating. "Please help me," she begged as she sat there in the same smelly, dirty clothes, even the baby had to be uncomfortable in Bria's belly. She hadn't even been able to stretch out for a week. Bria heard the sound of the door opening up and she prayed it was someone coming to rescue her.

"Wassup, my nigga?"

She watched Cheese give some one five and Bria tried her hardest to see this person's face; when all of a sudden, she found herself panicking for air.

"Main," she cried as he stood in front of her face with this devilish and slick ass smirk. That nigga, Main, had only one motive from the beginning and that was to bring pain. "It was you," Bria cried out hysterically, "why would you do this to me, Main?" she asked as this nigga pulls up a chair to sit down.

"Did you ask yourself why when you took all of my fuckin' money and dropped off the face of the earth when I needed you the most?" he asked, causing her pain to become more unbearable and she knew she didn't have the answer to his question.

"Main, please…I'm pregnant, please let me go!" she was now pleading with this nigga.

"Not before I get everything I lost fuckin' around with you; not to mention, the heartache Bria, I really loved your ass; and you broke the code, so what did you really expect me to do?"

Main continued to sit there chopping it up with his nigga, Cheese, whom held Bria hostage, along with the other HP niggas.

"Look here, bruh," he said, handing Main the bag containing the money. "Haze picked this up yesterday and I counted it making sure it's all there," said Cheese as Main rubbed his hands together at the sight of money; but of course, his greed wanted more.

"What the fuck is that noise?"

They made their way into the room where Bria was, only to find her throwing up everywhere.

"Bitch, what the fuck you doing?" Cheese screamed out at the sight of having to clean all that up.

"I'm sorry, I couldn't help it," said Bria in between gags. "I am pregnant in case you forgot."

Main laughed as if the shit was really funny, but in reality it wasn't.

"Look here…clean that shit up!" he ordered, "I'll be back later," Main uttered as he left out the door never looking back. He had no remorse for Bria at this time; all he wanted was what he felt belonged to him and Donny was going to pay up.

"Hurry up, Chance. We do have an appointment and the photographer isn't going to hold our spot," announced Storm as she put the twins in their chairs. Chance finally brought his ass down the stairs looking good as a bitch in his Akoo outfit and smelling even better. Storm couldn't do nothing but smile and shake her head; if they weren't running behind, she would have fucked him right there because he always turned her on. Storm, Chance and their twins, looked just like they had stepped off a magazine cover as they waited for their turn to take pictures.

"Baby, it's packed as a bitch in this mall today; the welfare checks must've come out."

They both laughed because that was the only time you saw the mall packed like this.

"Sanchez family?" the receptionist called out, directing Storm to take her family back. What felt like two hours really was one, but the way the twins acted slowed them up. But they completed their session, which, by the way, turned out beautifully.

Macy's had a sale that day and Storm wanted to go; but of course you know Chance's ass didn't. He tried to say it was because he didn't want to walk to the other end of the mall, but we all know men hate shopping with their women. Whatever he needed to do to keep Storm happy was done as they pushed the double stroller while window shopping on their way to Macy's.

I have a family; Storm thought to herself, this was something she never felt would happen. The feeling that ran through her body at that time was unexplainable, and nothing was going to ruin her day. *But never speak to soon.*

"Look, boo!" shouted Storm as she ran toward the infant section. "This is what I want for the boys," she explained pointing to the new double bed crib.

"Whatever you want, baby," he answered, handing her his black card; but all Chance really wanted to do was leave the fuckin' mall. As Storm and Chance approached the exit to the store, who would have known his ending would just begin.

"Daddy," called out a child whose voice sounded familiar to Chance's. "Daddy, daddy!" the child called out again, but this time the voice sounded closer as Storm stops and turns around.

"Hey, daddy!" called out CJ as he jumped into Chance's arms while Storm stood their looking very lost.

"Daddy?" she asked, looking dead at Chance and he didn't know what to do.

"Yeah, daddy!" answered Lizette as she walked up from behind and Chance knew this wouldn't end well. He wished, at that moment, that he had powers to click himself away; but the fact is that this meeting was long overdue.

"What the fuck is going on, Chance?" asked Lizette, "and who is this bitch?"

"Bitch?! I got your bitch. The only bitch I see here is you!" snapped Storm. "Because I'm his wife!" she informed as she grabbed his arm clutching it tight.

Lizette stood there laughing to hold back the tears and from swinging because everyone, but Chance, was in the dark about this. The looks on those two women faces showed Chance that he'd fucked up big time now and what was he going to do.

"So you went out and got married, nigga, without inviting your son to the wedding?" questioned Lizette.

"Umm, excuse me? His sons are right here!" Storm said, pointing to the stroller containing Chance and Choice as Lizette could have ripped Storm's heart out of her chest.

"What the fuck you mean, 'sons' bitch! I'm the only one with his child."

They both cut their eyes over at Chance who stood there holding his head and not saying a word.

"Nigga, you got two seconds to say something or I'm gonna smack the shit out of you!" threaten Lizette and even though Storm was pissed at him, she damn sure wasn't going to let some other chick hit her man.

"Look, Lizette, go home ok," said Chance as he kissed CJ and turned to walk away. "and *yes*, these are my sons," he made sure he got that out as Storm followed behind him. Lizette screamed and cursed, but this altercation was far from over; in fact, it was just beginning.

Storm stayed quiet the whole ride home as the scene from the mall played over in her mind.

How could he keep something like this for me?, she thought to herself and she damn sure wasn't going to rest without answers. Chance wanted to say something to her so bad, but judging from the look on her face and the way she slammed his truck door, he knew now wasn't the right time.

"Alright, mommy's here," she said to the twins as they became fussy from needing a diaper change. Chance stood in the doorway of the nursery, watching Storm's every move.

"Baby, can we talk?" he asked, but Storm remained quiet until the twins were sound asleep. She wasn't about to argue in front of her children. Storm bumped past Chance as she walked into the kitchen, and of course he followed her in there too.

"Janay, please…can we talk?" he begged again and without warning, he was hit with reality.

Bang.

Storm threw a plate at his face, only grazing him as it smashed up against the wall.

"Fuck you, Chance!" she screamed and cried. "How could you lie to me the whole time, you bastard? And that text, and those strange phone calls…all of it was a lie and you've had a child the whole time but didn't have the audacity to keep it real with me!" she felt angry and wanted him to feel the same thing. "I'm sitting up here thinking my babies were your first, and all the time they're number two and three."

"Boo, I'm sorry. I didn't want to lose you," he pleaded, down on his knees as he tried to hold Storm by her legs.

"Get off me, Chance! My trust for you has been broken. I hate you. I hate you!" she punched on his back as she fell to the floor in rage. Instead of picking her up, Chance just stayed down beside her and once again tried to hold her close.

"Janay, please…I'm sorry. I love you so much baby. I was scared. Please believe me," he started to cry. They sat there in the middle of the kitchen floor as Chance began to explain everything. What was once a happy home had now been shattered and at this point, all Chance could do was pray for forgiveness and hope that Storm wouldn't leave him.

*****

"Wassup, Lizzy?" said Byrd as he opened up the door to D-Nyce Studios. "Donny's in the back with Keyz."

As she made her way down the hall, Rain's stomach did flips; she hated to be the bearer of bad news. Donny was in the middle of doing what he did best as he made eye contact with his sister. He informed Keyz that he'd be right back; all he wanted was for Rain to have some good news.

"Wassup, big sis?" he said as he kissed her on the cheek. "Please tell me we have to go get Bria," he asked, which made Rain choke up even more.

"Baby bruh, sit down," she pulled out the chair which Donny felt couldn't be good. "I need you to think long and hard Donny; who are you beefing with?" she asked, but Donny didn't understand what she meant.

"Come on, sis…you know me, I'm not down with all that shit; you feel me? I don't have a problem with anybody, but what's wrong? Why would you ask me that?"

"Baby bruh, this shit is personal, and it's toward you. These niggas want more money," expressed Rain as tears began to fall down Donny's face and he fell to his knees. All he wanted was his baby's momma back.

"Sis, I swear I don't know who these niggas are or why they fuckin' with me," Donny continued to cry like a five-year-old baby because he was slowly dying inside.

"Excuse me, D. There's a Penny here to see you and she said she's Bria's sister."

Donny invited her back even though he wasn't in any shape to talk.

"Donny!" Penny called out in surprise of the state he was in. "Please tell me my sister's ok," she asked, taking a seat beside Rain.

"Well, she's not fine, but she's alive and I need to know does Bria have any enemies that we should know about," asked Rain, "because the kidnappers are demanding more money."

"What the fuck you mean, *more money*?" Penny snapped. "Didn't y'all already pay them the fuckin' million?"

"Yeah, we did," said Rain. "But now they want more and I believe this shit is more than just personal on my brother."

They all had to put their heads together to figure this shit out. Bria was approaching her eight month, and without care, so they knew her condition couldn't be good. Penny suddenly remembered a conversation her and Bria had about Bria's old boyfriend that had gotten out of jail and was blackmailing her real bad. Could this be the situation that is related to this shit? But if it wasn't… Penny felt like it was time to come clean if it could save Bria's life.

"Donny, I just remembered something," said Penny as he and Rain were talking amongst themselves.

"Yeah, wassup, Penny. I just want my baby back," he expressed and that was it for Penny, she couldn't hold Bria's secrets at this point, it was life or death for her and that baby.

"I think I know who's responsible for this and let me tell you why," Penny begins as Rain took her glasses off to listen.

"When Bria and I were sixteen years old, she began dating this big-time drug dealer who gave her everything she wanted at her age and more. He was known for robbing niggas and taking over their turfs and one day Bria went with him. She didn't have a clue what it was that this mutherfucker was up to as far as making her participate in the robbery, but that trifling ass nigga did get her involved. He made Bria hold the gun to the guy's wife's head while the guy emptied his whole stash totaling two hundred and fifty thousand dollars. Bria said she was so scared. Her hands shook slowly as she tried to keep them still because the trigger was being hugged by her finger." Penny paused, dropping her head down to the floor.

"So, what happen?" Rain was like, *come the fuck on*.

"Somehow, the guy got loose from his grip and started to tussle for the gun as Bria stood there still with the wife at gun point. She screamed for them to just stop and of course, you know men…they didn't. The gun ended up going off and Bria said all she remembered doing was screaming and clutching her hand not thinking and, *pow*…another gunshot went off, blowing the side of the lady's head off."

Rain and Donny just looked at each other because they both were in shock. They had no idea the past Bria had come from, and this was only the beginning.

Penny continued, "Two years after that incident, Bria's boyfriend went to prison and he left all his money with her to keep and hold him down while he did his bid, but Bria did the total opposite instead. She left town with all of his money and used it to start a new life. She never went to visit him; in fact, she broke up with him all together you might as well say. I mean…shit; it was like she fuckin' vanished. Six months ago, she told me that he was out and apparently he was now making music," then Penny paused, looking up at Rain and Donny both then saying, "He makes music for you, Donny. I'm talking about Maliki."

"Main?" Donny jumped up on his feet. "You mean to tell me that he is responsible for this?" Donny punched a hole in the wall. All this fuckin' time he's been playing me?" Donny snapped as Rain tried hard to calm him down.

"He's been blackmailing Bria this whole time," said Penny. "Most of the money you've been giving her has gone to him, but he told her if she didn't do what he wanted, that he would tell you and the police about the killing. But what scared her the most was losing you."

"So, if you knew all of this, why didn't you tell me when we spoke on the phone?" asked Donny, "We could have been ran up on these niggas, Penny."

She started to cry. "I know. I'm sorry. I didn't know if she was missing at first and I don't like telling my friends or family member's secrets."

Rain could understand her loyalty; but at this point, that shit goes out the window. Donny and Rain had heard enough and it was time to put a plan into action.

"If that nigga, Main thinks he can out smart us, he's got another thing coming," Rain was mad as shit. She swore that her past was behind her, but it's bitches like this that was the reason why she had to go back. Rain kissed Donny and told him she'd get up with him later because it was something she had to do. He said, *ok* while he and Penny kept talking; but inside, Donny knew his sister was up to something.

* * * * *

"Am I really ready to do this again?" Rain asked herself as she sat outside in her truck. Everyone who knows Rain knew how much she loved her family and there wasn't any level she wouldn't go to if crossed wrong. She hadn't even talk to Storm's ass all day, so neither knew the damages of the other. As Rain picked up the phone to place a call to New York, a cold chill ran through her body; but was it God or the Devil, good or evil; something was trying to give her advice. Rain wasn't listening; all she wanted was for this nightmare to be over for her brother.

"Wassup, boss?" said Tip. "Long time…how you been?" he asked Rain; no matter what Tip will always love her.

"I need you and Doc to get to Virginia," was all that she said and he knew for her to request them it had to be bad.

"No problem, boss. I'll get that nigga and we'll be on the next thing flying out," he said.

"Call me when you guys land," Rain hung up, she'd explain what was up when she saw them. After speaking with Tip, she then put a call in to Hamp and Lee telling them to meet at her house by noon tomorrow since they lived right there in Richmond.

"I never thought I'd be back on this road," said Rain as she drove to Storm's house. *I got to let her know what's up with our brother now! Why the fuck are my sister's lights off in here.* "Storm, where are you?" Rain yelled out as she made her way inside.

"Storm…Chance!" she called out their names but still no reply as she walked toward the kitchen. "What the fuck!" yelled out Rain as she clicked on the kitchen light. "Why the hell are you sitting here in the dark?"

Storm was sitting there with her head down on the table. "Sis, are you alright?" she ran over and that's when she noticed that her face was full of tears and of course, Rain wanted to know why.

"Storm, where are the kids? What's wrong? Talk to me," Rain didn't know what to do as her sister poured her heart out through tears. She sat down beside her sister to hold her as Storm calmed down enough to begin to talk.

"Chance has another baby, sis and he kept this shit from me this whole motherfucking time," Storm explained to Rain what had happen earlier that day at the mall and somehow this day seemed like a twilight zone because the devil was fuckin' with Rain hard.

"Ok, calm down," she consoled her sister, handing her a glass of water to drink.

"I'm here now and we're going to get through this together like always; but I need you to try and hold it together long enough to help our brother. Doc, Hamp,

Tip, and Lee will be at the house by noon tomorrow."

Storm's eyes got big as shit and she was almost scared to ask. "Sis, why are they coming here? What's up?" she became frighten as she looked into her sister's eyes which told stories, but Storm wanted to hear it from Rain's mouth.

"Sis, trust me, everything is going to be ok; but right now, you have a lot going on so I need you to go get some rest and I'll explain when we all are at the house."

"Ok," Storm agreed, she knew that Rain had her and so if she said rest, that meant she was on watch. Rain made sure her sister was straight, and then she left to go home and fuck her husband!!

"Would you bring your slow ass on!" yelled Tip as Doc kept macking to some Virginia hoe.

"I'm coming, bruh," Doc said as he ran over, but turning back around for one more ass glance.

"Damn," Doc said, putting her number in his pocket, "that bitch got hella ass, my nigg."

He and Tip both watched her walk away.

"Her Name is Vanessa and she's a virgin, but I guess I'll be popping that cherry!"

All that nigga cared about was fucking and murdering as they both laughed, making their way to the limo drove by Nizzy.

"Wassup, yo? Damn you getting black," said Nizzy…always messing with Doc as they dapped five.

"I can still mack more hoes than you!"

They laughed while Doc helped Nizzy put the bags in the car and Tip checked in with Rain.

"So, Nizzy…where the hoes at and I know you got a shit of them!" joked Doc, but indeed, Nizzy was a ladies' lady.

"Mane, it's bitches everywhere. Shit…I got my own ice cream parlor myself."

They all laughed.

"What you want – chocolate, white, Spanish, or Chinese?" Nizzy was a fuckin' clown, but she knew on the real that Tricia would fuck her up if she found out Nizzy was trying to creep. "Let's get to the bottom of what boss wants and then we can party at Club Benji's."

"Come on, Rain!" Storm screamed, "They're here," she announced in reference to Nizzy pulling up as well as Lee and Hamp too. Storm opened the door for everybody. Inside, they all were happy to see each other as small talk was made, but the celebration was cut short once Rain came into the family room. By the look on her face, it wasn't a smile so they knew somebody was dying and it wasn't one of them.

"I know we said that this was over, but niggas think they can just play all over my family,"' Rain begins to explain. "My brother Donny's girlfriend has been kidnapped and I need my boys to find her for me. We need her back fast because she's pregnant with my blood, which is y'all's blood too."

You could see the seriousness in her eyes and hear it through her words.

"The nigga that did this shit is an ex-artist of my brother, and evidently, this nigga has more than animosity in this shit; he's on some payback. I'm loving this shit, and it's got to come to an end."

They knew when Rain put an order out, it was game on right away; mostly starting off with one of their old fashion stings.

"Doc and Lee, I need you to watch this nigga until he leads us to Bria's whereabouts and then you report back to me. Tip and Hamp, you two are responsible for getting her out safe and sound whether you have to kill someone or not. Bria is pregnant you guys, so please…I need her safe and unharmed," said Rain. Being that this was her first nephew or niece from her baby brother, Rain wasn't taking any chances.

"As far as I know, this nigga is personally tagging my brother and my stomach can't take any more of this shit, we need to end this quick."

The boys knew she meant business as she handed them the address to Main's shop and crib.

"So, between one of you…I expect to have her back safe soon, because we've never been defeated. I know we not starting tonight."

Ever since Ricky, they hadn't killed anyone but lil local ass niggas, but it's nothing like an assignment from the queen. After giving out her orders, she let the boys loose; but this time, Nizzy was involved. That night, Doc and Lee took their position right outside that nigga Main's house and them niggas were beyond focused.

"Can you fuckin' believe that boss is back in business?" said Lee, getting excited as usual.

"Hell, naw, my nigga. I thought she was done; so for her to return…this is some real shit that she had no choice but to handle this way," said Tip and he knew her better than any of them.

The night grew long and slow, nothing seemed to be happening. Just as Doc and Lee fired their last blunt, they saw that nigga, Main, leaving his house.

"It's 11:45 p.m., and this nigga backing up like he in a hurry about something," said Tip as they ducked down so that the passing headlights wouldn't shine on them. As soon as the coast was clear, they followed that ass. The followed that nigga to CVS as they watched him enter and exit with only one bag. The next stop was to this old abandon building; which, judging from the one light, there was someone in there. The building was so secluded that there wasn't any way they would have found this shit just by riding around. Doc and Lee waited until Main went inside and then they went up the back and they could hear the moans of a female in pain as they looked in and saw Bria.

"Please, take me to the hospital," Bria cried out. "I think something is wrong with my baby!" she weakly yelled out as Gee kept playing his game.

"Shut the fuck up, bitch ain't nothing wrong with you and if you think I'm taking you to the hospital so you can snitch, you got another thing coming," he told her. Bria continued to beg seeming like everything was hopeless, but she wasn't gonna die in that building. Main finally made his way in the room as Doc and Lee sat watch.

"As soon as this nigga isn't paying attention, we gone make our move," said

Doc as he pulled out their masks. "Put this on, nigga," he threw one over to Lee, as well as a black shirt to cover that bright ass neon green one that he had on. "Nigga, why did you wear that shit in the first place?" Doc joked.

"That's the first shirt I grabbed and dipped."

Main had gotten comfortable sitting with Gee, and they were into that PlayStation 4, ignoring the cries of Bria as they got harder. Doc and Lee made their way up the back stairs and stood in front of a door that happen to be unlocked, but they could see Bria through the glass.

"Ok, there she is, but we have orders to just watch."

"Fuck it, I say make an executive decision, my nigga. This girl can't wait any longer; and besides, we can take these niggas."

Lee had a point; they watched Main and Gee who were now conversing away from Bria about something, and then Gee started to leave.

"Aight, my nigga…make sure you go straight home, because tomorrow you got to pull shift all day," Main let him know because he hated sitting around this bitch and their other nigga backed out tonight. "Shut the fuck up!" Main yelled at Bria as Gee made his way out the door, not paying attention to the fact that it was cracked. Once he pulled off, Doc and Lee decided to call this in and follow him.

"Damn, that girl in pain, my nigga. We need to call Tip and Hamp right now," said Doc so they could go and get Bria while Main was there by himself. As soon as Lee put the call through, them niggas bounced. Doc and Lee wanted to continue to see what Gee was up to because getting Bria back was just the beginning of their plans. By the time Rain was finished with Main, he'd never fuck with anyone else again. Doc and Lee had no idea how much they'd hit the jackpot by following Gee; see there was something that nobody knew about them. The information was found out through Club Benji's a year ago, and he, nor Main never said shit to anybody.

Rain hadn't got the word yet on what these two nigga were witnessing. At that very moment, Gee parked in from of the club and got out grabbing a security jacket from the trunk; and *yes*, that's the same Gee.

"This bitch ass nigga!" Doc and Lee both expressed as they gave each other looks of hate for a snake.

"This nigga got a nerve to be working for Main and still showing up for work here," Doc was mad because Gee was playing Rain dirty. "Pussy ass bitch, I swear, watch that nigga gone pay," he said, as they did agree on making that executive decision to snatch Gee getting off, and that wasn't part of the plan, but oh well, *fuck all them niggas*.

"Look at your dumb ass bitch," said Main as he laughed at Bria in pain. "How does it feel to be kicked when you're down; huh? Ain't that how you did me when I got locked up?" he sat there eating on chips as Bria now lay on a pissy blanket covering the concrete floor. She was barely breathing at this point. She needed medical attention fast. Main had no idea that the party was almost over, he was too busy still talking shit to Bria when the knock at the door caught his attention for the moment. Without thinking, Main opened the door right up because nobody but his boys knew of that place until now.

"Peekaboo, bitch," he was greeted by the barrel of two 9s in his face; not giving Main time enough to pull for his shit at all.

"What the fuck, niggas! I don't have any work," Main began to explain, thinking that he was being robbed.

"Shut the fuck up, pussy! Now where is she?" Tip started pushing Main back from the door and instructed him to take them to Bria. Main did what he was told, but he was now scared as shit. He had no clue what these niggas were going to do to him and the next shift change wasn't until 7:00 a.m. and it was only 1:30 a.m.

"What they fuck!" Oh shit, mane…shortie is fucked up!" Tip and Hamp both had guns still drawn when Tip handed Hamp his gun to keep both of them aimed on Main, while he attended to Bria.

"Hold on, shortie I'm going to get you to the hospital ASAP," Tip said to Bria. Her eyes were barely open; she tried to cry, but couldn't. "Hamp, hold that nigga still and put a call to Rain; tell her to meet me at the hospital," Tip ran to the car with Bria in his arms, he knew there wasn't any more time to waste for her. He placed Bria on the back seat and told Nizzy to go inside and stay with Hamp. She was in the car with them, but as she made her way up to the back of the building she heard a sound.

Pow!

One shot rang out loud as fuck and Nizzy took off to make sure it wasn't Hamp. She wasn't surprise to find Hamp standing and Main's ass bleeding on the floor from a gunshot to the knee, but Hamp wanted to really put it in his head.

Tip forgot he told Hamp to put the call through to Rain; by the time this nigga got down the street, he was on his second call, but straight to voice mail it went both times. Tip knew the best thing to do was get Bria some help, so he left Rain a message.

"Get me some help please!" Tip ran inside the emergency room screaming as doctors and nurses came out of everywhere. They put Bria on a stretcher and immediately rushed her back, but they informed Tip not to leave because they would need some information on Bria.

"Come on boss, answer the phone," Tip had already passed panic as Rain finally answered this time. Tip was talking so fast that Rain couldn't understand a word that he was saying and it was causing her to get scared.

"Slow down, what's wrong?" she asked.

"Bria's in the hospital in labor, boss; and she don't look too good," he expresses. "We're at Chippenham hospital," Tip heard the phone hang up and he knew that help was on the way.

"What's going on, Tip?" Donny asked being the first out of the car. He wanted to see Bria, that was all he wanted at that moment, but Tip explained everything to him as they waited. He explained that Hamp and Nizzy had Main's ass chained the fuck up and finally the doctor and Rain entered the waiting room at the same time. Everyone's heart began to pump harder.

"Johnson family?" Doctor Cambridge asked as Donny replied.

"That's me. I'm her fiancé, but we are all her family."

Those words meant *talk nigga* they had waited long enough to see Bria.

"I'm sorry to have to tell you this, but Bria didn't make it."

Donny's whole body went numb as Rain and Storm quickly stood beside him, holding him up as their brother broke down in pain.

"What about the baby?" asked Rain.

"Well, there were some complications from being born weeks early, but right now, he's doing ok," Doctor Cambridge explained. "We have him on oxygen right now."

The doctor offered to only allow Donny to go back to Bria at this point, so he could have some time with her and the baby for a finale. They took Donny back to meet his son first; the little boy lay quietly in his crib looking right at Donny like he already knew who he was.

"Give me a minute, Mr. Johnson," said the doctor.

"My name is Peters, sir," said Donny, not being rude, but just informing, that's all. He turned back around to continue gazing at this beautiful view in front of him some more. Donny reached down, picking up his son for the first time; as the tears rolled down his face, he inhaled the smell of his son.

"Wassup, lil man, this is daddy," he kisses his son on the cheek as the soft baby hair rubs Donny's nose. "We got to name you without mommy's help, son, so let's try to think like her," he smiled, knowing her spirit was present in the moment. Donny requested to see Bria. Still carrying his son, he headed out into the hall as the nurse showed him to where Bria's room was. Doctor Cambridge was passing and he headed back to him.

"Take your time, sir," the doctor expressed; he could see the hurt all in Donny's eyes as he thanked the doctor while walking slowly over to Bria's bedside. Immediately, Donny pushed the nurse button because he felt himself becoming weak at the sight of Bria's badly battered body which reviled some of what they'd done to her.

"Yes, sir," the nurse came rushing in.

"Can you please bring me his bed," Donny asked wanting to make sure nothing happened to his son. The nurse quickly returned and placed the baby in it for him.

"Anything else, sir?" she asked as Donny shook his head *no*, but his eyes were still planted on Bria as the nurse turned to leave.

"God bless you, sir," she said as she shuts the door and that's something Donny really needed at the moment.

"Baby, I'm sorry. I'm sorry," he sobbed. "Look at what those bastards did to you, boo," he wipes his hand over her forehead touching her hair. "Baby, our son is so beautiful. Thank you very much for giving him your life for me and I wish I could have you both, but I can't because God has spoken and He needs you more."

I never heard a man cry the way Donny was over Bria's dead body in that room as he got down on his knees grabbing Bria's cold hard hand.

"I now take you as my forever wife, Bria Johnson, and I'll always love you."

This man's heart was shattered and then he still had to pull it together to raise their baby alone.

"Mr. Peters, sir," Doctor Cambridge interrupted, "it's time for the baby's next oxygen treatment and it's important that we keep him on this schedule to get his level up so you can take your baby home with you," he smiled at Donny and Donny's face smiled back, but his heart still wasn't grasping what the hell had just happen.

"As for his name have you decided on one yet?" the doctor asked as Donny paused for a split second.

"Briaon Edward Peters," Donny announced as the doctor wrote it down on the paperwork for Donny.

"Well, sir, I know this has been a very overwhelming day, so little Briaon will get one more day of treatment from us and then he'll be all yours. Ms. Johnson's body can lay in the morgue for up to three days and then the State will automatically cremate if we haven't reached any family, so just let me know what you're going to do soon," Doctor Cambridge extended his hand. "Pray, young man," he said as Donny kissed Bria for the last time, but kissing his son was just the beginning and he left.

Rain was the first person in the waiting room to spot Donny coming as she jumped up running toward him.

"Are you alright, how's the baby, what he look like?" Donny was asked as Rain and Storm both rushed him.

"I'm cool and he's cool, sis; but right now…" he turns to look Rain in her eyes "where that nigga at? I'm finishing him myself."

Donny had never killed anybody in his whole life, but shit…this here was very personal and Rain knew she couldn't stand in his way on this one.

"I'll take you there. Let's go," Rain walked off. Storm, Donny and Tip followed as Rain began putting calls through to Vick. She told him to shut down the cab company and bring the boys to the abandon building where Hamp and Nizzy held Main.

* * * * *

Doc and Lee sat outside Club Benji's until they spotted Gee's ass leaving, and you goddamn right they grabbed that nigga up.

"Snitches die like rats, mutherfucker!" Doc's voice was what he heard, but he didn't see shit as they run up behind him. They, too, were in route to the place for show and tell; too bad this situation wasn't fun. Niggas could hear Main yelling as they made their way into the building. Rain knew Hamp and Nizzy were giving him the blues, but now it was really time to pay. Instantly, upon entering, Donny hooked off on that nigga, knocking his gold fronts out his mouth and Main started to laugh.

"So, he does have heart; huh, bitch?" Main talked a lot of shit as Donny two pieced his ass, yet again; but on the third time, Vick and Tip grabbed him by the arm to calm down.

"Bitch, I got you, Main."

There weren't any words to describe how Donny felt at that moment; this nigga had just killed his whole life's plan.

"You killed my wife and could've taken my son."

"Oh shit, that *trash* didn't die," Main was a cold ass nigga as Rain, Storm and Donny charged toward him; but Doc and Lee coming caused a slight delay.

"Boss," they both called out as they pushed Gee into the room and Main's eyes, along with everyone else's, got big because they all knew Gee from the club.

"This nigga working with Main, boss," the boys said together and Nizzy wanted to kill this nigga herself for this shit because he worked mainly under her and he was a snake. Neither Rain nor Storm could believe what they were hearing.

"What the fuck did you just say?"

Oh, she heard it the first time, but she wanted to hear it again because this mutherfucker was a leak all along in her face.

Tip and Hamp tied Gee down in a chair next to Main.

"So what…you two became best friends through me?" said Rain. "Y'all really thought that y'all's strength could out weight mine; huh?" she asked, standing in front of them both and they sat there staring at each other not saying a word.

The sight of the two of them continued to nauseate Donny even more.

"Bitch!" he punched Gee right in the eye, "Answer my sister when she's talking to you," he said, but Gee just kept right on laughing in their faces.

"Well, since you two think shits funny and you don't want to apologize to my family, I guess this meeting is adjourned then," Rain smiled as Nizzy and Hamp grabbed Main and Gee by their shoulders, holding them back against the chair tightly and Rain nodded at Vick to give Donny his gun because he didn't have his own on him.

"Please, don't kill my brother," Main barely could speak.

"Your brother? Nigga that ain't your fuckin' brother!" said Donny.

Gee finally chimed in, "We are brothers, real brothers. We found out last year that our mom gave him up for adoption," stated Gee as Rain began to smile.

"Is that right? Well, brother…" she turns and says to Donny, "you hold the weapon so what would you like to do for this family?" she asked Donny as he now stood in front of the two of them.

"Are you your brother's keeper?" he asked them both and they still just sat there smiling so Donny asked the question one more time. "Are you your brother's keeper?"

Still silence was all they got.

"We are," was what Storm and Rain answered on their brother's behalf at that moment as Donny pulled the trigger with perfect aim twice. One slug to the face of each brother ended their new relationship. Just like that, what was supposed to be the beginning chapter had turned out to be the end.

CHAPTER 7

Family Secrets

Every family has secrets that have greatly impacted their lives; some of them are just very well kept. Denise's family had a great way of painting family images of them to the outside world, but behind closed doors there was usually hell to pay.

It took Donny almost three days to locate Bria's family, and it almost turned out bad; but luckily, Penny was able to locate Bria's mother. She let the rest of their family know what had happen and they were all coming in for the funeral. When Donny brought Briaon home for the first time, some of Bria's family had managed to get there and they came to the house to meet him, and boy was he spoiled from both sides instantly.

The day of Bria's memorial service was a day that Donny will always remember. What was supposed to be the best time of his and her life, turned out to be the second saddest of Donny's. He had no choice but to pull through it. He held the service at a very small church; big enough to hold Bria's loved ones. Donny held Briaon the entire time; he even went up and said some words for her with Briaon in his arms because they were now joined.

Bria's mom and sister gave Donny their word that they would be there to help and as great as it sounded, he knew they weren't even there for Bria when she needed them, but Donny just accepted their offer. Donny was going to make sure that no matter who was in Briaon's life, he would always feel his mom around him.

* * * * *

Even though Main and Gee were dead, those Highland Park niggas were enraged over that shit; especially how they say the rats ate through Main and Gee's body by the time they were found…they said that shit was pure torture. Donny wanted to show them the same hospitality they bestowed upon Bria. Now it was time for Donny to begin his journey as a first-time single parent and he just hoped that things would cool down with this shit while he chilled back for a bit and focused on Briaon.

The next couple of months were hard has hell on Rain and her family; raising a new born baby wasn't easy. Donny was still grieving over Bria and that shit was really fuckin' with his brain. Donny wouldn't eat; he really didn't sleep, all he did was be with Briaon and stare out the window while the baby slept.

Playing games with Rain could really get you fucked up, but when you mess with her kids… shit like that would get you killed. Denise's father, David, had better stop before he finds out the hard way about her wrath. Rain still hadn't met Denise's family, and she and RJ had been living together for months now; but Rain always knew what was going on. She would get the stories of how strange and nasty her father was toward her son because RJ had a very open relationship with his mother.

When Denise's parents found out that she'd moved out, her father flipped his wig something terrible. He called her phone every day for a week straight and she still wouldn't pick up, so this mutherfucker would just show up at her job. Denise wasn't ready to talk to him because she knew what his plan was and that would be to talk her out of it; but for once, she wanted to be happy. Because of all this, David decided to cut her off from the family, which most of them wouldn't give a fuck anyway. Charity and Rena maintained their communication with their sister dispute what David's order were; they knew that it was time for her to grow up and become the woman that she was deep inside.

Tre, DJ, and Sharod really didn't get into their sisters' lives unless shit was getting physical then they would be fuckin' somebody up.

Gloria, Tiara and Legally were the happiest out of them all; them bitches didn't give a fuck if Denise ever came back around as long as they had David all to themselves. They didn't care what this was doing to Denise.

"So, son, what's been going on? How's things with you and Denise?" asked Rain as her and RJ had lunch at Rico's Kitchen.

"I'm ok, mom. I mean *we're* ok," he quickly corrected to include Denise in his life. "We would be even better if her crazy ass father would grow up and allow her back around her family," RJ expressed as he ate his water crisp salad. "Mom, I just don't know what to do to help her," he sounded stressed.

"Well, baby, I think it's time our family meets hers," said Rain. "What about that house warming party I wanted to give you two? I think that would be a good idea to make this happen," she waited for RJ to respond, he knew that shit wouldn't work with David's ass.

"I don't know, mom…with Denise not talking to anyone but two of her sisters, I don't think her dad would let anyone else show up." RJ knew that Denise's dad was not the easiest person in the world to please, but the main thing was her family's dark secret that RJ didn't want his mother to find out about.

"You don't even have to tell Denise. I'll act like it's a surprise and do all the work myself. I can send the invites and everyone can just be shocked when they see each other; that way they can't plan their actions."

RJ knew his mother really meant well, but sometimes her ideas could be over the top; but he also knew she wasn't going to let up on this.

"Ok, mom…since you think this will help."

"Sure it will once they meet me," she starts to smile pretty, "how can they not want to join our family."

"Be my guest; but I don't have anything to do with it. Ok, mom? "Me…I'm just showing up."

RJ didn't know how Denise would react about this shit, but what could he do, this was his mother. Rain and RJ wrapped up the rest of their lunch for later because they both had meetings to get to, but of course, Rain went into full planning mode. She knew Denise's name, so finding her family's address wouldn't be hard; after all, this is Queen we're talking about…and she knows how to get whatever she wants.

* * * * *

That evening at home, Rain was into what she was doing so much that she didn't even hear Vick come in as he crept up behind her, placing his hands over her eyes.

"Boo, did I scare you?" he asked from the way Rain's whole body jumped.

"Yes, you did. You always get me," she laughed as they both passionately engaged in a kiss.

"What you been up to all day?" he asked, licking his lips and taking a seat at the kitchen table with Rain.

"Invitations?" he picked one up. "Nice, but what's these for?" he asked as Rain checked the guest list over and over.

"It's for RJ and Denise's house warming party," she continued writing as she talked; partially because she didn't even want to see Vick's facial expression after she'd said those words, but she knew more questions were coming, so she cut that nigga short before he could even ask. "I decided to throw them a surprise party. I think that's its time I meet her family, especially her damn dad," she said, "and besides, we could use an old fashion barbeque in this family after all we've just been through."

Rain knew Donny probably wouldn't come out to attend it, but he'd sure eat the food. Vick began to shake his head.

"Baby, I know you and your ideas and I hope you're not up to something."

Rain was known for doing that, she sometimes went too deep in on a situation but her main goal is always to protect. Rain was amused at how well Vick really knew her ways.

"Baby, I promise you everything is going to be perfect," Rain closed the lap top and left it along with the invitations on the table as she stands to walk away.

"Well, daddy…know that all my work is done for the night, how about you working on me," she smiled and Vick's nasty ass almost flipped the table over jumping up. He knew that this was an *I'm gonna fuck the shit out of her night* and he was all in.

Vick's muscular shoulders began to pulsate nice and slow as he picked Rain up in his arms. She laid her head on his shoulders as her hands glided smoothly down his back. The scent of that new Usher cologne filled her nose.

"You smell so delicious," Rain whispered in Vick's ear.

"Oh, I do; huh?" he kicks the bedroom door open with his foot and placed Rain with care on the bed so that the games could begin.

"Are you wet for daddy yet?" Vick asked Rain as he took two fingers and rubbed them inside her pussy. "Umm," his manly moan sounded out into her ears which caused her body to quiver.

"How deep can you go, daddy?" she joked around; she knew Vick liked challenges. She pulled the strap off her dress causing it to fall to the floor.

"Lay down," he instructed Rain. I swear my girl knew how to pick good dick! "Before I stroke that pussy so deep, let my lips taste your juices."

Vick was nasty and that's one of the things that drove Rain crazy. Rain was moaning very heavy off the rip. Shit…Vick's mouth hadn't even touched down yet. He spread her ass cheeks apart and dug his tongue so deep in her ass hole and then into her pussy that she thought it was his finger as Vick's mouth began to swallow Rain's soul through her vagina.

"Oh, my God…I can't stop shaking, baby," Rain expressed as her lower body rocked Vick's head side to side. Vick took his tongue, licking all the way from her pussy to her toes, as he sucked on each one passionately. With Rain's left leg stretched up in the air, Vick inserted his thick manhood, causing her toes to curl inside his mouth. She straddled his dick. Vick's strokes were like thunder. Rain grabbed his leg and he went in deeper as her always manicure nails engraved his back with lust, causing her body to lose control.

"Fuck this pussy; it's yours, daddy!" she threw that that back and Vick knew he couldn't hold back too much longer.

"Oh, baby…I can feel the wetness running down my dick!" Vick moaned as his dick throbbed hard inside Rain. "Damn your shit is so good." Rain had Vick's mind going crazy that night. "Shit, baby…I'm about to cum!" Vick moaned as he pulled Rain's body in tighter so she could feel the warmness of his seeds filling her pussy walls. She knew she was going to sleep good after that!

* * * * *

"Damn, it's cold as shit out here!" complained Clover about the weather, which this nigga always fussed about something. Clover Decou was one of those niggas with big time connects in shit overseas, mostly because he was always spying on somebody. This nigga was involved in so much stuff that he was tied to business all over. Because of his computer knowledge, he could find out anything.

"That's what I get for being a smoker," he played around as he stood out front the restaurant waiting on Chuck who was always running late, but this time, he sounded serious when he called Clover.

"Bout time your ass got here, I was about to leave," he gave Chuck a high five as they made their way inside Chow-Lou and took their seat. Clover could tell that Chuck's ass had been party already from the smell of alcohol that leaked from his pores. Clothes all wrinkled, Chuck never came out like that in public, so something had to be going on with him.

"What's going on with you, nigga?" Clover didn't waste no time asking as Chuck tried to straighten his appearance up.

"Mane, I've been fucked up ever since I lost my job because of this bitch that I want to talk to you about," Chuck stated. "I want you to find this bitch name Elizabeth Wales or Lizzy for short. This bitch must die and I do mean that because I want to be the one that does it," Chuck was serious, but he had no idea who he was really fuckin' with. "Christina Tulio is paying me one million dollars to find and get rid of that bitch, Lizzy, as well as locating her grandchildren. If you help me, I'll split it with you 50/50, but I need my life back and I can't until I pay that bitch back.

Clover sat there thinking about what this nigga had just said and knowing the background of the Tulios…if they were involved, shit was real.

"Ok, I'll do it, but only because I fuck with you; otherwise, I wouldn't touch a Tulio case," he said. "I ain't trying to have no business with them. Do you have a photo of this Lizzy woman?" he asked as Chuck slid it across the table to him and Clover just stared.

"I remember her!" he shouted out quickly. "I was on a job in Bora Bora and I was sitting at the bar when I noticed this woman that I thought looked familiar," he began to tell what happen. "It was the wrong person, but the guy she was with started to flip out and shit, so I just left it alone."

Chuck was taking it all in, but all he wanted was Lizzy's head on a platter and he didn't care how it got done, but he wondered what guy she was with.

"I never heard of her having a husband, so I don't know what man she was with out there. Last I heard, she was close to a lady name Janay. She's known by Storm, which is the aunt to the Tulio grandchildren," said Chuck as Clover took down all names, gathering every piece of info that he could.

"I'll get right on it and contact you in a few days with something," said Clover as he stood up from the table to leave.

"Go home and shower; get yourself together, my nigga. You don't want to face the enemy looking like that," he explained and Chuck knew he was right as he sat there finishing his drink and thinking because this was what he'd been waiting for and now he was close.

* * * * *

Rain and Storm spent the entire morning shopping for RJ's house warming which was two days away and Storm was glad to get out the house and help. Her whole life has switched to being all about Chance and Choice, which meant time for herself didn't exist.

"Mane, sis, it's so beautiful out here today," expressed Storm. "I'm glad Chance has the boys because I needed a little break."

They both laughed as they walked through the parking deck at the mall.

"Where the fuck did we park?" Rain was getting pissed, it was hot as hell and they had like twenty bags between the both of them; the shopping addiction was real!"

As they continued searching, Storm heard someone say, "Yeah, that's that bitch! Fake hair wearing asshole; I bet she won't confront me without her boo around," she heard the bitch laugh, but she didn't have a clue who they were talking to, that is until she turned around saw it was Lizette. She was with two other bitches gritting hard, but Storm just flashed a smile and kept walking.

"Who is that?" asked Rain, seeing her sister's emotions switch up instantly and she knew something was wrong.

"That's Chance's other baby momma, sis; but don't worry, she ain't nobody," said Storm, "she's just trying to push my buttons," she added as they finally spotted the car.

"There it is, damn my feet were burning," Storm tried to laugh it off as she and Rain put their bags in the car.

"You got something you want to say to me, bitch?" Lizette came up from behind them as Storm and Rain looked at each other.

"First of all, don't come up on my goddamn truck talking shit, bitch; have you bumped your head?" Rain asked as Storm became angry by this.

"Who the fuck are you questioning!" shouted Lizette. "You need to stay the fuck in your lane and mind your business before you catch *her* ass whooping," she said.

Did this bitch just threaten Rain and Storm at the same time? Storm never spoke a word, but she kept eye contact. Little did Lizette know what was coming next.

"Let's go, Lizette. These bitches don't want none," one of her friends said and that's when Storm lost it. The force that went through Storm's fist as she put it into Lizette's temple was powerful as fuck. Lizette's head hit the back window of the next car as Storm grabbed that bitch up by her whole face. Her two punk ass friends attempted to try and jump in, but as soon as they made a move, Rain grabbed them both by their ponytails and before they could even touch Storm, they were eating the soles off of Rain's Jordan's as she stomped the shit out them both.

"What the fuck you gone do again, bitch?" screamed Storm as she tried to reconstruct Lizette's face.

"I'm tired of your shit, bitch!"

Pop, pop, pop, was the sound of the blows they gave them bitches, and by now it seemed like the whole mall was watching; of course you know that someone called security. Lizette's two friends were out fuckin' cold. Rain tried to stuff them bitches inside of the Sears sign as they lay bleeding in the street unconscious. By now storm was crying and fighting, I guess she was releasing some well needed stress on Lizette's ass while she tried her best to fight back, but those lil ass hits didn't even phase Storm. She was so far in on the fight that she didn't even feel Rain pulling her off of that bitch. Storm swung, accidentally hitting Rain in her face.

"Bitch, what the fuck!" Rain grabbed her arm. "It's me Storm, let's go twelve's coming," Rain wasn't playing, if it's one thing she hated, it was the fuckin' police. Rain pulled Storm over to her truck as they got in and left the scene. Shoppers were all outside recording the whole damn thing on their phones and I bet somebody's gonna do something stupid.

"Oh my God, bitch, that felt so fuckin' good!" said Storm as she checked her makeup while Rain drove a hundred miles per hour to get back home.

"You better be glad you're my sister, because I would have fucked you up for hitting me in my face," Rain warned as they both started laughing.

"Aww, I'm sorry, sis," she reached over and kissed Rain's cheek. "You know I love you, but your ass is crazy because I didn't even see you fuckin' them other bitches up. All I knew was that blood was on you shirt and it wasn't yours," she said and Rain was really pissed about her shirt. That shirt was a four hundred dollar Gianfranco Ferre shirt that was now ruined cause of some hating ass bitches.

"But, oh well, they the ones got to recover," Rain and Storm joked, but they knew Vick and Chance weren't going to find this shit funny at all.

They felt like their women were queens and that type of fighting was beneath them and they have killers for shit like that. Storm had her car parked at Rain's house already, so when she pulled up, Storm got into her car and left…making sure she was the first to tell Chance the news.

"Baby!" called out Storm making her way into the nursery where she knew he would be with the kids. "There you are," she said as he lay on the carpet sleeping with Chance and Choice also asleep on top of his chest. "Aww, look at my men," Storm stood in the door way smiling. *I don't even want to wake them,* she thought to herself; so instead, she went to prepare dinner.

As Chance snored lightly, the scent of what his beautiful fiancé was in the kitchen preparing woke him up, as well as Choice's diaper soaking through his shirt. Chance changed the twins and got them comfortable in their chairs then it was off to see what mommy was up to.

"Umm, baby," Chance announced his entrance as he kissed Storm on her lips. "Got it smelling good up in here, momma."

Storm smiled at him as she kissed her sons, taking them in the family room.

"Boy, get out there and take your seat," Storm smacked Chance's hand as he snuck food out the pot.

"Alright, baby," he laughed taking his seat at the table' he loved Storm so much.

Miss Thang showed off with dinner; I guess it was part of her buttering him up process before she told him the news.

Pan sautéed chicken, vegetables and herbs, with loaded baked potatoes and a Caesar salad and let's not forget her famous homemade cheddar biscuits. Chance's eyes gazed in on the meal while Storm continued pouring them a glass of Moscato. Dinner started out a lot unusual that evening with Storm's conversation very minimal and Chance noticing he was the only one doing most of the talking.

"Baby, what's on your mind?" he got tired of short answers as Storm placed her fork down on her plate eyeing him.

"Ha, well…" she smirked, "there's no easy way to tell you this so I might as well just say it."

He was confused as shit hoping whatever it was he wouldn't have to shoot anyone behind it.

"Your baby momma, plus two of her friend tried to jump me at the mall today with Rain."

Chance's jaw fell into his hand.

"What the fuck you mean, boo?" he continued to ask, but Storm cut him off explaining there was more.

"We fought, babe. I had to beat her ass and I know you don't like me fighting, but what was I supposed to do, get my ass beat?" she expressed in questioned and continued. "Rain had to beat the shit out of her friends trying to jump their ass in our fight, and you know my sister, that shit definitely wasn't allowed."

Chance sat there with his hands on his head, but quiet for a second and Storm was nervous.

"Fuck!" he slams his fist on the table. "Fuck, Fuck, Fuck, mane!" he screamed again and this time causing the babies to cry. "Baby, you mean to tell me this bitch really ran up on you after I distinctly told her to stay in her fuckin' place which is CJ's mother and that's all," he said to Storm as she sat there now sipping on her wine. "Were people out there when y'all were fighting?"

"That's a dumb question, Chance," replied Storm. "It is a public place," she shook her head, "practically the whole damn mall was outside," she stated and that made him even madder.

"Baby you don't understand, that bitch has a sister that is a RPD detective and we don't need any problems with them niggas fuckin' with us," said Chance.

"Oh well, that's not my fault; she started it with me first. Is it my problem that she didn't win?"

"No, I'm not saying that, baby. I just don't want this to get out of hand, but don't worry about it, I'm going to fix this shit!" he said, getting up from the table and grabbing his Pea Coat and keys. "I'll be right back."

Chance kisses Storm as he leaves out the door slamming it behind him and leaving her still sitting at the kitchen table. The way Chance's truck tires sounded screeching out of their driveway made Storm jump up and grab the phone.

"Please, pick up," she prayed as Rain's phone rung and the boys had started crying again.

"Hello," answered Rain.

"Sis, oh my, God…he snapped out. Yo, Chance is mad as shit and he's gone over that bitch's house now!"

Rain just stood there holding the phone. "What the fuck? He gone kill that bitch, mane?" she finally said as Vick walked in the room.

"Who gonna kill a bitch, baby?" he asked plopping down on his side of the bed.

"Um, Um…" she began to stutter and Storm knew her sister hadn't told him yet.

"Go ahead, sis…let him know just in case he wants to go and get Chance before he does something stupid," Storm said to Rain as they hung up the phone.

"Wassup, boo, who was that?" Vick asked as Rain sat down beside him,

"That was Storm and I need to tell you something and I know you're not going to like it," Rain begins to talk.

"Me and Storm fought Lizette and two of her friends today," Rain said it out her mouth.

"What the fuck?" Vick sat up like lighting, checking Rain's body for any bruises.

"I'm fine, baby. They tried to jump my sister and you know that shit don't stand, but now your brother has gone over there and I think he'll kill her."

Vick jumped up.

"Shit, boo, let me get to this fool!"

Vick kisses her and leaves too; now Rain and Storm were both sitting at home worried.

*****

When Chance pulled up at Lizette's house, he saw her sister Lavette's Honda already parked out there and he knew he'd have to deal with this bitch too.

"*Knock, Knock*, he slightly banged on the door and you guessed it…Lavette was the one who answered it.

"Ha, ha, ha, this mutherfucker finally decides to show up," she announced as Chance brushed passed her hard. "Where the fuck is your punk ass bitch who tried to jump my sister?"

This bitch done went and lied that quick goddamn it's only been hours in. Chance just stood there staring at Lizette as she sat on the couch holding an ice pack to her face because the whole left side was swollen.

"Why the fuck you lie, Lizette; huh?" Chance wanted to smack her ass next as she kept looking away at the TV and that's when Lavette tried to speak on her behalf, but Chance shut that bitch up quick. "You and I both know how your sister can be and we both know she tried to jump my fiancé," he expressed. "Didn't you?" he asked her again.

This time she yells out, "So what if I did?"

Dumb ass bitch, got her sister bout to press charges, Chance thought to himself because he knew that's what Lavette had planned.

"Zette!" said her sister as she walked over beside her, "Why did you lie to me? You know how much trouble I could have gotten into if I filed a false report?" Lavette began to explain, but at that point, Lizette didn't hear shit that was being said; all she wanted to do was take her anger out on Chance. "Sis, do you hear me?" Lizette continued to sit there in a daze and this time the door bell rung. "I got it, bitch," Lavette said to Chance in reference to him reaching to open the door. All eyes sat to see who it was; as soon as the door opened, Lizette's ass leaped up off the couch and on to Chance's fuckin' back.

"I hate you, bitch. I hate you!" she screamed as she pounded Chance in the back of his head with her fist, while Lavette and now Vick had to grab that crazy bitch off of him.

"Zette, let him go!"

"Get this crazy bitch off me, bruh!"

Everyone was yelling out everything as they tussled and Vick's strong ass yanked Lizette by that eighteen-inch Remy as she fell back onto the fuckin' floor.

"Bitch, you're sick, I swear!" said chance as Vick helped him up off the floor.

"Get the fuck out my house, mutherfucker!" Lizette cried in anger as her sister held her in comfort.

"With pleasure, bitch. Now stay the fuck away from Storm and I don't want no shit with the law Lavette because it's clear who's the crazy one here."

Chance and Vick walked right out the door without shutting it back. Chance and his whole family had had enough of this bitch and her many attempts to try and get him back; but now, hopefully, she gets the fuckin' point.

"Where the fuck you come from, bruh?" Chance asked Vick as they stood outside near their cars.

"Rain told me what happen and I thought you were gone kill that bitch; especially with CJ being at mom and dad's house," said Vick as they both shook their heads laughing.

"Well, let's just hope nobody recorded that fight and everything should stay quiet," Chance expressed as he pulled a blunt out and lit it.

"Let me get home and let my wife know everything is good," Vick got inside his car and Chance followed in his own. "I'll hit you in the morning, my nigga."

"Thanks, bruh," said Chance as he sped off down the street bumping Rich Homie Quan's, "Get the fuck out my face." Vick just smiled and pulled off too, it was time to go home and chill.

*****

We all wear mask to disguise painful past events that may make us feel ugly without it. There comes a time when in order to move to the next level in life, the mask of protection has to come off and you must face the person you truly are. The problem is, some people have worn their shield for so long that their inside true self has become forgotten.

Denise's dad was one of those people who disguised himself from everyone besides his family, because if corporate America knew just who he was inside… they would be sick. After this little mess, it was time for Rain to focus back on the party because the invitations were already sent out. They had food and decorations, even the guests had started to RSVP; all that was left to do now was put this shit in action. Rain hadn't spoken to RJ the day before, but she knew they received the invites because he texted her.

"Let's just hope everything goes well," Rain said to Storm as they finished up the final touches on their hair.

"Where is Aaliyah?" Storm asked.

"She's in the nursery with your sons." They both laughed at how much she loved babies.

"We look beautiful, I must say, sis."

"I agree," Storm checked out her body in those Gucci Jeans. "Let's go party!"

Outside most of RJ's friends had already started to arrive as the gift table got packed fast. A couple of unfamiliar faces also graced them with their presence, but the guests of honor hadn't even arrived.

"There you are, baby," Rain noticed RJ walking through the yard as she kissed her son on the head.

"Hi, Denise, you look great baby," Rain kissed her too as she started to notice people she knew there.

"RJ why are my cousins, Kim and Shawn, here?" Denise whispered as they made their way into the party; but before he could answer, she was rushed by them.

"Hey, cousin," they all kissed and hugged as Denise felt her stomach knotting up.

"Hey, what are you guys doing here?" Denise was in search of some answers.

"We all got invitations to come to your housewarming party."

Denise turns to look up at RJ who was very quiet the whole time.

"Oh, really? How nice. RJ, can I talk to you for a moment?"

They both excused themselves as Rain stood watching from a far.

"What's this, baby?" she asked him and he didn't want to lie any longer.

"My mom put this together for us, boo, so that our families could meet," and with those words Denise began to choke.

"Family? What you mean?" Just as she asked her question…

"Hi, I'm RJ's mom and you must be Denise's parents," Denise heard that shit from outside as they both just stood looking at each other. As Denise hit the backyard her eyes locked with her dad and she wanted to cry immediately, but she held it in. They walked over; all her sisters and brothers with their families came to support her or rather act like it.

Rain took Gloria by the hand. "Come on honey let's go have a glass of champagne and chat."

Storm leads the way while Charity and Rena walked off with Denise. Everyone else except David and RJ went to raid the food. The guests were mingling, and nobody got hurt; this was turning out to be a very god party after all.

"Hello, young man—the one who stole my daughter away from her family," said David.

Here his stupid ass go with his attitude toward RJ, but he wasn't going to be the one who fucked up the party, so he played nice.

"No, sir, I didn't steal her away. I'm just trying to love her that's all," RJ replied back as he sipped on his Patron Gold; even Gloria was over there laughing with Storm and Rain having drinks while Tiara and Legally talked shit from across the yard.

"Sir, I'm trying to get to know you, but you're making this very hard. I don't want any trouble with you," RJ said as David took his glasses and slowly lowered them.

"Look here, sonny," he placed his hand on RJ's shoulder, "my daughter was fine without you, I gave her all she needed," David had the nerve to say.

"Nasty, bitch," RJ mumbled.

"Boy, what did you say?"

"Now hold on…I'm nobody's boy, so check yourself!" snapped RJ and the heat between the two was now rising.

"Look, I've heard all that you have given her, mane, and frankly, I don't want to relive that shit again," RJ walks off and goes over to where his mother is.

"How are you beautiful ladies doing?" RJ kisses his mother.

"We are good honey; your mother and aunt are a blast," said Gloria. "I haven't laughed this much in years."

"Well, that's good, Ms. Gee. I told you I had one of the coolest families," he confessed as he and David still remained eye contact.

"Let me go over and get your husband," Rain said, always trying to bring peace; but why the fuck she had to go messing with David. Vick and Chance were on the court with Denise's brothers, they had even started to relax. David was so far gone staring at RJ that he didn't even see Rain come up from behind dancing around him.

"Excuse me, sir, you're mighty handsome; may I have this dance?" she smiled as Marvin Gay played loudly.

"I'm good, thanks."

That was one rude mutherfucker. What harm was it to dance?

"Ok, then let's talk parent to parent; why don't you like my son?"

"Your son isn't what I pictured for my daughter," David replied and Rain wanted to knock his ass out.

"Well, my son is everything that you should want for your daughter because I raised him right."

Rain knew the type of man she'd groomed and this man had one more time to be disrespectful at her home.

"Look, lady, I really don't want to be here," he finally said.

"Well leave, mutherfucker!" was heard loudly over the music as Rain yelled, causing the all of the guests to stop in their tracks.

Vick immediately left the court to go and check on his lady and to their surprise, Gloria just kept sitting with Storm. Vick didn't even have to say a word when he walked up.

"Gloria, let's go," he knew what time it was by the redness in Vick's eyes and he hadn't smoke or drank all day. Denise and RJ stood behind Rain and Vick as David stood alone for the first time.

"I'll see you at home, dear," Gloria uttered out and he knew she hated to feel embarrassed. "Goodbye," Gloria snapped; so instead, Tiara and Legally got up and left with him and for a few minutes more, everyone stood and looked at each other, but it took Chance to be the goofy one

"Oh well, let's eat."

In the middle of pure silence, everyone couldn't do anything but laugh. Inside, Gloria was a little scared; but there was something about Rain and Storm that touched her and she realized that not everyone was all bad. Gloria felt like the time had come for her daughter, as well as herself, to live their life from under David's controlling ways. *Shit, Gloria...you're the woman you better learn your power!* The rest of the party went spectacular, even old Gloria got her buzz on.

"Denise," Gloria stopped as they were leaving, "I'm sorry," she grabbed her daughter's hand. "I should have been there for you. I should have stopped it all," she continued to say with tears in her eyes.

"I forgive you, mommy," Denise gives her a hug and a kiss, and for the first time, Gloria was Denise's mother.

"Alright now, Rico baby," Gloria wipes her eyes and smiles, "Love my baby right."

"Yes, ma'am. I'm on it, Ms. Gee," he said as Sharod and DJ helped their mom to the car. Denise felt as though she were on top of the world.

"Thank you, momma," Denise laid on Rain's shoulder.

"You're welcome, baby. I was hoping you wouldn't be upset at me for this," she said.

"Not at all," and you could tell Denise meant it by the smile on her face.

"I hope your mom and dad will be alright tonight," Rain said as RJ hugged Denise from behind.

"They're gonna be just fine!"

* * * * *

Meanwhile at the house, David had another idea for Gloria's ass when she got home; but little did he know, she wasn't the same Gloria that left and after tonight he would remember that shit. Charity and Rena grabbed their mother's shoes and purse as Gloria's son's helped her into the house.

"Come on, momma," laughed Sharod at her stumbling over her own feet.

"Mom, it sure is nice to see you loosen up in life again," DJ couldn't believe that this was Gloria.

"It feels good, son. And I really like those sisters. I bet it was fun to have a twin," she said falling down on the couch in their family room as David made his way down the stairs.

"What the fuck has gotten into you?" David calmly asked Gloria, but the look on his face didn't say *calm*.

"Look, dad," said DJ, "she had a little fun…so what?" he meant that shit. "Why don't you leave her alone and try talking tomorrow," he tried to suggest while Gloria sat right there smiling. By now Tiara and Legally came down to join them so now everyone but Denise was there.

"Son, I'm talking to your mother, not you, so mind your fuckin' business!" David told DJ and he kept his respect for the moment, long enough to see what his mother would do.

"Get up," David went over and grabbed Gloria by her shirt, but she yanked away. "Get your ass up, I said!" David pulled her arm.

"Leave her alone, dad," the kids all screamed out and this time Gloria did get up.

"Ok, David, I'm up; now what?" she looked up at him. "I said leave me alone."

David smacked Gloria hard as fuck in the face. I think he was even a little stunned. Gloria stood up not crying or anything.

"Fuck you, you nasty dog! I'm done being your little arm candy. I've sat back long enough, but not no more."

They all were in amazed at how Gloria was talking. I think David's was more of disbelief.

"You will not continue to hurt me or my daughter any longer."

Of course Denise's other siblings were lost.

David gave Gloria a look as to say, *Bitch you better not,* but she was a woman fed up.

"I won't let you rape Denise anymore. I just won't sit back and let you keep fucking my daughter."

DJ and Tre, even Sharod's defenses were up.

"Momma, what the hell you just say?" Tre asked and all David could do was turn and leave the house. This nigga had no words to say to them after that. There wasn't a dry eye in the room as guilt set in. They all knew the hard times that they gave Denise coming up about being his favorite and now they really knew why.

"I know how you all must feel right now; believe me, I feel the same way," expressed Gloria; she too didn't know what to really say for allowing this to happen in the first place. "I hope you all can forgive me, but most importantly, please try and love on Denise a little more, she's been through enough."

Gloria walked upstairs to go to bed. Her job was done, she came clean to her family and all she wanted now was to move forward making good memories with her children.

Chapter 8

Shuffle

"Mr. Peters, Doctor Walthrust will see you now," announced Raven, the receptionist at New Beginning's mental health clinic where Donny's been going twice a week since Bria died. He made his way inside the office and took a seat.

"Hello, Donny," Doc greeted.

"It's always a pleasure, sir," Donny was very quiet today and Doctor Walthrust knew something would come out in the session.

"Well, let's begin where we left off. How are things at home with raising little Briaon?" he asked.

"Things are going real good for the most part, Doc; he's my little prince," expressed Donny. Briaon was his reason for living, but he had other things on his mind.

"Can we switch gears for a minute, Doc?" asked Donny. "I have something I want to get your advice on."

Doctor Walthrust nodded as a sign to continue and Donny took a sip of his water and began.

"You already know the background that I came from and the one I'm trying to create, but mutherfuckers are truly trying my life, Doc," said Donny, knowing Doctor Walthrust wasn't up on his slang and judging from his face, he was lost on its meaning. "*Trying my life* means pushing me to snap resulting in dumb shit and I have Briaon, Doc. I'm all he got."

"Donny, your hiding," Doctor Walthrust pointed out. "Now tell me what's going on?"

"Niggas are trying to kill me; they have been looking for me and my son with a fifty thousand dollar ransom on our heads. I haven't been back to work at the studio. I left Keyz in charge and he tells me repeatedly that strange dudes keep popping up wanting to meet with me, supposedly about signing to D-Nyce Studios," but Donny knew who they were, only Main's goons were out for revenge.

"Donny, this is serious; what are you doing to protect yourself and make sure little Briaon remains safe?" Doc asked.

"We've been at my sister house which is a very safe place, but I don't want to put her life in jeopardy," said Donny, "but Rain isn't going for us separating."

He was right, Donny knew Rain would kill before losing him so he hadn't told her but it was time for them to talk.

"Doc, I love my family and the only way I see it, there's two scenarios which are kill them, or leave the city."

Doctor Walthrust continued to listen in on all of Donny's feelings as he made notes to later process, but he knew Donny needed to figure something out quick.

"Well, Donny, ultimately the final decision is up to you; but I do feel that you should talk with your sisters and come up with a solution right away because things could end up out of hand," he continued to give him some instructions before it was time to go. "I'll see you back in a week because I'm going on vacation, but if you need me, you have my personal number," said Doc and he hoped Donny would get through this ok. Donny knew he and Rain needed to talk, but the hard part was figuring out how to say it.

A lot of things had become strange inside Denise's parent's house; it was just like David's ass didn't exist. Of course Gloria's still had her attitude with that nigga, but now none of their children were speaking to him at all.

David sat in the kitchen, cigar in one hand and drink in the other, trying to figure out just how all this had blown up in his face.

"That punk ass boy and his family," David said under his breath. He was pissed the fuck off at the whole situation, but mostly he wanted to get to Denise.

"Hello there, son," he said as DJ walked in, taking a banana from the table.

"So you're still not talking to me? I said I'm sorry, what else do y'all want me to do," said David as DJ stood there looking at his sickening ass.

"Dad," he said, "and I call you that because I carry your name and I don't want to be disrespectful…" DJ was still in his feelings. Denise is his sister and he felt like as the oldest, he should have protected her. "We are not the ones that you need to be apologizing to. What about Denise, you know your daughter that you raped," expressed DJ. "When you're ready to talk to her, then you can talk to me," he said as he walked right out his father's face. DJ and his siblings all felt pain, but it came in the form of different lesions. It's crazy how their dad was the one who lacerated them.

"You look nice, mom. Where are you on your way to?" asked Tiara as she stood at the door watching Gloria get dressed.

"Thanks, baby, I'm going to have lunch with your sister Denise, would you like to join us?" Gloria knew Tiara and Denise needed to talk because they used to be very close growing up.

Tiara stood quietly, "Yes, I want to go, there's something I'd like to say to her," she confessed.

"Great, baby, here," Gloria said, handing Tiara her keys.

"Go start my car, I'll be right down," said Gloria. She was excited to see if those two would get along.

David cut his eyes at Gloria as she left and it killed him that he didn't have mind control over her anymore. At this point, all he could do was attempt to fix this.

*****

Denise arrived at the restaurant ten minutes ahead of time and it had been long since she enjoyed her mother's attention. As she ended her call with RJ, letting him know she made it safe and Denise thought that she was seeing things.

"Tiara," Denise called out as she and Gloria approached the table, "what are you doing here?"

"Hello to you too, sister," Tiara greeted as they took their seats and the waitress came for their drink orders.

"What's going on, mom? Is everything alright?" Denise didn't know if they were setting her up and David would pop out from nowhere.

"Your sister wanted to come along, dear," Gloria explained, "and she has something she wants to say to you."

Denise had no idea what happened after the party as she looked over at Tiara for conversation.

"I'm sorry, sis, I'm so sorry," Tiara began, "for all the years I've hurt you by not being there and now we know what Dad has been doing to you."

Denise looked at Gloria.

"Mom had to let go of that pain and I'm glad that she did because I can stop hating or blaming my sister for attention that you didn't even ask for, and I want you to know I love you."

The tears came down Denise's face. *Is this really happening, God?* she asked in her head, she never imagined this day would come.

"Thank you, Tiara, that means a lot to me and I really miss the close bond we had," said Denise, she wanted so much to get that back with her sister. Denise tapped her eyes so her makeup wouldn't run. "I'm starving, let's eat!"

They all began to laugh. This is what Denise has always wanted.

* * * * *

Aye, this is Chuck. Fuck life, fuck you; leave me a message if you fuckin' want too.

Clover hated Chuck's answering machine.

"This is the fourth time I've called you, nigga; and I haven't gotten a call back. I hope your ass just drunk and everything is ok; but anyway…I found the location of that Janay girl and I'm going to take a trip out there next week to see if our Lizzy's there too. Hit me ASAP, nigga."

Clover hung up, he hated doing jobs once people fall off, but again…that is his boy. Chuck and Clover had history together and that's the only reason why this nigga even cared.

Clove, being a detective, loved to search the latest news on Google or any other social media site and of course his favorite was Facebook. As he browsed his timeline being nosey, he spotted a headline that caught his eye

"Club Benji's owner BRAWL at the mall"

What the fuck? Clover thought to himself, "World Star got this shit," he said out loud as he clicked on the link and began to watch the show.

Niggas had no idea that someone leaked a video of Rain and Storm beating those bitches, but sure enough, that shit had 2,300 likes already and it had only been live for four hours. Clover watched in full detail and he could've fallen out his chair when he spotted Lizzy fighting too.

"My, my, my…must be my lucky day; these bitches made my job real easy," he said as he slammed the top of his computer down getting excited.

Since Chuck hadn't called him back, Clover decided to go ahead with plans to go to Virginia and keep all the information until he talked to him.

After that shit ended with Gee and Main, Storm had no choice but to bring in new help for Club Benji's, so she hired these two niggas from the West end. Cash and Red, straight from Idlewood Avenue, but don't let the White boy fool you… they were killers. So what better plan to join in with more.

One sure way for word to travel fast…put it on the internet and if Clover knew about the video it wouldn't be long before Storm and Rain's people found out.

"Anybody seen Nizzy?" asked Red as he walked through an empty Club Benji's.

"Check the office!" T-Dub yelled from VIP, but Red had already looked in there.

"I guess she stepped out this bitch for a minute," said Red, plopping down in one of the plush swizzle chairs. "Deja Vu strikes again. Good ole faithful Facebook." One of Red's friends who knew he worked at the club tagged his ass in on the video. "Dammmn!" he smirked, holding his hand over his mouth. Red thought that shit was hilarious.

"Mane, they gave them bitches the business" #MyBossaG!! this stupid nigga had a nerve to fuckin' comment.

"I wonder if Chance knows about this?" he picks up his phone. "He gone fuckin' bug out," he says as he dials Chance's number.

"Yo, what's up?" answered Chance, "Everything all good?" he asked and Red explained that he was fine but what he'd seen was not. He began to share the fact that the video was all over the web.

"Yeah, boss, on World Star…that shit got mad likes too. I just wanted to make sure you knew what was up," he expressed as Chance looked over at Vick who was waiting on him to get off the phone and finish business, but now he could see that Chance's attitude just shifted gears.

"Red, thanks my dude, let me call you back; but better yet, I'll see you at the club later," said Chance as he ended a very upsetting call and he wanted to see what his brother thought about it being out.

"Bruh, tell me why Red just said the video's out all over the fuckin' internet?" Chance began to explain to Vick who was now mad at this shit too. They both felt like this could be bad for business, as well as bring heat to the girls and they both loved them sisters to death.

Vick suggested they wait until later to tell the girls.

"Bring it up at the meeting tonight," he suggested, "just to have everybody on alert," said Vick, "because I'd hate to kill a nigga in a crowded room."

Chance agreed. He knew the girls needed a clear head tonight, so he and his brother went back to finishing their business before time came to be at the club.

*****

"Hush, little baby, don't say a word, auntie's gonna buy you a mocking bird," Rain walked the floor singing and rocking Briaon to sleep so that she and Storm could leave for Club Benji's. Donny had been gone all day and she knew he went to the doctor, she just didn't know what he had to do after that.

"Shh, I just got him to sleep," she said as she laid Briaon in his crib so aunt Storm could kiss him.

"Come on, sis, leave him be," said Rain as they heard Donny coming in the door. Rain dimmed the light and put a crack in the door; it was now time to switch from auntie to boss. "Hey, baby bruh."

Donny kisses them both as they walked into the family room where he was.

"Where you been all day?" asked Storm putting on her coat.

"Nowhere…my appointment and then I just rode around; but before y'all go, can I talk to you?" Donny asked as they gave him their full attention. "Now before y'all say no, please just hear me out," Donny began to say. "I'm tired, sis, and I don't want Briaon to grown up in hiding," which makes sense, "and these niggas ain't going to stop looking for me, so I guess I got to keep killing; huh?" he asked knowing that they didn't want that for him and the baby. "I got to get out of here, sis, before they find me and my son," he was concerned about his baby. Donny remembers a lot from his young life with Jackie and Keith. "I don't want my son raised with no parents."

Rain and Storm looked at each other because they knew he was serious and a lot of what he said made sense.

"Baby bruh, you want to take you and the baby away from us and live somewhere else where you have nobody? That's fuckin' crazy!" she was pissed at the thought of not having Donny in her view every day. You know Rain loves her baby brother!

Donny was tired of all the killing and he didn't want to be a part of that shit anymore. "Can you just think about it," Donny asked as Rain and Storm headed for the door.

"I love you and I'll think about it," she said. "Briaon's sleep in his room."

She slammed the door ready to go and really have a drink now.

*****

All of the lights, all of the lights.

You would have thought that Jeezy was in Club Benji's tonight as many mutherfuckers were lined up to get in when Storm and Rain arrived, so they decided to go through the back.

Everything was in place and everybody looked great, but Rain's mind was still branded on Donny.

"Wassup, boss?" greeted Nizzy meeting them at the door. "Vick and everybody are waiting on you two," Nizzy added, following behind them for protection.

"Do you see that line, baby?" Rain approached Vick, giving him a kiss and Storm went over to Chance.

"Yeah, I did, boo; you'd think that we were taking food stamps to get in."

Everybody laughed, but Vick kind of had an idea where all these people came from.

"Tonight, as you all can see," said Vick, "it is definitely going to be a packed house and I need security on top of y'all shit tonight. I don't know if y'all heard, but there's a video out there of Lizzy and Storm whipping some bitches ass," he continued as Storm and Rain wondered how it came out, this was the first they'd heard of it. Chance gave Storm a look to say that everything was alright, but of course, Rain was going to want more details later.

"Let's party."

He adjourned the meeting so Nizzy could go and open the doors.

Everybody in the club "turned up" that night, and if it wasn't for Yetta double ordering the shipment, the bar would've ran out of liquor. They had people visiting from Norfolk and Hampton; shit, I even heard Florida was in the house too, and the night couldn't have been more perfect for them. Damn, people can be so fuckin' nosey; but oh well, they made a fuckin' killing this here night and Nizzy was even amazed when she did the final count.

"Maybe beating ass can help you get rich," she joked and she handed Storm the printout from tonight as they were leaving.

"We did well, boss," said Nizzy, "whatever had to happen," she started to smile at Storm hard, "just had to happen," she was happy that it did occur…shit sometimes mess does sale.

Nizzy made sure that all the doors were locked; all with the exception of one, as she made her way toward the storage in the back and opened the door to let Merlot in. Word is that Nizzy broke it off with Tricia and now that sexy human was back on the market.

"Wassup, boo?" said Nizzy, admiring her ass while she swung it walking in.

"Don't, *boo*, me. I was at that damn door freezing, what took you so long?" Merlot asked as she walked up on Nizzy pressing tightly against her body.

"I'm sorry, but my boss was still in here, baby; but why don't you let me make it up to you," suggested Nizzy. *Damn, that girl makes me wet every time I talk about her.*

"And how are you supposed to do that?" Merlot asked as she felt Nizzy's hand going under her dress.

Just as Nizzy remembered, Merlot wasn't wearing any panties. Nizzy picked Merlot up off her feet.

"Baby, what are you doing? Put me down," Merlot giggled as Nizzy placed her down on top of the bar. Merlot kept looking around nervously, scared to death that one of Nizzy's bosses would come back while she was busy indulging in the taste of Merlot's neck.

"What's wrong?" she stopped, noticing the decrease in Merlot's moans.

"Chill, boo, my people are gone home for the night, and besides, they trust the kid," she kissed Merlot on her soft lips. "Now come on and serve me. I'm at the bar and I'm thirsty," she expressed and within seconds all Merlot knew was that she felt Nizzy's tongue traveling toward her now running pussy.

Nizzy partook on sucking that clit as she stroked her head using all the right motions.

"Oh, baby," moaned Merlot. "Ain't nothing like your head, Nizzy. I swear!" she said as the erotic act had her mind blown. It felt so good as Nizzy began taking her tongue to the next level which ended up being Merlot's nice, juicy titties and she played around her areola. She tickled her nipples with the tip of her tongue; mane, Nizzy used the fuck out of that body organ as it slurped up the taste of Merlot. While sucking on her breast, Nizzy eased two fingers into Merlot and the more she pumped them in her, the more her volcano erupted.

"Now, she's ready," whispered Nizzy into Merlot's ear as she unbuttoned her Armani black slacks. That twelve-inch dildo rose hard on its release as Nizzy gently inserted it into her pussy. Merlot laid back, body hanging backwards off the bar as her head swung in a waving motion.

"Fuck me, Nizzy…give me that dick, don't hold back, you said you were at the bar."

Merlot talked dirty and that shit sent Nizzy's fire into full blaze. The more she demanded, the harder Nizzy worked and I know she enjoyed their view from the bar mirrors as she worked them walls right; surprisingly none of the glasses fell down.

"Oh shit, damn, boo, this pussy good!" said Nizzy.

Are you sure she's a fuckin' girl; you got some real men who don't throw dick like that and she still manages to treat the hot pocket polite.

"I'm about to cum, stay right there, don't move!" Nizzy ordered.

"Ok, daddy, I'm cumming too," announced Merlot as their moans echoed throughout the empty club.

Heavy breathing and sweating…Nizzy didn't want to take the dick out, but she knew after a certain time, the alarm company would call if it was activated, so now it was time to really lock up Club Benji's.

* * * * *

You cannot see a snake in your grass until sometimes it's too late; and if it's poisonous, it might just bite or hurt you in some way. That is what makes human snakes so dangerous because they occasionally have a way of making themselves invisible. A snake will never let you in on their intentions up front; they will act as if they are your friends, or even family, just like no threat is posed until it's judgment day and they suddenly come on with their attack.

The snake in Denise's family was none other than the head and in this case he was moving for the physical one last time.

It had been a week since the disaster at the housewarming and David hadn't seen or talked to Denise, so his urge for her couldn't hold back too much longer. He had tried to call her cell, he even went to her job, but she just kept refusing to see him right now and I'm guessing he had enough.

On this particular day, David and DJ were the only two at the house and he was shocked when David asked him to show him where Denise lived, and of course, DJ wanted to ride. David said that he thought that it was time they made up. The car ride over was silent as fuck. DJ really didn't have shit to say to his dad and if it wasn't for Denise, he wouldn't have gone. DJ couldn't do anything about their past growing up, and he felt as if he'd betrayed his sister, but he would protect her if he could now.

"Are you coming in?" asked David as he got out the car.

"I'll just speak so you two can talk, this is long overdue," DJ replied, walking up to Denise's door and knocking. David stood behind him as Denise opened the door.

"Hey, bro, what are you two doing here," she asked hugging DJ but keeping her eyes on David's nasty ass.

"I rode with dad to show him where you lived because he wanted to talk to you," DJ turns to walk back to the car.

"I'll be out here, sis," he said as Denise invited David inside.

David looks around to see if RJ was there, "Where is your boyfriend?" David asked as Denise stood in the middle of her living room, arms crossed like *bitch please hurry up*.

"He's out, dad, but what is it that you want to talk about?" she cut right to the point.

"Ok, then, I want to know why aren't you answering the phone for my calls and why would you go against me?" asked David.

I thought this nigga was coming to apologize, Denise shook her head.

"I don't have to answer to you, dad. I'm a grown ass woman!" she snapped for the first time as David's sick ass began to smile.

"Grown woman; huh?" he expressed as he rubbed his hand down the side of her face.

"Move," she pushes his hand down, but instead of stopping, he grabbed her arm.

"Didn't I tell you when you were nine years old that your vagina belonged to me," he grabbed her right between her legs and had the nerve to smell his fuckin' hands. "Sweet smell, just like I remember."

Damn shame as Denise started to shake and cry.

"Why can't you let me live? Don't you think you took enough from me already!" she yelled.

"Dad, I need you to leave," she said, pointing toward the door, but David's ass didn't budge.

"You're mine, Denise. You came from my dick and if I want to give you some of it, I can," he snatched her close and Denise became really scared.

She never fought David back in her life; most of the times when he was raping her, Gloria was standing outside her door so no one would come in. That's how fucked up he had her mind too.

"I miss my pussy," he whispered in her ear. "Now be a good girl and do as your father says. Lie back on the couch!" David demanded and it was almost like this time her feet got stuck on the ground because she couldn't move and that pissed him off even more at that point. "Lay the fuck down," he used a firm pitch tone as Denise felt her body being pushed back onto the sofa and David's big ass climbed on top of her.

DJ was in the car bumping Lil Wayne's, *I'm not human* as Denise was inside screaming for his help.

"Get off of me!" she fought and it felt good not to lay there while her father penetrated her. "DJ help me please, help me!" she screamed and punched at David as he took his hand pressing it down on her mouth just as RJ pulled up outside.

"Stick up, nigga!" DJ tried to scare RJ as he made his way up to the door to go in.

"Oh shit, wassup, bruh? Turn that shit down, nigga," he laughed at how loud DJ was playing the music as he opened the door while DJ now followed closely behind him.

"I'm going to turn it down, nigga; let me go in and get pops so we can leave because I got to pick the kids up at 7:00 p.m.," said DJ as he walked in with RJ and what they saw made the music shut off in their minds.

From that moment on, everything to DJ seemed to move in slow motion as they caught David in the act of trying to rape Denise. DJ never moved to go and pull him off of Denise, all he did see was RJ running into the other room for his gun.

"DJ, help me please!" Denise's teary eyes interlocked with her brother's.

POW, POW, POW, POW, POW.

DJ emptied the clip into the back of his own father being the one who finally did save Denise from him. The sound of the gun going off scared the shit out of RJ and all he could think about was getting to Denise to make sure that she wasn't the one hurt. As RJ turned the corner from the bedroom he spotted Denise in DJ's arms and all he could do was drop to his knees.

"Thank you, God," he silently whispered, making his way over to comfort hysterical Denise.

"It's over, sis, its over," said DJ as he rubbed the back of her head while it rested on RJ's shoulder now. "I might go to jail for a long time now because of this shit," DJ expressed, "but it was all worth it if you ask me," he hung his head down. "I wish I could have stopped it sooner," he confessed and Denise didn't want her brother to go to jail for doing the right thing, she needed him more than ever now.

"Is there something I can say to the police to make them see that it wasn't your fault?" she cried, standing next to her brother, looking at David's body face down on the floor. DJ knew that the cops weren't going to hear that shit. RJ started to think of something that could help them out and then he remembered his boy, Ben.

"I got a friend with a chop shop, he'll help us out. He'll burn that nigga's bitch ass body so there's no evidence; but you two gone have to control y'all family," suggested RJ.

Damn, he is his mother's child, taking charge just like Rain.

DJ and Denise looked at each for conformation, "Let's just say that nigga got mad and left," DJ brought up the idea.

"I'm cool with that," Denise paused, "I'll be my brother's keeper," she hugged him and he kissed her on the head. "This will be our secret forever."

They both pinky swore!

"Alright, bruh, come on and help me wrap this nigga up," joked RJ, "Mutherfucker gone start stinking my house up in a minute."

They covered David's body in three quilts. Denise stood watch as her past became buried and now she could really move on.

"Baby, go ahead and get cleaned up; try to rest while me and DJ take this ride," RJ instructed as they both kissed her and picked up David's body, carrying that nigga to the trunk to drop him off. They drove for about forty-five minutes until they reached Charles City, Virginia where RJ's white friend, Ben, was located.

Ben knew anytime that RJ pulled up, it was about business and money, and it didn't even take long for him to catch on. RJ explained to Ben everything that had just taken place and once he hit him with three stacks, it was fuckin' show time.

DJ watched as Ben loaded David's ass on the table and politely slid that bitch into the incinerator.

"Can I shut the door?" that was DJ's only request and Ben stepped off to the side.

"Be my guest," he said as DJ shut the door slowly because he wanted to watch as the flames ate through what use to be David!

CHAPTER 9

Looking Ass Nigga

"No need for revenge," someone once said.

Sit back and wait, those that hurt you will fuck themselves one day, realest shit I've ever wrote, and I knew this is true because of David.

DJ, Denise and RJ were the only ones that knew the real truth about what happened on that day, and of course, their silence wasn't going to be broken. They went on about life like nothing had ever changed and the way DJ staged everything was pure genius. He drove David's car back home that evening before anyone else got there and he parked it like it was never moved. DJ went to his house, took a shower and got dressed, heading out to the club with some friends.

To him, this was an *I'm sorry* gift to his sister for not seeing the signs at first; and of course, the rest of the family still felt very betrayed over what David had done.

Gloria was even like *good* when they found out he'd left town. DJ explained his version to the truth which was that David snapped.

"He came down stairs talking shit, mom, saying things like...fuck you and us," he made himself sound sad. "Dad said he was tired of kissing our asses and that he could go start over somewhere else, so he grabbed his brown luggage," (which DJ had already disposed of) "and he got in a cab and left without saying where he was going or anything to me, mom."

He made it sound so convincing as Gloria laughed it off replying, "Good Ridden."

Neither she nor her other children really gave a fuck after all the shit that just came out about him who would. They still had all the money in their possession and Gloria even empty like three bank accounts as well as changed her will over to her children; they all, in some strange way, felt free.

*****

"Hello, sir," the flight attendant approached Clover as he laid his head back against the seat. "Would you like Chicken or Steak?" she asked as a privilege of first class, but this nigga declined her offer, ordering an Absolut Citron on the rocks instead. This nigga was preparing to catch a mouse.

Clover left New York for Virginia without a word to anyone or even hearing back from Chuck's ass, which meant nobody knew he was on his way there. Dangerous grounds alone. This nigga must be out of his mind, then on top of that, he had no clue as to who he's really, really chasing, because Lizzy's part of the equation is quarter, and nobody had any idea there was still La'Rain. Yeah, he's a detective, but that doesn't mean shit because Rain's a different breed bitch. She would kill his mother in front of his face if she had to, but Clover really didn't do the proper homework. He saw a couple of pretty harmless looking bitches and he stereotyped them; *Big Mistake*.

I'm guessing that this nigga had a smooth first class ride; shit, he drank himself to mutherfuckin' sleep.

"This is your captain speaking; at this time will you please buckle your seat belts as we prepare for landing in Richmond, Virginia."

This nigga woke up quick, smiling hard as fuck; but he had no idea where the fuck he was. Some detectives have the advantages of traveling all over the world in good or bad parts, but that nigga, Clover, hadn't seen anything really but the good. He dealt with clients trying to catch their spouses cheating and he always ended up following them on some goddamn island. This nigga had no clue what the streets of Richmond had to offer and still he decides to chase the big bad wolf. Clover made his way through Richmond International Airport, and of course, he rented a car, so it took him about fifteen minutes to pick that up. Marriot Broad Street was a nice place to stay, mostly paid or celebrity people stayed there.

"Welcome to the Marriot, sir; are you checking in?" greeted the check-in clerk.

"Yes, ma'am, Clover Decou," he said, handing her his ID and credit card as he looked at her body up and down. She must've seen right through his perverted ass way, because she cut him short real fast with the mean evil eye, like *nigga I don't think so.*

"Here you are sir, room 303; and the elevators are right this way," she directed, "please enjoy your stay.

Clover went up to his room and took a shit, shower, and shave, then he did a little more research on Lizzy. Sometimes the cyber world can be a good and a bad thing when it comes to promoting your business; it's funny, but the internet is like a talkative female and it tells everything.

Coming from a long trip and checking into your room, most humans are ready to eat. During Clover's Google search on Elizabeth Wales, Rico's Kitchen pops up.

"Hmm, let's see what this menu is talking about," this sneaky bastard already had it in his mind that he was going even if the food wasn't his choice; I guess he had to humor himself. Gathering the address, his phone, gun and keys…off he went to start being a spectator.

"Good evening, will you be dining in or is this pickup?" Latoya cheerfully asked, and of course Clover wanted a table in the corner. "Right this way, sir," she said as she showed him to his seat and he followed while looking all around. "Here you are, sir, your server will be with you shortly," she turned to walk away.

"Who runs this place?" Clover stopped her in her tracks.

She faces him and says, "Her name is Janay Peters," she never showed a sign of an attitude, plus, she was scared as to why he had asked. "Is everything alright, sir?" she asked, just making sure for herself.

"Yes, ma'am, everything is great. I just think it's beautifully decorated inside of here that's all."

Latoya smiled, "Well enjoy your meal, sir," she said as she left.

"Ok, Janay, I got you in my trap too," he said. "Y'all bitches really think you have game," he talked to himself as he looked over the menu to find something to order. Ten minutes later and still no server and Clover had to go to the bathroom as his veins began to poke out his head from anger. "Look…fuck this, I'm going to drain the wiz; this bitch taking all day," he got up and left his table.

The bathrooms in Rico's Kitchen were positioned on the side, away from the dining area because one thing Rain hated was restrooms that were around people eating food. Clover made his way through the almost packed room as he looked around in search of familiar faces, but there weren't any in there. Once he got in front of the restrooms, he could hear conversations from the kitchen staff and someone kept calling out Tommy or Mr. Wales. He decides to peep into the swinging doors of the kitchen to see if he could get a look at this Mr. Wales, and a full staff had come to work that night which meant the kitchen was packed.

"Tommy, Steam Lobster Sous, Chef Jermaine called out as Vick turns around to give it to him.

So, you're Mr. Wales, Clover said, remembering him from Bora Bora. Clover's hot breath fogged the door glass as he spoke. "I got your ass too, you rude mutherfucker," as he begins to laugh, Clover thought he was going to have a fuckin' party bring them down.

"Are you lost?" walked up Kimmy, a night shift waitress.

"Yes, I'm looking for the bathroom."

"Right behind you, sir," she said as she carried a heavy ass tray; all she wanted was for this nigga to move out her way.

Close call dumb ass, you lucky she was busy or else she would've told Vick about that shit.

Clover went to take a piss and returned back to his table just as his waiter walked up.

"Hello, sorry about the wait, I came here once, but you were gone. My name is Jason and I'll be your server this evening," he said as Clover just sat there staring him up and down. I guess he wanted to make him wait now.

"I'll have the southern style smothered chicken and gravy, with rice pilaf and baked potatoes," he said smart, but Jason kept it real cool with his ass.

"Would you like butter and sour cream with that?" he asked.

"Yes, if it's not going to take extra-long to get."

"Ha," Jason said, "will that be all, sir?"

"Yes, Clover gritted on him hard as the young man walked away.

"I hate young ass waiters; he needs to carry his ass back to school somewhere," Clover said as he heard a voice from behind.

"Hello, baby."

Clover listen in and for a minute he thought someone was trying to holla at him, as he turns around to see Lizzy hugging a regular customer, then she made her way toward the front.

"And there is Lizzy. My, my, my, my, what a beauty in person," Clover said to himself.

Nigga, kill yourself; even on his best day Rain would walk right past his ass so he might as well wipe the droll from his chin as her PHATY bounced by.

Rain walked up to the hostess booth to let Latoya know about a big reservation on its way to the party room and Clover was all up in her face.

"I'm meeting Janay, so hit me on my cell if you need me," Rain said to Latoya, walking back passed his table, but this time she glanced in his direction. She didn't think anything of it because new people ate there all the time. Clover watched her leave through the back door. In intense speed, Clover jumps up from his table and left right out the restaurant not saying a word to anybody. As he started up his car, he saw Rain at the stop sign and that's when he began his suicide chase. Not getting too close, but staying within reach, Clover rode with that fuckin' Escalade. Left, left, right, right, Clover wasn't letting her get out of his sight; he would have killed himself trying not to lose her truck.

Brandermill Woods, he followed Rain right on in as she made her way over to Storm's house to pick her up for their sister date to the movies.

Beep, Beep, "Come on before we be late," Rain teased from the truck as Storm made her way toward her.

"I'm coming; I had to get the babies straight."

"Hi, sis," she kisses Rain's cheek and shuts the door.

"Bumping that new Kesha Cole I see," she said as they sung almost every song on the damn album; they laughed, not really on watch mode at that time because to them, there wasn't any reason to.

Clover sat in his car as they walked through the parking lot and he watched as they went into the theater.

"I love my job. Snake ass nigga, Karma can be a fat bitch."

That nigga forgot all about being hungry, besides the hot dog he got out and brought, he never had anything else; all he did was sit in that car until he spotted them coming out.

"Come on Lizzy, take me to your house," he adjusted his seat so he could get ready to pull off and follow them again. This time from Storm and then to Rain's house.

"Ah ha, got you now, Elizabeth Wales. Chuck is going to love what I have for him," Clover laughed. "I think tomorrow I'll really go back for my meal," he said, as he pulled off he felt like he had enough information for tonight.

* * * * *

"Hello," Rain answered with her deep sleep voice, it was 6:15 in the fuckin' morning. "Hey, Cream, what's wrong?"

"Nick called out and there's no way I can open and run this place on a Saturday breakfast rush by myself, Ms. Lizzy," that was Cream's way of saying, "you need to come in" to the boss.

"I can be in by 9:00 a.m., but I have to work at the club tonight, so I'm not going to be able to stay long, but I'll get someone else to come before I leave," said Rain as Cream was relieved and thanked her, then Rain hung up and laid the fuck back down.

Nine o'clock Rain had said, yeah, right, try 10:30 a.m., but shit...Rain was the boss.

"Hey, Cream," she said as she walked into her office to put her stuff on top of her desk. "You found anybody to come in yet?" Rain questioned her.

"No," Cream replied, "I'm calling down the list now!" she yelled from across the hall, but all that was suddenly put on hold for Cream to go and handle a rude customer.

"I'm coming, Cream!" yelled Rain as she saw her run past, "let me get this phone call," Rain was looking at her phone as her whole facial expression did a 360.

"What the..." she paused; it had better be just routine checkup. "Wassup, Trix, you good?" Trix was Rain's private investigator that made sure her back was secured at all times. Of course a real queen makes sure she's protected and ain't no fuck boy gone just run up.

"Hey, baby, you got a minute? I really need to fill you in on some information I peeped yesterday," Trix explained. "I did my homework on a nigga and I think y'all might know who the fuck he is."

Rain was lost.

"No him? Who's him?" she asked, "and why would you be doing homework when I haven't given any assignments?"

"When you left the restaurant last night, some mutherfucker followed you out, so I wanted to know who or what the fuck he wanted. His name is Clover DeCou and he's some type of detective from New York City and I know that Janay is from there, so maybe it's her he's following. I'll be on the lookout for that nigga today," Trix was ready and not playing as Rain requested a picture of Clover which he faxed right over to her and they hung up.

Hmm, she said to herself, picking up the phone as she noticed Clover's face from last night. Changing her mind instead, Rain waited. *I'll get his report for today and then tell Vick what's going on.* Rain went on about her morning helping Cream through the rush, Tommy's Saturday breakfast at Rico's Kitchen was the bomb.

"Lizzy, catch that end table for me, please!" Cream called out as she cleared the dishes from another table.

"Welcome to Rico's," Rain stopped mid-sentence as she now locked eyes with an unknown enemy. "What can I get you?" she wanted to cut his dick off and serve him that little shit, and Clover actually knew who she was.

"Short staff, huh?" he made small talk, not even knowing she was on to his ass.

"No, some of our workers are sick with the flu; you know it's a lot of that going around. You sure you want to eat here?" Rain sarcastically said because she wanted his snake ass gone, but even that didn't make this nigga get up and leave.

"I'm good, I already had my flu shot, but I'll have the western omelet with home fries and grits; oh, and can I get some orange juice wit that?" he tried to be nice.

"Coming right up," she storms off and puts the order in, then Rain went to call Trix!

"This mutherfucker really wants to die," she talked light as she stood by the kitchen watching him. "He's in here about to eat now, Trix."

"Oh for real?" that nigga Trix bust a U-Turn in the middle of the intersection on his way to Rain. "You want me to touch him, boss?" he asked.

"Naw, this one's for me," she laughed. "Just keep tabs on his every move and I do mean stay close," she instructed as her thought process was now overtaking her.

"Here you are, sir," the waitress brought him his food as Rain sat at the hostess station keeping her watch guard up until this nigga finished eating and left.

"I see you, Clover," she laughed, shaking her head as he got into his car. "We will soon meet face to face," Rain never told anyone anything about Clover as she finished the remaining morning rush with Cream.

Clover went back to his room so he could rest and get ready to hit the night scene for information and he could finally bring this ship into harbor. *A bunch of Non-Mogul niggas acting like they had a plan*, Clover thought to himself, not knowing that he had now become the prey. Nobody even knew where the fuck Chuck was.

"Oh shit, about time this nigga called. Wassup?" answered Clover, "Where the fuck you been?"

"Mane, I've been handling some business with a lady friend," said Chuck, but look…my phone is dying and I'm on my way home. I'll call you as soon as it charges," Chuck cut him off as he waited in rush hour traffic.

"Cool, make sure you do, I got some real good for you Chuck," informed Clover as they hung up so Clover could go and get ready.

In pursuit to Club Benji's, Rain's phone went off inside of her purse while she rode in Vick's truck with him.

"Where you at, boss?" Trix asked as she told him she was on her way there.

"I see that nigga, Clover, heading into the club; so he's got to be following Janay."

This nigga was really pissing Rain off now just to know that he's fuckin' with her sister.

Who is this mutherfucker and what does he want, she thought to herself as she gave Trix orders on what to do next.

"I'm on my way, don't touch him, let his ass mingle and I'll take over as soon as I arrive."

"What's wrong, baby?" asked Vick as the look of rage consumed her face.

"There's this detective from NY that's been following me for two days and Trix just said he's at the club right now. He doesn't know that we're on to him, and I don't know what he wants."

Vick kept driving, not saying a word until Rain called out to him.

"Can I shoot him in the head?" Vick was serious as shit, he was gone walk in the club and straight pop that nigga right there.

Rain doesn't like a sloppy performance, so she suggested talking it over with management. Chance and Storm pulled up at the same time, you know Rain filled them in on the news so that they all could be on the same page. As they entered, everything went as normal routine as Nizzy always made sure of. They talked like they do every opening night, but tonight they put them on to this in-house pig. Cash suggested slipping him a mickey and then kidnapping the mutherfucker so then maybe he'd confess up to what it is that he wanted.

Rain thought that it would be a good idea. "Let him chill, get comfortable and think he's still watching me, but the whole time I'll be enjoying watching him and that's when we'll make our move."

I love that queen, her brain power is so brilliant and if bitches only knew that's how a queen rules, smart in sequence, a queen doesn't like disorder. Everyone was cool with the instructions, Nizzy was even told to let Yetta know to double the alcohol in whatever Clover ordered.

"I'm dropping my surprise later on tonight," Rain expressed as Vick stood there grabbing his dick.

That girl could rule me any day, he was thinking and if you ask me that's a smart man.

"Who would throw away a woman with the character of a Hope Diamond, which ranked top four out the most expensive ones in the world valuing at 350 million, so what does that tell you about loving Rain.

Trix was already up in their VIP section when everyone else arrived, so they sat and had a couple of drinks. They didn't have to worry about anything right now because Nizzy was all on that nigga. Even though Rain was having a good time, she was still paying attention, *Never be Defenseless to the Enemy.*

"Come on, baby, let's dance," Vick offered.

"Yes, my dear, let's do it!" she hopped her sexy ass up, looking good from head to toe in that all-black fitted Versace mid-quarter cocktail dress that Vick had especially made for her. *Need I mention the black spiked Louboutin pumps?*

"Wait, baby, pass me my hat," Rain stopped. "If I'm going to do it, I got to do it right."

Storm and Chance laughed as Trix stood at the top watching Rain's every move.

"I love your hair when it's wrapped. Your so fine, wife."

She couldn't do anything but blush.

Oh, how I love that man, Rain thought as they danced to "Love in this club."

Clover must've ran low on money, because this nigga left the exotic side, which I thought he was there on business, but I see his business must've been slapping that ass. As he made his way over to the bar and sat down, Nizzy had already put Yetta on, so it was now ready, set, and go.

"Let me get a Patron Gold on the rocks and make that two," Clover ordered as Yetta smiled sexy.

"Sure, baby, coming right up," she said as she went to make his drinks. Clover turns around to face the dance floor.

"Ms. Lizzy, I sure wasn't expecting you to be in here tonight," Clover smirked, looking like the Grinch that stole Christmas with his shady ass.

"Look at the happy couple; Chuck's gonna have so much fun with them. I hope he fucks that phat ass bitch first," he spoke about Lizzy just as Yetta set his drinks down.

That'll be fifteen dollars," she said as he gave her his credit card and Yetta wrote the numbers down just in case.

"Here you are, sir," she hands it back to him.

"Aye, pretty lady, can you start me a tab?"

"Good choice," says Yetta as they both began to laugh, but Clover didn't know that the joke was on him.

"Baby, can we sit down?" Rain slowed up in her dancing as she and Vick both were out of breath so they went back up to VIP. Nizzy came up to check in with Rain and to let her know that this nigga was down there getting wasted.

"Go tell Cash it's time," she said to Nizzy and you can take it straight to Yetta.

"10-4, boss," Nizzy replied, I swear she was the right candidate for this job. Rain took her seat center stage in the lounge and she had a great view of that dumb ass bitch.

"There you are, Ms. Wales," Clover leaned back against the bar as he sipped his life away.

"I see you, too," Rain was saying as well, sitting pretty with her sister beside her. She couldn't hear a word Clover was saying, but she could read his fuckin' energy and that was one of the powers she possessed. Vick and Chance went down to the lower levels to do a round, when all of a sudden, Chance came up with this great idea.

"How's it going?" he spoke to Clover as he walked up to the bar and Rain was wondering what the fuck was this nigga doing; but she didn't make a move, she just sat there and waited to see what happen.

"My name is Tim," Chance started a conversation.

"Clover," this nigga answered short.

"Ok, cool. I'm here on business and I wanted to get out and this place seemed to be the talk of the town."

"Yea, I heard," said Clover. "I'm just passing through myself from Michigan."

Liar and Chance already knew that he was as Storm begins to worry.

"I see what he's doing," Rain said to Storm as they sat having drinks.

Diversion, she thought, "Beautiful choice, baby," Storm expressed, "and that's why I love that man."

They both laughed as Clover and Chuck continued to chat.

"Baby, I'm tired of playing with this bitch; let's finish this so we can go home."

The queen needed her rest and Vick put the nod through to Nizzy and it was on.

"Aye, one more round," Chance ordered for them and Yetta knew to specially hand make Clover's. Rain signaled the DJ to play one of her favorite songs that it took her back to when Donte was running things. As the song began to play, the words filled the air in the entire club, making the old heads go wild with cheer.

* * * * *

But let us leave these two young men to sit and reflect on the fate of the world; for life as we know it my brotha, must go on. And so the hustlers continue to hustle, and the playas continue to play.

That's my shit, yes," Clover sang along as Chance said, "Fuck it," and joined in with him.

"Perfect song for the occasion, sis," Chance said underneath his breath as he and Clover continued to sing and drink.

I'm a man today, can't nobody tell nothing, got a hold on life, I'm taking each day by day, being strong, know just where I'm going to as I get higher and higher.

"Yes, I remember those days; don't you?" he elbows Chance. "I used to smoke so much weed, dude," Clover began to confess his past like he had a new BFF, but little did he know that song was the tell of his life as Rain and Storm continued to watch as he forgot all about his job plus those pills had him feeling real good.

Rain smiled as he laughed and conversed while drinking his trap to doom.

"Cuz, I'm too cool (too cool), and what they say is true; oh, I'm full of smoke.

Watching my life go down.

The words played as Rain watched the performance of Clover's life.

Watching my life go down.

As it continued to play, Clover finished that drink and ordered another; at this point, his vision was getting blurry. Chance had left; well pretended that he did, because they knew that this nigga would be out quick.

Club Benji's began to get empty for closing; it was almost 3:00 a.m.

"Woo," Clover tries to catch his balance, having a hard time getting up to leave as eyes still focused on him from the lounge.

"Wassup, my man? You good?" Nizzy approached nicely. "You need some help getting home?" she knew damn well that he did after those two Oxycottons that Cash got and Yetta crushed them both into one drink—double Patron…it's a wonder if that nigga didn't die.

"Look, I must've drunk too much, but my car is outside in the parking lot," Clover's drunk ass informed. "Can you please just help me get outside," he thought all he needed was fresh air to sober him up, but *sorry honey, not gone work!*

After Nizzy exited the club with this fool, she ran into Chance already standing outside by Clover's car and he noticed him already acting like they'd been buddies forever.

"Hey, there is my friend, Tim," this was easier than they thought; being a detective, they believed this nigga would be on his shit.

"Ok cool, let Tim get you home. I just had to get you outside the club," said

Nizzy as she handed him over to Chance; which was all a part of the plan.

"Come on, my dude," I'll drive you home and just chill there," Chance suggested and Clover gave him his car keys and got in.

"I need to make one stop to get some clothes," Chance said and then they were off. Clover was so gone, once Chance hit the heat, that nigga was out cold and he didn't have any clue where they were going.

4317# Chance typed in the code to the gate that allowed him into Uncle Bob's Storage. When he pulled up, Rain, Vick and Storm were already there with the door to lot 233 pushed up in the air. They even had a thin ass mattress in there to lay him on, what they called, comfortably.

Chance picked him up, took his body and dropped it down on the mattress and his head hit that concrete floor hard. Vick and Chance tied up his mouth, hands and feet; this nigga never moved, but I know he gone have a headache in the morning as they all started exiting to leave.

"Leave the light on, but well…bolt lock this bitch up," said Rain and her storage unit was privately off by itself.

So no one would even heard this nigga if he rolled against the door, but she knew she'd be there in the morning when he woke up.

"I'll get my questions answered in the a.m., but right now, let his ass sleep that shit off; can't talk to a half-dead man."

Vick shut the door and locked it; now it was time for *name that spy*. When Rain and Vick got home, Aaliyah was already there asleep in her room as Rain peeped in.

"Look at my princess," she shut the door and went into her room to sleep herself; she knew all that had to be done tomorrow.

* * * * *

"Wake your ass up," Rain kicked him in his back while Vick stood there that cold early morning with her.

"Uggh," Clover squirmed, trying to figure out what was going on and why was he freezing. "Where am I?" he mumbled through the tape as Rain told Vick to remove the mouth guard so she could hear him clearly when he spoke. "What do you want with me?" he was pissing on himself as well as wondering how he ended up trapped.

"You tell me what the fuck is going on!" Rain yelled in anger. "You have been the one that's following me around, so what the fuck do you want" she questioned Clover and he couldn't figure out how she knew.

Did I spill the beans last night? he thought, but nobody could answer that for him. "Look, I was told to find out where you were for this guy name Chuck."

Immediately Rain knew who the fuck that was.

"He wanted you for getting him fired and Janay for the Tulio's grandchildren," Clover was telling everything because he didn't want to die in that storage room.

"These bitches never stop, do they, honey?" asked Vick as Rain smiled but shook her head no.

Quiet as a mouse, she turns to look outside the storage. *Do they know that I'm alive*? she thought to herself. *Or are they really just after Lizzy?* she wondered, but what did they want with her children.

Rain instructed Clover to get Chuck on the phone, "Tell him you found me and that he and Christina need to get to Virginia quick," said Rain, making it seem like RJ and Aaliyah were in trouble, but she never let Clover know who she really was. Vick untapped his hands and feet, handing him the phone to use.

"Call them now, mutherfucker!" said Vick and he wasn't playing.

"Here we go again with a hater on his wife," Chuck's phone ranged out one time and he picked it up. "Where the hell have you been, Clover?" he immediately snapped off, "I called you like six times yesterday."

"Main, I know! I was knocked out asleep. I think I'm coming down with a bug," he lied as Vick held his 9mm to Clover's head waiting for a reason to pull that trigger as he continued, "Look, I found Lizzy and Janay in Richmond but I need y'all to get out here quick because some things are not good with her grandchildren," he laid the foundation; Clover knew that Lizzy meant business.

"Ok, ok…I'm gonna call her now and I'll let you know what time our flight gets in," Chuck jumped up and down while letting Clover know he had his money. "You deserve it, dog."

They both laughed, but on Clover's face fell tears.

"Yes, got you now, bitch!" yelled Chuck referring to Lizzy as he called Christina's phone; but the first two times it went straight to voicemail. I'll try one more time, he thought as he went to dial her number, but on this attempt, she was calling him back.

"Hey, honey are you ready to travel?" Clover shocked Christina.

"And what actually do you mean now?" she asked him in return.

"I found your grandchildren."

Christina dropped her wine flute as it shattered all on the floor, "Chuck, don't play with me," she smiled, "are you serious?"

"Yes, they are in Virginia with Janay, but Clover's telling me that things are not looking good," he reported. "You need to come get them."

That's all Christina needed to hear. "I'm there, Chuck, and we can take the Tulio's private jet," she wanted to get there fast. "Janay would pay for whatever's wrong with them and Lizzy's gonna get hers too," said Christina, she blamed her for ruining her life.

Christina told Chuck to meet her at the airport in an hour and not to be late because she was anxious to see Rico's kids. Chuck and Christina both packed faster than they've ever done before as Christina was stopped by Steven leaving out the door.

"Mom, where are you going?" he startled her as she left, Christina wanted to keep all of this a surprise.

"Son, I don't have time to talk right now; I've got an important meeting."

Steven wondered where she was heading with luggage, but he just let his mother go. He knew how much Christina hated to be badgered. Steven helped her put her bags in the cab as she kissed him on his face and left. Chuck texted

Clover, letting him know they were on the jet and that they'd be landing in an hour and when Vick saw this, he told Clover to text back the address and room number to the Marriot and also that a limo would be picking them up.

"Baby, get this nigga over to the hotel room and if he tries anything funny, kill him," Rain told Vick; she knew that Clover had to walk through the hotel lobby, untapped of course, so she didn't want any funny business.

"I gotta go over to the house for something and I'll meet you at the room," she left as Vick told Clover, "Let's go. Don't try me because I'll kill you. Now get in the car," Vick held the gun to his head as he got in. As they drove to the hotel, Vick kept telling Clover not to try anything dumb; especially if he didn't want his eighty-nine-year-old mother raped and murdered because he'd have a junkie do it if he thinks he was playing. "Just try me," said Vick and Clover promised that he'd follow all orders and that he goddamn did.

This nigga walked in the hotel past security and a real cop, and he didn't do or say shit as they made their way up to room 303. Approaching her house, Rain called Storm and Chance so that they could attend this final meeting; and of course you already know that they were going to be there. She pulled into her driveway texting RJ before she got out.

Your grandmother is in town and she's trying to kill me, so I would like for you to be there too.

She hit send and before she could unlock the door to the house, RJ texted back, but Rain proceeded in the house to inform Aaliyah. Subjecting children to negative statements about their own parent, especially when she's raised them with her all, violates the most basic job you have as a grandparent and that is to protect their heart."

When RJ and Aaliyah think back on all the negative things they'd ever heard Ricky or Christina say concerning their mother, they knew that there was no real way that they ever loved them at all.

"Damn, it's nippy," complained Christina as she put on her five-thousand-dollar mink and Clover carried the both of their luggage to the limo which was outside already.

"Hello, glad you had a safe trip," Cash was the driver. This nigga turned white boy real quick. "Clover has instructed me to bring you to the Marriot, room 303; he's already there expecting you," Cash played his part to the fullest; he even had the proper voice on. Christina and Chuck planned the whole way there they really thought they could out smart Storm. "Here we are people," Cash opened up their door, "don't forget the room is 303."

"Oh, we won't," Chuck's ass was sober now. He couldn't wait to see the look on Lizzy's face when they busted her and he cuts her fuckin' heart right out her chest.

"Damn, Chuck you're a little mad, huh?"

Chuck and Christina walked straight into the Marriot, nonstop to the elevators and up.

"Right here," Christina stopped him as he sonic walked past, this nigga couldn't wait to see Clover.

Knock, knock.

Chuck did the honors; he was excited to be one step closer to seeing Lizzy as the door opened. "Hey, nigga, we're here," Chuck dapped Clover up, never noticing that he wasn't smiling as Christina walked in behind him.

"Get off of me!" they both tried to fight, as Vick and Chance grabbed them both from behind and instructed Clover to sit back down in his chair as they slammed Christina and Chuck down in one too.

"Clover, what the fuck is all of this!" screamed Chuck as Christina sat there scared, clutching her purse.

"It's out of my control now," that's all Clover said as Rain, Storm, RJ and Aaliyah walked out the bathroom and Christina looked as if she'd seen a ghost.

"What are you doing here, Abuela's babies?" Christina jumps up to hug them, but Aaliyah pushes her back down, which surprised her because they always were so close. Chuck became nauseated as he started to vomit all on himself.

"Don't move, you bitch!" said Rain.

"Here I am, you want to kill me? The both of you wanted Lizzy; huh?"

They all sat there quiet as a mouse and that shit made her even more pissed. Rain had been trying to escape this family for years now, and even under a new name, they still were coming.

"You..." she walks in front of Christina, "You wanted Janay so that you could get your hands on my children," said Rain and I swear Christina had a mild heart attack as she became deranged.

"What do you mean, *your children,* lady?" Christina asked. "Their mother died years ago," she uttered as the three thought this was some type of game.

"Bitch, pardon my back," as Rain turns to face her kids which were behind her. "Is your mother dead?" she asked.

"Hell, naw!" they both kissed Rain on both sides of her cheek. "Our mom had to form a new life in order to keep us safe from your bad blood," expressed Aaliyah as she and RJ told their mother to step back because they wanted to make sure Christina knew that all this was coming straight from them.

"Abeula, you have never done shit to help us ever since our dad died, so how dare y'all two try and take our mother yet again; first your husband, and now you too," they both shook their heads; it was now time for them to be heard.

"Nieto y Nieta...I'm sorry for the past, but I always loved you two," Christina tried to butter them up with what she thought they wanted to hear, but she must've forgot they ain't little kids playing in her backyard anymore.

"I had no idea that Lizzy was Rain until now, but I wasn't trying to hurt her personally," she began to cry as Aaliyah told her brother she was done with these lies and shit.

Aaliyah spoke up, "Fuck what they have to say at this point because Lizzy is Rain," her daughter blurted out as RJ reached underneath his shirt and pulling his gun.

Without a word, RJ shot all three of them in their heads; they were tired of people trying to take their mother away.

Rain ran up to him as gun smoke filled the air; evidently, RJ and Aaliyah had this shit planned all along. Rain had no idea her son was going to do this.

"Son," she whispered in his ear. "Let it go, it's over now," she said, still shocked because this was her son's first kill and out of the three, one was his grandma.

"Mom, I'm sorry; we couldn't lose you again."

"Yeah, we just couldn't, mom," Aaliyah comes in on the hug. "You are our everything," and what Rain felt at that very moment was bittersweet emotions; of course, she never wanted her kids to get a body on their hands, but she understood her son's reason for pulling the trigger!!

CHAPTER 10

Identity of a Queen

The next couple of days, Rain stayed quiet trying hard to hear from God about what had just happen. She took this time to reflect on everything she and her family had been through and it was then that she realized there was one more chapter to close. What better time than to do it now, in this moment, while they were already ending things.

"What are you doing?" she went into Donny's room and lay out on his bed playing with Briaon.

"Giggle, giggle, goo," Briaon kicked and played as Rain told her brother everything that had happen the last couple of days and how God woke her up to a lot of things about life.

"That's good, sis. I'm glad it's all over, now you can finally be happy," Donny said as he looked out the window at the sky. Rain knew her brother was in so much pain and it was time to put an end to all of that once and for all.

"Get you and Briaon packed," she said.

"Why? Where are we going?" asked Donny and Rain told him.

"To take a family vacation, baby bruh; you need some fun in the sun."

Donny slightly smiled, even though that's not what he felt like doing; it was still better than being stuck in the house.

Rain called Storm who knew what was up as she got her family ready to meet everyone at the airport, two hours later they all left. Rain, Vick, RJ and Aaliyah, along with Donny and Briaon, loaded up in the limo; but something was off about everyone else. They all laughed like never before and the feeling was so unexplainable.

"We're here," said Rain who happened to be the quietest as Storm, Chance and the twins were already standing there by the jet.

"Why y'all waiting out here?" asked Donny, "You could have just gotten on the plane," he said, but Storm had other plans.

"We're not going, baby bruh; we just came to see you off," she said as Donny turns around to face everyone else.

"Here," Rain handed him a suite case containing two million dollars. "Go live your life. I love you," she cried. "Hell, everyone was crying at that point. He hugged his sister real tight.

"Thank you," Donny cried as Storm walked up.

"I love y'all two and I promise we'll be just fine," he said as Aaliyah held on to Briaon.

"We know you will," they said to their brother and they didn't want to let him go, but he needed to hug everyone else.

They watched as Donny and Briaon boarded the jet, and even though they were hurt, Rain knew her brother deserved to be happy no matter what it took to make that happen; she never put a price on her love. As the jet took off, Rain felt half of her soul fly away. Rain didn't want Donny to tell them where he was going.

"Call me when you get to your place of living," was the last thing she said to him as they kissed and parted ways, but Rain knew it wouldn't be long before she got a call.

The limo ride home to a house without Donny caused Rain to think of how much strength all this has given her; but inside, you never know how much bullshit you can take until you have gone through it.

* * * * *

"I know I can't tell you what it's like to be me; hell, even I had to hide behind my own words. I had to learn how to get past my own enemy which was fear, and that's how I learned to be a queen. I'm sorry it took me three books to share my secret with you, but this queen will only travel in silence. In order to have seen my plan through, I had to hide myself from you. Now the stories have been told and I'm feeling less drained, "Oh well, I guess I'll tell you that…

I AM LA'RAIN… and I put a note in his suite case!

STREET CHRONICLES

G STREET CHRONICLES
PRESENTS
TURNT
Out
EVERYTHING THAT GLITTERS AIN'T GOLD!
MONIQUE LOVE
"AUTHOR OF DOPE GIRL'S AMBITION SERIES"

We'd like to thank you for supporting G Street Chronicles and invite you to join our social networks.
Please be sure to post a review when you're finished reading.

Like us on Facebook
G Street Chronicles
G Street Chronicles CEO Exclusive Readers Group

Follow us on Twitter
@GStreetChronicl

Follow us on Instagram
gstreetentertainment

Email us and we'll add you to our mailing list
fans@gstreetchronicles.com

George Sherman Hudson, CEO
Shawna A., COO

G STREET CHRONICLES

43853099R00191

Made in the USA
Middletown, DE
20 May 2017